BELIEVING THE DREAM

Books by Lauraine Snelling

Hawaiian Sunrise

A SECRET REFUGE

Daughter of Twin Oaks   *Sisters of the Confederacy*
The Long Way Home

RED RIVER OF THE NORTH

An Untamed Land   *The Reapers' Song*
A New Day Rising   *Tender Mercies*
A Land to Call Home   *Blessing in Disguise*

RETURN TO RED RIVER

A Dream to Follow
Believing the Dream

HIGH HURDLES

Olympic Dreams   *Close Quarters*
DJ's Challenge   *Moving Up*
Setting the Pace   *Letting Go*
Out of the Blue   *Raising the Bar*
Storm Clouds   *Class Act*

GOLDEN FILLY SERIES

The Race   *Shadow Over San Mateo*
Eagle's Wings   *Out of the Mist*
Go for the Glory   *Second Wind*
Kentucky Dreamer   *Close Call*
Call for Courage   *The Winner's Circle*

Lauraine Snelling

Believing the Dream

BETHANYHOUSE
PUBLISHERS
MINNEAPOLIS, MINNESOTA

Published by Bethany House Publishers
A Ministry of Bethany Fellowship International
11400 Hampshire Avenue South
Bloomington, Minnesota 55438

Printed in the United States of America

ISBN 0-7394-2871-3

DEDICATION

Believing the dream is dedicated
to all my readers who want to know
what happens next with the Bjorklunds.
So do I.
Thank you for the opportunity to find out.
Blessed to be blessings,
all of us.

LAURAINE SNELLING is an award-winning author of over forty books, fiction and nonfiction, for adults and young adults. Besides writing both books and articles, she teaches at writers' conferences across the country. She and her husband, Wayne, have two grown sons, four granddogs, and make their home in California.

Bjorklund Family Tree

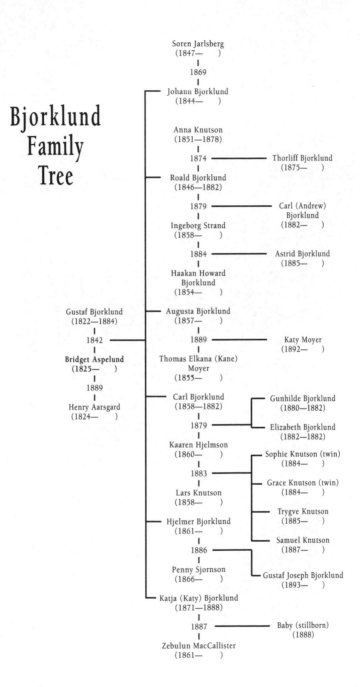

Soren Jarlsberg
(1847—   )
|
1869
|
Johann Bjorklund
(1844—   )

Anna Knutson
(1851—1878)
|
1874 ———————— Thorliff Bjorklund
| (1875—   )
Roald Bjorklund
(1846—1882)
|
1879 ———————— Carl (Andrew)
| Bjorklund
Ingeborg Strand   (1882—   )
(1858—   )
|
1884 ———————— Astrid Bjorklund
| (1885—   )
Haakan Howard
Bjorklund
(1854—   )

Gustaf Bjorklund   Augusta Bjorklund
(1822—1884)   (1857—   )
| |
1842 ———————   1889 ———————— Katy Moyer
| | (1892—   )
Bridget Aspelund   Thomas Elkana (Kane)
(1825—   )   Moyer
| (1855—   )
1889
|
Henry Aarsgard   Carl Bjorklund   Gunhilde Bjorklund
(1824—   )   (1858—1882)   (1880—1882)
|
1879 ———————— Elizabeth Bjorklund
| (1882—1882)
Kaaren Hjelmson
(1860—   )   Sophie Knutson (twin)
| (1884—   )
1883
| Grace Knutson (twin)
Lars Knutson   (1884—   )
(1858—   )
Trygve Knutson
Hjelmer Bjorklund   (1885—   )
(1861—   )
| Samuel Knutson
1886 ———————   (1887—   )
|
Penny Sjornson
(1866—   )   Gustaf Joseph Bjorklund
(1893—   )

Katja (Katy) Bjorklund
(1871—1888)
|
1887 ———————— Baby (stillborn)
| (1888)
Zebulun MacCallister
(1861—   )

CHAPTER ONE

—————⊗~⊗~⊗~—————

Northfield, Minnesota
November 1893

Perhaps today there'd be a letter from home—from Anji.

Thorliff Bjorklund stared out at the snow-blanketed yard behind the office of the *Northfield News*. Yesterday the mud matched his mood, and today, well, how could anyone feel like burnt oatmeal when the world sported a new coat of white? He turned back to his room, made the bed, and grabbed his books off the desk. If he didn't hurry, they'd be late for school, and the teachers at St. Olaf College did not approve of tardiness.

With the red muffler around his neck that his little sister, Astrid, had knit for him, gloves knit by Bestemor Bridget, and a black wool coat sewn by his mother, he was a walking testimony to the love of the folks back home. He squinted his eyes against the sparkling world, eyes of such an intense shade of blue that many people who knew referred to them as "Bjorklund" eyes. So why didn't they write?

His breath formed white clouds in front of him as his long legs made short distance of the blocks to the Rogerses' house, home of his employer and benefactor, his wife, Annabelle, and his daughter, Elizabeth, Thorliff's constant sparring partner. If he said black, she said red. His jaw squared at the thought, and he shook his head. *Women, how do you understand them? Anji, how do I understand you?* One minute he wanted to write and pour out his love for her, the next he swore never to write again—not after the telegram he'd received from her.

More than a month had passed since she told him not to come home. She didn't want or need his help caring for her injured father.

He rang the doorbell, stamping his feet to remove the snow.

"Good morning, Thorliff. You're late." Elizabeth Rogers, her wavy hair bundled tight in a crocheted snood, beckoned him inside. "You can eat your breakfast on the way. Father has gone to harness the horse to the sleigh." Her gray eyes snapped with challenge, and a smile had yet to call the dimple in her right cheek out from hiding.

"Snow too deep for you?" He knew the barb would hit home.

"If you had to wear wool skirts and layers of petticoats, you wouldn't ask such a silly question." Her laughter said she knew the darkening red of his face was due to her offhand comment of her unmentionables. She led the way back to the kitchen, where Cook handed Thorliff a cup of steaming coffee.

"God dag."

"Mange takk." Thorliff had removed his gloves on the way down the hall and now cupped both hands around the hot mug. "This feels as good as it tastes." Only with Cook did he ever speak Norwegian now, and that rarely. While there were classes at school still conducted in Norwegian, they had to do with the language, history, or literature of Norway. All else was taught in English.

"I made you a packet to go." Tall and spare as the words she used, Cook handed him a cloth-wrapped package. "There's enough there for your dinner too."

At a shout from outside, Thorliff took a couple quick sips from his coffee cup and handed it back to her. "Takk."

He held the door for Elizabeth and followed her out, flicking a wave to Cook as he closed it. The cold bit his nose as soon as he stepped off the porch.

"Good morning, Thorliff. I hope that cantankerous furnace kept you warm last night." Phillip Rogers, his straight nose and high cheeks already red with cold, finished tucking the wool robe around his daughter's legs. "Coldest we've had this year, and along with all this snow, I thought you two could use a ride up the hill this morning." He climbed into the front seat of the sleigh, tucking his heavy wool greatcoat over his legs.

"Thank you, sir. I added coal to the furnace before I left and set the damper on half. The water was frozen in my pitcher this morning."

The horse snorted, sending out a white cloud, and picked up a high-stepping trot that set the harness bells jingling.

The sound only reminded Thorliff of home. This morning everything reminded him of home, and here he thought he'd gotten over that. When they hit the grade going up to Manitou Heights and the college, the horse dug in, slowing to a walk so as not to slip.

"Good thing I had him shod last week. Put the winter calks on his shoes." Phillip turned to smile at his riders. "You two sure are quiet this morning."

"I have a philosophy recitation first period." Elizabeth spoke from her nest in the rear seat. "I feel that if I don't hold my head just right, all that I memorized will drain right out."

Phillip laughed. "That's my girl." He turned to Thorliff. "And you, son, what about you?"

Thorliff half shrugged. Confessing that all his thoughts since rising had to do with home seemed extremely inappropriate. After all, the last thing he wanted to do was offend his host and employer. "I have an idea for a story for the paper."

"Good, what's that?"

"What if you ran a contest for a Christmas story, the winner or top three or some such being published Christmas week? I thought maybe you could have different divisions, according to age, you know." He sent Mr. Rogers a sideways glance, hoping for some sign of approbation. When he received a nod, he continued. "I thought perhaps you could ask some teachers from Carleton and St. Olaf to be the judges."

"And would there be prizes?"

"Isn't being published enough?" Thorliff thought back to his first acceptance letter and to the excitement he'd felt the last couple of years after sending off stories. How he'd run all the way to the Baards' farm to tell Anji. He jerked himself back to a sleigh in

Minnesota, leaving thoughts of the summer fields of home in Blessing, North Dakota, behind.

Phillip nodded. "Maybe so, maybe so."

"I checked the back issues. You've never done anything like this."

"Got to hand it to you, young man, you are indeed thorough. That's most important in a newspaperman."

"Thank you, sir." Thorliff dredged up a mite of courage. "I . . . I could write up an article regarding the contest." While writing for the paper was a dream for the future, he'd not expressed a desire to do so immediately. Perhaps Mr. Rogers didn't see him as capable of that. Perhaps he was being too forward. Why hadn't he just kept his idea to himself to use in his own paper someday?

Sleigh and harness bells jingled. The horse snorted as he reached the crest of the hill.

Why didn't I keep my mouth shut? Showing off, or what? Thorliff swallowed a sigh.

"I think that's a fine idea." The voice from the backseat caught him totally by surprise. "So are you going to do it, Father?"

"Of course." Phillip glanced over his shoulder. "I said I would."

"No, you said that Mr. Bjorklund was thorough, which is fine and good, but you didn't answer his question."

Thorliff clapped his jaw shut. Elizabeth said all that . . . for him? Would wonders never cease? And Mr. Rogers said "of course," like, like . . . Thorliff felt like leaping from the sleigh and bounding through the snow, bounding over those tall elm trees that bordered the street and perhaps even a building or two.

"Oh, well"—Phillip turned to Thorliff—"can you have the article ready for typesetting tomorrow? We'll run it on the front page."

"Ah, of course."

"We'll do a thirty-point title, and unless something momentous happens to bump it to the second page, take six to eight inches. That way you can cover all the rules."

"Ah, rules. Yes, sir." Thorliff gathered his things and stepped from the sleigh with a nod. "Thank you for the ride."

"Elizabeth is good with rules. She'll help you."

"Yes, sir." He turned to assist her, but she waved him off.

Elizabeth threw back the robe and stepped from the sleigh. "Good thing my recitation is in my first class this morning." She retrieved her satchel of books. "Remember to contact Mrs. James regarding that ad. I wasn't able to reach her. And remind her she has to pay for the last one."

Phillip Rogers made some kind of noise, and the look he sent his daughter brought forth a peal of laughter. He touched the brim of his black Homburg, clucked the horse forward, and headed back down the hill.

As he did every school morning, Thorliff looked up to the imposing tower atop the mansard roof of the college. The entire red brick building, affectionately called Old Main, resembled a European fortress or castle, but in his mind the tower pointed to God himself.

"Mr. Bjorklund, would you please stay after class?" Mr. Ingermanson, who taught freshman English, stopped at Thorliff's desk as he handed back the papers he'd graded.

Thorliff fell off the dream ledge he'd been enjoying and nodded. Now what? Had his paper been so terrible? He wanted to tuck it into his bag but forced himself to look at it instead. Not good but not terrible either. He thought back to the glowing comments Pastor Solberg used to write on his papers. Life sure was different here. He had yet to receive a glowing comment on anything in any of his subjects. He took notes through the lecture and waited until the others had filed out. Benjamin, the young man who sat behind him who'd become his friend, gave him a commiserating look as he passed by. Thorliff shrugged, then rose to stand in front of the teacher's desk.

"Sir?"

"Ah yes. It has come to my attention that you are from North Dakota."

"Yes, sir. From Blessing, a small town near Grafton."

"Are you by any chance related to the family that makes the cheese?"

"Yes, that's my family. My mother started the business." Thorliff felt his shoulders relax as a sigh of relief escaped.

"Good, good. I have a favor to ask." Mr. Ingermanson, receding dark hair combed straight off his brow, leaned back in his chair.

13

At Thorliff's nod he continued. "Will you be going home for the Christmas holidays?"

"Yes, sir." *Unless Anji sends another message to the contrary, then I may never go home again.*

"Fine. I know this sounds strange, but could you bring back a wheel of cheddar cheese?"

Thorliff nodded, at the same time wondering how he would carry it on the train.

"My family just loves that cheese, and it would make a marvelous Christmas present, albeit a bit late." He smiled. "I will pay you whatever the cost."

"I will write and ask Mor to keep one aside. Christmas season pretty much cleans out the cheese house."

"Thank you, young man, I do appreciate that."

"You are welcome. Is there anything else?"

"Yes, one thing. Your answer to question five presented a very interesting thought line. You think for yourself and present your views clearly and persuasively. A fine thing in one of your age. You are dismissed."

"Thank you, sir." Thorliff barely resisted clicking his heels together once outside the door. A compliment. He'd finally received a compliment on something he'd written. And wouldn't Mor laugh about the cheese order.

He ate his dinner in the study room along with others who brought their own meals instead of eating in the dining hall.

"So." Benjamin sat down next to him and opened a packet of sandwiches. "What did Inger the Terrible want with you?" Benjamin was as dark as Thorliff was fair, with woolly caterpillar eyebrows above deep-set hazel eyes. His hooked nose reminded Thorliff of one of the workhorses at home, but the smile that made grooves in Benjamin's cheeks was totally irresistible.

"He wanted me to bring back cheese from home. My mor makes the best cheese in the country."

"She ships to Minnesota?"

"Our cheese goes all over the country. And it's possible our wheat was ground into flour for your bread."

"How big did you say your farm is?" Benjamin started on his

second half of sandwich, the first disappearing in three bites. "Half of North Dakota?"

"No, it's just that most of our wheat goes to flour mills in Minnesota." Thorliff laid down his roast beef and cheese sandwich and popped one of the molasses cookies into his mouth. "If they'd pay decent prices for the wheat, the farmers would be able to keep producing."

"I heard they're having a bad drought again on the prairies."

"Yes, they've had hardly any rain this fall, so the snow had better be deep." Thorliff returned to his sandwich, then pushed back his chair. "You want a cup of coffee?"

"Sure." Benjamin held out his mug.

Thorliff took the two cups up to the large gray graniteware pot that simmered on the stove and filled them both. When he returned another student had joined them.

"Mail's in if you are interested."

Thorliff set his cup down. "I'll be right back."

"Hey, Thorliff, pick mine up too, will you?" Benjamin raised his voice to be heard over the hubbub.

Thorliff waved one hand to signify he'd heard and joined the ranks of students checking their mailboxes in the dark oak-paneled hall. When he twirled the handle of box 316 and opened the little door, he could see two envelopes. Anji—could one be from Anji? He withdrew them both and checked the handwriting, cutting off the sigh before it took wings. One from his mor and the other from Pastor Solberg. At least he'd heard from home. Two weeks without a letter seemed like half a year. But why nothing from Anji? Sorrow seeded resentment, and resentment sprouted instantly into anger. And to think she had promised to write him every week. If that's all the stronger her word— He cut off the thoughts and checked the glass on Benjamin's box. Nothing.

"Sorry, your box was empty." Thorliff took his place at the table and wolfed down the rest of his sandwich.

"You look mad enough to chew railroad spikes." Benjamin snagged one of Thorliff's cookies. "Nothing from your girl again?"

Thorliff shook his head. "She's not my girl any longer." He and Benjamin had filled each other in about their home lives during their dinner meetings. While Benjamin was from Stillwater, a lumber town not far away, he stayed with a family in Northfield and clerked at the dry goods store. He'd invited Thorliff to come home with him on weekends, but so far Thorliff had declined the invitations, choosing to work at the newspaper instead to improve his typesetting and breaking down skills. Now he was nearly as quick as Elizabeth.

"I need to get to class. Glad you enjoyed my cookies." He gathered up his books and ate the last cookie before Benjamin could appropriate it.

"They treat you better than the Bachmans do me." Benjamin tried to look soulful, but his wiggling eyebrows made Thorliff snort. Climbing the stairs to the classrooms on the second floor, Thorliff rehearsed a blistering letter to send to Anji. Since he was a few minutes early, he slit the letter from Ingeborg open with a blade of his pocketknife and pulled out three sheets of paper: one from Andrew, one from Astrid, and one from his mother. He read the news of school and farm from Andrew and tales of the new kittens and some of the new students at the deaf school from Astrid, who signed her letter, *I've been missing you so much, and your stories. I hope you love school as much as I do. When you come home for Christmas, it will be the very best ever. Love, your little sister, Astrid.*

Thorliff swallowed the lump in his throat while guilt chuckled on his shoulder. Here he'd been angry at Anji, but he hadn't written personal letters to his brother and sister. And he had only written Anji one letter after the telegram. When she didn't answer, he didn't write again.

He unfolded his mother's letter.

My dear son,
    I do hope this letter finds you well in body, mind, and spirit.

He stopped reading and with a sigh glanced out the window. Snowing again. No sparkling sun, no glimmering drifts today. Hearing the others coming into the classroom, he folded the letter and put it back in his pocket where it burned until he had time between classes to finish reading it.

    I am sorry to have to remonstrate you in a letter like this, but why have you not written to Anji? She fights so hard not to let the hurt show, but I can see it in her eyes. She is carrying

16

such a heavy burden, even though the Mendohlsons have moved into the Baard soddy to be of help. I must say that I am disappointed in you.

Thorliff gritted his teeth. *Why did I not write? I did write. Could my letter have gone astray? Has Anji written, and I didn't get them?* Raging thoughts twisted his gut. He returned to the letter.

Joseph is wasting away. I think his heart broke when Agnes died, and then the fall crippled him, leaving him with no will to live. Metiz says he will be gone before spring, and while I hope she is wrong, I cannot wish this life on him when he has heaven and Agnes to look forward to.

Ingeborg continued with other news, but Thorliff returned to the beginning. Was she right? A worm of contention whispered so low he had to stop breathing to hear. *You're a man now. What right has she to scold you like this? Is it really any of her business?*

Why is this your fault? Where had that voice come from?

Thorliff tried to turn to his studies. He opened two books to their proper places, straightened his pencils, and folded his muffler and stuffed it back in his pocket. Steam hissed in the radiator under the tall window. Normally he could shut out all the surrounding noises and study, but today . . . He broke the lead on his pencil and took out his knife to sharpen it again. He skinned his hair back with a desperate hand, read the same paragraph three times, and still had no idea what it said.

With a sigh, he took out paper and started to write.

Dear Anji, I . . .

"Thorliff, Father is here to take us down the hill before this storm turns into a blizzard." Elizabeth beckoned him from the doorway.

"I'll be right there." He put his papers away and shrugged into his coat. Promising himself he'd finish the letter later, he clattered down the stairs.

"Why can't you let me know where you are going to be?" Her words matched her frown.

Was every female in the world angry with him? Thorliff schooled his face to blankness and held the door for Elizabeth. His right eye twitched.

CHAPTER TWO

Blessing, North Dakota
December 1893

"I miss Agnes so much, I . . ." Ingeborg Bjorklund shook her head.

Penny, her sister-in-law, nodded. "Me too." Penny lifted long-awaited baby Gustaf to her shoulder for a burp. Penny's hair, straight as wheat and just as golden, was braided and coiled at the back of her head. "How she would have loved holding this one. No one loved babies like Agnes. I always thought Tante Agnes would be here forever." Penny leaned her cheek against her baby's head, the near white hair almost invisible. She raised tear-filled blue eyes. "She was too young to die yet."

"Ja, and too broken to live." Ingeborg had listened to her dear friend talk of heaven and the glories there. While the rest of them had not been ready to let her go, Agnes had looked only forward, bit by bit fading from this life, preparing for the next.

Ingeborg wiped her eyes. What a paradox, to be so happy for her friend who'd gone home and yet miss her so terribly. "You remember when you all first came here? You so young and lovely even then, with a smile fit to charm the birds from the trees. The

18

boys and Thorliff were friends from the first moment. When Joseph said he guessed this was as good a place to settle as any, I wanted to sing and dance. Had no idea Agnes would become the best friend I could ever have."

"Ja, and we've done a lot of singing and dancing. Weddings and harvest parties. I know Tante said so many times she was glad the wandering bug went on and left them behind."

Ingeborg heard Andrew's whistle for Paws. "School's out."

"Eh, how the time does fly when we're together." Penny looked around the kitchen, the yellow-and-white-checked curtains at the windows, the braided rag rugs on the floor. "Your place is so welcoming, like someone with arms wide open. Every time I come, I go home feeling rested." Penny shook her head. "Strange and wonderful."

"That's because at home you are always listening for the tinkle of the bell over the door to the store. Customers coming and going." Even before she and Hjelmer were married, Penny opened her store by the railroad tracks. Now it was famous for selling everything a family needed, including Singer sewing machines.

"True. How is that new student of Kaaren's doing? Hjelmer said he never saw one so angry as George McBride."

Ingeborg, aproned from shoulder to ankle in white, brushed a tendril of hair from her cheek. She wore her hair long and braided like so many of the local women and coiled around the rear top of her head like a halo without the shine.

"Hjelmer said that? When did he see him?"

"He and Olaf were out to Kaaren's school, measuring for some new desks. All hers are for children, not big enough for a grown man like this new fella."

"Did he talk to him or what?" Sitting back down at the oak table, Ingeborg pushed the plate of molasses cookies down to her guest. The teakettle sang its own tune on the back of the stove where a pot of stew perfumed the house.

"A bit. He's hard to communicate with, but Mr. McBride reads lips some. Since we all learned sign language along with Kaaren for Grace, I forget that others don't have that advantage. Uff da, the things we take for granted."

The baby started to fuss a bit, so Ingeborg reached for him and crisscrossed the cozy kitchen, jiggling the baby and crooning to him at the same time. How she would love to have a baby again, but God hadn't seen fit to bless them that way. She'd carried a resentment in her heart for several years until one time she and Agnes had a real crying session over their lack of conceiving and decided to give up hoping. While Agnes's last baby had been still-born, Ingeborg lost hers early on in a runaway accident in the fields. They'd both decided to forgive themselves and accept God's forgiveness too.

She could hear Agnes, plain as if she sat right where Penny was sitting like she so often had. *"Not like we can do anything now, and God in his mercy knows best. Fighting against God is a real waste of time, you know?"* This time Ingeborg used baby Gustaf's gown for a crying towel.

"Mor." Eleven-year-old Andrew and Astrid, only eight, burst through the door. "There's a letter from Thorliff. Read it quick." They grinned at their guest, matching blue eyes sparkling with delight. "Hi, Tante Penny."

Astrid stopped in front of her mother and reached out a finger for Gustaf to clutch. "Hi, baby. You sure look happy." She moved her finger in a circle, then tickled Gustaf under his chin as his smile widened.

"Oh, good. I'd like to hear that, and then I must get on home," Penny said. "If the mail is out, Mr. Valders is right busy." Anner Valders worked in the bank and the store, since an accident during harvest took part of his arm.

Ingeborg handed back the now cooing baby and, with a knife, slit open the envelope, taking care so she could use the inside of the envelope for writing paper. She sat down at the table and unfolded the precious page from her eldest child.

"My dear family,
Thank you for the letters, which mean so much to me. I feel a world away instead of only a few hundred miles. I'm sorry to hear there has been no rain, but if you have as much snow as we do, there will be moisture in the earth for spring seeding. I read the *Farmers' Almanac* here in the library, and it says that 1894 will have more rain. The sad thing is, it says there will be more flooding due to heavy snows."

"How can a book predict weather way ahead like that?" Andrew, already taller than his five-foot-seven mother, set the cookie jar on the table.

"I don't know, but I've heard it is pretty reliable. Someone at the Grange swears by it." Ingeborg looked up from her reading and shook her head when Andrew came up with a handful of cookies. "One at a time, please."

Astrid nudged her brother. "Oink, oink."

He nudged her back, none too gently.

"If you two will settle down, I will read some more." Ingeborg waited, then resumed. She read about Thorliff's contest for the newspaper and the stories that were already being sent in and how there had been a skating party at the school.

> "We had a huge bonfire on the shore of a small pond, well frozen, and someone brought out a hockey puck, so we used brooms to sweep it back and forth. Our team won, but not because I made any goals."

"We need to make a pond by the barn like we used to." Andrew dunked his cookie in the cup of coffee he'd laced with cream and sugar. "That was fun."

"Keep reading, Mor." Astrid, braids tied with blue ribbons that matched her eyes, leaned over her mother's shoulder.

"Ah, this part is for me." Ingeborg read silently for a bit, then continued aloud.

> "I will not be home until just before Christmas, as Mr. Rogers has asked me to write an article about the writing contest winners."

"Then he'll miss the Christmas program." Astrid plunked herself down on the chair. "And we're doing one that he wrote a couple years ago." She propped her chin on her hands. "I hate Thorliff being gone."

"I don't ever want to leave the farm, school or no school." Andrew reached over and tickled Gustaf, getting a wide smile from the round-faced baby.

"Me neither." Astrid dipped her cookie in her mother's coffee. "Does he say more?"

"Just that he's looking forward to seeing us all." Ingeborg folded up the letter. "Was there any other mail?"

Andrew shook his head. "I better get out to the barn. Did Bell have her calf yet?"

"Haakan said most likely tonight. Astrid, we need more wool carded. Bestemor is knitting faster than I can spin it."

"Ellie could maybe come help." Andrew stopped at the doorway.

"I'm sure her mother has plenty for her to do."

"I could go ask."

"Andrew just wants to see Ellie again. He always wants to see Ellie." Astrid made a face at her brother.

"She's my best friend." Andrew made his comment as if that should be as clear to everyone else as it was to him.

"I'll go get Sophie and Grace, Mor. The three of us should be able to get that whole fleece done."

Astrid shrugged into her coat and ran out the door, flapping her hand in farewell. "Bye, Penny, Gustaf."

Penny sighed. "Well, I better be going. Looks like you have plenty to do." She tied a woolen knit cap on her baby's head.

"I'll get your horse hitched. Where's Far?" Andrew took another cookie.

"Over helping Lars with the steam engine."

By the time Penny had the baby and herself all properly bundled up, the jingle of the harness said Andrew had the sleigh up to the house.

"Here, take some of these cookies for Hjelmer."

"He loves your cookies. You ever think of baking for the store again? Ever since the baby, I just don't find the time, and those railroad people sure do like to stop for cookies and cheese and whatever else I happen to have on hand."

"Let me think about it. With the cheese house slowing for the winter, I might find the time." Since milk production fell during the winter months, there was less to turn into cheese, both from their farm and the others who shipped milk over in cans and took back whey to be fed to livestock. While they had butchered five head of hogs, they'd shipped three times that many to Grand Forks to the stockyard. The remaining three sows and boar would feed well on the whey from the cheese house.

Ingeborg hugged Penny good-bye and helped settle her in the sleigh with the baby bundled under an aging buffalo robe. "You come again soon. Taking time for a real visit was such a treat."

"For me too." Penny turned the horse toward town, the sleigh bells jingling across the snow, now blue-tinged with the oncoming evening. Magenta, gold, and fiery oranges and reds streaked the western horizon, using the clouds as a palette.

Ingeborg stopped on the steps to appreciate the burst of glory, then hurried inside to get warm again, hanging her heavy wool shawl on the peg by the door.

"My land, but the temperature is dropping fast. We're in for a real cold spell."

Astrid and her two cousins burst through the door, panting from their run across the small pasture between the two houses.

"Mor, did you—" pant, puff—"know Grace can run faster than anyone?"

"No, I didn't know that." Ingeborg wrapped an arm around each of the twins and hugged them to her. "Bring the carding paddles in here by the stove so I can help as I make supper. You are staying for supper, right?" She directed the question to Sophie, who nodded hard enough to make her braids flop. With Sophie every movement flowed fast, like a creek down a hillside, while Grace was the still, clear pond that invited one to sit beside it and think.

"We'd rather stay here. I don't like eating with Mr. McBride there. He's not very nice, even though Mor has had talks with him." Sophie's amber eyes snapped under straight thick eyebrows.

"Mor said we have to love him with Jesus' love, but sometimes that isn't easy." Grace, her hair two shades lighter than Sophie's Jersey brown, tipped her head slightly to the side, as if begging for understanding as she signed the words, her fingers flying in her agitation.

"You are right, Gracie, lots of time, loving someone isn't easy." Ingeborg made sure she was facing Grace and that she spoke distinctly since her hands were busy with her cooking.

Grace flashed a smile that was heart stopping in its loveliness. Grace could say more with a smile and a lift of an eyebrow than many people could say in two minutes. She hugged her aunt and followed Astrid to retrieve the paddles for carding from the parlor, where the washed and dried fleece filled a basket in the corner. Taking a set of paddles with fine wire teeth, each girl pulled a hunk of wool off the fleece, laid it on her paddle, and began the smooth motions that pulled out the tangles and laid the fine strands of wool all in the same direction so it would be ready to spin.

"Mor is teaching the deaf students to card and spin wool," Sophie announced. "She said that it's something worthwhile, and you don't have to be able to talk. I think Onkel Olaf will teach the boys wood carving."

"What about the girls?" Astrid stopped her stroking. "I like working with wood."

Sophie shrugged. "But that Mr. McBride—he doesn't want to learn anything. I don't know why he stays."

Grace laid down her paddles so she could sign. "He stays because he hopes this will help him. But he is afraid."

"Afraid of what?" Ingeborg stopped stirring the stew in the kettle on the stove and looked over her shoulder.

Sophie shrugged. Grace squinted her eyes to help think better.

"I'm not sure. Maybe because people have laughed at him and said he was stupid."

"How do you know that?" Ingeborg knelt in front of her niece.

Grace shook her head. "I don't know." She laid slender fingers over her heart.

"Has anyone ever done that to you?"

"A little." Grace studied the flat wooden backs of the carding paddles.

"It was that Toby Valders and his brother. Andrew slugged him a good one before Pastor caught them." Sophie shook her head. "I ha—" She glanced at her aunt from the corner of her eye. "I don't like him one bit."

"Ah." Ingeborg rocked back on her heels, struggling to hide the smile Sophie's quick change in words had brought. *Another one of those times my son fought for the underdog.*

"Andrew got in trouble, but he warned Toby that he'd beat him to bits if he said anything like that again."

24

"And did he?"

"Not yet."

Grace watched the discussion before her fingers flashed her comments. "Toby told me he was sorry."

"Told you?" Ingeborg paused. "Oh, you mean he can sign too?" Maybe there was hope for the boy after all. She knew Anner Valders wouldn't tolerate that kind of behavior if he knew it was going on. *Was Pastor Solberg not talking with Mr. and Mrs. Valders?* She thought a moment. Pastor Solberg hadn't mentioned Andrew's transgressions to them either. *Oh, my son. How do we teach you there are other ways to settle things than with your fists, even when you are in the right? And I don't blame you a bit for wanting to beat that Toby into the dirt. How could he be mean to Grace, of all people?*

Grace reached out and put her hands on Ingeborg's cheeks to turn her face so she could see. Slowly, with intense concentration, she spoke. "I am right about Mr. McBride."

Ingeborg fought the tears as she watched Grace work so hard to talk. She turned her face to kiss the little girl's palm. "I know, Gracie, I know." *Father, you have given us such a treasure in this little child. Help us to keep her safe.*

CHAPTER THREE

"So how is Mr. McBride doing?" Kaaren Knutson, Ingeborg's sister-in-law and headmistress of the deaf school, turned from sliding freshly baked bread from the pans and lining them up on a flat wooden rack to cool. She dipped her fingers in the softened butter and spread the butter over the tops of the loaves. "There now." She wiped her hands on her apron. "So?"

Ilse Gustafson shook her head and sighed. "He . . . he gets so angry he cannot think straight. And his fingers . . ." She shook her head again. "Like boards they are, stiff and stubborn." Her own fingers, fluid like water, danced through the alphabet for sign language. She brushed a drift of mouse brown hair back from her forehead and tucked it into the sides caught back in a bun.

"I know, and other than praying for him, I'm not sure what to do either. He has been spoiled by his mother, and I have a feeling he is sure his father hates him. Some people do not do well with a child who has an impairment, as you well know."

Ilse nodded. *Oh, Lord, how families can hurt each other just because a child can't hear or talk or some such. Please help me deal with this man. There is just something about him.* . . . She brought her attention back to Kaaren. "Excuse me, my mind just took off all by itself."

"Mine does that too. Especially when there is someone I am overconcerned about."

"You think I am overconcerned here?" Always quick to doubt her own value, Ilse's high forehead wrinkled, and her pale blue eyes grew anxious.

"Oh no, dear child, never." Kaaren took the steps to reach Ilse and draw her close, her hands automatically patting the girl's back, noting the shoulders still so thin the bones stuck out too much like angels' wings.

"Ilse, are you not taking time to eat again?" She drew back and lifted Ilse's chin with one finger.

"I think I am, but then someone calls, and I go help and then get busy, and—I'm sorry."

"Ilse, you do not have to be sorry. I am the one who should apologize. Forgive me for taking advantage of your generous heart. You work so hard, and I appreciate you beyond words. This school would not function were it not for you."

"Ah, I . . ." Ilse wiped her eyes on her apron. "Mange takk." She drew a scrap of cotton from her pocket and blew her nose. "And to think I came here asking about Mr. McBride."

"Ja, well, we must solve that problem too, but I think our Father in heaven is more needed with him than we are, although we get to be His hands." She pointed to a chair. "Sit. The coffee is hot, and the bread is calling." The two, working as a team as they'd learned so well in the two years since Ilse left the boarding-house and came to help at the school, quickly had the bread sliced and buttered, cheese cut, and coffee poured without either telling the other what to do.

When they sat at the long table covered with a red-and-white-checked cloth, they both sighed at the same moment, looked at each other, and laughed.

"A moment's sit-down is such a pleasure." Kaaren pushed the plate of bread over to Ilse. "Help yourself. Where is Mr. McBride now?"

"Out with Lars. I should be baking cookies so we will have plenty when the children return from school."

"Ja, and I should be starting supper." Kaaren picked up her coffee cup and inhaled the steam. "Back to your question regarding Mr. McBride. I am truly hoping that the wood-carving lessons with Onkel Olaf will be a turning point. Something tells me there is an artist hiding behind that angry face and we just have to keep looking until we find a way to let it out."

As soon as the deaf students could sign, they attended the Blessing School with the local children, taught by Pastor Solberg, who signed as he spoke. Mr. McBride, however, at twenty-eight, was too old for school, so they took Onkel Olaf up on his offer to teach the man woodworking.

"You think so, really?"

"Ja. And when spring comes, perhaps working in the soil will help him."

"He sure hasn't taken to milking cows." Ilse shook her head.

"No, but did you see his face when the calf was born? Like he'd seen a miracle, which every birthing is, far as I'm concerned."

"Ja, but he does the milking anyway." Ilse propped her elbows on the table and took another bite from her bread and cheese. "I remember being angry."

"When?"

"After Mor and Far died on the ship and I was all by myself. Until Bridget took me under her wing, I was so scared."

Kaaren took a bite of bread and studied Ilse. "Are you saying you think Mr. McBride is afraid?"

"Did I say that?"

"Not in so many words, but I think that's your meaning."

"How do you know things like that? The meaning behind the words, I mean." She smiled at stumbling over the ideas.

"Well, I will tell you, it is much easier now to figure out what you mean, because you talk more. No longer are you that ghost of a girl who tried always to be invisible." Kaaren pushed the bread plate back to Ilse. "Have some more so you don't fade away."

Ilse took another slice and rearranged the cheese to give herself time to think. "So what could he be afraid of? He is a big man."

"I'd say that he is afraid he will not learn the sign language and that he will have to go back to his father as a failure."

"That will never happen. I will not allow it." Ilse could feel her chin tighten. She bit down hard on the bread, chewing as though she were ready to fight the father, who had not even had the courtesy to bring his son to the deaf school, sending him instead with a servant. At the time she'd been a bit overwhelmed at the thought of such wealth, but no longer.

"I'd like to give that *old* Mr. McBride a piece of my mind."

"Me too. And I'm sure that one day we shall have that opportunity. But for now, let's get his son able to communicate."

"But if the father or mother doesn't learn sign language, who will he speak with?"

"Good question." Kaaren brushed the crumbs off the tablecloth and into her waiting palm, then dusted them onto the plate. "That's why I believe we need to add to what we offer. We must teach families too, at least one member besides the deaf one. I know we send home the book, but how many people take the time to learn like we had to in the beginning?" Kaaren nodded, her mouth pursed, one finger stroking her chin, eyes half closed.

Ilse rose and quietly began putting things away. Much earlier she'd learned to recognize Kaaren's deep-thinking actions. Something good would come from their discussion, something really good.

When she heard Mr. McBride come in through the door, she fixed a plate with the leftover bread and cheese and poured a cup of coffee. Perhaps with a bit more encouragement, including food, George McBride would be more amenable to bending his fingers again.

That evening, when supper was finished and everyone had pitched in to do their share of the chores, the Knutson family and all the deaf students gathered in the parlor that had been enlarged enough for everyone to have a seat. Lars and Trygve, his elder son, carved new wooden spoons for the cooks, and Samuel, the baby of the family at six, played with a kitten from the batch who lived behind the kitchen stove. Kaaren took up the book she'd begun reading a few days earlier and turned to where they'd left off, reading *The Adventures of Tom Sawyer* aloud while Sophie signed so the deaf students could enjoy the story too.

"We have a black man living here in Blessing too, huh, Ma?" Trygve, setting his carving in his lap, interrupted the story. "I like Mr. Sam."

"The Lincolns are fine folks," Lars said around the stem of his pipe, which as usual had gone out.

"How come some people don't like them or Metiz and Baptiste either?" Trygve asked.

"Because they are stupid."

"Sophie, how can you say such a thing?" Kaaren kept her place with one finger and frowned at her daughter.

"Well, they are. Toby Valders said something mean to Lemuel, and he had no right to do that. He's not just stupid, he's mean too."

"Me and Andrew are going to—" Trygve clapped a hand over his mouth.

Lars took his pipe from his mouth and set it on the table beside him. No one in the room moved, not even George McBride, who'd been tapping his foot where he sat over in the corner.

"Now, Trygve, finish what you were about to say." Lars looked straight into his son's eyes.

Trygve stared down at his hands. "We want to teach Toby a lesson, one that he remembers for a good long time."

"And what are you going to do?"

Trygve shrugged. "Don't know yet."

"I see. And what has Pastor Solberg been teaching Andrew and Toby?"

"How to chop wood?"

Kaaren kept herself from smiling at the innocent look Trygve gave his father. She put her arm around Samuel so he could lean against her shoulder. *Lord, help these sons of ours to learn to love peace and seek righteousness, not with their fists. There must be a way to get through to Toby.* She remembered the day the two little boys had been discovered stealing food from Penny's store. They'd hidden on the train coming out of the slums of New York and finally made it to Blessing before getting caught. The childless Valderses had adopted them, and life had never been the same in Blessing.

"Don't you think chopping wood is to help them consider what they've done wrong and to help them learn to live right?" Lars rested his elbow on his knees and stared intently at his son.

"Oh." Trygve played with a curl of wood. "But Far, sometimes Toby is mean to Grace too, and—" His sister laid a hand on his arm and shook her head no.

"He is too."

One of the other children stood and came over to Kaaren, standing by the arm of her rocker until, with a smile, Kaaren put her other arm around the girl.

"It's all right." She spoke slowly and clearly so the child could lip-read. "I think we should talk about this later, or we'll never get our reading done tonight. Trygve, you get the Bible and turn to First John. Sophie, let's read." She opened Tom Sawyer to the page they'd been on and continued reading, the kitten purring in her lap while Samuel stroked its fur.

When finished with the chapter, Kaaren took the Bible from Trygve and began reading. " 'Beloved, let us love one another: for love is of God. . . .' " When she finished, she said, "This is what God has to say about the way we are to live. By tomorrow night I want to hear some ideas from all of you on how we can live that kind of love right here in our home and at school. Now let us pray.

"Father God, we thank you for loving us, even though some-times we don't love others like you ask. Show us ways to be more loving and help us always to be thankful for all the things you have given us. In Jesus' name, amen."

Kaaren looked around the room. "Now, all of you get to bed, and I'll be up in a few minutes to tuck you in." Her eyes stopped at Grace. *Something is cooking in that girl's mind. I wonder what she is up to.*

Later, as she sat on the edge of her bed and unpinned the long braid of golden hair she wore around her head like a crown, she yawned and rolled her head from side to side.

"Long day?" Lars lay on his side, enjoying their nightly ritual.

"No more than usual. How did Mr. McBride do out in the machine shed with you?"

"Doesn't take much instruction to clean rust off the machinery and oil it."

"He's not slow, is he?"

"Not that I can tell. His father just didn't take any time with him. What a waste. He has to learn patience, my word, but he has to learn patience." Lars ran his fingers through the hair she was brushing one hundred strokes. "He likes working with the horses, though. Perhaps he could apprentice to Hjelmer at the blacksmith."

"That would give him a trade, not that he needs one for money, but it would give him a feeling of usefulness." Kaaren turned and rested one knee up on the bed, her long flannel nightgown covering her feet too. "I've talked with Onkel Olaf, and he will start him on woodworking next week. Let's give him a chance at both things and see how he does. Ilse is determined he is going to learn to sign, no matter how frustrated and angry he gets."

"The poor man hasn't a chance with all of us ganging up on him." Lars lay back on his pillow. "Hurry up and get under the covers before you freeze and I have to warm up your feet. As Matthew said, let today's troubles be sufficient for today."

CHAPTER FOUR

Northfield, Minnesota

"I can't believe all these entries."

Thorliff watched as Elizabeth sifted through the stack of envelopes. When he came up with the idea of the Christmas story contest, he'd thought perhaps twenty entries would be a goodly number. Instead, they received that many in a day sometimes. He had listed all the entries in a ledger that included the day they arrived and which category they fit under. Schoolteachers had assigned this as a composition to their students, both colleges were well represented, including faculty, and the people of the town and the outlying countryside were dredging up their Yuletide memories as well.

"Father says we've received twenty-five new subscriptions to the newspaper, thanks to the contest." Elizabeth looked over her shoulder to Thorliff. "This was a pretty good idea."

What? The prickly Miss Rogers giving him a compliment? Thorliff pulled the ledger out from under the counter. "Thank you." But at times he wondered if he would have suggested the contest if he'd had any idea of the avalanche of entries they'd get. Or that the work of it was going to fall to him. Tomorrow was his turn to recite in Bible class, and while he was prepared with questions of his own, he had yet to formulate an answer to the teacher's question.

"Do you need some help?"

He blinked and looked sideways at her. "Uh, yes. That would be very nice."

"So what is your system?"

"I open the envelope, decide which category the story fits in, enter it in the ledger, and then place story and envelope in the proper box." He motioned to the row of four boxes on the shelf under the counter.

"Okay, how about if I open them and hand them to you for entry?"

"Good." Standing at the counter, they set to the task, with Elizabeth slitting all the envelopes with a letter opener and creating a pile with the envelopes on top of the pages.

"How is school going for you?"

Thorliff nearly swallowed his Adam's apple. Why was she being so pleasant? "Good." *Not really, but what should one say? Of course if I'd hear from Anji, perhaps I would feel better about school. Come on, dolt, think of something polite to say back. Good, wonderful, brilliant repartee.* "And for you?"

"Could be better. I wish St. Olaf had the science classes I want to take so I didn't have to trek down the hill midmorning and then back up. Wasn't so bad in the fall, but with all the snow we've had . . ." She waved a paper in front of him. "Wait until you read this one."

Thorliff had heard her refer to medical school before at other times but had never asked her about it.

"How are things going?" Phillip Rogers shut the door before more snow blew in and stamped his feet to get the snow off his boots. "Brrr. Such miserable weather. I told Tom to bring the sleigh back in an hour, so I hope you will be done by then."

"I will or else it'll have to wait until tomorrow."

Phillip hung his coat and muffler on the coatrack and set his wool fedora on top. "How are the entries coming?"

"We need to begin reading them and sorting out the best. I asked the teachers at Carleton and St. Olaf if they would read the top three or four in each category." Thorliff motioned to the four boxes.

"Good grief, that many? And the final deadline is when?"

"Tomorrow."

Phillip massaged his chin for a moment. "I know what we'll do. Tomorrow, if the two of you can take the time, we will take the boxes home, have supper, and spend the evening reading. I'm sure Annabelle will help us. Elizabeth, why don't you ask Thornton if he would like to join us. We'll make a party out of this."

Elizabeth glanced at Thorliff out of the side of her eye. "What do you say?"

I say I have homework to do. "I-I guess that would be all right. Perhaps the next day I can take the finalists up to Mr. Ingermanson, and maybe Thornton would take the ones to Mr. Jordan." Though Thornton Wickersham attended Carleton, Thorliff had met him one night while skating at the pond with Elizabeth.

"And if they can get the results back to us over the weekend, we will publish the winners in next week's edition. Perfect."

"What if you printed the runners-up this week and the winners next week?"

Phillip paused in flipping through the entries. "Thorliff, that brain of yours must never be quiet." He clapped Thorliff on the shoulder. "Good idea. We'll prolong the suspense."

"You better plan on printing extras of those two editions. People will buy more than one so they can send copies to all their relatives." Elizabeth yawned and stretched, locking her hands behind her and pulling her shoulders back. "The accounts are caught up. There are some invoices you need to pay there in your basket, and Mrs. Jamison called. She wants to talk with you."

"About what?"

"I don't know. She insisted on talking with you." Elizabeth strode to the shade-covered windows and peeked out. "Tom's not here yet."

"I can call for him if you are ready."

"Please." Elizabeth rubbed her upper arms. "I'm already tired of winter, and it's just begun."

Thorliff locked the door after they left and turned out the gaslights. Making his way down to the basement, he threw several large chunks of coal into the furnace, half closed the dampers, and headed back upstairs to his room. At least there was a heat grate near his desk so he could stay warm while studying. He reviewed his lesson on Matthew for Bible class, wondering if he dared ask the question he and Benjamin had been arguing about, and spent half an hour memorizing his verses. Since he'd memorized most of them in school in Blessing, this was review. He paced the floor, " 'Blessed are the peacemakers: for they shall be called the children of God. Blessed are the pure in heart: for they shall see God.' " He dragged his hands over his scalp. "No, it's the other way. Pure in heart comes first."

He was still murmuring the "blesseds" when he fell asleep under the woolen patchwork quilt he'd brought from home.

"And you have a question, Mr. Bjorklund?"

"Yes, sir." Thorliff swallowed hard and heard Benjamin shuffle his feet. "Sir, in the Old Testament we see Jehovah, the God of creation but also the God of judgment and wrath. How then can He be the same being as the God of love in the New Testament?"

"And this question has been bothering you?"

"Yes, sir. All through school." Thorliff forced his body to remain still.

"I see. And you believe you are in a position to question the living God?"

"Well, sir, He says in Job to come and discuss with Him."

"And in Job doesn't He also ask where you were when the stars were put in the heavens?"

"Yes, sir."

"Then I would suggest that you read all those passages again and see if you are in a better position than Job to question. Is that clear?"

Thorliff could feel the heat creeping up his neck. *Why didn't I just keep my mouth shut?* He sat back down, gritting his teeth but keeping from glaring at Professor Schwartzhause. After all, he'd invited them to ask questions. And this was the one class in which he'd not been ashamed of his exam scores.

"Tomorrow, Miss Jacobson, you will recite. Class dismissed."

As all nine of them filed out of the classroom, Benjamin muttered for Thorliff's ears only, "Sorry for that. Should have asked some of the sophomores if this would work in this class or not."

"I don't believe God gets angry when we ask questions. He is bigger than that. Why, Abraham didn't just question. He argued with Him. And got God to change His mind. So did some of the other prophets. Aren't we supposed to learn from their examples?"

"Maybe by the time we get to the New Testament, we'll get some answers."

That night after supper at the Rogerses', Thornton, Thorliff, and the family split up the contest boxes and quickly sorted out the entries that were not in contention with the finalists. Since the largest box was the children's, Elizabeth and Thornton took that one.

"At least ours are shorter," Elizabeth said, handing him a stack of papers.

"So what exactly are we judging them on?" Thornton asked, his head bent to reading, the firelight haloing his curly hair.

"Originality, quality, does the story have a good conclusion, is it really a story with a beginning, middle, and an end or just a picture of life." Thorliff rattled off the requirements without looking up.

"Do you have a check sheet or something to score them on?"

"No."

"This is all very subjective, then?"

"Oh, Thornton, just choose the top three or four from your pile, and I'll do the same, then we'll compare." Elizabeth shook her head. "It isn't like they are winning a college scholarship or a packet of money or something."

"Now, dear, let's not be . . ." Annabelle Rogers, dark hair smoothed back and bundled in a black crocheted snood, looked up from her chair facing the fire.

"Thank you, Mother, let's just read."

The crackling of the fire, the whistle of the wind amongst the eaves, and the whisper of papers being shuffled were the only sounds for a time, but other than the wind, they were friendly sounds. That and the warmth of the room after an excellent supper made Thorliff fight to keep his eyes open. He caught a yawn and looked up in time to see Elizabeth do the same, then heard Mr. Rogers give the slight start that meant he had about dozed off too.

"I'll ring for coffee, or we'll all nod off." Annabelle pulled the cord in the corner.

Elizabeth put her papers down and went to stand in front of the fire. "I've done fifteen, and only one really stands out, so I've divided those I've already read into good, possible, and no chance."

"I'd say that makes rather a good division." Phillip was reading the stories from older folks. "I have one here that really jerks the heartstrings. If nothing comes better, that's the winner in my group."

"You have to choose three."

"Oh, that's right." Phillip gave his daughter an exasperated look over his half glasses. "Such a stickler."

While the coffee helped, everyone was yawning by the time they finished.

"Thanks, Tom, for coming out on such a cold night," Thorliff said, stepping out of the sleigh. In the last year, since the installation of the telephone, Tom had divided his time between working for Dr. Gaskin and the Rogerses.

"It's all right."

"And thank you, Thornton, for delivering the manuscripts to Mr. Jordan for me and for your help with the judging."

"Quite all right."

Thorliff waved as the sleigh went on to the Muellers' house, where Thornton lived with his pastor uncle and his wife and sons.

Thorliff, however, still had to finish a composition that was due in the morning. His employer's "well done" as he left this evening helped somewhat to alleviate the nagging sting of his teacher's words earlier in the day. From now on, Thorliff promised himself, he would keep his mouth shut in class except when called on. *But if God didn't intend for me to think, why did He give me such an inquisitive mind?*

By the time he finished the composition, he felt wide awake so he began a letter to Anji.

Dear Anji,

I must confess that I have no idea what is happening between us. You sent me that telegram that sounded as if you never wanted to see me again, and when I wrote to you, I never received an answer. I have decided to write again in the hopes that my earlier letter was lost and you are feeling as bereft as I. Surely the love we confessed for each other is stronger than these difficulties. In fact, perhaps these are the tests we must go through; as silver and gold are purified by fire, so are we.

And should the unthinkable be, that you no longer love me as I do you, then I must know that too. I think I am over the worst of the homesickness that plagued me through October. While I did not expect school to be easy, I have been surprised at the difficulties I have experienced. Just today I was castigated rather severely for questioning what I see as the disparity between the vengeful and judgmental God of the Old Testament and the God who is love of the New. I am not the only one with questions. There are others who discuss with me in private. As you know, Pastor Solberg welcomed our questions, saying that when we question, it is like flint on flint, sparks fly, and we all become wiser. He said that God is not afraid of our questioning and loves us anyway. After all, Thomas doubted, and as I understand, only when doubting leads to disbelief is there a problem. All my questions create an awe in me that the God who created the universe also created me and desires that I commune with Him.

I have been reading Christmas stories entered in our local newspaper's contest, and many of them make me even more wish for home. Though I want to come home for Christmas, some days I doubt that I can leave my job, while on other days I would give up the job and school itself for a glimpse of your sweet face.

Greet your family for me. I have joined my prayers with
yours that your father would heal enough to be free of the terrible pain he is suffering. I know you must miss your mother
terribly.

All my love,
Thorliff

Without rereading what he'd written, he addressed the envelope and, while the ink dried on the envelope, folded the paper to
insert and seal. When he crawled under his quilt, he was sure this
would be another of those nights rife with questions and devoid
of sleep. But in the morning he knew he'd not prayed for any
beyond those of his immediate family before falling into the comforting arms of rest and refreshment.

They had to reprint more copies of the paper with the runners-up stories and so doubled the run for the finalists. When one
customer suggested they print all the stories in a small book, Phillip handed that project over to Thorliff.

"What do you think? Is this something that you can do?"

"Before Christmas?" Thorliff felt his heart leap to racing speed.

"No, no. I know that is impossible. But we need to keep that
in mind for next year. I think this first edition could come out in
January during the winter doldrums. We could look for other
places to sell it besides the newspaper office. Olson's Bookstore
would be a natural."

"What if you designated a portion of the cover price to go to
a local charity? That would extend the Christmas spirit into the
new year."

"Thorliff, where do these ideas of yours come from?" Phillip
stared at his young worker with an amazed expression.

Is that good or bad? Thorliff wasn't certain if he was to be castigated or congratulated. Unsure, he kept silent.

"Now, do you have any suggestions as to which charity?"

Thorliff let out the breath he wasn't aware he'd been holding.
"I don't know the town well enough, but scholarships are always
needed at the colleges. As you know, St. Olaf was pretty close to

closing its doors this fall. Reverend Ytterboe is out canvassing for financial assistance."

"Thank you. I shall ask my wife. She would have suggestions for this also. Son, you are increasing our good name in Northfield. Thank you."

The bell tinkled over the door, and a child entered the newspaper office. He laid his pennies on the counter. "I would like two more copies of this week's paper. My sister is one of the story winners."

Phillip winked at Thorliff. "See?" He reached under the counter where they had a stack of papers stashed. "Here you go, lad. And tell your sister congratulations from us."

The boy dashed out with a quick wave over his shoulder. His cheery smile reminded Thorliff of Trygve—and home. Home, where Christmas secrets abounded as everyone made presents for the others and tried to keep them from guessing, where Mor and Astrid would be baking goodies and pulling taffy, where they would have made snow candy by now and dipped small candles to light on the tree. At the school they would be practicing for the Christmas program, the program that he always used to write but didn't write this year for the first time since the school began.

What would he give for Christmas gifts if he did go home?

Chapter Five

December 21, 1893

"So, Thorliff, are you going home for Christmas?" Mr. Rogers asked.

Elizabeth Rogers watched the young man's face as he struggled to find an answer to her father's question.

"Ja, I plan to take the morning train tomorrow."

"I thought you decided not to." She dropped the last of the capitals from Thursday's edition of the *Northfield News* into their cases. The ancient printing press still used individual type that was hand-set on a long slug line and had to be put away when the paper was finished printing.

Elizabeth brushed a lock of hair off her face with the back of her hand. "That means I have to help pick next week, and here I thought to have some time off."

"You've had time off. I've been doing most of the picking all month." Thorliff sighed. According to her, he did nothing more than clean and keep the furnace going, and here he'd written the final article about the winners of the Christmas story contest, and made sure the judges received their entries, and catalogued all the entries, and come up with the idea in the first place.

Along with keeping up with his classes.

"How long will you be gone?" She snapped the case closed, and he shoved it into the slot where it belonged.

He looked to Mr. Rogers. "How long may I be gone?"

"I could sure use your help with the New Year's edition." Phillip Rogers consulted the calendar on the wall by his desk. "Can you return on Wednesday the twenty-seventh?"

"If I need to."

"Your little sister is going to be mad at you." Thorliff had told Elizabeth of his family on some of the evenings when she worked on the accounts and he either cleaned up the newspaper office or put away the used type.

She had told him about her dream of becoming a doctor. While the sparring continued, they had developed a friendship of sorts, wits honed to a sharper edge due to their repartee.

"Are you ready to head on home, dear?"

"Any time." All of a sudden Elizabeth felt like someone had stolen whatever energy she had left, leaving her noodle limp. She trapped a yawn behind her fingers, remembering at the last moment that she hadn't washed yet. She turned to her father. "Do I have ink on my face?"

"Only a little." Phillip glanced up from searching his pockets. "Have you seen my—" he turned back to the desk—"here it is." He removed an envelope from his pocket and handed it to Thorliff. "Merry Christmas, son."

"Why . . . why, thank you."

Elizabeth tried to stifle her look of surprise, but her father caught it. One raised eyebrow dared her to say anything.

She rubbed the inside of her cheek with her tongue and headed to the necessary to remove the ink from her face. *Father has never given the boys that work here a Christmas present. Why is he starting now?* Not that Mr. Bjorklund was a boy really, even though he'd grown thinner through the fall instead of muscling out like Cook insisted he should. When she returned, her father had donned coat, muffler, and gloves, and stood waiting, holding her coat. Thorliff had disappeared.

"Where'd he go?"

"Down to stoke the furnace."

"Oh." She pushed her arms into her coat sleeves and removed her muffler and hat from the coatrack by the front door.

"Did you need him for something?"

"No." *I was going to wish him a merry Christmas is all, but then he'd probably make some comment that would make me want to give him a shove. Thorliff is so exasperating; why can't Father see that?*

Instead, here her father was giving the man a gift of money for Christmas. Not like her mother hadn't already sent a plate of Cook's Christmas treats. Ah, the krumkakar, the sandbakkels, and fattigmann, plus the julekake they would enjoy on Christmas morning. One thing about Cook, she never spared the butter.

"Are you ready, my dear?" Her father touched her arm with a gentle hand.

Elizabeth bit back a sigh. This year, for the first time since Cook came to them, she'd missed out on helping with the Christmas baking. Being a junior in college took more time than she'd imagined, and not just studying.

She shook her head at her father's questioning look and headed for the stairs to the basement. "Merry Christmas, Mr. Bjorklund." All the emphasis on the mister, knowing that would make him smile.

"And to you, Miss Elizabeth." His use of her given name made her smile.

Just as she turned away, he started up the wooden stairs sided on one side by a wall and a wooden handrail on the other.

"Really, a most blessed Yule." There was no teasing tone in his voice, only the richness of one friend sharing with another.

"Thank you." She struggled for something more to say, but when the words failed her, she turned instead to let her father usher her out the door. For some odd reason, a lump clogged her throat.

"A fine young man, is he not?"

"I guess." She ducked her chin into the muffler that covered her face clear to her eyes. *Pray for a safe journey for him.* The inner voice caught her by surprise.

Why? What could happen? He would get on the train here, change in St. Paul, change again in Grand Forks most likely, and then . . . How come lately that still, small voice had been coming more frequently? Ever since her visit with Dr. Morganstein in Chicago, she'd noticed a change and wondered why. Could it be the influence of the woman who radiated love in action?

"I should have had the sleigh brought round." Phillip Rogers picked up the pace. "It's dropped twenty degrees since we came over after supper."

"But not much wind." Speaking, even through the muffler, let sharp knives attack her throat.

"Good thing."

By the time they reached the front gate, they were both breathless from inhaling frigid air. Annabelle Rogers threw open the door before they reached it.

"Oh, my dears, I was about to send Old Tom with the sleigh." She stepped back out of their way. "My land, the cold is ferocious."

Unwinding their mufflers and removing coats gave Phillip and Elizabeth time to catch their breath. Annabelle hung their things on the walnut coat-tree, then turned with a wide smile. "I have a surprise for you."

The look in her eyes made Elizabeth want to put her coat back on.

"Not company."

"Why, yes. Thornton came by, and I thought you'd be home earlier, so I asked him to stay for . . ." Her voice trailed off, then regained its normal forcefulness. "Coffee and cookies."

If he brought me a present, I am going to . . . to . . . It's your own fault if he did. Remember, you invited him to join you in that courting conspiracy. Any courting man would bring his intended a Christmas gift. Just because you don't take the game seriously, remember that he has gone out of his way to make it look convincing.

Elizabeth wished she could stuff a rag in that little voice that played at being her conscience. She'd just wanted to get her mother to call off the matrimony police. Asking Thornton to enter into a pretend courtship had seemed just the thing.

And it worked, didn't it?

She forced a smile to lips that wanted to snap and followed her chatting parents into the parlor. The roaring fireplace drew her like children to light.

"Good evening, Elizabeth." Thornton Wickersham stood, setting his eggnog on the whatnot table beside his chair.

"Good evening, Thornton." She almost added the *mister*, but surely they'd progressed beyond that. "Cold out, isn't it?"

"Bitter." He came to stand beside her, both of them with their backs to the heat. "I would have come for you had I known you were at the office."

"Thank you, but the walk home was good for us." *Liar. You could hardly breath.*

"Do you want hot cider or eggnog?" Her mother had taken her place at the tea tray. "Or rather coffee?"

"Hot cider sounds wonderful." Since her gloved hands had been protected by her dyed rabbit muff, that was about the only warm part of her. But the thought of a hot cup was appealing.

Before she could take a step, Thornton had crossed the room to fetch the cup for her.

"Here you go."

She glanced up at him, about to say something biting, but swallowed the remark into a meek "Thank you," her mother's dogged training in manners winning out.

"Elizabeth, are you not feeling well?" The twinkle in his amber eyes warned her more was coming.

She rubbed her forehead, trying to banish the beginnings of a headache before it became full blown. "Just tired." Taking a sip of the cider wafted cinnamon and nutmeg through her senses. She inhaled again. Along with the pine fragrance from the tree, cedar from the garlands outlining doorways and windows, and vanilla from the candles burning on the mantel, the house wore a potpourri of Christmas smells. She inhaled the steam from her cup again, feeling the muscles in her neck relax. Knowing which ones needed to let go and making them do so were two different operations entirely.

"Thank you, dear Thornton, this indeed is just what I needed."

He cocked an eyebrow at the *dear*.

She drowned an almost giggle in her cup. Her mother had heard.

Thornton leaned closer. "I'm preaching at the Congregational church tomorrow evening. Will you come to hear me?"

As a minister in training, Thornton often preached at some of the churches in town, but more often at smaller outlying congregations.

Elizabeth glanced at her mother, who nodded. Agreement came easily if her mother thought an event might add to the romance she assumed to be budding between her daughter and this "fine upstanding young man," to quote her mother.

Guilt twanged.

"Elizabeth, any chance you might grace us with some Christmas music?" Her father leaned back in his chair. "'We've been so busy, it seems like weeks since I've heard you play."

"That was me playing with the choir at school."

"Along with the orchestra. How about a private concert?"

"Of course." With a smile she placed her cup in Thornton's extended right hand and crossed to the ebony Steinway in front of the drawn red velvet drapes. The piano was placed so she could see out to the gardens when she played.

Stretching out fingers and loosening her hands and arms, she took her seat on the bench, not bothering to place sheet music on the rack. She knew what her father wanted—a medley of his favorite Christmas carols, and for those she needed no music. Placing her fingers on the keys took her beyond the doorway into another world, a private place where she floated on the notes. Stroking the keys like a lover might his beloved, she segued from melody to melody with nary a pause, her eyes closed, the better to feel the ecstasy.

Her teachers, her mother, and sometimes her father had all encouraged her to continue with her music, but her entire being pleaded to become a doctor. Music was for delight. Healing people was her mission.

She ended with "Silent Night," letting the notes drift off like a memory.

"That was magnificent." Thornton leaned against the piano, reverence deepening his gaze.

"Thank you." Opening her eyes took a concentrated effort, staying transported with the dream was much easier.

"I must be going before I wear out my welcome."

"Did you walk?" Phillip roused himself from his reverie.

"Yes, but my uncle's house is not far."

"I'll have Tom hitch up the sleigh. If you slipped and fell on the ice or some such nonsense, you'd freeze before you hit the ground." Phillip hefted himself to his feet. "Thank you, my dear. That was magnificent."

Moments later, hearing the jingle of harness bells, Elizabeth picked up her insistent cat, Jehoshaphat, and clutched him under her chin as she walked Thornton to the door.

"I'll see you tomorrow night then?" Thornton took her hand.

"Not in the front row."

"Surely my intended should sit up close to the front." His waggling eyebrows made her giggle.

She put one finger to her lips. "You don't have to go that far," she whispered. "She believes. She believes."

"Your gift is under the tree."

She pulled her hand away. "I was afraid of that. Why did you—?"

"Isn't that proper?" He donned a stricken look.

She stepped back, still shaking her head. "Good night and merry Christmas." Now she'd have to come up with a gift for him. And she had planned on staying home tomorrow doing a whole lot of nothing. What kind of monster had her game of pretend created?

CHAPTER SIX

Blessing, North Dakota

"Thorliff's coming home, Mor, Thorliff's coming home." Astrid danced about the kitchen, twirling in place before the stove.

"You be careful you don't fall in the oven."

"Mor, I can't fit in the oven no more." Astrid tweaked her mother's apron strings as she spun by again.

"If you've got so much energy, you can haul in two more loads of wood. Why is Andrew late again?"

Astrid stopped spinning and swooping. "Ah . . ."

Ingeborg turned from checking the chicken baking in the oven. "Astrid?"

"Ah, I'll get the wood." The girl dashed from the room, snagging her wool shawl off the peg by the door as she ran by.

Ingeborg sighed and wiped her hands on her apron. What had that young son of hers gotten into now? She crossed the room to look out the window. The sun already hung low in the west, painting the scattered clouds in shades of vermilion and cerise. The snow on the ground caught matching tints. Surely Pastor Solberg wouldn't keep Andrew into dusk?

Astrid dumped the first armload into the woodbox and

hustled out for the second before her mother could ask her anything else.

Ingeborg picked up her rolling pin again and gave the sour-cream cookie dough another two passes. What could be going on with Andrew? Cutting the cookies, she tried to figure out ways to help her younger son deal with his too quick responses with his fists. Could Haakan talk with him again? She shook her head. Haakan thought Andrew's method of championing the underdog quite remarkable, to the point of giving him lessons in fisticuffs. Should she talk with Pastor Solberg—again? Somehow it didn't seem fair that Andrew be set to chopping wood when the altercation was really someone else's fault.

She sighed and picked up the thread of an ongoing conversation with her Lord.

"It really isn't fair, you know. But I understand he has to learn better ways, and I do try to help him see that." She made a mouth shrug. "And yes, I suppose the woodpile gives him time to think on other ways." She stopped cutting cookies to lift them to the cookie sheet with a pancake turner. "But then, if I know Andrew, he uses that time to figure a way to get even with that Toby Valders."

"Who you talking to, Mor?" Astrid paused in the doorway, the pieces of split wood weighing her down. "I know, you and God, huh?" At her mother's nod, she added, "About Andrew again, ja?"

Ingeborg could feel the corners of her mouth tilt up. The look on her daughter's face would make any mother laugh. When and where did Astrid learn to cock her head and raise an eyebrow just so?

"Have a cookie."

Astrid dumped her load in a woodbox that looked close to becoming kindling itself.

"You don't have to worry—"

"I don't worry!" Ingeborg interrupted her daughter to receive another roll of the eyes and slight headshake. "Excuse me."

"Like I was saying"—Astrid's grin held a wealth of secrets— "Andrew isn't at school, but you can't ask me where he is 'cause then I'd have to break a promise, and you don't ever want me to break a promise 'cause you said a promise is a sacred thing, and I—"

Ingeborg held both hands in the air, a sure sign of surrender. "Enough."

Astrid picked up two cookies still warm from the oven. "These sure are good. You make the best cookies anywhere." Her grin pleaded with her mother to not ask more questions. "After all, it is almost Christmas."

"Oh." Ingeborg felt a grin tickle her cheeks. "Guess I never thought about that." At Astrid's slow shake of her head, Ingeborg clarified. "For me, I mean."

"Now, you know I didn't say nothing."

"Anything."

Raised eyebrows and rolled eyes. "Anything."

I wonder what he is making for me? Ingeborg knew she was nearly as bad as the children when it came to delight over presents. Why, the year Haakan surprised her with a Singer sewing machine . . . such finagling he'd had to go through to keep her from buying one herself.

"What are you smiling about?" Astrid snatched another cookie.

"Just thinking back to other Christmases."

"I sure do miss Thorliff. He would have written a new Christmas play if he was here." She sank down on a chair and propped her elbows on the table. "Just ain't the same without him here."

"Isn't."

"That's what I said."

"No, you used ain't, and that is not proper."

More eye rolling. "Sorry. How come we have to say everything right? Other kids don't. Lots of the grown-ups don't neither."

"Either."

This time a sigh. "They don't."

"I know, but Tante Kaaren worked really hard to make sure we all learned to talk English right. I believe that since we live in America, we should talk like good Americans."

"That's what Pastor Solberg says too." Astrid traced a finger trail in the flour on the table. "Toby Valders said a bad word today and got his mouth washed out with soap, and then he had to write

on the board fifty times. Used up two whole pieces of chalk."
Ingeborg sighed.

Forgive me, Lord, but I sure am grateful you didn't let Penny and Hjelmer adopt those two, no matter how disappointed she was at the time. And now look, you blessed them with Gustaf, the pride of Bridget's heart. They had named their little son Gustaf after Hjelmer's father, who had died after most of the family emigrated to America. *How Penny would have managed those two ruffians along with her store is beyond me. But then, who but you knew all that in advance?*

Ingeborg slid her flat pan into the oven under the rack holding the roasting chicken. All the while she glanced out the window, checking the barns where the men, including George McBride from the deaf school, were busy milking. Andrew should be out there too. Did Haakan know where the boy was so he wasn't worried?

Astrid wrinkled her forehead, her book on the table as she studied for the morning.

"You may light the lamp if you want."

"All right. But let me finish the chapter first."

That alone told Ingeborg her daughter wasn't doing her arithmetic. Like her brothers, she loved to read.

"You could read aloud. Goldie and I like stories too." Ingeborg nodded at the orange-and-white-striped cat curled on the rug by the stove. At his name, the animal opened his eyes and treated them to a throat-inspecting yawn. The barbs on his tongue gleamed as he rolled and stretched that too, then began to straighten his fur.

"It's about a jumping frog contest. Do you know where Calaveras County is?"

"Some place in California, I think. Ask Andrew. He read that story a couple of years ago."

"We could have a jumping frog contest in the summer. The bullfrogs from over in the swamp jump real good."

"Sure you could."

"The jumping frogs of Walsh County." She wrinkled her nose. "Doesn't sound as good, does it?"

"Who cares. It would be fun. We could do it just before

52

harvest starts. We'll need a party about that time anyway." Ingeborg pulled her cookie tray from the oven and looked up at the sound of boots kicking off the snow on the back porch.

"Andrew's home." Astrid gave her mother a "don't you say anything" look before the cold draft preceded Andrew into the kitchen.

Thank you, Father God. I do feel more comfortable when all my chicks are home again. Please watch over Thorliff as he travels.

She tried to ignore the glances that Andrew and Astrid swapped, including the giggle from her daughter. "How was school?"

"Good." He snagged three cookies as he went by. "Good." This one came from a mouthful of crunchy cookie.

"Is that all you can say?" Ingeborg put an arm out to stop him on his way past.

"No, mange takk." Another mutter around a full mouth, as he'd just stuffed in the third cookie. He paused, ducked around his mother's arm, and reached for more cookies. "Tusen takk?" His eyebrow arched at the question.

"Oh, go on with you. The cows are waiting."

"I sure hope Thorliff gets home before a blizzard hits."

Me too, oh Lord, me too. She shut the oven door and took down the kerosene lamps from the shelf behind the stove. "Astrid's going to go blind if we don't get some light in here." She glanced over at her daughter, who had her nose so close to the pages that Ingeborg had no idea how she could read at all. Taking the scissors, she trimmed the wicks and lit them both with a spill lighted from the stove. Setting the chimneys back in place, she centered one on the table and kept the other to light the stove area. All the while she fought to keep her inner shivers to just that. Even after all these years and all the blizzards they'd been through, the memories came howling back with the wind.

That terrible second winter when they'd all lived in the soddies, Carl and Kaaren with their two little girls in theirs and Roald, Thorliff, and her in the first one. They'd been housebound, some days not even making it to the barn because the blizzard was so severe and prolonged. When she closed her eyes, she could still hear the howling of the wind, but so much less now that they lived in a snug house. Many families had been sick, and when the blizzard broke, Roald took the mule and rode out to check on the other families. Carl and the two girls died of the fever, Kaaren bordered on insanity, and Roald never returned.

The black pit of fear and despair nearly brought her down too, but by the grace of God, the four remaining Bjorklunds had made it through. At times the abyss yawned at her feet again, but she'd learned to let God close it and keep her safe—most of the time.

Andrew thumped back down the stairs and headed for the barn in a rush. He knew he was late, and while Haakan most likely had agreed to the tardiness, Andrew knew better than to take advantage of his father's good nature.

Later, when they were gathered around the table, the supper finished, Haakan clasped his hands above his head and stretched. "Takk for maten."

"Velbekomme." Ingeborg made the age-old response with a smile as she brushed his shoulder with her hand on her way to finish clearing the table.

"Astrid, your mor needs help."

"Ja, just a minute."

"No, now." At his quiet command, she shut her book and picked up the remaining plates and silverware.

"I was just trying to finish the story so Grace could have the book tomorrow."

"That is kind of you, but chores come first."

Ingeborg refilled the cookie plate and set it back on the table, at the same time refilling her husband's coffee cup.

"Ah, you do me good, wife." Haakan patted her just below her apron strings as she went by. "You think Thorliff is really coming?"

"He said he would."

"I know, but that was before—"

"Before what?" She turned from shaving curls off the soap bar into the dishpan steaming on the stove. She smiled at Astrid as she took her book into the parlor.

"Before, well, you know, the Anji thing."

The Anji thing. What a way to put it. Ingeborg tried to gather her thoughts sent awry by his doubt that Thorliff was indeed coming. Surely he would have sent a telegram if something happened to keep him in Northfield. Of course they would understand if he had to work, but the thought of not having everyone home for Christmas made her heart hurt.

"He'll be here." Now if only her heart would agree with her mind. *Please, God, bring him home, but mostly keep him safe.*

"Of course he will." Haakan dunked another cookie in his coffee. He leaned back, rocking the chair on the two hind legs until the squeal from the wood earned him a warning stare. "Are they both upstairs?" He'd dropped his voice to a whisper.

Ingeborg shook her head. "They're by the stove in the parlor."

"The box came today."

"You saw Penny?"

He nodded. "I hid it in the machine shed."

"Good." So strange it seemed to order Christmas presents from as far away as Chicago or Minneapolis, when for so many years, they'd made all their own gifts. But this year she'd wanted to give Astrid a real doll, one with a porcelain face and curly hair. The set of books they'd ordered for Thorliff would make his eyes sparkle, and the wood-carving tools for Andrew . . . ah, such pleasure she would have watching their delight on Christmas morning.

Another box had come earlier, one her dear husband knew nothing about.

"Why are you smiling so?"

"Nothing. And don't you go pushing. It's almost Christmas, remember?"

His chuckle made the secret even more fun. Surprising Haakan was hard. He seemed to have a second sense about gifts.

"Bedtime." She crossed to the arch that led into the other room. Andrew looked up from his papers.

"I'm almost done. Sure wish Thorliff was here to help me. He thinks writing stories is fun." From the tone of his voice, obviously Andrew didn't.

Astrid closed her book with a sigh. "That was such a good story. I bet Thorliff could write just as good though."

"Someday he will. I'll be up to hear your prayers in a minute." Ingeborg returned to the kitchen to dump out the dishwater and pour the rinse water into a bucket to reheat in the morning. She folded the wet dish towel and hung it on the rod behind the stove.

"I'll bank the stove." Haakan closed his Bible and crossed his hands on top of it. At the quiet in the kitchen they could hear the wind prowling and whining about the eaves. The sound made her feel even more snug and safe within the walls of their home.

"You'll be in to bed soon?"

Ingeborg felt the tingle raised by the special tone in his voice.

"Ja, soon." Strange how after ten years of marriage she still felt like a young bride when he spoke like that. She climbed the dim stairway, light from the children's lamps beckoning her upward.

She peeked in on Andrew first. He shut his book when he saw her in the doorway. "Just think, Thorliff will be here for almost a week." He glanced at the side of the bed his older brother used to occupy. "You think he and Anji will make up?"

"I don't know. I don't understand what the problem is."

"He could write to her and make things all better."

"How do you know so much about this?" But she knew that was a rhetorical question. Andrew listened, plain and simple.

"Gus said she cries a lot. I don't like that Thorliff makes her cry." He shook his head.

Ingeborg sat down on his bed. "I think Anji has more to cry about than just Thorliff." At the thought of Agnes that leaped into her mind, Ingeborg swallowed back the tears. And if she still struggled with the grief, so much more for Anji.

Andrew cocked his head. "You think Manda and Baptiste are okay?"

"Sure they are. Mrs. Solberg had a letter just last week."

"Can Metiz read?"

Ingeborg studied her son's face. "No, I don't think so." Always so concerned about others, what was he leading up to now?

"So does she know how Baptiste is?"

"Yes, Mrs. Solberg read her the letter, along with one written to her."

"Good." Andrew slid down and pulled his covers up around his shoulders. Not long and his feet would be hanging over the end of the bed like Thorliff's had at the last. If Andrew had his way, aging Paws would be up here instead of curled in a box behind the stove. She stood and bent down to kiss his cheek. "Good night, son of mine. God keep you."

"I prayed Thorliff would get here all right."

"Me too." She blew out the lamp. "Perhaps tomorrow." She patted his shoulder, missing the hugs he used to give her. Bone crunchers some of them were before he realized how strong he was becoming. Just this fall he had passed her in height, and last week she'd had to let down the hem in his pants, and they were still too short. *Perhaps if Thorliff has grown, he has pants I can cut down for Andrew.*

Astrid left the warmth of her covers to kneel at the side of her bed, resting her cheek on her mother's knee when Ingeborg sat down. She murmured her prayer in Norwegian, then ran down the list of those she cared for, "Bless Mor, bless Far . . ." clear down to the cat now curled on the end of her bed.

"Mor?"

"Ja?"

"It's only four days until Christmas."

"I know."

"And Thorliff isn't home yet."

Ingeborg nodded, meeting Astrid's imploring gaze. "He better hurry or he'll miss Christmas." A frown dug in above her nearly white eyebrows.

"He better get here before the blizzard."

Amen to that. "How do you know we are going to have a blizzard?"

"Far said so." And if her father said it, in Astrid's eyes, that was next to God talking.

"Yes, please, Lord, bring our son home before the blizzard." Ingeborg barely repressed a shudder that tried to shake her clear to the bottom of her soul.

CHAPTER SEVEN

On a Train West
December 22, 1893

The sea of white continued to eternity.

Thorliff made himself return to his book rather than stare out the train window. Hoarfrost rimmed the sides, sending feathers out to take new territory. He'd already scraped it away once. At least he didn't have to study. Exams were over, as was his first term. He'd made it through. What a relief.

"Grand Forks. Next stop, Grand Forks."

Thorliff watched the conductor sway his way down the aisle, stopping to answer a question posed by a man most likely a drummer, from his appearance. The salesman looked a mite familiar, perhaps one of those who frequented the Blessing Boarding House.

Why, Lord, can I not read here? I can with the babble of students in the reading room or even when the press is running. His thoughts roamed back to the pressroom where the antiquated press tried to shake the walls down. But there he could concentrate on his books and listen for the slightest change in the printer cacophony that signaled trouble, trouble that occurred with dismaying regularity.

Taking the printer apart, fixing the problem, and putting it back together came after he'd learned to set type, put away type, clean the rollers, and grease the gears. Greasing the press wasn't a whole lot different from greasing the combine or the steam tractor. If the part moved, grease it, was his father's maxim. Who would have thought his hours helping his father and uncle Lars with the farm machinery would be put to use with a cranky printing press?

Thorliff's stomach rumbled, even louder in his ears than the clackety-clack of train wheels on rails. The screech of applied brakes let him know the train was indeed nearing the Grand Forks station where he needed to change trains. They crossed the bridge over the frozen Red River, and steam billowing past his window from the braking reminded him to fetch his satchel from the rack above his head and slide his book into the outside pocket. He hadn't needed to pack much for such a short visit.

When he stepped to the platform, a snowflake floated down and settled on his nose. The gray sky promised a multitude.

When he made his way to the counter to buy something to eat, he glanced around at the waiting passengers. Wouldn't it be a surprise to see someone he knew?

"I'll take a hunk of that cheese and two slices of bread, coffee if you have some."

The woman behind the counter nodded. "That there is Bjorklund cheese. You ever heard of it?"

"Ja, I have." Should he tell he most likely helped make that wheel of cheese?

"They make the best cheese anywhere. Better even than Wisconsin." She handed him his dinner. "That'll be forty cents, please."

Thorliff kept himself from shuddering. Like his bestemor always said, *They rob you on the railroad.* And that was true whether buying food or shipping grain, cheese, hogs, whatever.

"Takk." He took his change, his mind spinning off to an article he could write for the paper. Alternately taking bites of bread and cheese, chased down by coffee that could almost be called hot, he made his way to a high-backed wooden seat, much like the pews in most churches. When he glanced up to the reader board, he shook his head. One hour to wait. Now dusk would fall before he could get home.

Setting his coffee carefully on the seat beside him, he drew his textbook out of his satchel and tried again to read.

A baby crying reminded him to take a sip of his now cold coffee. He glanced in the baby's direction to see a young man and woman trying to comfort a quilt-wrapped infant. The baby was having none of it, screaming as if they were beating him. The young mother got up and took her unhappy offspring to the necessary.

An arrow of sorrow pierced Thorliff's heart. That could have been him and Anji in a couple of years if she hadn't cut him out of her life like she had.

Unbidden, thoughts of Anji took over his mind. Graduation, her speaking so movingly, their first kiss, holding her hand, walking through the fields, laughter, the times they had danced together before he knew her to be more than a good friend.

Was college worth giving her up? Not that he'd given her up at all. She was the one who refused to let him help. She was the one who said not to come home. She was the one who failed to answer his letter.

Somehow, dredging up any anger was beyond him. He would be seeing her soon. Surely they would be able to talk again, to iron out their misunderstandings.

He forced himself to return to his history of the early church, not the most inspiring reading for one whose mind had a tendency to fly across the miles to home. When the train finally chugged into the station, he nearly leaped up the steps.

Never had the miles passed so slowly. Gray clouds hung low over the white-sheeted prairie, heralding an earlier than usual dusk. As they left the lights of town behind, the houses grew farther apart. Those he saw already had lamps lit, and all had smoke rising from chimneys. Surely many of the families were doing their last minute Christmas baking, the houses redolent with cinnamon, cardamom, and cloves. Mor would have apple cider simmering on the back of the stove, perhaps a roast in the oven, fresh bread on the counter.

His mouth watered at the thoughts. He should have asked his family to leave his skis at the boardinghouse in Blessing. *Why do I always have such good ideas so long past the time to make them happen?* He shook his head and continued to stare out the window.

"Hey, aren't you young Bjorklund?" The conductor stopped beside his seat.

"Ja." Thorliff kept his finger in the book to mark his place as he glanced up at the blue-clad man.

"I thought so. Henry Aarsgard, he married your grandmother, right?"

Thorliff nodded again.

"That Henry, he sure thinks the world of all of you. No more than if he was truly your own kin. You went away to school, to college, right?"

The man needed no more than an occasional nod to keep on talking.

"Does my heart good to see my old friend so happy."

"Do you see him often?" Thorliff wished he had his pencil and paper out. Somehow he sensed there was a story here—he just wasn't sure what it was yet.

"Your grandmother, she's about the best cook anywhere. Why, just the other day she sent a basket of cookies and breads and such for those of us who knew Henry. Even had some of that Bjorklund cheese in it. Your mor makes that, right?"

Another nod.

"That Henry, he is some lucky fellow." The conductor glanced up in response to someone's call. "Coming." He raised one hand in acknowledgment, then turned back to Thorliff. "You give Henry my best now, you hear?"

"I will."

"And a blessed Yule to you and all of yours."

"And you." As the man took two steps along the aisle, Thorliff called him back. "Sir, I don't know your name."

"Just tell him Sig. He'll know."

"Yes, sir, Mr. Sig, I will."

As the train steamed north, Thorliff put away his book so he could identify every place and look for changes. One farm looked deserted. Was that the family Mor had written about that gave up and went back East somewhere? Or did they go back to Norway? He couldn't remember. Either way, one of the Bjorklunds had most likely bought up his land. There'd be more fields to work come spring.

With the river frozen over, most likely his father had started cutting ice and hauling it to the ice house. Since there were no more trees to cut within hauling distance, the sawmill no longer ran in the winter. He knew that he'd missed the trek over to Minnesota to cut the Christmas tree. He shook his head at his fancy. Of course the tree was already decorated and waiting in the parlor to light the candles on Christmas Eve.

I missed all of the preparations this year. The thought tugged his spirits downward. In spite of the concert at school with both the choir and the orchestra, he still didn't feel like this Christmas was real.

Even printing out the booklet with his Christmas story for those at home hadn't made him feel in the Christmas spirit. *So why not?* He asked himself the question for the whatever number of times.

Anji. Her name echoed in his heart. The closer he got to home, the stronger her name rang. At school he'd been able to keep so busy he could ignore his heart, at least part of the time, but not here with the clackety-clack of the train.

"Blessing. Next stop, Blessing, North Dakota." Sig smiled as he swayed by.

Out across the white-drifted prairie Thorliff could see the Baard farm and on beyond that, the Bjorklund barns. The train slowed. The silver blue of twilight shadowed the drifts. If he craned his neck, he could see the grain elevator up ahead. Steam billowed past his window as the engineer applied the brakes, the screech a more sure announcement than the conductor's call. The snow-shrouded elevator, Onkel Olaf's furniture shop, and out the window across the aisle, Bestemor's boardinghouse. The station. Thorliff reached for his satchel and stood. Strange, but he felt in another world or at least another time period than Northfield, as if he'd traveled through a telescope back in time. In spite of his knowing better, the feeling persisted that nothing had happened in Blessing while he was gone. It had remained frozen in time like children playing statues.

He swung down, using the bar by the door with his free hand. "Thorliff!"

He turned at the calling of his name to see a horse and sleigh waiting at the far end of the platform.

"Astrid?" What was she doing driving the sleigh like that, a little girl like her?

She whipped the reins around the whip stock and leaped from the sleigh, her braids bouncing from under her red knit cap as she ran toward him. He dropped his valise in time to catch her when she threw herself into his arms.

He fought the burning behind his eyes and sniffed. Surely the cold, that was all. "Astrid, how did you know to meet me?"

"I've been coming every day since school was out. You almost missed Christmas." She released her stranglehold on his neck to lean back and see his face.

At her accusation, he could do nothing but nod. "I know, but I'm here now, and I think you've grown a foot since I left."

"No, already had two, didn't need another." Her saucy grin said she knew just what he meant, but just because he was a big college man, he wasn't above being teased.

He grabbed her again and this time swung her around in a circle like he used to do when she was little. Only now he held her by the waist and the spinning almost sat him down in the snowbank.

They ignored the train leaving and arm in arm headed for the sleigh.

"Do you want to stop and see Bestemor first? Or . . ." Her eyes grew round. "You haven't seen Gus."

"Gus?"

"Penny and Hjelmer's baby boy." Patience colored her tone.

"Sorry."

"He's the sweetest baby in the whole world."

Thorliff shook his head. "No, I think I'd rather just go home."

"You want to drive?"

"Ja." He glanced toward the church and school. "Pastor Solberg isn't in town, is he?"

She shook her head and climbed up into the passenger side of the sleigh. "No, he's at home, but said to come on out any time you wanted. We'll see him at service on Christmas Eve."

Thorliff tried to focus on her words, but all he could think about was Anji. Should he stop now or come back later?

"Mor will have supper ready when we get there. She's made rommegrot just for you."

Sitting himself on the sleigh's seat, he grasped the buffalo robe at their feet and pulled it up over his sister's legs. "Good, I haven't had any since last winter." He unwrapped the reins and pulled slightly to back the horse so they could turn and head for home. He'd have to go see Anji on the morrow. If his mor was beating rommegrot, they needed to be there when the butter came.

"The men should be done with chores by the time we get home. They started early." She touched his arm. "You haven't forgotten how to milk cows, have you?"

He clucked the horse to a trot. "Astrid, I've only been gone for three months, not a lifetime."

"Seems like one." Her sigh caught his heart. "Nothing's been the same with you gone." She scooted closer to him. "Andrew shoved Toby Valders headfirst into a snowbank the last day of school. Toby was some mad, but he had it coming. Pastor Solberg had told Andrew if he hit Toby again, he didn't know what he was going to do with him, but Andrew didn't hit him."

"Does Mor know about this?" Thorliff jerked his thoughts back from Anji and looked at his little sister, who was no longer very little.

Astrid shook her head. "You won't tell, will you?"

"No. I'd like to have dumped Toby on his head any number of times."

"I think Toby doesn't like being short when so many of the boys are getting tall."

This girl sure has a good head on her shoulders. "Where did you come up with an idea like that?"

She shrugged. "Just thinking, that's all. Oh, and one day he told Andrew, 'You think you can do anything just 'cause you're so big.' "

"Astrid Bjorklund, you don't miss a thing, do you?"

She rubbed her red nose with her mittened hand. "That's good, isn't it?"

"Ja, that's good." The jingling of the harness bells rang out across the prairie. Errant snowflakes bit their faces as they sped over the drifts on a direct line toward home, the fences buried in frozen white.

"Sure must have been cold here already."

"Ja. Pa says this looks to be one of the coldest winters since we came here. Our house and Tante Kaaren's are much warmer than most."

"That sawdust in the walls really helps, doesn't it?"

"Here comes Paws." The dog yipped as he bounded across the snow.

Thorliff stopped the horse with a *whoa*. "Hey, Paws, come on boy." The yipping dog tried to leap up into the sleigh but had to scrabble with his back feet to finally make it. He scrambled onto Thorliff's lap, his tongue busy in spite of the whimpers coming from his throat.

"I think you missed him."

"Ja. I haven't had a dog greeting like this since . . ." He left off his thought and thumped the dog on the ribs, at the same time rubbing ears and head. "Good dog, Paws, good dog." *He's getting old; his face is almost white, and he almost fell.* He wrapped the dog in a one-armed hug.

"He missed you too."

"Aw, he greets everybody like this."

Her snort more than expressed her opinion.

With Paws back on the ground and trotting beside the sleigh, his doggy grin expressing pure joy, they drove on up into the yard.

"I'll take care of the horse." Astrid reached for the reins. "You don't want to go getting your good clothes dirty."

"No." Thorliff turned to look his little sister in the face. "I will change and come to help."

She shrugged. "Don't want to leave him out in the cold and wind too long."

Thorliff couldn't believe his ears. Who did she think he was, or better yet, who did she think she was? "Hey, Astrid, this is me, Thorliff, your big brother. I was taking care of the horses before you were born." He patted her on the shoulder. "I'll be right back." "I just want your visit to be nice."

"Mange takk. It will be, and taking care of the horse will feel real good." He grabbed his valise and, climbing from the sleigh, took the three stairs as one. The door opened before he could touch the knob, and he nearly dove through it and into his mother.

"I was coming as fast as I heard the bells." Ingeborg hugged him, then stepped back to cup his face between her hands. "You are home at last." Her chin quivered, and her eyes turned suspiciously bright.

Thorliff nodded. "I am home, and if I don't get right back out there, Astrid is going to put the horse and sleigh away."

"So what is wrong with that? She does it all the time." Ingeborg shut the door and drew him into the kitchen. "They'll be up from the barn in just a few minutes."

"I'll be right down, then." Thorliff hugged her again and headed up the stairs, stairs that were steeper and narrower than he remembered. He threw his valise on the bench by the wall and shucked his good clothes as fast as he could, then pulled on his old pants still hanging on their peg on the wall, along with a woolen shirt. He changed boots faster than he ever had and clomped back downstairs. His chores coat, too, still hung on the peg, this time by the back door.

"Back as soon as . . ." The rest of his words were lost in the slamming of the door.

The horse and sleigh were gone, so he trotted on down to the shed where Astrid had already backed the sleigh into its place and was unhooking the harnessed horse from the shafts.

"I said I'd do it." He lowered the shaft to the ground.

"I know, but this way we'll be done sooner. I thought you might like to go over to the big barn and say hello to those milking."

He walked beside as she led the horse into the stall waiting for it. Together they removed the harness, and while he hung it on the pegs set in the posts of the barn wall, she dug out a can and poured the oats into the feedbox set in one side of the manger.

The horse on the other side nickered his request for a feeding too, so she gave him a small bit.

"You didn't do all the work," she reminded the dark bay gelding as she squeezed by him on her way out of the stall.

A barn cat twined about her boots as she and Thorliff started for the door. A blast of frigid north wind made them both duck their chins into their coat collars. Snow swirled and stung their faces, making it hard to see beyond their feet. They followed the shoveled path to the main barn and fought with the wind to open the door.

Bursting through the small door beside the wide double ones, they laughed at the same time and stamped their boots. The warmth of a barn full of cows and the quiet with the door closed made Thorliff pause. The telescope had switched ends on him. Now Northfield lay at the tiny end, and he was home.

"Thorliff, you came." Andrew looked up from pouring milk from the bucket into the strainer set on top of the milk cans. A bit splashed over as he poured fast, set the bucket down, and met them halfway down the aisle.

Thorliff reached to shake his brother's hand, but Andrew grabbed him in a hug instead.

"Thorliff," Haakan called from behind one of the cows. "Over here, milking Jezebel."

"He's the only one who can." Andrew kept his voice down. "She kicked me halfway down the barn."

"Did you put the kickers on her?" Thorliff stopped behind the only Holstein in the barn.

"Of course. Didn't do no good." Andrew and Thorliff stopped where they could see their father, forehead clamped into the cow's flank, fingers stripping the last of the milk from the now slack udder. The cow switched her tail and shifted her back feet.

Haakan grabbed the full pail and rose all in one smooth motion before she could move farther.

"At least she gave you a warning." Thorliff stepped back out of his father's way.

"Here, please dump this." Haakan handed the froth-filled bucket to Andrew, then drew Thorliff into the circle of light from the kerosene lantern. "You've lost weight."

"Ja, some."

"Don't they feed you there?"

"Ja, they do." Thorliff looked into his father's eyes, somewhat shaded by the poor light. Was there a shine there, one that most likely matched his own?

"Good to have you home, son."

"Mange takk." Thorliff cleared his throat. "You need another hand?"

Haakan shook his head. "Just finishing. Why don't you and Astrid go on back up to the house."

"I can haul the milk cans to the springhouse."

"Only this one left." Andrew joined them again. "I took the others on the sled. You hear that wind?"

They stopped talking to listen. A northerner howled around the eaves of the barn, shrieking like banshees wanting in.

"Hit like a freight train, didn't it?"

Haakan checked the world outside the door and laid a hand on a shoulder of each of his sons. "We have a problem. We've got a whiteout."

"The line isn't up to the house yet." Andrew closed his eyes. "I was going to do that this afternoon, but I forgot."

In spite of the warmth of the barn, Thorliff shivered.

CHAPTER EIGHT

Blessing, North Dakota

"I can't see a thing." Astrid's voice quivered.

"Whiteout. Thorliff, you take the lead. Just stay on the shoveled path. The sides will keep us safe this time. We're going to rope up though, just in case."

Thorliff reached for the coiled rope hanging on the wall. "You want I should pound stakes as we go?"

"I'm sorry, Pa." Andrew sounded close to tears.

"I know, but this is the way we learn our lessons. I should have checked myself to make sure. We'll be all right. At least I sent George and the others home early."

Thorliff tied the end of the rope around his waist and then looped it around Astrid's. When he handed the rope to Andrew, he managed a pat on his brother's shoulder. "We've been through worse."

Andrew nodded and roped himself in.

"Now I'll tie the end to the hook outside the door and then I'll pound the first couple of posts in. Andrew, once you reach the house, give three tugs. Land, this storm came down faster than any I've ever seen."

Thorliff and Andrew both pushed against the door to get it open and then staggered as the wind fought to slam them back inside.

Shuffling his feet along the shoveled-out path, Thorliff could feel the snow depth already over the tops of his boots. The path would be filled within the hour at this rate.

After what seemed an hour but he knew to be only minutes, he felt a break in the solid wall of snow and knew that to be the path to the springhouse. Pushing forward, he caught the opposite side of the path and continued until he banged against the steps to the house.

"Go on in." He shouted to be heard over the roaring of the wind and handed Astrid up the steps where Andrew helped her open the door to the porch, which they'd added to and enclosed since he had left for school.

Ingeborg, her shawl wrapped around her head and shoulders, stepped from the house into the porch. "I was beginning to worry."

"I know, but everything is all right." Thorliff clapped his mittened hands together to dislodge the snow. From the pinched look around his mother's mouth, Thorliff knew she had progressed beyond the point of beginning to worry.

"No, it's not, Mor. I forgot to put up the line this afternoon after Pa reminded me." Andrew stood hunched over, as if braced for a solid pounding about the head and shoulders.

"Then you've learned a good lesson. Where is Haakan?"

"Driving in the posts to hold the rope."

"I'm going back to help." Thorliff tugged on the rope three times, waited for the answering tug, and tied the end to the wooden railing built along the steps.

"That's my job." Andrew clung to the rope.

"You wait here in case one of us needs a spelling."

"If you bring some posts this way, we could all do it."

"Good. I will if Pa agrees." *That boy has a good head on his shoulders* was Thorliff's last thought as he stepped back out to battle the wind. The cold burned clear down to his lungs with every breath, even though he kept his long scarf wrapped around the lower part of his face. Ice pellets daggered any skin bared to the elements. Keeping his hand on the rope, he followed their trail back toward the barn.

"Get more posts." Haakan shouted in his son's ear to be heard above the shrieking wind.

Thorliff continued on to the barn, the gusts pushing him forward, then fought that same wind with all his strength to open the door. The snow drifting in front of it joined forces with nature to keep him out. Once inside he leaned against the wall for a moment, dragging warm air into lungs that felt like ice crystals. The roaring wind called him back outside so, grateful for the still burning lantern hooked over a nail in a post, he found another sledgehammer and, carrying the stakes, dove back out into the fury. He handed some of the posts to Haakan and followed the rope back to where Andrew waited to pound in spite of the storm. Without the rope they'd never make it back and forth between barn and house to care for the livestock.

By the time he and Haakan made it to the house, his eyebrows wore a curtain of ice, and he could barely feel his feet. Sweat, trickling down his back from the exertion of pounding the posts through the ice crust, felt like an icicle stabbing him when he removed his jacket.

"Thank the Lord you are all right." Ingeborg helped them remove and hang up their outer things, then poured them each a cup of coffee. "Your hands and feet—no frostbite, is there?"

The three men checked their hands and faces for white spots and wiggled their toes in their socks. "Nope, just pure cold is all."

"Did you blow out that lantern in the barn?" Haakan turned to Thorliff.

"Yes, sir. Didn't think we'd be going back."

"Good." Haakan rubbed his hands together over the heat from the stove. "Sure hope everyone else was ready for this. This is the first winter alone for the Baards. I should have checked on them."

"Joseph is able to advise even though he can't do anything."

"Ja, if he is awake." Haakan scrubbed a hand over his hair.

At the mention of Anji's family, Thorliff paused his hand rubbing and turned so the heat warmed his backside. *Anji, with a blizzard like this, when will I see you?* He knew how much time it took to water cattle and horses by hand. In the early years they had kept a hole cut in the river ice so they could lead the animals down there to drink. Now with the well, they would haul water from there and melt snow on the stove for the house.

"How are they all doing?" He studied the cream- and sugar-laced coffee in his cup, one of his mother's antidotes for intense cold. Normally he drank it black.

"Well as can be expected. Neighbors helped with the fall work."

That wasn't what he really wanted to know, but asking after Anji would—would what? They knew he loved Anji.

But did they know she no longer loved him? The pain in his heart flared anew, like a stove fed a pitch-drenched stick.

"Anji asks after you." Ingeborg's look made his ears burn. "Was there a reason you no longer wrote?"

Thorliff stared at his mother, fighting to keep the anger from staining his face. "*I* no longer wrote?" His voice squeaked on the last word. What had Anji been telling them? Did they not know of her telegram for him not to come home? Did they not know of the anguished letter he'd written after that, the letter that never received an answer? And then another letter, even though he hadn't heard from her.

Thorliff clamped his jaw to keep the words from rushing out.

Haakan cleared his throat. "Ah, Mor, I think what Thorliff and Anji do is beyond our . . . our . . ." He laid a hand on her shoulder with a gentle shake of his head. "They're grown up now, you know?"

The look she gave him said clearly what she thought of how grown up they were, but she nodded. "If we don't eat the romme-grot soon, it will be ruined. Astrid, refill the coffee cups while I fill the bowls."

After they said grace, Thorliff sprinkled more cinnamon on the rich feast in front of him. He dipped his spoon down through the melted butter and into the rich, creamy mixture that tasted like nothing else but what it was, rommegrot. He savored each mouthful, letting it melt on the back of his tongue and slide down his throat.

They had served traditional Scandinavian delicacies at the Christmas festival at school, but now he realized something he'd known but never really appreciated. His mother was one of the best cooks anywhere. He took a slice of bread and laid the soft cheese, made especially for Christmas, on top. Again, he took the time to enjoy the bite of the cheese and the yeast-rich bread. No wonder people on the railroad had wanted to buy his mother's cheese. He took the spekekjøtt, sliced so thin you could nearly see through it, from the passing platter and laid it over the cheese. They'd hung the haunches of lamb to dry in the upper rafters of the barn as soon as it grew hot enough and left them there until fall. Dry, hard, he'd heard it called a poor man's ham, but in his mind the two were as different as horses and cows.

"Thorliff!" Astrid nudged him with her elbow.

"What?" He blinked, his focus jerked back to the table from wherever it had roamed.

Astrid giggled, then handed him the bowl of applesauce. "I thought you might like some of this."

He spooned some onto his plate and nodded his thanks before passing the bowl to Andrew. "Where is Hamre?" Some cousin he was, not even aware when one was missing from the table. Cousin Hamre had lived with them since he came from Norway.

"Over to Kaaren's." Ingeborg glanced around the table to see if anybody needed something more. "I think he kind of likes Ilse."

"Now that would be a fine match." Haakan held up his bowl. "More, Mor?"

Astrid giggled at her father's quip.

Ingeborg laid her hand on the back of her husband's neck as she took his bowl, giving him a smile that Thorliff realized she kept for Haakan alone.

The smile and the hand, tokens of love that persisted through the years. And grew. Would he and Anji ever have that kind of love? How was it different from the heat that burned his hand whenever he touched her? Thorliff rested his chin in his hand. With the warmth of the stove and his full belly, keeping his eyes open took more effort than he had to give.

"Do you want dessert?" Ingeborg reached over his shoulder for his plate and bowl. "Astrid baked an apple pie just for you."

He double blinked and sat up straight to look across the table to his laughing brother. "Ja, please."

"Good thing or Astrid would have smacked you one." Andrew held up two fingers.

"No, you only get one piece." Astrid stood to help her mother clear the table. "And if you aren't nice, you can count on a little bitty one." She held her thumb and forefinger about an inch apart.

"You can give me the extra part of his." Thorliff winked at his brother.

Astrid set the pie pan on the table in front of her father. "See, I even made an apple out of dough." She pointed to the apple shaped crust in the center, surrounded by slashes for steam vents. A light dusting of cinnamon and sugar glistened in the lamplight.

"Astrid, you're an artist."

She shook her head and rolled her eyes. "I just like to bake and make things look nice."

Thorliff gazed at his little sister. *You're growing up, and I'm not here to see it. What would happen if I stayed, didn't go back to St. Olaf? It would certainly save a lot of money. Far used to be so against my leaving, I wonder what he'd say if I decided not to return. Would it make a difference with Anji? Has the blizzard hit Northfield too? Or only tried to smother us here on the Dakota plains?* At a lull in the conversation, the wind seemed to increase its fury. Or had he just not noticed that it had been howling all along?

Too many questions, too little mind left. He smiled up at Astrid when she set the first piece of the pie in front of him. "Shouldn't this be for Far?"

"No. Tonight you are the guest of honor."

"Tomorrow, however, you get to milk cows." Andrew nudged him under the table with his boot toe.

"So enjoy the honor tonight." Haakan accepted the second piece from his daughter. "Mange takk."

"You're welcome."

When they'd all been served and the coffee cups replenished, Thorliff cut the flaky crust with his fork. He scooped the bite to his mouth and looked up to see Astrid watching his every motion. He chewed and swallowed, making sure his face changed not a whit. Looking down, he cut another bite.

"Thorliff." Her wail made him laugh.

"Can't I tease you anymore?" He licked the tines of his fork.

"Umm. Best pie I've had for a long time." Pictures of Cook fixing his supper and packing his dinner box cascaded through his mind as he took another bite. Cook loved to make sure he got enough to eat, but even her pastries were no match for this one. Could it partly be because he was home and everything tasted better here, eating with his family instead of by himself at the newspaper office or in the dining room at school?

"Thank you, Astrid. And you are an artist, only with dough and flour and such."

"She draws real pretty too." Andrew scraped the pie juice from his plate. "Are we going out to check on the stock?" He looked to his father for an answer.

Haakan shook his head. "Not tonight with that blizzard the way it's howling. Everything was shut up tight. Let's just pray it dies out by the morning."

CHAPTER NINE

December 23, 1893

But it didn't.

Ingeborg cupped her elbows with her hands, grateful for the thick woolen sweater her mother-in-law, Bridget, had knit for her. The wind, the horrendous, vicious wind that tore at the house, seeped in through the tiniest of cracks, stealing the warmth and blowing frigid blasts that took her back through the years—back to when Roald died.

The pit—the eternal black pit, she could feel it, could almost see it on the edges of her vision. It had nearly squeezed the life out of her those years ago, and it always waited for her to succumb again. The fear of it made her shudder with an icy chill that even the roaring storm could not dispel.

"Mor?"

If Ingeborg turned quickly enough she knew she would see the darkness slithering away, gnashing its teeth at the interruption.

"Ja." Ingeborg sucked in lungfuls of life-giving breath and, grateful for the reprieve, reached out to her sleepy-eyed daughter. "What is it?"

"Where's Far?"

"He and the boys fought their way out to the barn to milk."

"Are you sure they made it?"

"Ja, three tugs on the rope."

"I dreamed that the blizzard covered our house right over." Astrid snuggled into her mother's embrace. "Like it did the soddy."

"Most likely covered the soddy again too." *Thank you, Father God, for our sturdy house and for banishing the pit by bringing my daughter to me. I will not fall in again, for you promised to deliver me. You did before.* Her gratitude swelled and forced the shimmering drops in her eyes to overflow.

"You are crying. What is the matter?" Astrid leaned back enough to gaze into her mother's face.

"Not sad, at least no longer. Joy perhaps?"

"For the blizzard?" The horror in the little girl's voice widened her eyes and mouth.

"We are safe, we have each other, and we are not sick." That other time, terrible sickness had taken Carl and all they'd found of Roald was his pocketknife. Surely God would not allow such tragedy again.

"And Christmas is almost here."

"Ja, I'm grateful for that too." She hugged Astrid one more time and set her back a step so she could cup her face with loving hands and smile into those eyes so blue. "Ah, Astrid, my heart, what would I do without you?"

"Be sad?" Astrid hugged her mother one more time. "I'll get dressed and help you with breakfast. Or do you think I should go help milk?"

"No, your far gave us strict instructions to stay in the house. He said the wind might just send us flying over the prairie." Ingeborg shivered at another screech at the eaves. "Go on and get dressed. Put on an extra petticoat and a sweater."

As Astrid left the room, Ingeborg took the sourdough crock off the warming shelf, measured out two cups to mix with milk, and set it back to grow again. Then she added flour, salt, eggs, and some bacon grease to the mixture for pancakes. If the dough set some before the men returned, it wouldn't hurt. The pancakes would just be lighter. The yeasty aroma of the batter made her sniff deeply in appreciation. If there was any batter left over from breakfast she would knead in extra flour and let it rise to make rolls for supper. Tomorrow was Christmas Eve—the candlelight service at church, and the children's program.

"Uff da," she muttered to herself. "And so much yet to do."

She took the copper boiler to the porch door and set it beside the new door to the outside. The wind pleaded for her to come out, whistling through any crack it could find, a sibilant siren's call to eternal sleep. She buttoned up her coat, pulled her hat down over her ears and, mittens in place, stepped outside long enough to scoop the boiler full of snow to melt on the stove. Before she finished, the cold had already penetrated her coat and muffler. "Uff da, indeed." She glared at the swirling snow. "You'll not take any of us, ever again." She turned and, with a grunt, slammed the door against the banshees and returned to her kitchen to slide her boiler to the back of the stove. They wouldn't have to haul water from the well to the house anyway, and if needed, they could melt snow for the chickens and the pigs too, even the cattle if necessary. But knowing Haakan, he had filled the barrels in the barn to water the stock in an emergency like this. She glanced up at the carved walnut clock on the shelf, their Christmas present one year from Olaf.

"Mor, how come they're not back yet?"

"They'll be in soon. The blizzard makes everything go slower. They'll water, feed, and clean out the manure before breakfast so they don't have to go back out there until evening."

"What about my chickens?"

"Andrew will take care of them."

"What if this lasts through Christmas?" Astrid finished unbraiding her hair to begin brushing it.

"Then we all stay snug in our own houses and go visiting later."

"Our presents will be late."

"I know." Ingeborg finished slicing the slab of bacon and wiped her hands on her apron. "Here, let me help you."

"Can you braid in these ribbons?" Astrid held up two red-and-green plaid ribbons.

"Ja, that I can."

The clock hands both pointed to the nine when Paws rose from his bed behind the stove, tail wagging, and made his way to the door. After the clomping of three pairs of boots, the door from the porch finally opened. Paws continued to wag his tail but no longer did he leap up and yip his greetings. His muzzle was near to white as the snow on the men's hats and shoulders, and the rest of his once caramel-colored face was faded like cloth left out in the sun too long.

"Thank the good Lord for a warm house and a secure barn." Haakan set a bucket of milk on the counter. "This nearly froze just between the house and the barn."

"So did my face." Thorliff leaned down to pet the dog, receiving a flick of tongue on his hand for the effort. "Aw, Paws, you've become an old dog while I was gone."

"Good thing we insulated the cheese house too. There was frost on the cans out there but not froze solid." Andrew unwound the muffler from his neck. "We fed some of the fresh milk to the hogs and chickens." He brought his basket of eggs to show Astrid. "Look, that one froze in the nest." An egg with a crack down one side lay atop the others.

"But my hens were all right?"

"Ja, and that rooster tried to get me again. He's about due for the stewpot."

"You just don't talk to him right." Astrid took the eggs over to the dry sink to clean them.

"Breakfast will be ready as soon as you are. There's plenty of warm water in the boiler for washing. Astrid, bring me the eggs from yesterday and then pour these freezing men some coffee. The cream is already on the table."

With her mind humming thanksgiving for her men being safe inside again, Ingeborg poured pancake batter onto the square flat skillet and moved the sizzling bacon from another frying pan onto a plate.

"And to think you made it home just before this blizzard hit." Ingeborg patted Thorliff's shoulder as she set the platter of bacon in front of him. "Our God is so good to us."

"Let's hope that train is stopped in some station instead of out on the prairie somewhere." Haakan smiled at his wife as she took her place at the other end of the table. "Now, let us give thanks. We have so much to be thankful for."

"I'm just grateful that wind can't get in here." Astrid shuddered. "It sure wants to."

Ah, this is such a far cry from what life used to be here. Ingeborg brought her thoughts back to the moment and joined in the table prayer. Now if only everyone else in Blessing, nay, in all of North Dakota and wherever the blizzard roared, were as snug and tight as the Bjorklunds.

"So, Thorliff, tell us what school is like for you." Haakan leaned back in his chair, patting his stomach. "Mor, that was mighty good."

Thorliff nodded. *How do I tell them without telling them all?* He ran a forefinger around the rim of his coffee cup and trapped a sigh before it could escape. The truth, always tell the truth. He glanced up from under his eyelashes to see if Mor had just said that again or if it was only in his mind.

She nodded, her smile encouraging him to begin.

"School is harder than I thought it would be."

Haakan looked up from tamping tobacco into the bowl of his pipe with his forefinger. "You mean harder to study or . . ."

"I study all right."

"You have time to study?" Ingeborg picked her knitting out of a basket she'd brought to the table and adjusted the four ivory needles that said she was knitting a sock. She caught the trailing yarn over her fingers and inserted one needle into the next stitch. When started, she raised her gaze to meet his, searching for the real answer behind his pauses.

"Ja, my work at the paper gives me a room of my own, like I told you in the letters. The night we print the paper, that is all any of us does, but other days I have time. You should hear that old press thump. Sounds almost as bad as our steam engine. But I can pick type now almost as fast as Elizabeth. That's Miss Rogers, my boss's daughter."

"She works there too?" A ring of smoke haloed Haakan's head.

"Ja, but not all the time." Thorliff shook his head. "She sure has strong opinions."

"She goes to St. Olaf too? I think you wrote?"

Another nod. "She is studying to be a doctor."

"A woman doctor?" Andrew looked up.

Just tell them about Anji. No, not for anything. Coward. The discussion in his head made him want to run right out into the blizzard.

"What does your school look like?" Astrid propped her chin on her stacked fists.

Ah, something easy. Thorliff turned slightly in his chair to see her better. Anything rather than the questions chasing like rainsqualls across his mother's face. "St. Olaf is on the top of a hill, so Old Main, the first and largest building, looks out over the countryside. It is four stories tall, made out of brick, with a beautiful tower pointing straight into the heavens. All of my classes are there. The dining hall is in the basement. I do a lot of my studying in the reading room, and my first room was on the top floor."

"Is it higher than our barn?"

"Ja, and with tall windows." He didn't add that sometimes he found himself looking out the windows at the oak and maple trees rather than listening to his professors. "I wrote you all this."

"I know, but I like to hear you tell about it."

The adoration in her eyes made him reach out and give a gentle tug on one of her braids. "I see you have Christmas ribbons in your hair. How lovely."

"M-mange takk." Her whisper tugged at his heart. How was it that now that he was home, he realized anew how much he missed his family. This day would be perfect if only he could talk to Anji and straighten out this mess they seemed to have made. Did she long for him as he did her, or had she banished him from her heart forever?

"Do you have friends there?"

Thorliff described the two other young men he usually ate dinner and sometimes studied with. "But one of them lives on the hill, and I live down in the town, so there is not so much time to be together."

LAURAINE SNELLING

"And you are pleased with your job?" Ingeborg passed the plate of molasses cookies around.

"Ja, more than pleased. I brought you a copy of the articles I have written. The Christmas contest was my idea, and it went over very well. Mr. Rogers said we picked up some new subscriptions because of it, and a couple of advertisers said they would like to work with us if we do it again."

"Will Mr. Rogers do that?"

"He said so. I'm going to suggest something similar for Easter." He nodded his thanks when his mother pushed the cookie plate closer to him. "I write the obits. . . ." At their looks of confusion, he paused and added, "obituaries, unless it is someone really well known, then Mr. Rogers writes it. He likes writing editorials the best, so perhaps I will get a chance to write hard news one of these days."

"There's a man come to town from Norway. He's staying at the boardinghouse, and he sends articles back to newspapers in Oslo." Andrew brushed the shavings off the animal he was carving.

"Let me see." Astrid reached for the figure. "A donkey."

"Ja, for the manger scene. I tried a camel, but"—Andrew shook his head—"I haven't seen a real camel, and I know horses, mules, and sheep real good."

"Well." Thorliff corrected his younger brother automatically, looking up in time to catch his mother's smothered smile. He cocked an eyebrow, and she shook her head.

Astrid stroked the carved figure. "You carve as good as Onkel Olaf."

Andrew reached for the donkey. "I need to take a bit more off the rump."

Thorliff and his mother swapped glances that left them both smiling. Haakan rocked his chair back on the hind legs in time to earn a swat on the shoulder as his wife went by on her way to replenish the fire in the cookstove.

"I know. If I break the legs, I have to fix them." He ducked away and brought his chair back upright. "Such bossy women in our family." But his smile said he was teasing, as did hers.

Thorliff watched the byplay between the two of them. Would he and Anji ever be like that? Showing love in little ways, sharing

82

good times in a snowbound house redolent with the fragrance of cooking ham and apples baking in cinnamon sauce? He refused to contemplate further and rose, stretching his arms above his head with a yawn. "How about I refill that woodbox?"

"Ja, and we better get to refilling the water barrels in the barn. Even the little daylight out there is better than none." Haakan copied his son's stretch and took his pipe to the stove to knock the ash into the firebox. Taking out his pocketknife, he scraped the pipe bowl clean and knocked the edge of it against the stove opening again. He set his pipe in the rack on the small shelf and drawer on the wall behind the stove where he kept his tobacco.

"I thought you'd stay in all day," Ingeborg said.

"Sorry. Let's go then, boys."

Once bundled up again, the three of them stepped out into the frigid blast. Haakan shook the rope free of the drifting snow and motioned Thorliff and Andrew to go ahead while he took the snow shovel and cleared the steps. When they got to the well house, Andrew began winching up buckets of water, dumping them into the buckets waiting to be attached to the yokes Thorliff took down from the wall. With a heavy bucket on each end, Thorliff adjusted the yoke over his shoulders and walked sideways out the door. Snow drifted in while the door was open. Haakan cleared the way for Thorliff as they leaned against the wind only to find the snow piled halfway up the front of the barn door. Thorliff set the pails on the icy ground while Haakan shoveled just enough snow for them to open the door and step into the sanctuary of warmth and peace. While Haakan shoveled more snow out of the way, Thorliff broke the film of ice in the barrels and poured in the buckets of water.

Back and forth they trekked until the barrels were full and the livestock all watered again. Every time he stepped back outside the first breath of icy air felt like a knife burning and stabbing deep in his chest.

"I think it's letting up some," Haakan said when he caught his breath again. He leaned against one of the timber posts, shaking his head. "This is some storm."

Thorliff listened. Had the wind really died down? He crossed to the door and pulled it open. Loose snow followed it in, but one

could actually tell it was slowing. The snow still swirled, but . . .
"The wind is dropping, like you said."

"Thank the good Lord for His mercy and favor."

Now I can go see Anji? The thought made Thorliff want to run
to the house, grab his skis, freshly waxed and ready on their pegs,
and schuss across the fields. He could be there in no time.

"And we filled the barrels in the worst of it." Andrew joined
his brother in the doorway.

"You're letting all the heat out," Haakan said.

Thorliff and Andrew rolled their eyes and stepped back to
close the door. "Is there anything else here that needs doing?"

"Ja, plenty, but Mor must have dinner ready for us so we will
eat first. Andrew, you gather the eggs, and Thorliff, you return the
yokes and buckets to the well house. I'll go check on the cheese
house if I can find it." They hadn't pounded in poles and rope to
the cheese house, knowing the milk could stay in the well house
for a few days. The straw and manure they'd banked against the
walls and on the roofs of the well house and cheese house, along
with the sod walls, kept the milk and cheese from freezing. At
least they hoped and prayed it would.

With the lighter sky, they could see the rope lying atop the
snow six feet or more ahead of them. While the well house was a
mound of white, the house itself loomed through the falling snow.

"It's stopping." Andrew burst through the door just ahead of
his older brother. He set the bucket, eggs nested in hay in the
bottom, by the cupboard and unwound his muffler.

"Mor, may we go skiing if it lifts?" Astrid turned from setting
the last knife in place.

"Or take the sleigh out?" Andrew hung his coat on the peg by
the door.

"We'll see. Fill the woodbox now and we'll eat. Where is
Haakan?"

"He's checking the cheese house. I'll get the wood," Thorliff
said when Andrew started to put his coat on again.

Instead of taking what wood was stacked inside along the
porch walls, he stepped back outside to the woodpile lining the
east wall. The stack reached clear to the porch eaves. He brushed
snow off the pile and loaded his arms. Three armloads and the

kitchen box was full, so he hauled in some more for the much depleted stack on the porch. Haakan joined him, and together they made sure there was plenty of wood on the porch in case the blizzard returned.

"They use coal in Northfield?" Haakan brushed the chips off his jacket.

"Ja, black dirty stuff. But it burns more slowly, and no matter how many trees, there would never be enough to cut to take care of the towns. Some places have steam radiators to heat the rooms. Like at school."

"Steam boilers, eh? Must have someone watching them all the time." The two stamped the snow off their boots and used the broom to brush off their coats. Haakan returned to the outer door and watched the snow falling.

"Better not plan on going anywhere yet. This could change any minute. Remember how fast it hit before." He slapped his leather gloves against his thigh. "I got a feeling it ain't over yet."

Thorliff glanced up at the skis and back to see his father watching him. Haakan shook his head ever so slightly and motioned his son to precede him into the warmth of the kitchen.

Does she even know I am home? Less than a mile away, and I might as well be in Northfield.

Just like earlier, they hung up their things, washed, and sat down to eat.

"At least we can hear ourselves think." Ingeborg set the last bowl on the table and took her place. At the first word of the grace, they all joined in.

The day before Christmas Eve and no company, no last minute preparations, no laughter.

At least not in Thorliff's heart.

CHAPTER TEN

"It's cleared enough. I'm going to see Anji."

Haakan shook his head, twin furrows deepening above his nose. "That's not a good idea. Look to the north. This is only a breather."

"On the skis I can be there in ten minutes. If it starts to snow again, I'll come right home." Thorliff pushed his sweater-clad arms into the sleeves of his heavy coat and wrapped a muffler around his throat. When he hazarded a glance toward his mother, he could read the fear in her eyes. "I promise I'll watch the weather." *I have to see Anji. Can't you understand? I have to!* He pulled his knit cap down over his ears. "See, the sun is even shining."

The last glance he had was his parents standing shoulder to shoulder, his mother's lips moving in what he knew to be silent prayer, Haakan shaking his head, and Astrid with her hands clapped over her ears and reading at the kitchen table.

Out on the porch he took the skis down from the pegs on which they were stacked and grabbed the poles hanging on pegs by their wrist straps.

Andrew joined him on the porch. "You sure you remember how?"

"Of course. You want to race me?"

"Nope. I'm not so hardheaded as to think I could outski a blizzard."

"You'll understand one day." Thorliff sat down on the steps to buckle the straps across his boots. "Thanks for keeping them waxed." He stood, checked his bindings and, with two strides, dug in the poles and started his journey across the drifts. Progressing cross-country with no fences to block him or roads to follow, he slitted his eyes against the dazzling brightness. The wind blew up crystals, and the cold knifed his chest, but neither mattered. He was on his way to see Anji at last.

He tried to pick up speed on the down sides of the drifts, but it was hard work going up drifts and even cutting through the deep snow where it hadn't drifted. The shushing sound of the skis against snow was as crisp as a bite out of a fall apple. With the wind at his back he covered the mile in fair time.

The barking dog announced his arrival as he skied around the house to the back door. No sitting on the front porch like they had last summer. No walking out across the fields. No Agnes. That thought caught him in the chest as he bent to unstrap his bindings.

"Thorliff, what in the world—" Knute bounded down the steps and clapped Thorliff on the back, nearly sending him headfirst into the snowbank. "What are you doing out here? The blizzard is coming back."

"Hello to you too." Thorliff propped his skis against the back stoop. "Besides, we have no guarantee the blizzard will return, and don't remind me to look north." He kicked the snow off his boots against the steps and, removing his mittens, stuck out a hand for shaking.

"Everyone, look who the wind blew in." Knute, taller even than Thorliff and filling out his shirt like a man, ushered their guest into the kitchen.

Anji turned from stirring something on the stove. "Thorliff, you're home." She started to move toward him and stopped.

"Ja, on the train yesterday. Then the blizzard struck, or I would have been here earlier." *Why is she looking at me like she's not sure who I am?* The desire to take her in his arms made his hands twitch. He studied her face. She looked tired, like she'd aged ten years in the three months that he'd been gone. Where had her warming smile and merry eyes gone, leaving behind trembling lips and eyes dull with fatigue, despair, what?

"Anji?" A quavering voice came from the bedroom off the kitchen.

"Excuse me. Pa needs something." She left the room in such a hurry he wasn't sure she just didn't want to stay.

"So how's school?" Knute sat at the table his father, Joseph, had made when they first came to homestead, making all they needed as had the other settlers.

"Sit, sit. Have coffee with us," invited Swen, Knute's older brother, although to look at them, both broad of shoulder and chest like the men they needed to be, it would be hard to tell which was which, they looked near enough alike to be twins.

Why can't I go in there with Anji? The thought crossed his mind and set his feet in motion. "I need to go greet your pa first." He stopped and looked back. "Watch the weather for me, would you please? If it starts to snow again, I have to head home."

"Ja, we will. You took a chance on that blizzard coming back."

"I know." Thorliff slipped into the bedroom, his nostrils pinching at the odor of just what he wasn't sure—sickness, dying by inches? One look at Joseph's skeleton lying in the bed told him it was the latter. If he hadn't known where he was, he'd have had no idea who it was.

Anji leaned over the bed, propping her father's head and shoulders up so he could drink from the cup she held to his lips with her other hand.

"Pa, Thorliff is home and he came to see you."

No, I came to see you. But he pasted a smile on lips that would rather shout his horror and went forward to take the old man's hand. "God jul, Mr. Baard. That was some blizzard yesterday, wasn't it?" *What do I say? I've known this man since I was a small boy and now . . .* His throat closed, and he looked to Anji for help. But she was gone.

"Thorliff?" The voice was so weak he had to bend to listen.

"Ja. I came home from college for Christmas."

"Sorry." His bleary eyes closed again.

For what? Thorliff laid the frail hand back on the covers. "Good-bye, Mr. Baard." Thorliff didn't know if he meant for now or until they met again in heaven, but surely no one could live long in the condition Joseph was in. Thorliff left the room and sucked in a deep breath of cinnamon-scented air as he walked to the table.

"H-how long has he been like this?"

"Ever since the fall. Must have broken his back in several places. He's in such pain all the time that Anji gives him the laudanum regular like." Knute slowly shook his head. "Things sure ain't been the same since Ma died."

"Do you like school?" Gus drifted over to stand by his arm.

Thorliff looked down at the little boy whose legs were sprouting out his pant hems. "Ja, I do, most of the time."

"I don't."

"Why not?"

"Reading is hard."

"Ja, some things are." *Anji, why are you so silent?*

"Arithmetic is too."

"I know."

"It's starting to snow again, Thorliff." Swen turned from the door with the news.

"I better go, then." He turned to Anji. "I'll see you at church tomorrow night?"

She shrugged. "Depends on how Pa is. You hurry now before you can't see." A bit of life sneaked into her words but not her eyes. "Thank you for coming to see him."

As he shrugged into his coat, Thorliff fought against the anger swelling his throat. *I guess if you don't care more than this, that is my answer.* "Knute, Swen, hope to have a better visit over Christmas." He clapped his hat on his head and hesitated for a moment, hoping Anji would see him to the door, but just then Joseph called again, and she headed for the bedroom door instead. When he looked to Knute, all he saw was a slight headshake accompanied by a one-shoulder shrug.

Outside, Thorliff threw his skis down and stepped first on one and buckled the straps, then the other, but all the while his hands were busy, his mind ran faster.

What a waste of time. Here I thought to work things out, and she can't even make enough time to talk with me. If that is what she means by love, I want no part of it.

Skis on, he dug in with his poles and headed for home. The wind had already blown enough snow to fill his tracks. And while it was snowing and blowing, it wasn't blizzard proportions yet.

Snow crusted on his eyebrows, and each breath burned his nose and pierced his lungs. He headed in the direction he knew to be home, knowing that if he overshot the farm, he'd run into the brush on the riverbank. While it was light enough to see, swirling snowflakes kept visibility to only a few feet. He skied, stopped to try to get his bearings, and pushed off again. Snow swallowed time and distance, and cold froze the sweat drizzling down his back. How could he be so weak in the knees and legs?"

Because you haven't been working hard enough. Not much different than starting up fieldwork after the winter off. The voice in his head drowned out the wind for a brief moment.

Living in town, especially in a town like Northfield in a river valley, shallow though it may be, had protected him from the winds and storms from the north. While he told himself all of this reasonable information, his mind tried to figure how far he'd come. Shouldn't he be home by now? He could most likely ski right into the barn before he saw it.

Fear tasted bitter on his tongue.

He stopped and shook his ski poles at the storm. "All this, and she didn't even take the time to talk with me. She knew I came to see her, not her father." The wind took his shouted words and hurled them right back down his throat. He leaned forward, gasping for air, ski poles dangling from the leather straps over his wrists as he cupped his mittens over his mouth to create a pocket of warm air to breathe.

What if I die out here? Serves her right. The crazed thoughts whipped around his mind like the blizzard that whipped around his head.

"Stop it! Just stop it!" He pushed off again. *Lord, surely you wouldn't have brought me home to die out here in a snowstorm. Like my father did.* The thought caught him by surprise. While Roald had been on a mule instead of skis, had thoughts like this come to him too?

He should have been home by now. If that thought had flitted through once, it had returned more times than she cared to count. Ingeborg clattered the stove lids onto the side so she could put more wood in the fire. *Father, please take care of him.*

"He most likely stayed at the Baards'." Haakan looked up from the journal where he kept records of the farm. He'd entered Bell's bull calf earlier in the month, and now he made a note of the blizzard on December twenty-second and twenty-third.

"You want some more coffee?" Ingeborg held up the pot.

"I guess." Haakan pushed his cup closer to her. He glanced at the clock again. "Half an hour since it started snowing again."

"Ja." She poured his coffee, chewing on the inside of her lower lip. Worrying, something she said she no longer did. *Lord, please take care of my son, for there is surely no way I can. But I swear when he . . . no, forgive me, I don't swear, but if he is out in this, he deserves a trip to the woodshed. Or at least a few hours splitting the huge chunks.*

Haakan stood and stretched, closed his journal, and put it back on the shelf above the trunk that Roald and Ingeborg had brought from Norway. He stopped on his way past, took another swallow of coffee, and headed for the back door.

"Where are you going?" Ingeborg glanced at the clock. It wasn't time to start chores yet.

"I'm thinking if he is near to home, he might hear the triangle. Too easy to ski right on by us in a storm like this."

"Or a gunshot?"

"We'll try the bell first." Haakan shrugged into his black woolen coat and wrapped a muffler around his neck. "You keep praying."

"Ja." Ingeborg prayed against the pit that seemed to lurk behind the stove right now. She fought the memories. *Lord, forgive my doubts, but I've been here before, now with my son rather than a husband. Please, keep him safe and bring him home. Oh, Lord God,* bring him home. But then, maybe he is safe and warm at the Baards', and they are having a real good visit. Perhaps he and Anji are working out their difficulties.

The clang of the bell echoed through her prayers.

All they'd ever found of Roald was his pocketknife and the bit of the mule's bridle. The wolves had taken all the rest. For so long she'd thought perhaps he was holed up somewhere injured or ill, but everyone searched every house and barn with no trace of the man who'd taken on the responsibility of seeing to all the neighbors. So many had died that winter, and in the spring some of those who made it through left, unwilling to fight any longer for the land that was supposed to be free. Free meant paid with blood and sweat instead of cash money.

"Is Thorliff all right?" Astrid leaned against her mother's arm.

"I pray so."

"He didn't stay at the Baards'."

"How do you know that?"

"He promised to come home, and Thorliff always keeps his promises."

Andrew came into the kitchen and headed for the back door.

"Where are you going?" Ingeborg asked.

"Out to relieve Pa. Ringing like that wears your arm off." Andrew slid his arms into the sleeves of his coat. "I think we should take the rifle out to the other side of the barn. Sound might carry farther that way. I'll ask Pa."

"Takk."

"Ja."

Astrid slid her arms around her mother's waist. Ingeborg wrapped her arms around her daughter and leaned her cheek on the top of Astrid's head. "I've been praying, Ma. God is listening, isn't He?"

"Ja, He hears."

While the bell continued to ring, Haakan blew through the back door, crossed to where the rifle lay on pegs on the wall, and took it down. He poured shells from the box into his hand to drop in his pocket. "I'll be out behind the barn. Send someone for me if he comes past without my seeing him."

"Ja." *Lord, please. Please!*

Haakan gave her a hard hug and, gun in hand, headed back out the door. The bitter cold blew across the floor and attacked Ingeborg's ankles, even through the wool socks that covered her legs. She shivered and hugged Astrid closer still. Her litany of *please, God, please,* flowed through her mind, gusty as the wind and just as imploring.

Surely I've gone by the farm. Where am I? While the wind came from the north, he knew he'd been skiing not so much against it but across it. Had the force of the wind sent him south? But it wasn't at his back. Thorliff stopped to figure where he might be. The river must be straight ahead. Or had the wind changed directions? The thought made his stomach clench.

Chapter Eleven

Northfield, Minnesota

I sure hope no one decides to have her baby now. Elizabeth stared out the window at the unrelenting snow.

"Got a foot or so," her father said when he came in from shoveling the front and back porches. He'd also been out to the stable to care for the horse. "I'm heading down to the office; you need anything from downtown?" When Elizabeth and Annabelle both assured him they were fine, he went out the door, whistling.

While the wind whistled around the eaves and blew drifts over the front fence, Elizabeth felt snug and safe in the chair before the hearth. She closed her eyes, enjoying the fire and the smells, redolent of Christmas. Peace seeped into her bones along with the warmth of the fire. Some time later she heard the bells of a sleigh as it turned into their lane and shortly after her father's voice teasing Cook in the kitchen. When he came into the parlor, he warmed his backside in front of the blaze.

"The telegraph says there is a terrible blizzard to the west of here in the Dakotas. Trains aren't running. Everyone's holed up to wait it out. I sure hope Thorliff made it home safely."

Elizabeth tapped her pencil against her teeth. *He must have. He*

left early yesterday. Lord, please keep him and his family safe. Jerking
her thoughts back, she picked up her physiology book and went
back to taking notes. Only by constantly reviewing could she
remember the names of muscles and know where they were
attached to the skeletal system. So in spite of the Christmas break,
she kept on studying.

"Dinner is ready." Her mother stood in the doorway. "Your
father is washing up now."

"All right." Shutting her papers in her textbook, Elizabeth set
them down on the floor by her chair and got to her feet only to
thump back into the chair. Her right foot refused to function. The
pins and needles of returning circulation stabbed, making her
wince. *Stupid, stupid. You know better than to sit on your foot for so
long.* She wiggled her toes and flexed her ankle and foot, wincing
all the while. Her mother would say it served her right. A lady
should sit straight, both feet together on the floor, not have one
tucked under her. When she could finally walk, she limped
toward the bathroom to wash her hands.

Cedar garlands decorated each doorway, held in place by red
bows and pinecones. The pine tree in the front window of the
parlor stood ready to be lit, a white candle in a holder clamped on
each bow. Elizabeth eyed the stack of presents as she passed. Only
through the sternest of admonitions had she kept herself from
shaking those with her name on them. But then, guessing what
was inside was half the fun. Perhaps she and her father would
indulge themselves in package shaking after dinner, when and if
her mother went upstairs for her *lie-down,* as she called it.

"So, my dear, is all ready for this evening?" Phillip flipped open
his napkin and laid it across his lap.

"I believe so, that is, if anyone shows up. I do wish this snow
would stop."

"I'm sure you're not the only one."

"I know, but this much snow makes me feel utterly . . . claus-
trophobic." Annabelle glanced around the table to make sure all
was in order. "Elizabeth, is everything all right?"

"Yes, of course." Elizabeth looked up from resettling her napkin and reminded herself to smile. What had happened? All of a
sudden she felt . . . she felt what? Strange, as if something terrible

had happened or was about to happen. Sadness washed over her like a heavy rainstorm. She shook her head and sat up straighter. *This is silly,* she admonished herself, all the while smiling again to both of her parents. Anything to banish the worried look they both sent her way.

"You know Cook's funny saying, 'A goose walked over my grave'? Surely that was what it was. Please pass the butter." She snatched a roll out of the basket and broke it open to let loose the fragrance of freshly baked bread. "My, doesn't that smell wonderful?"

Conversation continued in fits and starts, nothing like their usual ease. When the meal was finished, Elizabeth couldn't leave the table fast enough. She paused in the act of pushing her chair in.

"Is there anything you need me to do, Mother?" *Please, don't say yes.*

Annabelle refolded her napkin and inserted it back in the silver napkin ring, obviously thinking hard. "No, I believe all is well. Your father has shoveled the front walk, and—"

"Looks to be done snowing," Cook announced as she pushed open the door from the kitchen.

"Ah, good." Annabelle brightened considerably. "You go back to your studying, and Phillip, you to your editorial. I shall go have my lie-down after all." She came around the table and linked her arm through her daughter's. "Even if there are fewer here than sent their RSVPs, we shall have a marvelous time. Have you any idea what you will be playing, besides Christmas carols, of course."

"I've adapted the 'Hallelujah' chorus from Handel's *Messiah*, and a couple other numbers as well. I do so love Handel's music."

"Wonderful." Annabelle stopped on the bottom step and glanced around the decorated rooms. "I do love Christmas. I wish we had these decorations up all year."

"The tree would drop all its needles, and then you would fuss." Phillip winked at his daughter as he passed the two of them on his way to his study.

"Oh, listen." Elizabeth darted to the front door and peered out the long narrow window flanking the oak door. "Sleigh bells."

Phillip joined her with a sigh. "Now I suppose you want me to hitch up the sleigh for a ride?"

"Oh, would you, Father? Mother, you want to come along?"

"No, thank you. I need to be fresh for this evening. You two go on and freeze your noses if you want." Annabelle continued on up the stairs while Phillip and Elizabeth donned their heavy coats, swapping chuckles like two children just let loose from school.

"Bundle up warm, now." Annabelle's admonition floated back down the stairs, making Elizabeth giggle into her fur hat before pulling it over her ears. "I'll get Cook to heat us a couple of bricks."

Within minutes Elizabeth and Phillip were snuggled beneath the bearskin robe, hot bricks at their feet, and joining the parade of sleighs that jingled their way down Main Street, flying hooves and shushing runners billowing loose snow and packing the rest.

"Let's drive past Doctor's house." Elizabeth waved at some friends turning into the convoy.

"On our way back." Phillip waved at someone and shouted "Merry Christmas" in return. He eased back on the reins as his horse sought to outpace the horse and sled in front of them. "Easy, boy."

Snow glittered, as if rejoicing at the return of the sun. Blue sky, so welcome after the days of gray, pine trees, bows weighted by snow, and icicles daggered from the eaves all caught Elizabeth's gaze as they jingled their way along.

Northfield shook itself and displayed its festive garments just in time for Christmas.

"Dr. Gaskin, are you coming tonight?" Phillip slowed the horse as the doctor waited in his sleigh to join the throng.

"Planning on it. Got to go check on that young'un Elizabeth took such good care of. He had the croup again before the snow hit."

Elizabeth gnawed her lip. *Should she offer to go along?* If she was late for the party, her mother would never forgive her. "Tell them Merry Christmas for me."

"I will. See you later then."

Phillip gave his daughter a slight shake of his head.

"You knew what I was thinking?"

"Your mother would have my hide tacked to the stable wall if I came back without you."

"Really?" Elizabeth couldn't resist teasing him. But obviously, neither of them wanted to be on the bad side of Annabelle and spoil her party.

As they left the sleigh riders behind and headed home some time later, Elizabeth pulled the bear robe up over her nose. With the sun already angling toward the horizon, she could feel the temperature dropping just as fast. Knowing that Cook would have hot chocolate ready for them made her shiver in anticipation.

Pine and cedar, vanilla and cinnamon, the potpourri of fragrances met them at the door. Elizabeth inhaled the aromas of Christmas clear to her toes, even before the warmth began to melt the snow on her boots. She shed her outer garments, hanging them on the coatrack in case there was any lingering snow.

"There you are. I was beginning to worry. You know our guests will be here before long."

Elizabeth glanced at the clock. Two hours yet. They were not late.

"You are planning on wearing that lovely red Christmas frock, are you not?" Annabelle paused in the doorway for an answer.

"Yes, Mother." A quickly caught sigh made her aware that she'd planned on the dark blue silk just because she'd known her mother would request the red. *Why am I so contrary?* A glance at her father caught the wink he sent her.

" 'A merry heart doeth good like a medicine.' "

She nodded and smiled back. Since her father so seldom quoted Scripture, she appreciated it even more.

And a merry heart she had indeed as she sat at the piano several hours later, welcoming their guests with the gift she enjoyed giving most, her music.

"Well, hello." Thornton's deep voice brought her out of her music-induced reverie.

"Thornton, I thought you were going home for the holidays." Thornton had left his family home in Pine City to attend Carleton College.

"The snow changed my mind, or rather the railroad's mind. I should have gone the day before like I'd planned." He leaned against the ebony concert grand, surveying the crowded rooms. With all the doors opened, the guests could visit in the parlor, the music room, the dining room, and the study. Her mother and father were still welcoming late arrivals, and Cook, in a brand-new ankle-length white apron, circulated among the guests with a tray of hot spiced cider and eggnog.

"Would you like some?" Thornton nodded toward the refreshments.

"Cider, please." Elizabeth segued into a Christmas medley.

He set the china cup in its saucer on the piano. "You know, if you ever used sheet music, I could turn the pages for you."

"Thank you, kind sir, but not these. Perhaps later." *Go make yourself useful, Thorny. Let me be.* The thought reminded her that she must never slip and call him that to his face. He could be Thorny only to her.

As if reading her mind, Thornton answered a beckon from his aunt, who had taken a chair close to the fireplace. Her pale face and rotund belly could no longer be hidden by a cloak or full dress. In spite of the social strictures, Annabelle had insisted she come, knowing how much Mrs. Mueller needed a respite from her brood of rambunctious boys.

Through half-shut eyes she watched Thornton bend down to hear her request and then nod and pat her shoulder. He did have nice manners and seemed to care deeply for his aunt and uncle. *So where are you going with this?* The thought intruded only slightly as the music flowed from her fingers stroking the keys. *If I were ever to think about marrying, perhaps Thornton would not be a bad candidate. It would certainly make my mother happy, ecstatic in fact, not that she wasn't already pleased with the friendship, always hoping for something more.* But men took a great deal of time. She'd seen that in every relationship she knew. *How could I possibly have both a busy practice and a marriage?* She wrinkled her nose and picked up the beat with "Joy to the World." Better to leave off even thinking along those lines.

"If you would like to mingle for a while . . ." Annabelle stopped by the piano. "Such a lovely gathering, don't you think?"

"Yes, Mother, everyone seems to be having a very nice time.

Have you seen Dr. Gaskin? He said he'd be by after a couple of calls."

"No, he hasn't arrived."

"Hmm. I hope everything is all right." Her thoughts traveled out to the farm and the young couple with the croupy baby.

"Could you please play 'O Tannenbaum'?" Cook whispered on her way past, her cheeks as bright red as the holly berries in the arrangement on the table.

Elizabeth did as asked, at the same time keeping one ear tuned to the doorbell. She'd just finished Cook's request and was about to stand up when she saw her father head for the front door.

"So you decided to take a break." Thornton appeared at her side with a glass of eggnog in hand. "Thought this might taste good about now."

"Thank you." She took the glass and raised it to her mouth but set it on a nearby table when she heard Dr. Gaskin's voice. "Excuse me," she said, getting up from the piano.

She arrived in time to see her father taking the physician's coat and Dr. Gaskin helping a woman off with hers. *Who is with him?* The thought flashed by to be answered when the woman turned around. Dr. Gaskin's nurse. "Why, Miss Browne, how nice to see you." Will mother ever have a fit about this. Elizabeth didn't dare look at her father for fear he would make some droll face and she would not be able to keep from laughing. He too knew this would cause a ruckus with Annabelle—and most likely every other woman in the place. Not even seven months had passed since Dr. Gaskin's wife died. And here he was escorting another woman.

"Nurse Browne had nothing else to do tonight, and I thought this might give her a chance to meet more of the Northfield residents, other than patients, that is." Dr. Gaskin smiled down at the woman beside him.

Elizabeth stepped forward. "What a nice idea. Miss Browne, why don't you come with me and I'll introduce you around." She sent a look to her father that said keep him busy out here or something.

"I would like that. Indeed, I would." Matilda looked around at all the decorations. "My land, but this is lovely. Such a lot of work you and your mother have put into this."

"Oh, Father helped some, and Old Tom. Mother loves Christmas more than any other holiday. Have you met my mother?"

Miss Browne shook her head. "Other than folks at the Methodist church and sick people, I've been too busy to get around much."

Thornton joined them as soon as they entered the music room. "Ah, now you must introduce me."

Elizabeth did the honors, and with Thornton on the other side of Miss Browne, they took her around the gathering, making sure she was always on the opposite side of the room from the doctor.

"Can I get you either hot cider or eggnog?" Thornton asked.

"Eggnog, please."

"Coming right up."

"Miss Browne, this is Mrs. Mueller. You met her husband in the study."

"Oh, we're old friends by now." Matilda leaned closer. "How are you feeling, deary? You look a mite peaked."

Mrs. Mueller nodded. "My back, it's been aching some off and on all day, but I so wanted to come to the party. I thought if I just sat back out of the way, no one would mind."

"No, they most surely wouldn't." Miss Browne sat down on the hassock in front of the chair.

Little does she know, Elizabeth thought. There will be buzzing over a woman in her condition coming out to a gathering. Sometimes I wonder where these folks think babies come from anyway. Like they suddenly appear after a woman has been in hiding for two months?

She watched as Nurse Browne, in the guise of holding Mrs. Mueller's hand, took her pulse, then looked around the room until she saw the doctor. Glancing back at Mrs. Mueller, Elizabeth saw her face go white as she laid a hand on her side. *Oh dear, trouble ahead.* Elizabeth crossed the room and knelt by the steel-jawed woman.

"Can I get you anything?" She kept her voice low.

"No, I want to hear you play the Christmas hymns, dear. I'll be fine." Mabel Mueller's smile gained strength, and she nodded, now that the spasm had passed. "Please," her eyes pleaded more strongly than her words. "Please don't tell anyone. I trust Miss

Browne here will keep me company."

Elizabeth cleared her throat. "Does your husband, I mean, Reverend Mueller know how you are?"

Mrs. Mueller shook her head. "I don't want to bother him. He needs an evening of enjoyment." She patted Elizabeth's hand. "It will be a long time yet. I should know. I've done this before."

Have you ever. Elizabeth wanted to run over and drag the doctor back to his patient, but she didn't want to make a scene.

Annabelle stood in the cedar-draped doorway and shook a string of sleigh bells. "Refreshments are served, and then we will have our evening's entertainment." She looked square at Elizabeth when she made her announcement.

"May I bring you a plate?" Elizabeth squeezed Mrs. Mueller's quivering hand.

"No. No, thank you, dear. I'd best not eat anything just now." She touched the young woman's hand as she turned to leave. "Please begin your concert soon, then I will ask the reverend to take me home."

"Oh, I will." Elizabeth looked across the room to see Reverend Mueller talking with another man as the two of them strolled through the doorway. He didn't even look her way, let alone ask his wife to join him. *Has the man no sensitivity for his wife at all?* The urge to run and grab him by the hand made her shake. *What is the matter with him?*

Elizabeth made her way to her mother's side. "Can I—" She stopped herself. No need for her mother to become involved. Most likely Mrs. Mueller was right. After all, she'd done it often enough.

"Yes, dear, what is it?" Annabelle left off a conversation and turned to her daughter.

"Ah, the party is going well."

"Yes, it is." She turned to answer a question from Cook.

Elizabeth faded into the crowd. Her mother was in her element. No sense to cast a shadow on the party.

"Are you all right?" Thornton materialized at her elbow, plate in hand. "I brought this for you." He held out one of the plates as an offering. "I reserved us a spot on the piano bench."

"Thank you. Let me get some more punch."

"I already put that by the piano." He motioned over his shoulder.

Elizabeth glanced up to catch laughter lighting his eyes.

"What?" *Do I have something on my chin?* She wanted to check in a mirror.

"Nothing, you just always look so surprised when I do something for you."

"Oh." *Now, why can't the reverend treat his wife like this?*

"What's wrong?"

"Why?"

"A frown just trampled the edges of your smile and stole the light from your eyes."

She could feel the blush race to her hairline. "Thornton, you must be a poet under your happy-go-lucky exterior."

"Who, me?" His eyes widened. "For a fellow who studies as hard as I, surely that is a misappropriated description."

Elizabeth cast a gaze heavenward. "Let's just go eat. I never win when you tease me like that."

"No, you just decimate my ego in chess and croquet."

"Have we played whist?" She settled herself on the walnut bench.

"No, and we won't. I have taken a vow to never again play cards or any other game with you. You always win."

Elizabeth looked across the room to Mrs. Mueller sitting with her head resting against the back of the chair, her eyes closed. *Would that I could win at every game, if I could be so bold as to think of doctoring a game.*

Mrs. Mueller's hands suddenly strangled the arms of the chair.

"Here, take this."

"But you've hardly eaten anything." Thornton looked from Elizabeth to her barely touched plate. "Surely there is time—"

"No, maybe not." She stood and, shaking out her skirt, sat back down on the piano bench and rested her fingers on the keys. "Please go and sit by your aunt, and when you see that she looks uncomfortable, go fetch Dr. Gaskin."

"What . . . you don't mean. . . ?"

CHAPTER TWELVE

Bless you, Thornton, you did as I asked without question.

Thornton made his way across the room, smiling and greeting folks as he passed but never getting sidetracked. He moved the footstool in place and sat in front of his aunt.

Elizabeth watched him smile and offer the woman a tidbit, then at her bidding went for something in the other room, returning with a cup of punch. So who is the more typical of the male species? Reverend Mueller or Thornton Wickersham, my father or—or Thorliff Bjorklund? Surprised that his name had sprung to her mind, she heard "Greensleeves" rippling from beneath her fingers.

One by one the guests made their way back to the chairs. Her father brought in more seats from the other rooms, as if they wouldn't hear her playing from the study or dining room.

At her mother's nod she hit several chords as an introduction and then went into the opening bars of "Hallelujah!" from Handel's *Messiah*. As the music flooded the room, the wonder of it made her soul smile. She forgot the people gathered, forgot her concerns for Mrs. Mueller, forgot everything but rising and floating with the majestic music. By the time she finished the final note, she had to wipe the tears from her cheeks as the guests applauded. She segued into other favorites and finally into Christmas carols, so everyone could sing along.

When the final notes faded away, her father handed her a handkerchief and reached for her hand so she would stand. "Beautiful, my dear, simply beautiful."

"Thank you." Elizabeth smiled and dipped her head in acknowledgment of her audience's appreciation. "Thank you all for coming. I know Mother has more refreshments in the dining room. We wish you all a most blessed Christmas, and may the Christ child reign in your hearts all through the year."

"If any of you has a favorite song that Elizabeth has not yet played or something you would like to hear again, you could ask her." Phillip glanced at his daughter to get her nod.

Elizabeth sat back down at the piano, her fingers automatically searching out the keys in rippling streams. At the same time her gaze returned to Mrs. Mueller, who smiled and nodded her appreciation, then clutched the chair arms again.

None of those around her were paying any attention, but about the time Elizabeth was going to rise and go to her, Miss Browne returned to her side.

Where was Thornton? Elizabeth's gaze roved the areas she could see. No father, no doctor, no reverend. They must be in the library or her father's office. Her eyes went back to Mrs. Mueller to see her clenching with another contraction. It hadn't been three minutes since the last. Her gaze collided with Miss Browne's. There was no time to take the woman home, not with the contractions this close and the weather as cold as it was outside.

She finished the notes as if nothing were wrong and rose from her bench, all the time glancing around, searching for her mother. She must be back in the kitchen. Which to do first? Find her mother or Reverend Mueller or a room for the birthing?

"Elizabeth, Mrs. Mueller is in distress." One of their neighbors stopped at her side.

"I know." Elizabeth crossed the room and knelt beside Mrs. Mueller. "Do you think you can walk up the stairs?"

"I am so sorry." Tears slipped out ahead of a groan. "I thought it would be hours yet."

"Don't you fret. Been a long time since a baby was born in this house. Can you walk?"

"I . . . I can try." Together Elizabeth and Miss Browne helped the woman to her feet.

"How can I help?" Thornton appeared at her side.

"Go find Dr. Gaskin and then my mother."

Another groan made her wince. Thornton made his way through the chatting guests, who were heading toward the front door in a leisurely fashion. How could they all be so unaware of what was happening?

Because Mrs. Mueller was the consummate actress, that's why.

The men came from the study and surrounded the three women.

"I knew I shouldn't have allowed you to come." Reverend Mueller spoke in a whisper that turned into a hiss. "Let's get you home immediately."

"No, you'll do nothing of the kind." Elizabeth heard the words coming from her mouth before she even thought them.

"I beg your pardon?"

A groan cut off their discussion.

"Where should we take her?" Dr. Gaskin asked Elizabeth.

"Upstairs or else to the study."

"I'll carry her." Thornton stepped forward.

"Don't be silly. She can walk." Reverend Mueller's strident voice made Elizabeth gnash her teeth.

"Walking might have been good a while ago, but not now." Dr. Gaskin looked to Thornton. "I'll help you. We can cross hands to form a seat and carry her up. Are you ready?"

The two men crossed their arms, and locking hands, stooped low for Mrs. Mueller to sit.

"I am so ashamed." Her whisper cut to Elizabeth's heart, but when she realized the woman's skirts were soaked, she understood even more.

"What's happening?" Annabelle joined her daughter.

"Her baby."

"Oh." Annabelle forged ahead of the men. "This way."

"I'm sure we could make it home before . . ."

Elizabeth turned to the minister, but her father stepped between them. After warning her with a frown and commiserating with a slight smile, Phillip took the reverend by the arm and led the blustering gentleman away. "Come with me to the study, and we'll let the women do their jobs here."

Elizabeth followed the others up the stairs. *What is the matter with that man? How can he be such a good man to those of his parish and so careless with his wife? That isn't what the Bible says about men of God, is it?* As she topped the steps, she reminded herself she needed to look up the Scriptures to see what was indeed written.

"Elizabeth, get more towels." Annabelle met her at the door to the guest room. "I've rung for Cook to boil extra water."

When she brought in the towels and two extra sheets, Dr. Gaskin motioned to her. "Do you have your black bag handy? I didn't bring mine tonight."

"Of course. I'll be right back."

A bit-off shriek shattered the stillness, sending speed to her slippers.

Really, with both Doctor and Miss Browne here, I'm not needed. But Elizabeth couldn't leave either, drawn back to the guest room in spite of her own admonishments. She had assisted Dr. Gaskin on enough birthings not to want to miss a thing. And she knew her presence would be a comfort to Mrs. Mueller.

After another hour passed and the baby no closer to making an appearance, she went downstairs to fetch coffee for those in attendance. At the bottom of the stairs she could hear male voices from the study, so she went to check on them also.

Her father and Reverend Mueller were seated in front of the fire, their discussion intense enough they didn't hear her enter.

"But you know the unions are not of God. Why do you say so?" Phillip leaned forward, his hands clasped, elbows on knees.

"I say that anything that improves the plight of the working man is a good thing. How can you dispute that?"

"True, but to say God has His hand in it?" Phillip stared at his guest over his steepled fingers.

"God has His hand in everything, no matter what we think.

He has not abdicated the throne and left it all to man."

"What do you mean by that?"

"The running of this world, of course." Reverend Mueller leaned back in his chair, fingers cushioning his chin.

Here he is arguing politics while his wife is up there struggling to bring another child into his family. What about good things for women, like not having a baby every year? Elizabeth kept her thoughts to herself but cleared her throat to let them know she was there.

"Excuse me, but may I get you anything? Coffee, Reverend?"

"No, thank you." He answered with barely a nod in her direction. As she turned to leave, he raised his voice slightly. "Lovely playing this evening, Miss Rogers. Such a gift you have. Any time you would like to come play for services again, you let me know."

"Oh, I will." *Be a slow day in Chicago before I do that again.* One more strike against the minister. She'd often fought off the memory of his "suggestions" on how she play the hymns. She either went too fast or too slow or too loud or too . . . there were always more too's.

And yet, most of his congregation thinks he can walk on water. Why, Lord, is it that he rubs me the wrong way? Reverend Johnson is such a wonderful man; I wish we attended the Congregational church instead.

Cook had the granite coffeepot hot enough on the back of the stove. She roused from her sleep in the chair when Elizabeth moved the coffeepot. "Why did you not ring?"

"I needed something to do with my hands."

"You could go to bed, you know. The nurse is helping Dr. Gaskin."

"I know. But if I can help in any way, I would rather be doing that." *I'd rather be up there helping, but they are working so well together.*

"You could go play for her. You know how Mrs. Mueller loves to hear you play the piano."

Elizabeth finished filling the silver pot and set it on the tray. Cook added a plate of cookies and picked up the tray.

"You go play. I'll make sure the door is open."

Elizabeth did as told, wishing they had kept Mrs. Mueller

downstairs so she could hear better. If this was soothing to her, more power to the gift of music.

But she couldn't lose herself in the songs, even caught herself stumbling in places, because she couldn't forget about the scene upstairs. While she hadn't heard any more interrupted screams, she hadn't heard a baby's first cry either. What was going on up there?

Cook climbed the stairs with something else. The argument in the study grew louder. Had her father doctored the coffee with something stronger? When had Thornton left? Or hadn't he?

When Cook came back down, she stepped into the parlor. "Mrs. Mueller is asking for you."

With a nod Elizabeth slipped away from the piano and, hiking her skirts, dashed up the stairs.

"How is she?"

Dr. Gaskin shook his head. "See if you can get her to push. We've got to get that baby moving."

Elizabeth leaned over the side of the bed and stroked the sweat-soaked hair off the pale forehead. "Mrs. Mueller, you asked for me?"

A brief nod and her eyes fluttered open. "Th-thank you." Her voice barely above a whisper, Mrs. Mueller reached for the younger woman's hand. "Please don't be angry at Reverend Mueller. He does the best he can."

Elizabeth ducked her head. *Had her feelings been that obvious?* All words fled her mind. What to say? Right now she wanted to take a horsewhip to the man. He hadn't even asked about his wife, as if she were nothing more than the drudge who worked at his house. Yet she'd seen him show such compassion to ailing members of his church. Why not his wife?

"You just think about getting this baby born. Doctor says it's time to push."

A faint nod. "I . . . I'm afraid . . . I d-don't have much . . ." She clenched both eyes and teeth against another contraction.

"Please, push! Push with all you have, Mrs. Mueller, come on." Elizabeth gripped the woman's hands as if she could share her own strength. "Push!"

"I a-m-m." As if drawing on her last ounce of strength, she

reared up, face, hands, body straining, her keening high and piti-ful in its weakness.

"Again. Here, push against me." Elizabeth pulled the woman against her and braced her back on the head of the bed. "When the contraction comes, push. Your baby needs you to push." The young woman whispered in the weary woman's ear and brushed the soaked hair off her forehead. *Lord God, help us here. Please give her the strength she needs.*

The next contraction gathered force and tore at the woman's body. With another keening, she pushed against Elizabeth's strength, crying against the agony. "G-God, h-help me."

With a gush of bright red blood, the tiny baby girl slid into the world, flaccid and still.

Nurse Browne snatched up the baby, being careful of the cord, and blew in the blue-tinged face. "Come, little one, you must breathe." When nothing happened, she shook the tiny form. "God in heaven, help this lamb." She dangled the child by the feet and slapped first the soles, then the minute buttocks.

"Doctor, she's not breathing."

"Dip her in warm water," Dr. Gaskin ordered over his shoulder as he fought to stem the tide of red. Rolling one of the towels, he pressed it against the flood and kneaded the belly to get the uterus to contract. "Come on, Mrs. Mueller, fight back."

Elizabeth kept one eye on the nurse swishing the baby in a pan of warm water and another on the patient. She stroked Mrs. Mueller's hair back again, coaxing her to respond, all the while fighting the tears that threatened to break loose.

"Get her husband up here—now!"

Elizabeth ran out the door and down the stairs. "Reverend Mueller, Doctor says you better come quickly."

"Is the baby born?" He rose and strode to the door, brushing past her.

"Yes."

"What is it?" He took the stairs two at a time.

"A little girl." She didn't say the baby had yet to breathe.

"Only a girl, eh."

Rage clamped hands around Elizabeth's throat and cut off her air, melded her hands to the banister and locked her knees. Only a girl? His wife fought to bring a baby to life, she might be dying, and he says 'only a girl'?

Only a girl! The words beat time with each foot she placed on a stair tread. She stopped outside the room to calm her heart and breathing, both of which were going full throttle, like a steam engine out of control. *Breathe,* she ordered herself. *Easy now. You can be of no help in this state.* She took a third deep breath and felt her shoulders drop from where they'd been pinching her ears.

She entered the room to see Reverend Mueller sitting beside his wife on the bed, the bed a sea of blood. Surely she had none left. The thought made Elizabeth half gag. Never had she seen so much blood.

Exhaustion painted blue shadows on Mrs. Mueller's gray-white face. The sheet over her chest barely registered breath.

But still she bled.

Dr. Gaskin looked up at Elizabeth, and a minute shake of his head told her far more than she wanted to know.

He'd given up hope. Dr. Gaskin, who insisted on hope until the last breath is drawn, had none.

"The baby?" Elizabeth's whisper was answered by Nurse Browne shaking her head, tears leaking over her rounded cheeks. The sheet on Mrs. Mueller's chest was still. "She's gone."

Reverend Mueller bowed his head. "The baby?"

Dr. Gaskin shook his head. "We did everything we could."

"I know." He turned to his wife, stroking her hair back, tracing a finger down her cheek. "God keep you." He ducked his head, and a shudder racked his shoulders.

Like a mother black bear defending her cubs, Elizabeth turned on him. "If you'd taken better care of her, this might not have happened. You wore her out with babies every year in spite of Doctor's warning."

"Elizabeth!" Phillip entered the room just in time to hear his daughter's attack.

"You act like—like . . ."

"Elizabeth Marie Rogers!"

She heard the voice from the other end of a long dark tunnel. God himself. But she didn't say that. She pushed by her father and ran across the hall into her own room.

Dear God, what have I done?

Chapter Thirteen

Blessing, North Dakota

Thorliff pushed off again, then stopped. Had he heard something not of the wind? He strained to hear, holding his breath. Nothing but the howling of the gale. He leaned forward to start again but stopped. He whipped the cap off his ears, the cold slashing into his sweaty hair. "Lord God, let it come again if it is what I hope."

The bell rang again, faint. The wind dropped, and this time he heard it clearly. Off to the left and slightly behind him. He pulled his hat back down over his ears and turned his skis at a right angle. A rifle roared closer than the ringing. Thorliff drove his ski poles in and pushed off again. The rifle spoke again, closer this time. He angled to his left and skied four, six, and ten strides when the rifle blast sounded almost next to him. A dark shape loomed out of the swirling white. The barn.

Thank you, God, thank you. I'm home. You brought me out of the wilderness. I'm home. Left or right. The door has to be near here.

The rifle roared to his right. Three strides, and he could see Haakan. "Don't shoot again, I'm here." He shouted to be heard above the wind.

"Thorliff! Oh, thank God. Thank God." Haakan threw his

arms around his son, thunking him on the back with the rifle butt. "Here, get in out of the wind. Are you frozen?"

Thorliff walked in on his skis, not stopping to unbuckle the bindings until he stood in the warmth of the barn. Haakan shut the door behind him. "Mange takk." He tried to sniff, but the sides of his nose didn't move, so he breathed through his mouth, as he realized he'd been doing for some time. He rubbed his nose with the back of his mittened hand and felt the ice fall away, likewise from his eyebrows.

Haakan knelt in front of him and undid the buckles of the straps so Thorliff could step off the skis. "Your mother is waiting."

Thorliff swiped at the tears running down his cheeks. "Pa, I was so afraid."

"I know. Us too."

"Forgive me for being so bullheaded. I left there as soon as it started to snow and thought sure I could beat it home."

Haakan put both arms around his son and held him close. "God is good to us this day. Come, Andrew's arm must be falling off by now." They could hear the ringing as the blasts of the blizzard fell and rose. "Can you walk?"

"Ja." Thorliff took a step and would have fallen had his father's strong arm not held him up. Together they made their way down the long aisle and pushed the north door open, the wind and snow trying to seal them in. With each step, Thorliff felt the life coming back into his feet, but when the blizzard hit him full on again, he staggered.

"Here, I will go first." Haakan, skis in one hand, used his other to clamp Thorliff's hand on the rope that led to the house.

Thorliff ducked his head and shut his eyes against the biting snow. One foot in front of the other, that's all he had to do. Hold on to the rope and put one foot in front of the other. *I'm home. Thank you, Lord, I'm home.* The triangle rang again. He stumbled against his father's broad back.

"You've got Thorliff!" Andrew screamed above the wind. He turned and yelled again through the door, then grabbed his brother's arm and helped him up the steps. Between Andrew on one side and Haakan on the other, Thorliff staggered into the kitchen and collapsed in his mother's arms.

Ingeborg hugged him for a moment. "Thank you, Jesus. Thank you, Father. Thank you, thank you." Between her and Haakan, they walked Thorliff to a chair and sat him in it, then Andrew unlaced his boots while the others stripped off his outerwear. "Get snow."

Astrid grabbed a pan and hurried outside to fill it.

"Do your hands have feeling?" Ingeborg squeezed Thorliff's white hands. He nodded and squeezed back. *Thank you, Lord.*

"Your feet?" Andrew removed Thorliff's socks and moved one of his feet in a circle and pinched his toes.

"Ja, I think so. They are full of pins and needles right now."

Using her thumb, Ingeborg pressed against his nose, his cheeks, his forehead.

"Looks like the end of his nose might be frostbit." Haakan took the pan from Astrid. "Go get a quilt off my bed."

Ingeborg cupped snow in her hand and applied it to Thorliff's nose and a white spot on one cheek. "If this is all you come away with, God protected you beyond belief."

Thorliff felt the shiver start in his feet and work its way up his body. He shook so hard his teeth clacked together.

"Good, your body is fighting back." Haakan wrapped the quilt around him. "You see any white marks on his feet?"

Ingeborg shook her head. "Andrew, hand me that lamp. Or rather, hold it down here so I can see." She carefully inspected his toes and his feet, then shook her head and began chafing them with her hands. "Astrid, dip some warm water into that pan, and we'll put his feet in that. Not hot, just barely warm." She rolled up his pant legs and set his feet in the enameled pan. "Too hot?"

Thorliff shook his head. "I-if I c-can just q-quit shivering . . ."

"No, that means the circulation is coming back." Haakan took one of the dish towels off the rack behind the stove and wrapped the warm cloth around Thorliff's head.

Ingeborg poured a cup of coffee, added two spoons of sugar and some cream, and held it to Thorliff's lips. "Here, drink this."

"You better put some of that whiskey in it. That'll warm his insides faster."

"You're right." Ingeborg fetched the dark bottle from the cupboard and added some to the coffee. "Drink."

Thorliff took a deep swallow and double blinked as the heat hit his throat. He swallowed again at his mother's insistence.

"Drink it all." She set it in his hands, and he gratefully cupped them around the heat.

Ingeborg opened the oven door, and they half-carried, half-pulled Thorliff's chair closer to the heat pouring out of the oven.

"Ah." He closed his eyes in bliss as the heat washed over him. Sip by sip he drank the potent brew and felt the heat curling in his middle, stretching out to his limbs with every beat of his heart. *So easy I could have missed* . . . He cut off the thought with the dregs of his cup. No sense worrying about what if. Just be grateful for what is. *In everything give thanks.* The Bible verse was easy to follow right now. To give thanks for his family, for the warmth, for the stove, for the wood to heat the stove, for the house that protected them from the fury outside, for the clang and the shot that had called him home. He could feel a tear trickle down his cheek. So much to be grateful for.

"We need to get to milking since there's just the two of us." Haakan nodded to Andrew.

"I'll help." Astrid looked up from pouring warmer water into the basin around Thorliff's feet.

"And so will I." Thorliff sat forward. The shudders had lessened, and the cold block inside him had melted. He flexed his hands and feet. "Everything is working fine." *Please, I really need to do this.*

When the four returned a long time later, Ingeborg sighed in relief. While she'd known they were safe in the barn and, thanks to the rope, could get back and forth, still fear lurked like a pickpocket, ready to take advantage of any doubt.

The blizzard lasted through the night, drifting snow so high they shoveled a tunnel out in the morning.

At the breakfast table after chores were finished, Haakan leaned back in his chair. "One good thing, all the snow really insulates the house. You can hardly hear the wind in here."

"Ja, we must be grateful for everything." Ingeborg laid both hands on Thorliff's shoulders. "And to think you are having no ill effects from yesterday."

"Well, I don't want to go skiing right now. In fact, I have no desire to go skiing any time in the near future." Thorliff flexed his fingers and twisted his wrists. "Although how one can lose so much milking muscle in three months is amazing." He rubbed the muscles on his arms. "I got a cramp on that last cow and didn't think I could finish."

"I bet Mr. McBride is real sad he isn't getting to milk." Astrid giggled around her mouthful of cinnamon roll. "Christmas won't be the same without everyone here though."

"Who knows, this might blow over by evening, and then we'll all go to church, same as ever." Andrew reached for another roll. "You make the best rolls, Mor."

As Astrid and Ingeborg cleared away the dishes, Haakan shook his head and punched Thorliff in the shoulder, a bit harder than a light tap. "One thing I got to tell you, son: No matter how wonderful she is, no woman is worth losing your life in a blizzard."

"Haakan!"

"Unless, of course, it's your ma there." The half smile he sent his wife didn't reach his eyes that bored into Thorliff's. "You can't love and comfort someone from the grave."

Thorliff nodded. He'd come to much the same realization before falling asleep. "Ja, you're right."

"I know we all got to learn by our mistakes, but I hope to heaven you don't ever do something so foolish again. Leastways not where your mother and I can hear about it."

Thorliff looked up in time to catch a shine in his father's eyes. Haakan went back to scraping the bowl of his pipe with his knife. *Ja, some mistakes can be fatal, that is for sure. I hope I never do something so foolish again too, but . . . Ah, Anji, what will become of us?*

CHAPTER FOURTEEN

Northfield, Minnesota
December 24, 1893

"I cannot believe you said that!"

"I'm sorry, Mother. Neither can I." Elizabeth felt the weight of her transgression dragging her down into the oriental rug under their feet. If she could sink through it, perhaps she could wriggle out of the room without anyone seeing her, and if she got stepped on, so be it. She'd earned being stepped on. Screaming at a guest that way, screaming at anyone like that, was beyond the pale for a young woman brought up with her standard. Let alone a Christian woman or a Christian, period. "But when he said 'only a girl' and the baby died and then Mrs. Mueller died, I wanted to strangle the man with my bare hands." She stared down at her hands, flexing the long fingers that searched out music for the soul and hoped to bring healing to the sick and injured. "Perhaps shrieking at him like a fishwife wasn't proper, but . . ." Elizabeth could hardly hold her head up, both from weariness and a remorse so heavy that if she wasn't sure she'd do the same again, given the same provocation, she'd have let it pound her right through the floor.

"I trained you better than that. A lady never loses her temper in front of others." Annabelle wore her stern look, tight about the mouth and eyes, that had always made Elizabeth flinch and wish she were somewhere else—anywhere else

Elizabeth couldn't bring herself to look her mother in the eye, instead worrying a hangnail on her right forefinger. "I am truly sorry. I shall write Reverend Mueller an apology immediately." She'd already been composing it in her head. "Will that be sufficient, or is there something else you think I could do?"

"I don't know." Annabelle rubbed her forehead. "I have a headache coming on, and here it is, Christmas Eve day. So much I have left to do. Even after we finally went to bed, I couldn't fall asleep right away. I kept wishing I had done something more."

"Like what?" At the look on her mother's face, Elizabeth knew the lecture was over, but the action not forgiven. She could feel herself switching into doctor mode at the pain evident on her mother's face.

"Oh, like realized what was happening and made her comfortable or . . ." Annabelle rubbed the spot again. "I don't know."

"How about if I mix your medicine and you go take a lie-down? You'll wake up feeling good again, so you can attend church tonight. Christmas Eve is your favorite service." As it is mine, and I really don't feel like going. *All I feel like doing is sitting in a corner and bawling. And sleeping for a week. And here it is Christmas and time to be celebrating.* Elizabeth rubbed her eyes that still carried a shovelful of grit in spite of washing them twice.

"Here, Mother, I'll mix your medicine. You'll feel better soon."

"I think of those poor boys with no mother to turn to. Poor, poor lads."

Elizabeth noted her mother didn't mention Reverend Mueller.

"Think I'll ask Cook to fix extra, and we'll take it over to them. Although I'm sure members of the church have already done that."

"With four boys, whatever is brought will disappear quickly."

"Will you get the door, dear? I just cannot be seen looking like this."

"Of course." Elizabeth did as asked. Pulling open the door to a solid white world under a gray sky, she motioned the man on the steps to enter. "How are you this morning, Doctor?"

"Same as you. Trying to figure what I could have done differently to somehow have kept that poor woman alive." He shook his head. "I forgot to tell you the other news last night. You know that croupy baby?"

Elizabeth nodded.

"He didn't make it either. Died during the blizzard when no one could get help. Those young folks are some despondent."

"But I taught them—"

"Sometimes steam tents work, but sometimes the only thing is a tracheotomy, and even that's not sure. But they couldn't get out, and they did the best they could by not sending someone else out to die in vain."

Tears smarted her eyes again. She sniffed and dug out a handkerchief. "What a terrible Christmas for both families. Can you stay for a cup of coffee?"

"No. I have calls to make before this weather gets any worse. One thing you learn if you want to be a good doctor. You try to figure if you could have done something different, and then you admit to the good Lord that He's in charge, not you, that you did your best. And then you go on. You can't let it eat at you, or you better go into another field. I've seen doctors eaten alive by circumstances they could not control. Life and death in particular."

Elizabeth's sigh let go half the weight, and another did the same. "But did you ever rail at one of your patients like I did?"

"No, but sure wanted to more than once. I can't hold you accountable for that." He leaned closer and lowered his voice. " 'Sides, between you, me, and the gatepost, he had it comin'."

"I thought he was a friend of yours."

"He is. Been so for the ten years he's been in town. But—" The doctor stopped and gave Elizabeth a pat on the arm. "I want to thank you for making Miss Browne feel so welcome last night. Thank your mother too. I better be off. And blessed Christmas in spite of all this."

"You too." Elizabeth reached up and gave him a quick peck on the cheek. "And thank you."

Dr. Gaskin huffed and turned to leave but not before Elizabeth caught the sheen of moisture in his faded blue eyes.

"God bless."

"Yes, lass. God bless."

Elizabeth closed the door behind him, glancing out just long enough to realize the snowfall had picked up. *Lord, please let us have Christmas Eve services. I need to hear the story and see the manger. I need to be reminded that you did indeed send your son as a baby. Two dead babies here this week. Are they really with you? I don't think I could bear this if I doubted that.*

After settling her mother with darkened shades, her powder mixed and drank, and a cool cloth on her forehead, Elizabeth trailed her fingers down the carved banister, straightening the cedar garland as she took the stairs slowly, one conscious step at a time, to the library, where she seated herself at her father's desk. *I wonder where he is.* The thought stayed just that, rather than translating into action, which was what her feet twitched to do. Walk in the falling snow, shovel the walk, anything was preferable to writing this letter. Heaving a sigh, she pulled out the drawer and rifled through the paper until she found a half sheet suitable for a note. In this case writing a book would not be sufficient. A *big* book.

Dear Reverend Mueller . . . She nibbled the end of her pen. *Get to it, ninny, and get it done so you can go play the piano or take a nap or bury your head in a snowbank.*

She dipped the pen point in the ink and continued.

> Please forgive me for shouting at you like that. I am heartily sorry to have added to your sorrow. Mrs. Mueller was always more than kind to me and to everyone she came in contact with. When I think of a good Christian woman, she is a shining example. Her faith and fortitude in the face of . . .

Calling herself several uncomplimentary names, Elizabeth scratched that out, set her pen in the ink and tore the sheet in half. Starting over, she wrote again, then stopped and chewed the end of the pen again.

"You want hot chocolate, tea. . . ?" Cook peered in the doorway.

"Tea would be good."

"Ja, and I fix the fire."

Only at the mention did Elizabeth realize it had grown chilly in the room. She raised her gray lace knit shawl back over her shoulders and returned to her mess. Taking up the ink pen again she noticed a gigantic blot desecrated half the words.

She wrinkled this paper up and tossed it, along with the first, into the fireplace. The flames flared and gobbled the paper, wrinkling it to gray ash. Gray ash, a good metaphor for how she felt.

Starting a third sheet, she wrote swiftly, closing with *I do hope you find it in your heart to forgive me. Sincerely, Elizabeth Rogers.* She waited for the ink to dry, being careful to avoid reading the words again so that she wouldn't feel compelled to rewrite the painful missive.

"There now, do you feel better?" Her father turned from studying the fire.

"Oh, I didn't realize you were here." She folded the paper and inserted it into an envelope. "I might feel better, but what about Mother? I cause her such distress at times."

"But not intentionally. Your heart is in the right place, my dear."

"Thank you. That helps—I think."

"Would you please help me replace the tree candles? I know that is on your mother's list of things to do before tomorrow's gathering."

"And would perhaps help me redeem myself a little?" She quirked one eyebrow.

"That too." Together they left the study, and Elizabeth fetched the candle box from the pantry.

"This one came mighty close." He held up a nub of hardened wax. "We need to keep better watch so we don't end up with a fire."

"Now, *that* would really fire mother off." The two exchanged small chuckles at the pun intended.

When Reverend Mueller stood up to conduct the Christmas Eve service, the entire congregation sucked in a breath, the whoosh could be heard distinctly. *What is the matter with that man?* She glanced at her mother to see her quickly cover her shocked look with her company face. Her father covered his choking spell with a genteel cough behind his hand.

"A blessed Christmas to you all. Grace and peace from our Lord and Savior Jesus Christ." While he lacked the normal Christmas smile, he seemed otherwise normal.

Elizabeth swallowed her ire, setting her stomach to roiling. How could he?

"I want to thank all of you for your caring for me and mine in this time of sorrow. Mrs. Mueller would be so touched by your generosity, as I am." He cleared his throat. "And now let us continue to rejoice in this night of our greatest gift, the birth of the Christ."

Annabelle put her hand on Elizabeth's arm, in comfort or to keep her from leaving, as Elizabeth started to rise. She sat back down and clamped her arms across her chest, ladylike or no. The nerve of that man! Had he no sense of propriety whatsoever? After glaring at him one more time, she set herself to listing the muscles of the arm and hand, graduating to the neck and head to take up the entire service. Other than singing the hymns and carols.

Following the benediction, she fled before she had to greet those around her. Her mother and father weren't far behind.

Christmas morning broke out the glitter, the sun striking diamonds from every tree limb and snowbank. A flock of blackcapped chickadees fluttered down for the crumbs Cook had thrown out.

Elizabeth stood at the kitchen window, coffee cup in hand, and watched their orange marmalade cat shake snow off each foot as he made his way toward the back door, totally ignoring the flitting and fluttering birds. She went to open the door for him even before he announced his need.

"Too cold for you, eh?"

Jehoshaphat chirped a response without even looking at her.

Tail in the air, he stalked past her as if she were there only to do his bidding, then sat on a rug behind the stove to begin his morning ablutions. He cleaned each foot first, chewing at a bit of ice between his toes before washing face and ears. Chest next, then nether regions until finished, when he stretched and crossed to twine around Cook's ankles, a practiced mew announcing his need for attention, of the food variety.

Elizabeth watched over the edge of her cup. So single-minded he, not wracked by the self doubts that had awakened her more than once during the night. Guilt and anger were terrible bed partners.

"Sad face for Christmas morning." Cook refilled Elizabeth's cup.

"I know. You heard about the service?"

"Ja. You eat, feel better."

"Did you send a basket over to Reverend Mueller's?" *I have to let this go.*

"Ja, Old Tom take it yesterday."

"Has he been around this morning?"

"Ja, got his coffee and julekake. I'll slice you some."

Elizabeth started to protest, then gave in. By eating she would stay on Cook's good side. While her mother had been civil to her the evening before, there had been a definite lack of warmth. Annabelle had been known to carry a disappointment into resentment, even stretching it to pouting. Even on Christmas. Until after the service, of course.

After a subdued breakfast, they waited while Phillip lighted the candles, then gathered in the parlor to open gifts. Elizabeth tried to be cheerful, but a pall of sadness hung over the entire house. She thanked her parents for the set of surgical instruments, forcing herself to sound more excited than she felt.

"This is awful. I just want to sit and cry instead of have a good time. And Mother, you have gone to such trouble to have everything nice for us."

"I know. I feel the same way. That poor woman. But I am grateful she was here with us rather than home by herself or with only the doctor in attendance. She was so grateful for your playing and for all of us helping her. That brings me comfort."

Elizabeth rose from her chair and went to kneel in front of her mother. "Thank you. I needed to hear just that."

Annabelle cupped her daughter's face in her two gentle hands. "We did all we could. You have to remember that. When you do all you can and ask God for His divine assistance, then you have to leave it in His hands. He alone has the power of life and death."

Elizabeth blinked back the tears that threatened. This was her mother talking, her mother who rarely referred to spiritual things. She turned her face and kissed her mother's hand. "Thank you." *Thank you, Father. I'll try harder to do as both she and Dr. Gaskin keep reminding me.* She turned and leaned against her mother's knees. "The tree is truly beautiful, is it not?"

That afternoon she and her father checked the candles again to make sure they were all in place for the last party of the season. After their guests left and the evening wound down, the candles would be removed for safety's sake. Before New Year's, the decorations would be put away and the tree set outside with suet balls and apples, studded with seeds, hanging from the branches for the birds' Christmas. Sheaves of wheat would grace the branches also, and dried corn on the cob would be added for the squirrels. As far as Elizabeth was concerned, preparing the tree for outside was almost as much a delight as decorating it with ornaments for the holiday.

Lord, I wish I could write a Christmas carol. Sitting down at the piano, Elizabeth let her fingers roam the keys. Her thoughts turned to one of the poems Thorliff had shown her. He was so shy about his writing. And yet he had brought so much joy to the people of Northfield who had sent in their stories and poems for the contest he dreamed up. Funny, she never thought much about him when he was here, but now that he was gone, he crept into her mind.

"A penny for your thoughts." Her father slid onto the piano bench beside her

"I want to write a Christmas carol." There, she'd said the words aloud. "Or rather, I want to compose a carol. Did you know that Thorliff used to write the Christmas pageants for his church and school in Blessing?"

"No, I didn't. What brought that on?"

"I was thinking of one of the poems that won the contest, the one about the little boy and the lamb. It cries for music."

"Yes, you would see that."

Elizabeth was already at the piano when the first guests arrived. Each year they held an open house on Christmas Day for those friends not invited personally to the earlier dinner party. She nodded her greetings and continued to play, losing herself in the glory of sound, eyes closed the better to feel.

"I think I come to this house as much to hear you play as to visit my good friends." Pastor Johnson, blond hair brushed over his expanded forehead and cheeks rosy from both the cold and the heat of the fire, stood slightly off to the side, a warm smile matching his voice.

Elizabeth smiled and nodded her greeting. *Talk to him*, a voice inside prompted. *About what? Don't be silly, you know about what.*

"Do you have a favorite?"

He half closed his eyes to think. "I heard your rendition of the 'Hallelujah' chorus was truly inspired. Would you mind playing it again and 'Mary's Prayer'?"

"Not at all." *Ask him!* How could a voice not even audible be so loud? "First I have a question for you." She swallowed and let her fingers go where they willed.

"Yes?" He leaned against the side of the piano, watching her through gold-framed glasses.

"Ah, this is hard."

"We have all the time, and no one else is paying attention."

"I know. I suppose you've heard that I screamed at Reverend Mueller the other night?"

"No. How would I hear that?"

"I was afraid it was all around town by now."

"You want to start at the beginning?" Pastor Johnson's voice came gentle and soft, like the smile he wore and the compassion in his eyes.

"He . . . he made me so angry that I . . ." She paused and felt tears burning the back of her nose. "Mrs. Mueller was so weak. This whole pregnancy wore her out, and Doctor had warned him she should have no more children. And when she went into labor here at our house, Reverend Mueller didn't even pay attention to her. She wouldn't tell him or let me tell him because she said he needed this time of relaxation because he works so hard." She could feel her jaw tightening. "And when the baby was finally born, and I told him he had a daughter, he said . . . he said"—she rolled her lips together— " 'Only a girl.' And then when the baby never even breathed and Mrs. Mueller died and he didn't even seem to care, I . . . I just screamed at him. I don't even remember for sure what I said, but . . ." She paused, the keys shimmering in front of her tear-filled eyes.

"How will I ever be a good doctor if I cannot control my tongue and emotions better than that?"

"Ah, dear child, such a heavy burden you lay upon your slender shoulders. Even doctors are not perfect, and a young doctor with a heart tender as yours even less so. But God does not call you to be perfect—"

"But the verse says, 'Be ye therefore perfect, even as your Father which is in heaven is perfect.' "

"But you see, the perfection comes from Him. Our Father grows us into that. Even James says the tongue is a raging fire, and if he found himself unable to control that little member all the time, should you do better than he?"

"Is that too much to ask?" She could feel peace sneaking up on her. At his smile she half shrugged.

"So what did you do?"

"Afterward, you mean?"

Again he nodded.

"I wrote him a letter of apology, pleading for his forgiveness. My mother is sorely distressed with her errant daughter who cannot seem to live within the bounds of propriety."

"And you have asked the Father to forgive you?"

"Of course."

"Then whether man or woman forgives you or not, you *are* forgiven. And you must act thusly."

She cocked her head. "Please explain."

"You must let the guilt go. In fact, order it out because you are living forgiven. You might go talk with Reverend Mueller later on. He may have totally forgotten the incident."

I wish, oh, how I wish.

"And have you asked your mother for forgiveness?"

"Of course."

"And she?"

"Well, let us say she is not speaking with me overly much."

Again his gentle smile. Gentle was always a word she thought of with Pastor Johnson, or she most likely would not have had the nerve to open this conversation with him. Love seemed to glow from him, like he was lit within by a light that never dimmed. *Lord, let my light be like his. Do I see Jesus shining from his eyes? Please, let me be like that.*

"Ah, young Elizabeth, God has great things in store for you, but the way to get there will not be easy. When God has our hearts, He holds us close to His mighty heart, and we begin to beat as one. Listen for His heartbeat, knowing it beats with love for you, no matter what."

She played on, letting the tears dry on her cheeks, her sorrow and joy both baptized with her music. "Thank you."

"You are most welcome. May you be blessed as you are a blessing to others."

Elizabeth glanced up to see Thornton coming into the room. She smiled, and he made his way to the piano, greeting Pastor Johnson as he turned to speak with someone else.

"Merry Christmas again. I'm surprised to see you today."

"I hadn't planned on coming, but"—he lowered his voice—"I had to get out of there."

"Difficult, huh?"

"So many calling. They bring something, pay their respects to Auntie, and then chat and eat in the parlor, where other ladies of the church make sure there is food and coffee set out."

"Your aunt is well loved." She almost said "was" but changed it. Mabel Mueller still lived, only now without pain, instead bubbling with joy in the presence of her Lord. Elizabeth thought a moment. Bubbling—would Mrs. Mueller bubble?

"I know that. Funny how most people have no idea what a saint she w-is." His eyebrow acknowledged what she'd said before. "I brought you something."

"You can't. You already gave me a present. And thank you. I've never had such soft leather gloves before."

"You're welcome. I saw this and thought only of you."

"Thornton Wickersham, you are carrying this charade too far." She leaned closer to make her point.

"It's nothing."

"Besides, I haven't given you your gift yet. It's under the tree."

"You didn't have to."

"I know that." She made a face and nodded toward the tree, glimmering in golden candlelight. Running an arpeggio and finishing with a lingering chord, she let the notes die out and rose, shaking her skirts out. A yawn caught her so by surprise that she barely got her hand up to hide it. Nodding and acknowledging the greetings and thanks from the guests, she made her way to the tree in time to see Thornton stand, her gift to him in his hands.

He carefully removed the ribbon and opened the shiny red paper, holding the leather-bound book in his hands. He read the title, tracing the inlaid letters with a fingertip, his voice reverent.

"If I can learn to write and preach like John Wesley, I shall feel I am fulfilling the calling the Lord has laid on my life." He held out his book. "How did you know I wanted this? If I could only think as clearly as Wesley, perhaps my sermons would change lives too."

"Perhaps, but I believe it is God who changes lives. We just use our gifts as he desires."

"Spoken like a true saint."

"Hardly." She watched him for a moment. "Is something wrong?"

"Ah, no." He shook his head. "Other than my aunt dying and my uncle acting like nothing is wrong and . . ."

"Grief does strange things to some people." She thought back to Dr. Gaskin and his spell of drinking. But he'd come out of it. "What do you mean?"

"In spite of the suggestions of his deacons, he preached the sermon last night and again this morning. His sister is coming tomorrow to take over the household, and then the boys will come home. They've been staying with friends. Other than mentioning that the funeral will be after the thaw like others, it's as if . . ." He paused, the candlelight reflecting in his eyes. "When I asked if he'd rather I found somewhere else to live, he looked at me like he couldn't understand what I meant. As if nothing had happened." Thornton rubbed his chin with one forefinger. "Strange."

Elizabeth wisely kept her opinions to herself. "Would you care for some of Cook's Scandinavian cookies? She makes them special for Christmas day."

"There have been so many callers." Thornton continued as if Elizabeth had not spoken. "She was much loved."

By everyone but her husband. Elizabeth snapped her teeth together. All she had to do was let her tongue loose again, and she would be even farther down on her mother's black list. Like six feet below the bottom.

"But back to your gift. I am grateful indeed that you listened to your instincts."

His whisper sent shivers racing up and down her back. *If I were truly thinking of marrying someday, this man would surely make a good candidate. He has become my best friend, and all because of a joke.* "I was afraid you already had this copy of his work."

"I shall treasure it." He folded the closed volume into the protection of his clasped arms.

What would it feel like to be wrapped close against his chest like that? She could feel her cheeks flame at the thought. *Elizabeth Marie Rogers, there is no way you can manage home, husband, family, and medical practice, so banish the thought from your mind. A doctor is what you will be. A good doctor. Please, God, I will be a good doctor, won't I?*

"I hate to break up the party, but it is snowing six ways from Sunday again." Phillip Rogers made the announcement, then turned to his wife. "I'll go get the sleigh hitched up for those who walked."

Within minutes the good-byes were all said, and only the smoke rising from the snuffed candles recalled the earlier party. That and the lingering scent of someone's perfume.

Elizabeth pushed in a chair here and picked up a cup there. She straightened the curtains behind the Christmas tree and checked to make sure all the candles were properly snuffed, finding one still smoking on a rear branch. To be safe, she went to the pantry for a bowl to put the spent candles in and returned to clear them off the tree.

"I thought you'd gone up to bed." Annabelle glanced around

the room now put to rights and started to leave again. She paused, gave her daughter a questioning look, took one step toward the door and, with a slight shrug that matched the furrow on her brow, crossed to her daughter's side.

"What is it sitting so heavy on you that you move like an aging dowager?"

"Now, that is an attractive picture." Elizabeth's smile twitched the corners of her mouth but never removed the bleakness from her eyes. Her sigh slumped her even more. *If I tell her my doubts, she'll just say play the piano and get married.*

"Here, let's sit in front of the fire." Annabelle took her daughter's arm and guided her to a winged chair, which she turned to face the fire now reduced to flaring coals. She pulled the hassock near and sat there herself, without picking up her needlepoint or even the napkin someone had dropped. Hands clasped in her lap, she waited, her brow serene in the flickering light.

Elizabeth did the same, but her fingers refused to stay clasped, picking at a bit of lint, smoothing a crease, nudging back a cuticle.

Finally Annabelle laid a gentle hand on her daughter's, forcing the activity to cease. "Is it so terrible you cannot tell me?"

If Annabelle had not been watching, she would have missed the minute shake of Elizabeth's head. One finger rubbed the first knuckle on the opposite hand. "Mother, sometimes I want it all, and I'm afraid I'm asking for too much."

The silence lay easy, punctuated by the whoosh and hiss of falling coals.

CHAPTER FIFTEEN

Blessing, North Dakota
December 24, 1893

"I wish Sophie and Grace could come, at least." Astrid glanced at the snow-shrouded windows and shrugged, a tiny shrug that meant she wasn't really whining, just wishing.

"Christmas Eve all by ourselves is definitely different." Andrew dumped another armload of wood into the box by the stove. He brushed the bark and sawdust off his jacket and into the box before taking his coat off and hanging it on the peg by the door. "That wind hasn't let up an inch. Tries to take my head off every time I step out the door."

Haakan looked up from a back issue of the *Northfield News* that Thorliff had brought with him. He was reading at the table. "They could come, but Lars and I decided taking a chance even with the guide rope was an unnecessary risk." Lars, Hamre, and George McBride had come to help milk the cows earlier in the day, and with the other students gone home for the holidays, the two families had been looking forward to all being together this evening. "We'll celebrate Christmas together when the storm blows out."

"But tonight we'll have Christmas by ourselves." Ingeborg checked the goose roasting in the oven and scenting the air with rich smells. She tweaked Astrid's nose as the girl inhaled the goosey fragrance. "A few more geese, and we'll have enough feathers for a new feather bed. I was hoping to send one back with Thorliff."

"Thanks, Mor, but I'm plenty warm with the quilts you sent with me." Thorliff exchanged newspaper sections with his father. "What do you think of all the unrest with the unions?"

"I believe in uniting for bargaining power, but violence isn't the answer either. If the rich wouldn't be so greedy, the working-man would give his best when treated right. Like the railroads and the flour mills." He tapped a finger against the paper on the table. "Kill off the farmers and there won't be any grain to haul or grind. We know as well as the railroad barons that there has to be profit to keep things running, but they better learn to manage better. Especially when times are tough like now. Drought can't be planned for."

"Astrid, you can start setting the table now. Let's use the new tablecloth and napkins." Hands protected by two large potholders, Ingeborg pulled the roasting pan from the oven and set it on the stovetop. When she lifted the domed lid, the crisply browned goose gleamed in the lamplight. "My, that smells good."

"You want I should mash the potatoes?" Andrew leaned around his mother to inhale the tantalizing scents.

"Please, and pour the potato water into that crock."

He rolled his eyes at her. That's what they always did, kept the potato water for bread making. "Yes, ma'am."

"Haakan, you want to hold the platter?"

Instead, he picked up the two long cooking forks and, piercing the goose on both sides, lifted it dripping from the roaster and transferred it to the platter. "Perfection. You want me to carve?"

"In a few minutes." She scooted the pan over to the hotter part of the stove, and when the pan juices bubbled, she poured in flour she had already mixed with water, stirring it all together to make rich brown gravy. "You could start taking out the stuffing. That bowl is warm for it." She nodded to the serving bowls sitting on the warming shelf.

Within minutes they were sitting around the table, heads bowed as Haakan offered thanks for the food and their safety, and asked for the same for all those buried under the blizzard.

Ingeborg added her own silent plea as visions of their earlier times flitted through her mind. *Thank you for all you have blessed us with. Thank you. Mange takk so many times over.* She joined her amen with the others. "Ah, so much we have to be grateful for." She patted Thorliff's hand. "And so wonderful to have you sitting here beside me again."

Thorliff nodded and turned his hand to clasp hers. "Thank you. My life here is certainly different from my one in Northfield. Someday you'll have to go there to see it in person."

"We will be there when you graduate." Haakan laid slice after slice of breast meat over on the platter. "Who wants the drumstick?"

"Me." Andrew passed his plate. "Both if no one else wants one. That's one good thing about goose, all dark meat."

"I'm as stuffed as that goose was," Haakan said when they finished eating and sat back in their chairs.

Thorliff reached for one more roll. "I eat so many of my suppers alone at the office that being together means more than the food. And no matter how good Cook is at the Rogerses', no one makes bread like you do, Mor."

"I made the rolls." Astrid nudged him with her elbow.

"Oh, then you have learned well."

"So you don't eat at the college then?" Ingeborg nodded to the coffee cups, and Astrid got up to bring the pot to the table.

"Cook fixes me a packet, and I eat with the other townies. I think my friend Benjamin sits beside me as much for the cookies Cook sends along as he does for my wit and wisdom."

Astrid plunked back down in her chair. "Are we going to open presents pretty soon?"

"You think some of those presents under the tree are for you?" Thorliff tugged on one of her braids.

"Yep. My name is on at least two." She propped her elbows on the table. "But I think there are more that are hid yet."

"Hidden."

She gave him one of those you-think-you're-smart looks.

"We'll open gifts after the dishes." Ingeborg stacked the dishes and carried them to the pan on the stove. Astrid and Andrew cleared the rest of the table while Thorliff answered Haakan's questions about life in Northfield.

"You know all the time I spent helping with the steam engine?"

Haakan nodded, his head wreathed in pipe smoke.

"Mr. Rogers couldn't believe how quickly I learned to take apart and put together that old printing press, but the work here trained me for that. Our engine here is a saint compared to that cranky thing."

"You like working on a newspaper?"

"More than I thought I would. Seeing those sheets of paper come out with the columns and type in order is like stitching grain sacks closed at the separator. You know you've accomplished something, sometimes at great odds. I prefer writing, but this job is teaching me a great deal. Someday I'd like to bring a newspaper here to Blessing."

"Really? You do want to come home to live?" Astrid juggled the plate she almost dropped.

"Ja, why? Did you think I was leaving forever?"

"Well, if you went to work for a newspaper in Minneapolis or Chicago or something, we'd never see you."

"Don't worry about it. I have to get through school first."

"Seems so strange not to be at church." Astrid leaned against her mother sitting in her chair.

"We'll have the program and everything sometime after Christmas."

"I know, but Thorliff might already be gone by then."

Haakan knocked the ashes out of his pipe. "Guess I better get the candles lit before Astrid has a fit."

"Pa!"

The three younger ones stayed in the kitchen until Haakan called them into the parlor.

Astrid stopped just through the doorway and clasped her hands under her chin. "It is most beautiful! Oh, how beautiful."

Thorliff, right behind her, laid his hands on her shoulders and squeezed gently. The tiny flames atop white candles shimmered against the green of the pine tree. Carved and painted wooden ornaments of stars, animals, and other figures hung from the branches, along with crocheted snowflakes.

"Your candles are perfect." Andrew took the first steps closer to the tree. "She spent hours dipping them all."

"We didn't have molds that small." Astrid looked over her shoulder up at her big brother. "I wanted the tree to be extra nice this year."

"It is." Thorliff squeezed her shoulders again and hugged her against him. "You did well." He nudged her forward. "See all those presents? You'd think we were a huge family for all those boxes."

"Come, let's read the Christmas story." Haakan beckoned them to the chairs. As soon as they sat, he opened the Bible to Luke and read in Norwegian. " 'And it came to pass in those days, that there went out a decree from Caesar Augustus. . . .' "

Ingeborg closed her eyes, the better to let the familiar words sink in. Such a simple story of simple people who had a baby. Only that baby was the Son of God. So she, like Mary, had saved so many things to ponder in her heart, to take out and delight in again so many years later, to take out and study, hoping each time to understand, and with understanding, accept. *Or is it the other way around? Acceptance first and then understanding, and sometimes still not understanding but rejoicing in the gifts God gives?* The thoughts made her open her eyes and look with love on each member of her family. So there weren't more. That seemed to be God's divine ordinance for her. So the storm bound them in. No matter. They were safe and warm and had each other.

She let a tear trickle down her cheek. *To sing His praises for what is, rather than weep and whine over what isn't. Lord, please help me to do just this—sing your praises no matter what.*

She heard Haakan's voice again. " 'And suddenly there was with the angel a multitude of the heavenly host praising God, and saying, Glory to God in the highest, and on earth peace, good will toward men.' " She murmured the words along with him, staring at the candles on the tree flickering in the draft from the window, or was the flickering due to the tears that continued to amble down her face?

"Don't cry, Mor," Astrid whispered, taking her mother's hand.

Ingeborg squeezed her daughter's hand. "Ah, but these are tears of joy, for I cannot think of the words to sing enough praise for what is welling in my heart."

Haakan closed the Bible and held it between his hands. "Your mother is right. So blessed are we. The Christ child came, and storm or no storm, He lives in our hearts even now."

"Amen." Ingeborg hugged Astrid and kissed her cheek. "And now I think we must open our presents, or someone I know will expire with excitement."

Astrid giggled. "I love Christmas." She knelt in front of the tree and reached for a package. "This one is for Thorliff."

As each opened a gift with the others looking on, the thanks arose like the smoke from the candles.

"Mor, Far, this is too much." Thorliff caressed the spines of the Dickens collection. The glow on his face made her and Haakan exchange glances of joy.

"All this for me?" Andrew picked up each of the carving tools as if they were made of spun glass and infinitely precious. "Tusen takk." He whispered the words as he laid the instruments back in the leather-bound case.

Astrid's package could be held in one hand. She opened it carefully, only to find a note. *Look under the stairs. Love, Far and Mor.* She looked to her parents as she pushed herself to her feet. "The cupboard?"

Ingeborg nodded, and as one they all rose to follow her into her parents' bedroom, where she turned the wooden latch and pulled open the door.

"Oh, look!" Astrid clapped her hands to her mouth before taking the two steps inside the closet to pick up a carved doll bed with a doll lying in state. The porcelain face wore a perpetual smile, and the hair was curled in ringlets. Astrid carried the bed to the rug and knelt to trace a finger down the curly hair and touch one of the porcelain hands. Black buttoned shoes peeked out from under the blue watered-silk dress and deep blue velvet coat.

"I've never seen a doll so beautiful."

"Pick her up." Andrew touched the cradle with his toe and set it to rocking.

"Andrew helped make the bed." Haakan stood with his arm around Ingeborg's waist. "I think she likes it."

Astrid leaped to her feet and threw herself at her mother and father, tears streaming and watering her smile. "Thank you! Oh, I cannot thank you enough." She reached up and squeezed hard, first her mother and then her father before dropping back to her knees to finally lift the doll into her arms. "I need a really special name for her." She looked up at Thorliff. "You have to help me think of one. You are good with names."

"Holly or Noel or Angel—Christmas names."

Astrid nodded. "Noel. I knew you would think of something perfect."

"We have more presents to unwrap." Andrew tugged on his mother's arm.

Thorliff picked up the cradle and followed the others back to the parlor. "I think we better pinch the candles out before they gutter."

"I wish I had made more." Astrid heaved a sigh as she pinched out one of the candles.

"There's always next year." Andrew started pinching out the higher ones. "This one was close."

Haakan brought a lamp from the kitchen, and they finished opening their presents.

"Haakan, your present is over in Lars's granary." Ingeborg held up her hands in a shrug. "Sorry."

"You can tell me what it is."

She shook her head. "No, half the fun is seeing your face."

"Ja, well, yours is over in Kaaren's cupboard. I knew you would find it here."

"Here's one for each of you." Thorliff handed the envelopes out. "Not much, but . . ."

Ingeborg opened hers. "Your story. Did you print this?"

He nodded. "Mr. Rogers let me use the press. I set it all up myself. The woodcut is from the college. They let me borrow it." He pointed to the intricately scrolled A. "They have an entire alphabet made by one of the early immigrants. Such a beautiful set."

Astrid sat on the floor and leaned against Thorliff's knee. "If the storm blows out and we can have Christmas Day, will you read your story to everyone?"

"I s'pose."

"Good, and maybe *A Christmas Carol*. It's in that set. I know 'cause I looked."

"Maybe. But it takes longer than one afternoon."

The only sad part of Christmas for Thorliff was not talking with Anji. He was beginning to doubt that would ever happen.

The storm blew itself out sometime before dawn, and by the time chores were finished, Hjelmer skied up to announce that church would be at eleven. That would give the church time to warm up.

But after the service, when Anji hadn't come with her family, Thorliff had to force himself to greet the folks around him. He answered their questions about school, about living in a big town, and how he liked newspaper work. Pastor Solberg greeted him with a hearty handshake and a thump on the shoulder.

"When do you have to leave again? I would like to hear more about your life at St. Olaf."

"I must be on the morning train on the twenty-seventh. I need to be back to help put out the special New Year's edition of the paper, even though school doesn't start for another week or more."

"Then we shall get together tomorrow, all right?"

"Ja, if the weather holds."

As the pastor turned to greet someone else, Anji's brother greeted Thorliff. "Sorry, Thorliff, but Pa took a turn for the worse during the night, and Anji can calm him more than any of us. It wasn't that she didn't want to come." Swen kept his apology low for Thorliff's ears only. "And with Anji, Pa always comes first."

"I see."

Swen took a step closer and leaned forward, dropping his chin. "Pa's been asking us to put him outside one night and let the cold take him home." His voice broke on the last word. "I-I can't do that. Some things you just can't do, but . . ."

Visions of the weary young woman he'd seen for such a short time had plagued Thorliff all morning. With all of the relatives meeting at Tante Kaaren's this afternoon, he knew he would not be able to leave.

After wishing everyone a merry Christmas as they made their way outside, the family climbed into the sled and made their way to Kaaren and Lars's house.

Thorliff sat stewing in chilly silence for a time. Finally he leaned forward. "Mor, have the neighbors gone in to help the Baards, other than with the fieldwork?" Like Swen, Thorliff kept his voice low, for his mother's ears alone.

Ingeborg nodded. "You know the Mendohlsons are there?" At his nod she continued. "Metiz and I have taken turns with Joseph, but he keeps calling for Anji and is so restless until she returns that we wonder if we do any good or not."

"But it helps Anji?"

"Some." She paused. "But letters from you would help more."

"I've written, but she never answers." *Only two letters. Be honest.* A conscience can be a worrisome nag.

"Perhaps she hasn't the time nor the strength at the end of the day, or the beginning. I ordered her to give him enough laudanum to sleep through the night, but he needs something stronger, the pain is so severe. I don't know how he keeps on. Sometimes I wish we had a real doctor close by."

Haakan stopped the horses near the back door of the Knutsons' house. "Everyone out."

Within an hour the large house was filled with enough people to make the windows pooch out. Sleds made of wagon boxes on runners instead of wheels lined the yard with all the horses tied in the barn and sheds. Laughter escaped out the chimney along with the smoke.

While the women bustled about the kitchen getting the food together, the men congregated in the parlor, and all the children headed upstairs to play.

"This family gets any bigger, we're going to have breathing room only," Kaaren said as she bumped elbows with Ingeborg at the stove.

"Good thing you have this addition. Who'd have ever dreamed those years ago that we would become this many?" Ingeborg shook her head. "And in such a short time."

"I've sliced the hams, and Penny is finishing the two geese. Should I mash the potatoes?" Goodie Wold slid the heaping meat platter into the warming oven.

"That would be good." Kaaren glanced over to where Bridget was slicing bread and stacking the plates high. "Ilse, would you please take care of the pickles and jams?"

"Metiz already did that, and I asked the girls to set the table." The first thing the men had done was set up two saw horses with plank tops to add to the long table already in place.

"Oh, good." Kaaren stopped and looked around to see what else had to be done. Nothing as far as she could see. The gravy bubbled on the back of the stove, the potatoes were almost done, the carrots and various other vegetables were ready to pour into bowls, the coffee pot was staying hot on the back of the stove, and stuffing from the geese was waiting in the oven.

A draft preceded Mary Martha Solberg's merry laugh. "Sorry we are late. Several of the cattle walked right up a drift and over the bars of the corral. We had to get them back in before they hightailed it. You'd think they'd be grateful for shelter in weather like this."

"They probably were getting cabin fever like the rest of us." Lars took their coats and laid them on the bed downstairs, being careful not to cover up Penny's Gustaf, who slept soundly with a pillow on either side to keep him from rolling off the bed.

"I brought the letter from Manda that Penny brought to church today. Metiz, there was one for you too."

"Good. I thought we'd have a letter reading after dinner, or rather after the presents. Otherwise the children will think they are being left out. Bridget brought a letter from Augusta, and I have one from Solveig. Good thing Christmas comes, and we work a bit harder at keeping in touch." Kaaren took up potholders and lifted the pot of beans from the oven. "Let's put the food on the table and say grace so we can eat."

By the time everyone had eaten their fill, there wasn't a whole lot left but a heap of dirty dishes, along with a mountain of pots and pans.

"We'll have dessert later and let the dishes soak while we open presents, if that is all right with you." Kaaren glanced at the line of children, who all nodded vigorously.

"You mean no more coffee yet?" Lars got a laugh from the others at his woeful look.

"I think we can manage. Into the parlor, everyone." Laughing and teasing over chairs and floor space, everyone finally found a place to sit, with George McBride perched on a stool in the corner. Ilse had kept him from going upstairs to his room with a hand on his arm.

The carved wagons Kaaren's uncle Olaf made for the boys were a hit, as were the rag dolls sewn by Mary Martha, the pastor's wife, for each of the girls. Everyone got mittens, scarves, hats, or wool stockings, the favorites being those made out of rabbit fur by Metiz. Hjelmer had made ladles for the women in his blacksmith shop, and new shirts for the men came from the sewing machines now residing in most houses.

Thorliff's printed story pleased everyone, and when Haakan brought Ingeborg a beautifully carved box she thanked him with a huge smile.

"Look inside," he said.

She lifted the lid to find a lovely cameo brooch. "Haakan, you shouldn't have." She kept shaking her head in disbelief while at the same time pinning it at the neck of her dress.

"Onkel Olaf made the box, but I cut and dried the wood."

"As he does for most all of my furniture." Onkel Olaf nodded, pipe smoke wreathing his head like those of several of the men.

"We should maybe make a run over to Minnesota this winter for both oak and pine, you think?" Haakan tipped back on his chair until he caught his wife's eye and, grinning, sat back upright. "But not right now."

"All right. Time for letters." Bridget, at age sixty-eight the oldest one at this gathering, pulled one out of the pocket of her apron. "This is from Augusta." She leaned closer to the sun-brightened window to see better. " 'Dear Mor, I know you will share this with everyone, so hello to you all.' "

George stood and headed for the kitchen as Bridget continued. Within moments Ilse followed, to find him staring out the kitchen window.

"Why did you leave?" She signed and spoke slowly, carefully enunciating to help with his lip reading too.

He shrugged, a frown digging furrows in his brow. "You know," he signed.

She nodded, burrowing into his soul through his eyes. "I will sign."

He shook his head, cutting the air with one hand. "Too slow." His fingers still lacked the fluid grace necessary to sign swiftly. "Too many." He thumped one fist on top of the other.

"You have to try."

He shook his head, locked his arms over his chest, and turned again to stare out the window.

Ilse tried to get in front of him, but each time he turned away. She glared at his back. "All right, be a stubborn, mean, angry man. I don't know why I keep trying." She spun on her heel and strode back into the parlor to join the others, calling him several uncomplimentary names in her mind.

Uff da, Kaaren thought. *Now what?*

Bridget continued to read from Augusta's letter.

"I cannot believe how quickly the time goes by. It seems like I came to America only last spring instead of more than four years ago. Kane and I were thinking of coming to visit this winter, but since I am in the family way again, we decided to stay put. I know how much you love babies, dear Mor, and little Katy is so bright and smiles and laughs all the time, so much the way I remember our Katy. She went from crawling to running, and while we cannot understand all her jabbering, she goes on and on. I'm sure she will be a storyteller like her grown-up cousin."

Bridget stopped and looked toward Thorliff. "She means you."

"I know, Bestemor. You think I should send her a copy of my story?"

"Ja, I was hoping you would get the hint." She returned to the letter.

> "All is well here. Kane is still raising horses for the army, but we have more cattle now too. With the steam engines, there is not as much call for oxen, but we still sell some. Our garden did well this year, so I put up as much as there was. We will not go hungry. I love the rolling hills here in South Dakota, and while we have no close neighbors, we get together sometimes. I wish we were closer to a church, but a village has not sprung up here like in Blessing. I wish you all a blessed Christmas and know that our Father is keeping you all safe.
>
> Your loving daughter,
> Augusta"

"She sounds happy," Hjelmer said. "When she started off in such a mix-up, I wasn't so sure."

"You think her getting on the wrong train was an accident?" Bridget looked over her glasses at her son.

"Well, ah, yes, it was a mistake she made, remember?"

"Ja, a mistake ordained by God so that she would meet the man He'd planned for her."

Hjelmer rolled his eyes. "I'll not argue on Christmas, Mor." But the slight shake of his head put the final punctuation on his thoughts.

"Okay, my turn to read before you two get into an argument." Kaaren waved her letter. "This is from my sister Solveig, who you'd think had fallen off the face of the earth, as often as I hear from her."

"Ja, since we no longer take cheese and eggs and such to the St. Andrew store, we never get up there." Ingeborg reached over and took the baby from Penny so she could play with him. "Sometime this summer we will go up there."

"Good." Kaaren unfolded the letter.

> "Dear sister,
> "I am so remiss in writing that you must wonder if we are still alive. But we are, and while the Bonanza farm that George

managed for so many years has been sold and broken up, George was given half a section for his years of working for the company. He bought the rest, so we own a section of land and lease another. George's brother has come to live here and help with the fieldwork. I have my chickens and a milk cow, just as you advised that every wife needs.

"The children are growing like weeds! Arne is seven and in school. Anne is five and wishes she were in school—she is teaching her dolls to read. Clara is three, and we will have another before summer. George has promised me some help before then. What do you hear from Norway? How are our family and the school? All are well, I hope. I am still amazed that my big sister is running a school for the deaf. What a blessing you are to so many people. Please write more often, and I will try to be more diligent in answering.

Love from your sister

and all of hers,

Solveig"

"Anne was just a little one when we saw them last," Ingeborg said, shaking her head.

"Ja, she was carrying Clara when they came." Kaaren folded the letter and put it back in the envelope. "Your turn, Mary Martha." She glanced up to see Grace leading George McBride back into the parlor, her small hand hidden in his. Grace's smile, so full of encouragement, made her mother send a prayer of gratitude heavenward. *A little child shall lead them.* The verse flashed through her mind and brought a sheen of moisture to her eyes. Kaaren looked over in time to catch Ingeborg's nod, her eyes bright too.

Grace sat George back down on his stool and, after patting his arm, took her place beside him, signing to Ilse to interpret.

That man doesn't stand a chance, Kaaren thought as she kept up her running litany of gratitude.

Mary Martha began to read her letter from Manda, the adopted daughter of Zebulun MacCallister, Mary Martha's brother. Manda had married Baptiste, Metiz' grandson, and they moved to Montana to ranch with Zeb. Mary Martha and John Solberg raised Manda and her sister, Deborah, when Zeb took off for Montana after his wife Katy died.

"Dear Pa and Ma,

"Thank you for the quilts you sent. We are grateful for them every night. While the weather is cold, we do not get the terrible winds that sweep down from the north in Blessing. We have built a log house of our own, and it is very snug. I train all the horses, and Baptiste keeps us all in meat and furs. He says this is a hunter's paradise, not hunted out like the Red River Valley. He and Zeb went on a horse hunt and brought back fifteen head. That, with the breeding stock we have, is becoming quite a herd. Although I never lived in mountains before, I know why the Bjorklunds dreamed of Norway. Such beauty I cannot begin to describe.

I know you are all together for Christmas, but you can know that we are happy and safe. Hopefully we will see you in the summer when we bring the horses to sell. We all send our love. Give Deborah an extra hug from me and tell her thank you for the letters.

Love,
Manda"

"That was pretty long for Manda to write." Thorliff leaned his elbows on his knees. "I'd love to see Montana. I hardly remember the mountains of Norway."

"Ah, high snowy peaks plunge right down to the fjords, with ridge after ridge of trees and farms wherever there is a flat place big enough. So different from here." Bridget closed her eyes, dreaming of the past.

"Do they have more snow than we do?" Sophie's eyes turned as round as her open mouth.

"Not usually. But many of the houses are built right into a hill, and the upper story is for people and the ground floor for the farm animals. That way everyone stays warm." Ingeborg smiled at her niece. "You would like it."

"Do we get coffee and dessert pretty soon?" Trygve asked at his father's prodding.

"As soon as the dishes are finished." Bridget got to her feet and led the way into the kitchen.

Looking back two days later as the train chugged south,

Thorliff wished he had been able to stay home longer. While Anji promised to write more often when he'd gone over to see her the day after Christmas, he had a feeling that things would never be as they were before. He took out his paper and started a letter, promising himself to write more often whether she answered or not. That's what friends did for each other after all. And it was obvious she needed cheering.

> Dear Anji,
> I hope you like my story and that it brings back good memories for you. I am so sorry to see your father suffering like he does. I know God is in His heaven and all is right with the world, but suffering like that brings up questions, at least for me. But then, you know me, the inveterate questioner.

He went on to tell her about his dressing down in class for his questions, trying to see the humor in it so that she would too. He reminded her that he'd left one of his Dickens books there and perhaps his mor or Kaaren would read to her father.

> Joseph seemed to enjoy the story when I read it, and that would give you a chance to do something else. I will write more when I get to Northfield. We are nearing St. Paul, and while there is plenty of snow here too, it is nothing like the drifts of Blessing.
>
> As ever,
> Thorliff

When he stepped off the train in Northfield, he felt as though he'd stepped back into his other world. What a paradox. Did he dare ask the teacher if that was part of Biblical truth, this telescoping of time and distance?

CHAPTER SIXTEEN

Blessing, North Dakota
January 1894

The pit, black beyond measure, yawned at her feet.

Ingeborg teetered, flailing her arms, reaching for some kind of rescue, any kind. The air swirling around her pulled at her skirts, tugged at her hair.

God, help! Her cry echoed the corridors of time, fading into nothingness.

"Mor! Are you all right? Mother!" Astrid shook her mother's shoulder once gently, and then with force. "Mor, talk to me!" Her voice cracked, a sob seeping through.

Ingeborg heard the voice as if from across a chasm, the chasm at her feet. As if something pulled at her very eye sockets, she stared into the void. Even God had left.

"Mor!"

The word shrieked in her ear.

"Mor! God, help us. Please, Mor, what is wrong?" The sob cut off Astrid's air. She patted her mother's cheeks, shook her again, both hands this time.

"Astrid?"

"Oh yes, Mor. It is me. Please, please open your eyes." Astrid collapsed into her mother's arms, shivering as though she'd just come from bathing in a snowbank.

"Astrid." Ingeborg's voice gained strength. "Little one, what is wrong?"

"Mor, you wouldn't wake up, and I heard you crying." Astrid burrowed closer, like a baby animal seeking milk from a reluctant mother.

Ingeborg blinked once and then again, stroking her daughter's braids with a trembling hand. *Where have I been? What happened?* She shivered. Was the door open to the outside? Why was it so cold in her room? She sat up, looking around. They were in the parlor, her knitting in a heap on the floor by the foot of the sofa.

"Hush, Astrid, it is all right now."

"B-but Mor, you were . . . you sounded like one of Tante Kaaren's puppies when they are hungry. What is wrong?"

Ingeborg shook her head. *What is wrong?* She glanced out of the corner of her eye, trying to catch a glimpse of what had gripped her with such deadly talons. A shadow slithered away before she could truly see it.

She clutched Astrid to her chest, raining kisses on her daughter's hair, her forehead, and her wet cheeks. "A bad dream, I think." A horrible dream, but dreams did not live on after awakening, did they? And if not a dream, then what?

She sucked in a deep cleansing breath and wiped the tears she'd not known were there with the back of one hand.

"Why are you home from school so soon?" But glancing out the window, Ingeborg knew by the shadows that some time had passed. The children were home from school, supper should be started, and here she'd been . . . She leaned forward and picked up her knitting, new wool socks for Thorliff, now a mass of knots, dropped stitches, and tangled wool.

Astrid stared from the knitting to her mother. "What happened?"

"I don't know, but I shall set it to rights later. How would you like a cup of hot cocoa? I think we both need one." She rose and brushed off her apron as if to brush off the vestiges of the dream. "Where is Andrew?"

"He stopped at the barn. Far called him."

Ingeborg dumped the rat's nest of yarn into the hand-woven basket Metiz had given her for Christmas and took her daughter's hand. "Perhaps you would peel apples for me, and we shall bake a pie for supper."

"After our cocoa?"

"After our cocoa." She checked the logs in the stove in the parlor, now chunks of shimmering coals. Where had the time gone? Attacked by shivers that stung like a hoard of angry bees, she took a chunk of wood from the woodbox and added it, along with two more, to the coals, then closed the glass-centered door and adjusted the damper. No wonder she'd been shivering. The fire had nearly gone out. *Lord, what happened to me?*

Walking to the kitchen felt like pulling her feet out of the swamp that formed near the river in the springtime, gumbo heavy on her boots. When wet, the black soil of the Red River Valley could bring horses, wagons, and machinery to a stop, let alone a human foot.

Ingeborg shivered again. *Lord, I feel cold from the inside out.* She rubbed her hands over the cookstove in the kitchen and checked the firebox to see coals there winking in a pile of gray ash. Opening the damper full wide, she took a piece of pitch pine and, with the heavy knife she kept on the warming shelf, shaved some curls onto the coals to start the fire more quickly, then added several small sticks. Smoke rose before the flames licked the curls, stinging her eyes, the pain feeling almost welcome, the heat a cause for rejoicing.

"You almost let the fire go out?" Astrid handed her mother the pot they always used for cocoa, her voice and face wearing matching question marks.

"I know." Ingeborg hugged her daughter around the shoulders. But she couldn't answer the questions unasked. Or wouldn't as she watched the red and orange flames eat the wood, turning it black.

Black like the pit. *Oh, God, please, not again. I cannot be trapped by that.* She closed her eyes for a moment. *You promised. Where were you? I called for you . . . to help me . . . to save me.*

149

She opened her eyes to see Astrid's face.

"Mor." Panic colored her words like the flames devouring the wood.

"Get the cocoa. Thanks be to God, he sent me an angel."

Astrid clamped her arms around her mother's waist, and the two of them stared at the fire a moment longer. "So pretty, aren't they? The flames, I mean?"

"Ja, that they are." Ingeborg laid her cheek on the top of Astrid's head, the hair, in the morning so tightly bound in braids, now tickling her nose. Then she set her daughter off with a gentle push and added more wood to the blaze. She set the iron lids back in place, first the divider, then the back lid, and finally the front, the clatter of them settling in place a welcome barrier to the now heating fire. "Bring the sugar with you too."

Together they spooned out the precious cocoa powder and sugar, added water to mix the two, and when that bubbled, added a stream of milk, Astrid stirring all the while.

The cat rose from its box behind the stove, arched and stretched, then wound itself around their ankles, a plaintive cry to be picked up.

"You silly thing," Astrid murmured as she snuggled the cat under her chin. The resulting purr made Ingeborg and Astrid share a smile and warm giggle.

That night when Haakan and Ingeborg cuddled spoon fashion, waiting for their body heat to warm the bed, he ran his fingers through hair he'd asked her not to braid. "What happened this afternoon?"

Ingeborg scooted her back more tightly against his front. She sighed, wishing she could just say nothing. "Astrid told you?"

"Ja." His breath tickled her ear.

"I . . . I'm not sure." She could feel him waiting. "I . . . guess it was a dream, but I don't remember falling asleep. I was sitting on the sofa, knitting Thorliff's stocking, and then I don't remember." She closed her eyes to see only black on her eyelids. "Oh." She could hear whimpering, feel the cold as if someone threw back the covers and she were in a snowbank. She pushed herself into

Haakan's warmth. "The . . . the pit. It came back. I was falling. I screamed for God to help. But nothing. No one! He promised m-me. He said He would never leave me nor forsake me but . . ." She swallowed a scream.

"Ingeborg, dear heart, you are safe. Here, with me, with us, you are safe. The pit did not get you. God answered. Astrid came. She found you." All the while he stroked her shoulders and arms, comforting her. "Shh, easy, you are safe. God did not fail you. Shh."

"Those years ago when . . . when Roald disappeared, I hardly remember how terrible that time was, but I do know that black pit nearly devoured me. Thanks be to God for Kaaren and Agnes. They prayed so and brought me back."

"They said you almost worked yourself into an early grave." He continued stroking her shoulder, relieving the tension so the muscles no longer quivered.

"I know, but I could not let the land go. I could not. We had worked too hard, dreamed of our own homes in this new land." Her words grew further apart.

Bit by bit the warmth seeped into her skin, her muscles, her very soul. His voice, his hands soothing. Her eyes drifted closed, and she relaxed against him, her even breathing broken only by a slight shiver and later a hiccup.

"Ah, my Inge, how I love you." Haakan sighed and whispered his own prayer for Godly protection before he joined her in sleep.

"Mor, are you really all right?" Astrid looked over the rim of her cup the next morning.

"Why? What are you talking about?" Andrew stared from his sister to his mother and back again. "Is Mor sick?"

"Now don't you worry. I am fine. Just had a fearsome nightmare yesterday."

"Yes, but it was in the daytime." Wrinkles covered Astrid's forehead. "You never sleep during the day, only when—"

"I am not sick. You are not to worry." Ingeborg crossed the room and stood between her two children, a hand on each shoulder. She squeezed gently but firmly. "You understand?" *Lord, how terrible to scare Astrid like that. What happened to me?*

Later, on the sleigh ride to town for her weekly quilting session, Ingeborg leaned close to Kaaren and told her what had transpired.

"It's from the blizzard, I expect," Kaaren said. "That winter we had such terrible blizzards, and with that flu, it is only through the grace of God that more people didn't die. And I was no help. Only you kept me alive."

"God gave us each other, that is all. And His Word that at times you had to shove down my throat." Ingeborg flicked the reins for the horse to pick up a trot, setting the harness bells to jingling a new tune.

Seventeen-year-old Ilse leaned forward from the backseat, resting her crossed arms on the back of the front seat. "None of you talk much about those first couple of years."

"There aren't many of us to talk about it." Ingeborg glanced at the young woman. "Metiz reminded me of Wolf's protection one day."

"What happened?" Ilse leaned closer.

"Wolf wasn't a pet really, but when he was half grown, Metiz had saved his life from a trap, so he adopted her and then the rest of us when we became her friends. We were his pack, I guess you'd say. Anyway, we kept the sheep in a corral by the sod barn, and about lambing time one year, we had a wolf attack. Wolf killed one of the attackers and chased off the others. We most likely would have lost the entire flock but for him."

"And then that summer he rescued Andrew when he got lost in the tall grass." Kaaren turned slightly so she could see Ilse's face. "Both were true miracles."

"Did Wolf die?"

"No, a couple of years ago he brought his mate and their pups back, as if to show us he was all right."

"We haven't seen him since." Ingeborg turned toward the store. "I have to drop off these eggs. Do we need anything?"

"Is Bridget coming? We could give her a ride."

"Ilse, why don't you run over and ask her." Ingeborg looped the reins around the whipstock. Since they now had a real sleigh instead of only a wagon bed on runners, she didn't have a brake handle. Ilse jumped from the backseat and trotted down the newly built boardwalk that ran in front of the store, the furniture warehouse, and the grain elevator.

"No stops at Onkel Olaf's now," Ingeborg teased, knowing that George McBride was there learning woodworking under Uncle Olaf.

Ilse just flapped her hand, sending both Ingeborg and Kaaren into a fit of chuckles.

"Her face must be red as a beet." Ingeborg hoisted the wooden egg crate from under the robe on the backseat and climbed down. "You shouldn't tease her like that."

"You're just jealous because I did so before you could."

"Indeed." Still grinning, Ingeborg mounted the steps to the store and opened the door, setting the bell above to tinkling.

"Who's there?" Anner Valders called from the banking room.

"Ingeborg. I've brought eggs." She inhaled the shop smells, from woodsmoke to leather, spices to tobacco, coffee, and the bite of vinegar from the pickle barrel to the right of the counter. Penny stocked whatever the folks of Blessing and those on the railroad needed. Saddles, hay rakes, and harnesses hung from the overhead beams, and back in the corner, clustered around the Singer sewing machine, fabrics of all design and color, along with threads and ribbons, beckoned every woman who came through the door. On a slow day Penny could be found there, her foot dancing on the clunking treadle, turning out whatever clothing her family needed. In the months prior to Gustaf's birth, the Singer had hemmed flannel diapers, blankets, and gowns. People coming through Blessing heading west were always amazed at the variety of goods sold in her store.

"Be there in a minute." Besides working in the store, Mr. Valders took care of the bank work, which due to the drought had not been overwhelming lately.

"Don't bother. I'll just set the crate on the counter. Has Penny already left?"

"About ten minutes ago."

"Takk." Ingeborg left the eggs and headed back outside, ignoring the part of her that wanted to see if Penny had gotten in a new shipment of sewing goods.

"He caught her." Kaaren waved to the sight of two people talking with their hands in front of Olaf's furniture shop. It was only through Ilse's painful patience that George was finally learning to sign with some dexterity.

"I catch glimpses of a different man now that he can communicate some and is learning a trade."

Kaaren nodded. "I was beginning to think it would never happen."

Ingeborg stopped in midstep into the sleigh. "And yet you kept him on?"

"Only due to Ilse's pleading and God not letting me send him back home."

"Hmm." Ingeborg settled herself on the seat and unwound the reins. "Shall we go get her or let her walk?"

"I'm coming," Ilse called. She signed one more thing to the broad-shouldered man, who signed back before opening the door to the furniture shop. He turned once more and waved at the two women in the sleigh before he disappeared inside.

"Well, I never . . ."

"I told you so." Kaaren raised an eyebrow. "Another of God's miracles."

"She's in love with him?"

"Ja, I think so, but you know Ilse. If ten words are needed, she will use two."

"And George?"

Kaaren shrugged. "If his face glowing like a gaslight whenever she comes near says anything . . ." Kaaren's smile dimmed. "I keep praying for him and for them, but I have to confess, I'd sorely hate to see Ilse leave the school."

"Ah, you mean if he chooses to return to his family?"

"Sorry to keep you waiting." Ilse clambered into the backseat. "Bridget already went to the church, along with Penny." She sighed. "And Mr. Moen."

"Mr. Moen is coming to the quilting?" Ingeborg clucked the horse forward. "Why, whatever for?"

Kaaren looked as surprised as Ingeborg felt. While they had met Mr. Ivar Moen in church the previous Sunday and knew that he was writing articles for a newspaper back in Norway about life in North Dakota in order to provide information for prospective Norwegian emigrants, Ingeborg had not expected this. In fact, she wondered why he had arrived in winter instead of waiting until spring when the farming started. As if milking, feeding, and repairing machinery weren't just as much a part of farming as working the land. She tightened the reins, and the sleigh squeaked to a stop. With the air still and the sky as clear a blue as only contrast with a white world can make it, she stepped from the sleigh and took the horse blanket with her. "I'll tie him out here; he most likely needs the sun as bad as the rest of us." She threw the blanket over the horse's back and, after slipping off the bridle and leaving it hanging around his neck, tied a rope from the halter to the hitching rail. She patted the horse's shoulder. "I'll bring you some grain later."

While she worked with the horse, the other two women gathered the baskets of food and sewing supplies to carry inside. Then mounting the steps to the closed church doors, Ingeborg glanced at Kaaren. "It's so quiet. Did no one else come today?"

Kaaren motioned toward the other horses lining the rail. "I think we're the last."

But instead of the normal laughter and talking, the ladies of the church were sitting quietly, as if waiting for the Sunday service to begin. A kettle of soup bubbled on the stove, along with a steaming coffeepot.

"Where are the babies?" Ingeborg caught herself whispering. She set her basket on one of the tables.

"Welcome. Come right on in." Pastor Solberg beckoned from in front of the altar. "I am just introducing our guest from Norway. After our opening prayer, I will leave you all to your stitching."

Ingeborg, Kaaren, and Ilse took seats in the back row. Pastor never came at the beginning of the quilting bee, only for the dinner afterward.

He rubbed his hands together and beamed at the only other male in the room. "Now, then, let us begin."

Ingeborg marveled at the beam of sunlight that lit the fine hairs on his head, giving him the halo that bespoke his calling. *Lord, so many of our friends are with you now. Are they wearing halos and singing your praises? Please watch over us.*

"Father God, we come before you this day grateful for your many blessings and the way you keep us safe."

Nodding, Ingeborg knew that if she raised her eyes she'd see the Lord standing right there in front of the church, praying right along with Pastor Solberg, just as though the two of them were best friends visiting each other. *Lord, yesterday I called for you. . . .*

And I answered.

I know that now, but I was so terribly frightened. I never want to see the pit again. I want to see only you.

"We thank thee for sunshine after storm. . . ."

Oh yes, your blessed sunshine, so bright after the days of darkness. You suppose that is why the pit returned?

"Keep us all safe, Father God, and thank you for bringing this special guest into our midst. Guide him as he sees firsthand the life you have given us in this land. Bless the fingers that sew here and give of our bounty to those less fortunate. Open our hearts this day to hear your word. In Jesus' precious name, amen."

Amen, indeed. Come, Lord Jesus. Ingeborg straightened and looked to the front again. *This man, this Ivar Moen, looks so sad. Lord, help him to find what he is looking for.* She stopped her thoughts. Why did that bother her? She glanced to her side to see Kaaren nodding at Pastor's introduction. Today would be different. The women would not feel free to speak their minds and hearts with a man present, and a stranger at that. She caught herself sighing.

"Thank you, Pastor Solberg, and all of you for permitting me to be here."

As if anyone asked us. Ingeborg Bjorklund, what is the matter with you?

"What is bothering you?" Kaaren leaned close enough that the whisper could not be heard by others.

Is it that obvious? She gave a tiny headshake, but Kaaren reached over and patted her clasped hands.

"All will be well."

Ja, I hope so. She forced her attention back to the man in front. Not tall by Bjorklund standards, but neither was he short. Not handsome but not ugly either. The man's saving grace from mediocrity was his full beard and mustache streaked with white among the umber. Somehow she thought him not old enough to be already graying, for his carriage was erect like a younger man and his voice strong as one who speaks to groups regularly. But his eyes, her attention returned to his eyes. If the eyes really are the windows to the soul, his soul lay parched like the land wounded by drought. The word *slain* slipped through her mind but slain did not apply to their land, for new life would come with the spring, watered by the melting snow of which they had an abundance. His frock coat and gray woolen pants looked more suited to a city symphony, and his hands looked to never have done an honest day's labor. At least not the kind of labor the people of Blessing were accustomed to.

"And so I thank you again," the man was saying in Norwegian, "for any who would be willing to answer a few questions regarding your life here."

Ingeborg glanced to where Mary Martha Solberg sat, a smile on her face that only her close friends would understand. It was the smile that said she had no idea what the man was saying. While she had learned some Norwegian, she still was teased at times for her slow southern way of speaking. And Norwegian with a southern accent was indeed a different dialect.

"Thank you and welcome." As this year's leader of the women, Penny Bjorklund stood and graciously added her greeting. She turned to the women gathered. "Pastor has asked us to continue our meeting as we always do so that Mr. Moen can visit with us and ask questions. Kaaren usually reads to us. Yes. Good." She answered to Kaaren's nod. "And now let us set up and get busy."

"You s'pose he brought a needle?" Ingeborg asked, loud enough that those in front of them chuckled too. Soon the sewing machine Penny had brought was humming in one corner, two quilting frames were set up with four women stitching away on each, and others were cutting or pressing.

Penny stopped by Ingeborg. "Have you seen Anji lately? I specifically invited her to be here today. She needs to get out of that house."

"Then who would take care of Joseph?"

"Surely Knute or Swen could do that for a couple of hours, not that he couldn't stay alone for a while, far as that goes."

"You want I should go have Andrew run over there?"

Penny pursed her mouth, a slight nod accompanying her far-away thoughts. "I guess not, but we need to make sure she feels part of us."

"What about Mira Mendohlson?"

"She's over at the soddy with Mrs. Sam, watching the little ones. Mrs. Sam offered, so we decided to try that. Leaves the mothers some time off for a change."

"Including you?" Ingeborg quirked an eyebrow.

"To be honest, yes. All those years I kept praying for a baby, guess I didn't realize how much time babies take."

"You do fine, carrying him around in the sling like you do."

"Ja, the store is different than the cheese house for instance. I don't know how you did it all back in those early days. Tante Agnes either. Sometimes I miss her so much I could scream. It's so unfair, she who loved babies and prayed for one for me all those years."

"I imagine she has plenty of babies to love in heaven." Kaaren, Bible in hand to begin reading, put an arm around Penny's shoulders and squeezed. "Today I think I'll just start with Psalm one and keep reading. Give us all a chance to sit at our Lord's feet and worship."

Penny watched as Kaaren made her way forward, stopping to talk with those who greeted her, her hand warm on every shoulder, and her smile as beautiful and comforting as the sun. "She not only reads and speaks wisely, she lives out her faith—none of that 'Do as I say, not as I do.' Wish I could be more like her."

"She went through the fire to get there, but even back when I first met her, she had a peace about her. Sometimes when she was so sick and I had to force food down her throat, I didn't think we would live through the winter. I had to ask her forgiveness for screaming at her, but short of holding her nose so she had to swallow to breathe, I didn't know what else to do. She believes God gave her a second chance at life and does far better than I do at continuing to thank Him for it."

"Well, the three of you were and are my heroes, or rather heroines. I hope Thorliff writes more stories about those early days.

We all need to be reminded so we can be thankful for what we have."

"God dag." Ivar Moen stopped beside the two of them. "I am sorry to interrupt, but I would like to talk with everyone here." His English was slow and halting, as if he had to think through every word, and his accent so heavy they had to smile.

"You can speak Norwegian if you like." Penny spoke before Ingeborg had a chance. She reintroduced herself and Ingeborg too. "This is one of the people you need to talk with. Ingeborg's one of the first settlers in our area."

"Mrs. Bjorklund." He bowed over her hand. "I have heard much about you. I am still being in trouble to keep faces along with names."

"Today we are starting with Psalm one." Kaaren raised her voice to be heard above the conversations around the room. Slowly quiet fell, and she began. " 'Blessed is the man who walketh not in the counsel of the ungodly, nor standeth in the way of sinners, nor sitteth in the seat of the scornful.' " She continued on with that psalm, and then went on to others.

Mr. Moen sat back and listened along with the rest, but Ingeborg noticed that some part of him was always moving, a finger tapping his thigh or a tick pulsing above his right eye. He leaned forward, elbows on knees, hands clasping and unclasping. She was tempted to offer him a needle and thread to keep his hands busy and perhaps lessen the strain. She drew herself back to listen to Kaaren's reading.

When Kaaren finished, Mr. Moen moved from table to table, greeting and visiting with the others. The women went about their quilting as usual, but the normal visiting and laughter didn't reappear until after dinner and the men had left.

"Whew," Penny said with a mock wiping of her brow. "Now we can be us." The others greeted her sally with chuckles and agreements.

"You mark my words," Ingeborg said on the way home. "I feel something real disquieting about Mr. Moen being here, and I have no idea why."

CHAPTER SEVENTEEN

Northfield, Minnesota

Sorry it has taken me so long to return to my letter, but getting the newspaper out is always hectic. Because it was a larger edition and a house burned down not far from here, and Mr. Rogers asked me to write an article about the fire at the last minute—forgive the clumsy sentence—I felt like I was on the cattle guard of a train engine pushing down the track and throwing aside anything in the way. I have the bumps and bruises to prove it. Another thing that slowed our progress was that we have two new machines here. Mrs. Rogers gave her husband a new printing press as well as a Linotype machine for Christmas. From the way I understand things, she has an inheritance, and he doesn't want it spent on the newspaper, so she gave him these much-needed gifts. What could he say? I think you can tell by the rush of my writing that I do indeed love working here.

Thorliff stopped and reread his entire letter, then dipped his pen and continued.

I promise to write more often, and I pray I can bring some lightness to your heart.

School won't start for another few days, and in the meantime I plan to work on another article, hopefully for *Harper's* again. The editor said he would like to see more from me. I brought all the stories I wrote when I was younger with me, and perhaps I can rewrite one of those to get it ready for publication. The library at St. Olaf has so many magazines that I can send things to, and perhaps I can earn money for next year. Wouldn't that be amazing?

Greet your family for me and know that I hold you close within my heart.

Yours,
Thorliff

He addressed the envelope while waiting for the ink to dry, at the same time remembering the look of utter weariness—or was it despair?—on Anji's face. *Why can't she let the others help her? Yes, Joseph wants her there and is more calm when she is with him. Lord, isn't that unfair?*

He shook his head and set the envelope on his desk. Fairness—did the Bible ever promise things would be fair? He thought back to all his Bible verses, all the reading he'd done. The Bible promised an abundant life, freedom, love beyond comprehension—but did it ever say fair? He thought to the Sermon on the Mount in Matthew, the "Blesseds," as he called them. *Blessed are the merciful: for they shall obtain mercy.* Mercy should be Anji's middle name, the very breath that she breathed. But where is it for her? Where was the joy promised for those who served the living God?

What was going on in her heart and mind? That was another question that nagged at him. They used to share their secrets, their dreams. Wasn't that part of love?

Questions followed him into sleep and rode him hard all through the night, leaving him wishing for rest that did not come.

He was already writing at the news desk by the time Phillip Rogers set the bell over the door tinkling at his entrance.

"Good morning, Thorliff." Phillip hung his hat on the coattree. "Cook sent your breakfast with me. She was hoping you would get some extra rest before school started again."

"I decided I needed to use this time wisely, so I've gathered a

couple of articles, stories actually, that I plan to send to magazines."

"I don't keep you busy enough?" After hanging up his coat and
muffler, Phillip laid the food packet on the desk. "I see you already
made coffee."

Thorliff stood. "I'll get it for you."

"No, I can—"

But Thorliff was already pouring two cups, one a refill. He
handed one to his boss and picked up his packet.

"Where are you going?"

Thorliff pointed to a table toward the back of the area crowded
by filing cabinets, bookshelves, and an armoire that held back
copies of the paper.

"Sit down here where the light is good." Phillip picked up one
of the papers Thorliff had written and, alternately sipping and
reading, nodded, smiled, and nodded some more before he picked
up another.

Thorliff opened the packet to find sliced roast beef and cheese
between two thick slices of bread spread with butter, two cinnamon buns with currants, and two hard-boiled eggs. "Cook means
to make sure I don't go hungry."

"She means to fatten you up. She's concerned that your mother
and father think she hasn't been taking good enough care of you."

"You're serious?"

"That's what she said." Phillip set his coffee cup down and,
using both hands, evened the sides of the papers by banging them
on the desk. "You wrote some of these back during school?"

"All of them. Just the top three I've edited and rewritten."

"I'd like to buy the one on the little boy lost in the tall grass."

"That was my brother, Andrew. He's eleven now and growing
like pigweed."

"I'll print it next week, and you can still sell it elsewhere."

"All right, but that's not why I laid them there." Thorliff swallowed a mouthful of sandwich.

"Did the wolf really find him, or did you make that up?"

"No, Wolf saved our sheep from other wolves one winter too."

"Wolf?" Phillip shook his head. "The old timers around here
will really appreciate these stories. So much like what happened

before the area was so settled." He pushed away from the desk. "I'm leaving for a meeting for newspaper publishers in Minneapolis tomorrow. Be gone three days. Much of the paper is already typeset, so you and Elizabeth should be able to finish up what we don't get done today. I'll be back in time for printing, not that you even need my help with that beauty in there."

"How can you possibly say that unions are good for our country?"

Thorliff shook his head. "If you lived in wheat country and saw what the railroads and the flour mills have done to the farmers, you'd be in favor of unions too."

Elizabeth glared at him through the yellow of the gaslights. "But look what is happening. There is rioting, and if a strike occurs, it could end up shutting down the country. You"—sparks flew from her eyes—"you really think that is right?"

Thorliff thought her hair might catch on fire with all the energy that radiated from her. "No, I never think violence is right." He thought a moment. "Well, not most of the time." A picture of Andrew bloodying the nose of Toby Valders flitted through his mind. Some people didn't understand words, only force.

"And I suppose the leader of the American Railway Union, Eugene Debs, is one of your heroes?" Sarcasm bit like a viper.

"Not at all." Thorliff bit back a stronger answer. *Sure, Mor, a soft answer turneth away wrath, but . . .* He sucked in a deep breath and slowed his words. "But if you had seen farmers leaving their land because the wheat prices and shipping prices gouged their hearts out, let alone the drought, you might perhaps feel differently. The Grange has been a good thing for the farmers, but it didn't go far enough. There wasn't enough support from the farmers or the politicians. The railroads and the flour mills united against us and . . ." He raised his shoulders and dropped them again. How to explain to her in ways she would understand?

"I don't know much about the Grange," Elizabeth admitted.

"It was formed to help the farmers gain a political voice to combat graft and usury by the railroad officials."

"You'd feel differently if you owned that railroad and those rabble rousers were cutting off your revenue."

"They aren't asking for the railroad, only for fair practices." Ever the one to try to see both sides of an equation, Thorliff tried. He'd idolized James Hill for pushing the railroads west, but at the same time, he seemed to care about the farmers and the land they were breaking and settling. *And I'm sure Mor said Mr. Gould had a part in the railroads. What if I were he?* Thorliff thought back to the college scholarships Mr. Gould had given to him and his classmates.

A story thread tickled the back of his mind. What if he were Mr. Gould? Or a poor farm boy, which he knew he wasn't compared to others, a boy who traded places with a rich young man and . . .

"Thorliff. Hello, Thorliff, where did you go?" Elizabeth snapped her fingers in front of his face.

He blinked and could see Elizabeth again rather than the two young men. How did they meet? Where? Why? The questions bombarded him. "Ahh . . ." *Come on, Bjorklund, you sound like an idiot, what is the matter with you?* "What did you say?" His finally focused look made him realize she was worried about him. Anyone would recognize the furrowed brow that reminded him of her father.

"I asked if you were all right." She spoke slowly, as if he were hard of hearing or perhaps missing a link in his chain.

A slight shake of his head, a little snort. "I . . . all right, you are going to think I'm crazy—"

"You've been working on that." But the glint in her eye told him she was now teasing. "Well?"

"You know when we were arguing?"

"We were not arguing. We were discussing."

He tried to cover another snort but didn't quite manage, which caused her to raise an eyebrow. "Look, sometimes stories just sneak in and grab me, tie my mind up in knots, and all I can think is, *What if.*"

"What if what?" She took a small step toward him, her gaze encouraging, a far cry from her former exasperation.

Thorliff shrugged and cocked his head. "Well, sometimes I have to dig and search for a story, and other times they leap into my head, people talking or laughing or . . . or sometimes even fighting, but this time I saw pictures. . . ." He scrunched his face into a shrug. "You don't really want to know. . . ." *Do you?*

"Thorliff Bjorklund." Her hands smashed into her hips. "Don't you go telling me what I want to know or do not want to know. I don't have stories that do this . . . this . . . what you're describing to me, but I have music in my head, and it pleads to be played. And sometimes it demands to be written down so that I don't forget it."

"You're a composer too?"

"Yes, but don't you ever tell my mother, because she'll insist that I play the piano, concert style, and I want to be——I *will* be a doctor." Her words rushed out almost as fast as his had.

"And doctors cannot play the piano?"

"Of course they can, but my mother wants me to be a world-renowned concert pianist, and I want to play for pure enjoyment, mine and others'."

"I see." Thorliff stroked his chin, unconsciously mimicking his father. "She has big dreams for you. Could you do that? Be a world-renowned concert pianist?"

"Possibly, but I would have to devote every waking minute to it, and I just don't have that kind of dedication."

"To music."

"Yes." She clasped her hands in front of her, fingers locked as if in prayer. "But helping a baby come into the world, stitching a wound, or setting a broken bone and seeing the relief and joy when the person feels good again—now that is the music I want to play." Her eyes pleaded for his understanding.

Thorliff felt a smile start down somewhere in his middle and work its way upward to tug at the corners of his mouth and crinkle his eyes. "Ja, stories and music must be cousins." He started to say "kissing cousins," but caught himself. Instead, his neck heated up, and he was grateful she could not see the red in the poor light. "I . . . I think I must get back to work." He motioned toward the printing press that sat in silent beauty. Compared to the old one, that is, which now resided in the storage room. However, even new, the press still required cleaning.

"Thorliff, have you thought of showing this story to my father?"

He shook his head. "No. Why, I haven't even written it yet!"

"Well . . ." She spoke slowly, obviously thinking the subject through as she talked. "I just have a feeling. You know he said he would buy stories from you. . . ."

He nodded. "Ja, he bought one before he left." His mind took off again. The rich young man and the poor young man. Trading places, trading lives. Surely someone had already written such a story. After all, as the Bible said, "There is no new thing under the sun." But could each chapter be an installment in the paper? Other papers had done such a thing. After all, that's the way Mark Twain got started, wasn't it?

"You want me to ask him?"

Pulling himself back to the present, he slowly shook his head. "No, I will write the first chapter and let him read it, then see what he says."

"Good." She dusted off her hands as if she'd just been cleaning or digging or something. "I'll let you get back to cleaning the press, and I'll finish editing the want ads. I have a feeling that when Father comes home from Minneapolis, he is going to be excited about what we've done."

I hope so. I most assuredly hope so.

At dinner on his first day back at school, Thorliff fetched his parcel prepared that morning by Cook as usual and took his place at the dinner table, only to be caught in the middle of another argument.

"Did you read what Arnet Morgan had to say this morning?" Benjamin bombarded him before he had even sat down.

"No, why?"

"Bjorklund, for a newspaperman, you don't keep up with news very well."

Thorliff settled himself and started to unwrap his box. "Did anyone make fresh coffee?"

"No, there was some already made."

"Pure sludge." He glanced around at his three friends. "What did I miss?"

No one responded to him, so he threw out a challenge to them. "So if you were in charge, what would you do differently?" Thorliff knew a question like that would get the others going again, and he could eat in peace. As he'd thought, the discussion raged around him, two men from the table behind them joining in. If they wouldn't have harassed him unmercifully for being a snob, he'd have chosen a chair in the corner so he could write and eat at the same time. As it was, he let the story play in his mind while he concentrated on demolishing the ham sandwiches, gingerbread cookies, and apple pie Cook had fixed for him.

"You don't mind?" Benjamin took the packet of cookies and passed them around. "We can't let Bjorklund have all of these. He has no idea what he is eating, let alone any appreciation of it."

Thorliff shook his head. Thank God Cook had a good idea of what young men needed for sustenance and provided enough cookies for half the room. He thumped the hard-boiled egg on the table so he could peel it.

"So how did you do on that Shakespeare test last term?" Benjamin propped himself on his elbows as the others left for their next classes.

"All right." Thorliff got up to get himself another cup of coffee. "You want some more?"

"Sure." Benjamin handed up his mug.

Thorliff waved at several greetings from passing students, poured his coffee from the gray graniteware pot steaming on the back of the stove, added a dash of cream to the mug poured for Benjamin, and made his way back to the table, all the while letting his mind play with the story. Why would they change places? Was one willing and the other not—then why? He always came back to the why. Rich but nasty, poor and good. What a cliché. But what if they were on a railroad car when strike breakers attacked?

"Thorliff, how can you be sitting there with your eyes wide open, and most likely your ears too, and not hear a word I say? Or are you just ignoring me, in which case I shall leave you to your whatevers."

"Sorry." Thorliff glanced up at the round oak clock on the wall.

"Oh, I'm late." He pushed back his chair and fumbled for his things. "Sorry, old man. Thanks for leaving me one cookie."

"I'd never let you starve. Tell Cook thanks from all of us."

Thorliff had just as much trouble concentrating in his Latin class. At least at home behind a team he didn't have to try to listen to a lecture when his mind was filled with a story. And this one promised to be a long one.

On the way down the hill after his last class, grateful for the sprinkled ashes so they didn't slip, he and Elizabeth both seemed lost in their own worlds. They reached the back door of the Rogerses' home before Elizabeth shook her head and stamped her boots free of snow.

"Sorry I haven't been much company."

"Hmm?" Thorliff looked down at her and half laughed. "As if I was." He held the door open for her. "I've never had such a long story come upon me like this."

"How is it coming?"

"I've started on it, but I just need time to write. Something besides school papers that is. I have one due for Ingermanson tomorrow, so tonight I must finish the rewrite."

"You know Latin, don't you?" They unwound their mufflers and hung their coats on the tree.

"Fairly well."

"Have you read any essays by Seneca or Pliny the Younger?"

"Some." Thorliff turned as Cook pushed open the swinging door from the dining room. "Benjamin said to thank you for the cookies. He shared them around most generously."

"Ah, that boy. He must have a hollow leg." Her chuckle meant she enjoyed feeding half the underclassmen at St. Olaf.

"Or three. He says the woman where he stays wouldn't recognize a cookie if it crumbled in her coffee."

Cook's chuckle rumbled from under her apron-clad bosom. "Never mind. I baked some sour cream cookies for you today. You take them in the morning."

"He needs some for late tonight too, Cook. He has lots of work ahead."

"Elizabeth." Annabelle entered the room, looking up from the list in her hand and smiling at Thorliff. "Good afternoon, young man. I hope you both had a productive day." She stopped beside Elizabeth, who was still taking off her boots. "Your father made it home a day early. He asked for you to come down to the office as soon as you got home."

"Ooh, and I just got my boots off. Did he say what he wanted?"

"No, sorry." Annabelle started to leave the room but stopped at the door. "It does smell delicious in here, Cook. Will supper be ready at six?"

"Yes, ma'am. Pork roast, like you said."

"And Mr. Bjorklund, will you be staying?"

"Ah . . . I . . ."

"Good. You can come back with Phillip then. He promised he would be home for supper tonight."

Thorliff looked at Elizabeth, who raised her right eyebrow in a perfect arch. As the door closed behind her mother, she whispered, "The queen has spoken."

"Now, you don't go being smart, missy. Your mother means well. Always."

"Not that I'd want to argue that, but let's get a bite to eat, and then I'll put my boots back on and see what it is the newspaper czar desires."

Cook flapped her apron at them. "And here I made apple kuchen special just for the two of you. You don't want any, eh?"

"Just try to keep us out of it." Elizabeth jerked on the tie of Cook's apron as she passed them on the way to the pantry.

"Uff da, such a saucy one." But her chuckle left no doubt of her affection.

———

"Father, welcome home." Elizabeth called her greeting even as the bell over the door announced their arrival. "I have brought you a treat."

Phillip stood from behind his desk to peer over the high front counter. "Hello to you and, ah, Thorliff, I'm glad you are here."

"And here I am the one carrying the treat. I think you shall not have it after all. I'll put it back for Thorliff to have later." She reached up to plant a kiss on her father's cheek. "You look tired."

Phillip sniffed the package she waved under his nose. "Apple something. Ahh."

"Kuchen, your very favorite." She set the parcel down and folded back the tea towel to reveal a large square of flaky pastry, apple filling oozing from the edges where the knife had cut. Cinnamon-sugar syrup had puddled on the plate and soaked into the towel. She whipped a fork from her pocket and laid it on top of the offering.

Phillip cut a bite and put it in his mouth, his eyes glazing in delight.

"No one makes better kuchen than Cook, even if she is Norwegian instead of German."

"And I have other good news for you too." Her eyebrow rose in Thorliff's direction.

He shook his head, made quelling motions with his hands. No, he mouthed.

"Thorliff is too bashful to tell you, but he is working on a monumental story that I believe you will want to run in the paper in installments." The words rushed out, sprinkled with laughter like the top of the quickly disappearing kuchen had been dotted with sugar.

"Oh, really?" Phillip laid down his fork. "Installments? What do you have?" His gaze drilled into Thorliff.

"It . . . it's not ready yet." Hands knotted, he took a step backward, glaring at Elizabeth's back. If only he could run out the door or at least disappear into his room.

"So, you minx, you've let the cat out of the bag."

His daughter shrugged, her head tipped slightly to the side. "He'd wait until it was too late to tell you, until the story had been polished to a brilliant sheen."

Her chuckle made Thorliff clench his teeth to match his fists.

Elizabeth paused for the coup de grace. "And been hopelessly out of date." She looked over her shoulder, beckoning him to come forward. "Please, Thorliff, tell him what your story is." Now she wore a winsome look, as if she hadn't turned his confidences inside out. And back again.

All right, Bjorklund, take it like a man and get even later. Why did I tell her what I was thinking anyway? He shook his head, but the silence in the room forced him to comply.

"It's fiction. A story." He glared at Elizabeth, which earned him another chuckle. She surely was enjoying herself at his expense.

"It's very good, Father." She'd leaned closer to Phillip, her eyes dancing in the light from the gas lamps.

"Let him tell me. You've caused enough problems already." Phillip sent Thorliff a look that bespoke centuries of men out-flanked by their friends or family of the female persuasion.

Thorliff thought of Astrid. She'd often worn that same look of delight he saw on Elizabeth's face. Delight at having flummoxed either of her brothers or both at the same time to make it the supreme attainment. "It started—"

"We were having a fight about unions." Raising her eyebrows, Elizabeth assumed an air of innocence.

"A discussion, sir."

"Ah." A nod accompanied the response. He turned to his daughter. "If you cannot wait for Thorliff to tell me his way, you may go write the obituary for old Mr. Thompson. The information is right there." He pointed to a stack of papers in the wire basket on the corner of his desk.

"No, thank you." Elizabeth sat back primly, as if to convince them of her sincere obedience, but her eyes gave her away. Hurry up, they seemed to say, why must you take so long?

"All right, this story came from a discussion about the unions, which I am sure my daughter instigated and made sure you understood her opinions on the matter. Opinions which I know to be vehemently antiunion."

"Yes, sir."

"And you, I take it, are on the opposing side?"

"Yes, sir." *Will I lose my job over this? Should I not fight for what I believe to be right? No, not fight, there is too much of that going on, but argue for?* He paused. *No, write a story about what I believe in.* He sucked in a calming breath.

"My story is of two young men—one of wealth, one of poverty—who exchange places on a dare or a bet."

"And I take it one is a union sympathizer and the other a member of the upper echelons of society?"

"Yes."

"How much have you written?" Phillip leaned back in his chair, the squalling of metal on metal loud against the hissing of the lamps. "One of these days I must oil this thing." He moved enough to create more agonizing shrieks.

Thorliff gave himself a mental order to take care of that when he returned from supper. "I've written a partial outline and part of the first chapter. There are still many holes to be thought out. Have you read Jonathon Swift's *A Modest Proposal*?"

Phillip thought for a bit. "Yes, a long time ago. Is this story you are thinking of a political satire like that one?"

"No, but having read more of his work lately, I—" *I dreamed of writing something that could make a difference in how people see things, writing that would have layers upon layers.* He brought himself back to the room, where two pairs of eyes studied him. "I'd like to do something similar."

"And if you can do so, I'd most surely want to publish what you write. Is there any way you can write a chapter a week? We'd run it in installments like Elizabeth suggested."

"But, but you haven't read it yet."

"I know. So where is your first chapter?"

CHAPTER EIGHTEEN

I knew Thorliff would do it, I just knew it.

Elizabeth flipped the *Northfield News* so the page stayed upright. She continued reading chapter three of *The Switchmen*. She finished the final line and closed the paper, not bothering to read the other news of the day.

"You finished it?" Annabelle entered the study carrying a tea tray. "I thought you might like some refreshment." She set the tray down on the desk and motioned toward the paper. "The story has started a stir. People who missed the first two installments are asking for back copies of the paper."

"And Father said we have at least twenty-five new subscribers." Elizabeth reached for the teapot. "You want milk with yours?"

Annabelle nodded. "I'll be right back. I won't disturb you if I sit here with my needlepoint, will I?"

"Of course not." Elizabeth poured both cups and added milk and one cube of sugar to each before leaning back in her chair, china cup warming her hands. No matter that the fire in the hearth snapped and flared and the furnace poured heat through the registers, she could not seem to get warm.

"Are you feeling all right?" Her mother reentered the room.

"Why?"

"It's hot enough in here to open the windows, and there you sit with a shawl over your shoulders and a hot cup of tea cradled in your hands."

"Yes, and Jehoshaphat at my feet, who's purring besides playing foot warmer." She stroked the cat's back gently with a wool-slippered foot. "He likes my slippers. You think the catnip I planted in the toes has something to do with that?"

"You didn't?"

"I did. Some that Cook had dried for him." Elizabeth sipped her tea, enjoying the fragrance as much as the heat melting down her throat.

"I'm sorry to hear about Mrs. Branson. She was such a sweet thing."

"Me too." *That's probably why I can't get warm. Her house was so cold, and watching her cough her life away . . .* "And there was nothing we could do. It seems with all the medical knowledge we've gained in the last years that we could have done something for her." She shivered at the memory of the trickle of blood that had come from the corner of the woman's mouth after a coughing spell.

Elizabeth could feel anger simmering just below the surface. Dr. Gaskin had warned her again that she must not take the loss of a patient personally.

"And you don't?" she had asked him.

"I try not to, but some do get through anyway." They both knew he was referring to Mrs. Mueller.

Elizabeth had tried to see his face in the silver dawn.

"If she had been willing to come to the surgery. . ." He had paused. "No, I cannot say that for certain, but Miss Browne is a mighty good nurse, and if we could have caught this before it went so far . . ."

His face looked as gray as the lightening sky. He turned his head. Elizabeth would never forget his eyes.

"That's the most important thing, to get some of these infections before they get entrenched. Folks don't have the money, so they wait too long. I'd rather they never paid me a dime if they would just come for help sooner."

Elizabeth took her hand from under the heavy robe and patted his arm. "Education is part of it."

"And pride. They don't want to take anything from anybody unless they can pay for it. Stubborn Norskys. And the Germans are no better."

"Nor the Swedes nor the . . ."

"Human nature, I guess." He pulled the horse to a stop in front of her house. "You go on in now and get some sleep. Things will look better after a rest and a good breakfast. At least that's what the missus always used to say."

And you still miss her, she thought. "And you'll do the same?" She tucked the robe back around his legs.

"For a bit."

She knew he'd be at work at nine when Nurse Browne opened the doors to his patients. "You have any surgeries today?"

"Not that I know of and no babies due in the next week or so. Of course that never kept some of them from coming. Babies come when they are ready, not when the calendar says. Thanks for coming along. I know you were a comfort to Mrs. Branson. You have a good way about you."

In spite of the cold, Elizabeth could still feel the warmth that his compliment had caused.

"You're not catching something, are you? That's what I worry about when you go off on these home visits with Dr. Gaskin." Annabelle watched her daughter over the rim of her cup.

Elizabeth didn't answer. She had no good answer, other than that's the risk doctors take. She had given in to her mother's request that she not go out on school nights unless it was an emergency.

She left the desk and went to stand in front of the fire, her back to the blaze, still sipping her tea.

"You should have stayed in bed longer." Annabelle pulled the fine wool yarn through the eye of the needle and began the methodical stitches that would fill in the background. She already had the blousy ring of roses finished.

Not for the first time, Elizabeth wondered how her mother could keep from keeling over from boredom at the repetition of inserting the needle, pulling the thread through, and pushing the needle down through the next hole, square, or whatever you wanted to call it. But since this was the twelfth chair seat besides all the pictures, footstool covers, and gifts she'd made, her mother must get some satisfaction from it.

Elizabeth would rather stitch wounds closed. But then, that would not appeal to her mother in the least. Her medical skills tended more to bringing tea and chicken soup, not that those weren't helpful.

Jerking her attention away from her mother, she asked, "Have you been reading Thorliff's story?"

"Of course. I read every word of the paper; well, not all the ads. I can tell who wrote each one, whether it has a byline or not. Each of you has your own style and viewpoint."

"Mother, all I write are obituaries and family news. Oh, and I help design the display ads."

"Your father appreciates your help, you know."

"I know." Elizabeth crossed to the desk to refill her cup. She held up the pot, asking without words if her mother wanted a refill also. Annabelle shook her head and continued stitching. *Father wants me to follow him in the newspaper business. Mother wants me to marry Thornton or some nice young man and become a concert pianist. Doesn't it matter what I want?*

Elizabeth Marie Rogers, quit feeling sorry for yourself. You know both your parents are supporting you to get the education you want. You can put up with a few sighs, looks, and innuendos. She made her way back to the chair and took up her pen. She had a paper due in her American Literature class, and for a change she hadn't finished it early. Finding time to read and compare Poe and Melville took longer than she had planned.

She'd much rather be studying physiology.

Sometime later Elizabeth heard the ringing of the doorbell.

"I'll get it," she called over her shoulder as she headed down the hall to answer the summons. Opening the door, she smiled as brightly as the sun on the snowbanks. "Why, Thornton, how nice to see you. Come in." Stepping back, she motioned him inside, then shut the door.

"I was hoping you might take pity on a fellow student and come along ice skating with me. If I have to read another line, I shall go stark raving, maniacally mad." He made a face fit to scare a young child.

"Now, really, it can't be that bad." She motioned for him to hang up his coat and scarf.

"It is in that house. Between Uncle talking on the telephone, the boys fighting, and the dog barking at the boys, I—well, I just left."

"You could bring your books to study here." She led the way into the parlor.

"Who was it, dear?" Annabelle entered the room and answered her own question with a pleased smile. "Ah, Thornton, it seems like ages since you were here. I shall order tea and—"

"Thornton has asked me to go skating."

"Oh, well, in that case we shall have tea when you return, or if you like, you could join us for supper."

"If you are sure that wouldn't be imposing."

"Of course not. I'll tell Cook. Now you bundle up well, Elizabeth. We can't have you coming down with something."

As Annabelle left the room, Thornton raised an eyebrow at Elizabeth.

"It's nothing, just that I was out on a call all night with Dr. Gaskin, and we lost a patient. I couldn't seem to get warm this morning after that."

"You can't let . . ."

She held up a hand, flat palm out. "Don't you start too. Knowing to do something and putting that into practice takes just that, practice. Some things are harder than others."

"I know." He gazed through the arch into the music room. "Perhaps this evening you could play for a while?"

"That I will. Now, if you are warm again, let's be off before the sun sets and the wind whips up." She heard a male voice in the kitchen. "Or I get asked to do something else."

"By all means." He held her coat for her. "Do you have your skates?"

"Here." She shoved her arms into the sleeves and turned to the closet where she pulled skates and boots out at the same time. Within a minute they were out the door, still pulling on gloves and tucking scarves into the necks of their coats.

"Oh, what a glorious afternoon. Thank you for getting me out of the house."

"And for me. You have no idea what it is like at Uncle's. I feel so sorry for the children, but at least they have their aunt Sonjia there now. She is young and lively."

She watched a cloud darken his face. "What is it?"

"Oh, nothing."

But she knew from the twitch of his upper lip that something was indeed bothering him. *Should I tease him out of his mood or find out what lies behind it?* As they strode down the street toward the pond, she thought some more. Rather than the usual half smile, his eyebrows drew a straight line across his forehead, two lines carved the sides of his mouth, and his usually smiling eyes made her think of storm-tossed Lake Superior.

"Thornton, what is wrong?" She stopped him with a hand on his arm. "I cannot keep up with you today, and you know I am a fast walker."

"Sorry." He covered her mittened hand with his own, still staring off in the distance. "It is not something you can do anything about. I'm not sure even I can."

Fighting against her nature to urge him on, she waited.

"Let's walk, or you'll get chilled."

"Only if you talk." She upped the candle power of her smile.

"I . . . I'm concerned about my uncle."

When he didn't continue, she prodded. "Yes?"

"I fear he is making a fool of himself. She is so young." He uttered the words with a noticeable lack of feeling, or perhaps the feeling was trapped behind a wall of propriety.

And any relationship is too soon. She ignored her jaw that wanted to clench. *No surprise this.* "Can you talk with him?"

"As in, 'Please pass the salt' and 'Do you think it will snow today,' of course."

But not as in, "What's wrong with you, Uncle?" Elizabeth clamped her teeth over her bottom lip. *Why can men be so smart in some things and so terribly dense in others?* "How can I help you?"

"You already are." He tucked her hand under his arm. "More than you know."

True to form, he tucked his cares away behind a wide smile, and they skated until the setting sun turned the snowdrifts to sparkling fire and then dimmed to the shades of her favorite pink rose with blue in the hollows.

"You will stay for supper?" She turned to ask over her shoulder as she opened the front door.

"Of course. I already agreed to that. And after we eat, you will charm us all with a private concert?"

"Of course. You know that is such a trial for me." She hung her skates back in the closet, along with coat, scarf, and hat, before sitting down on the dark oak Parson's bench to pull off her boots.

"Let me." Thornton knelt before her, taking her boot in both hands to pull it off. He glanced up at her to find her studying him. "What? Am I some bug under your microscope?"

"No, not at all." Their eyes locked.

"Oh, there you are." Annabelle dusted off her hands as she came down the hall. She stopped midway, trying to hide a smile. "Excuse me if I am interrupting."

"No, not at all." Elizabeth turned with a smile, one that she didn't feel any further than an upturning of her mouth. *What is hiding back there, dear friend, behind the smile you so glibly apply?*

"We had a marvelous time skating, Mrs. Rogers. You should have come along."

"Everyone was out." Elizabeth tucked her boots under the bench and stood, wishing she could move back the clock to moments before and yet grateful for that impossibility. Surely Reverend Mueller wasn't behaving improperly?

That evening Cook came to the door of the parlor where everyone, including Thorliff, had gathered. "Supper is ready."

"Thank you," Annabelle answered, laying down her needle-point. She raised her voice to be heard over the discussion raging in front of the fireplace. "Excuse me. It's time to go eat now." When no one responded, she rose to her feet and took her husband by the arm.

"Wh-what?" He obviously didn't want to be interrupted, the resentment that flashed across his face told her that, but when he realized who had tried to get his attention, he pasted on a smile and rolled his eyes. "Sorry."

"No, you're not." She leaned against his shoulder.

He patted her hand and stepped between the three young people, who had yet to hear her summons. "Enough talk, everyone. Supper is ready, and there will be no arguing over the food."

Thorliff's neck grew red, and he took a step backward. "I-I am so sorry. I—please forgive me?" His eyes pleaded for Annabelle to release him from his misery. At her smile and nod his eyes spoke his gratitude.

"Thorliff, you didn't commit mayhem or murder. Not that your precious unions haven't done just that, but—"

"Elizabeth." The tone of her father's voice made her clamp her jaw shut. She glanced up to see Thornton hiding his glee behind his hand, as if he'd coughed or was about to.

"Just for that, you don't get dessert." She poked Thornton's arm with a stiff finger. "Come, Thorliff, you at least take current affairs at their proper seriousness, not like someone else we know here who is arguing just for argument's sake."

"No more unions, no more worry about keeping St. Olaf open. We will have nice quiet supper conversation." Annabelle glanced up at her husband. "Right, dear?"

"What else is there?" Elizabeth muttered under her breath.

"I heard that." Annabelle didn't even bother to look over her shoulder as she and Phillip led the way into the dining room, the three younger bringing up the rear.

By the end of the meal, even Thorliff was turning down Cook's encouragement to have another helping.

"You two young men need plenty of fuel to walk home in the cold." Cook backed out the door, a stack of plates on her tray. "I bring in dessert now."

Thornton groaned. "Does she want us to pop?"

"No, but you can be prepared to take food home with you. When she knew you would both be here, she cooked plenty extra." Phillip leaned back in his chair. "A fine meal, my dear."

"Tell Cook, not me." Annabelle tucked her napkin back into the silver ring. "Let us adjourn to the music room. We can have our dessert in there."

"No time for the males to enjoy a cigar?" Phillip rose quickly enough to pull out her chair.

"And cognac? No, I think not." Annabelle smiled up at her husband. "You wouldn't want to corrupt two such fine young men, would you?"

Elizabeth shook her head and rolled her eyes. "As if you enjoyed a cigar anyway, Father. And if you did, it couldn't be in the music room. Smoke is not good for my piano."

"Really?" Thorliff asked.

Elizabeth cocked her head to one side. "Yes, if I can get away with it." She made a face. "I hate cigar smoke. A pipe is fine, but cigars, ugh." She made her way to the piano and settled onto the bench, lifting the keyboard cover in the same motion. "Is there anything special you want?" She looked from one young man to the other, both of whom leaned against an opposing leg of the instrument.

Thorliff shrugged. "Anything. I just enjoy whatever you play."

Thornton leaned on one hip. "Something gentle, please. No crashing chords or thundering arpeggios."

"As you wish." She loosened her fingers, stretching them in front of her, and proceeded to bring forth laughing brooks and spring rains, flowers dancing in the meadows, and birds serenading their mates.

While the others enjoyed their coffee and apple pie, Elizabeth lost herself in the symphony of sounds, segueing from piece to piece, creating the graceful melodies that wove one into the next, and dreaming of nothing and everything, becoming bathed and saturated with song. When the last notes died away, she opened her eyes, returning slowly from the land she lived in when she played. She looked up to see tears pooling in her father's eyes,

approval in Thornton's gaze, and awe deepening the blue of Thorliff's eyes.

"Thank you, my dear." Phillip brushed the back of his hand
across his face. "I think you play more beautifully all the time. Just
amazing."

"Thank you." She could barely lift her hands from her lap, and
her head seemed weighted by a storm, as if with the cessation of
music, all her energy had floated away on the lingering notes.

Phillip rose to check beyond the draped windows. "I'll get out
the sleigh if you boys like. Looks to be pretty cold out there." The
moon painted dark shadows on the pristine snow.

"I can walk, thank you." Thorliff stood and turned to Annabelle. "Thank you for inviting me to stay."

"You are indeed most welcome." Annabelle laid aside her
needlework. "Cook fixed a packet for you." Annabelle smiled. "She
is determined that you fill out." Her hands sketched a wider form.

"She feeds me well. At school they fight over the cookies she
sends."

She smiled and reached out to pat his hand. "Will we see you
in the morning?"

"Ja, for sure."

The two young men walked out together but parted at the
next corner since their homes were in different directions.

After bidding Thornton good evening, Thorliff picked up his
pace, his breath clouding before him. Thinking back to the music
that still played in his soul, his mind skipped across the miles to
Blessing. Guilt pinched and stung. He'd not thought of Anji all
evening. In fact, he wasn't sure she'd been part of his thoughts at
any time during the day either. She would have loved the music.
Why didn't she answer his letters? He'd sent two since returning
to Northfield from Blessing.

CHAPTER NINETEEN

The blizzards might as well have continued for all the time Thorliff had for winter fun like skating, skiing, or tobogganing.

Unable to keep up with his deadline of a chapter a week, his story *The Switchmen* had to be extended to every other week. His fans sent letters to the editor wondering why they had to wait so long.

Eugene Debs, founder of the American Railway Union, became a household name as he created more tension between the unions and the employers. The nation fell deeper into depression with gold losing ground and some saying the silver standard was to blame. Railroads and many other companies went bankrupt and employers laid off more workers so that the numbers of unemployed swelled to unheard-of proportions.

At St. Olaf, following the catastrophic news the previous autumn that the Lutheran Church would no longer support the school, rumors abounded about doors closing or both the college and the academy either shutting down or cutting back.

Thorliff sat with the other students in the chapel and prayed with everyone for God to bless their efforts to keep their school in session. *Where else will I go?* The question died aborning when President Mohn assured them God would find a way. Thorliff nodded. *Such total conviction he has.* President Mohn closed his speech with his favorite line, "Remember, boys, remember the college." He sent Reverend Ytterboe on his quest to churches and families to raise the funds to keep the college operating.

After writing an article for the *Northfield News* regarding the college's plight, Thorliff tried to ignore the turmoil around him— the chapters of *The Switchmen* that tried to take over his life, working at the newspaper, concentrating on his lessons. Each day he checked for mail in his box, only to be disappointed when nothing came from Anji. He reread the one and only note she sent in response to his post-Christmas letter, seeking to see something else between the lines that he hadn't seen before.

> Dear Thorliff,
>   I too am sorry for the blizzard. Thank you, though, for the letter. I was beginning to think you did not want me to write to you anymore since you never answered the last one I sent you.

Thorliff shook his head and rubbed the grit from his eyes. *Mor must have spoken with Anji by now and told her I hadn't received another letter last fall.* If only they'd been able to really talk over Christmas. He stared out the window of his room, the sides and sill framed in drifted snow with frost feathers and swirls glazing the pane. A streetlamp outside cast a faint golden tinge through the window, making the frost painting sparkle and wink.

So tell her yourself. He groaned at the advice. *But it's not fair. Should I be the only one writing? After all, she's the one who spurned my offer of help last fall. And I've written another letter that she has yet to answer.*

So write another. The inner voice would not leave him alone. *Remember your vow to write to her whether you heard from her or not.*

"One more, and that's it. If I don't hear from her, I shall know that she has changed her mind about loving me." *Remember your vow.* He wished he could brush that voice aside.

"And not kept her word." Weary of arguing with himself, he sat down and wrote again.

Dear Anji,

 I have not heard from you, and this grieves me beyond measure. If you did not receive my letter of January 20, then this is to replace it. But if you did, how can you not find it in your heart to respond? Are you ill? Mor has not written of illness, other than your father's, and I am so sorry to hear of his persistent suffering.

 I told you about the ongoing story that I am writing for the newspaper. Between work, school, and the adventures of *The Switchmen*, I am running to keep up much of the time.

 Greet your family for me.

As ever,
Thorliff

He folded it, addressed the envelope, and placed it in his coat pocket so he would not forget to post it.

Thorliff groaned when he glanced at the clock Mr. Rogers had given him. *How can time go by so swiftly?* He dug at his eyes with one hand and opened his Greek textbook with his other. Two chapters to read, and then he could devote some time to his story—the story he'd rather write than work on anything else.

He woke up several hours later, shivering, with his head on his desk. The furnace needed stoking, and the crick in his neck bit him every time he moved his head. After taking care of the furnace and setting the dampers for the night, he undressed and crawled into bed, heartily wishing for a warm brick from the oven at home to warm his feet. As he did every night, he prayed for Anji, but this night all his other regular petitions faded before the need for sleep.

When he arrived at the Rogerses' house in the morning, he greeted Cook and took the steaming cup of coffee she handed him while pointing him to sit at the table at the same time.

"Elizabeth is running late today."

"Ah." The first sip of coffee burned his tongue. "Mange takk." He smiled up at her when she set a plate of pancakes with maple syrup in front of him, two eggs on the side and a slice of ham. "I really have time to eat all this?"

"Yes. I'll be taking you up the hill." Phillip strode into the kitchen, settling his tie and straightening his suit coat. "How's your next chapter coming?"

Thorliff swallowed his mouthful of pancake, wishing he'd not been asked the question. "I'll have it ready for you in the morning."

"Won't give us much time for edit and rewrite."

"I know." *I'd have had more completed if I hadn't written to Anji. What am I to do? I cannot continue to be torn like this.* The sour taste of resentment overrode the flavor of the sweet maple syrup.

The thought plagued him through the ride up the hill and on into the afternoon. He caught himself dwelling on it, rather than the lecture, mulling it over when he should have been studying. That night after finally turning out the lamp but before crawling under the covers, he fell on his knees beside the bed.

"Lord, I cannot handle this. I am being torn from within, and all my without is grinding to a halt. I'm getting behind in everything, and sometimes I feel so angry, I could curse and fight. Is this what love is supposed to be? If so, I want none of it." He braced his forehead on his clasped hands. Cold seeped through the rug and into his knees. "Lord God, this is what I felt. What she said last summer—it was a beautiful thing. So why does she not answer? Why can't I live up to my vow and not let her lack of correspondence bother me?"

He waited, listening with all his being. As if floating on a breath so that he inhaled the words, he sensed a response.

Thorliff, my son, are you going to trust me?

Thorliff held his breath. Nothing more.

"Of course, I trust you. Haven't I always?" His words stopped his heart. *Have I been trusting Him?* Condemnation rode his shoulders with spurs raking his sides. His eyes fought to close, his tongue heavy, his heart weeping.

"I-I'm sorry. Forgive me, please. Instead of trusting you, I have been railing against you, against the things that are happening, things over which I have no control . . . no matter how much I want to. Please show me how to trust, Lord. I *will* trust you in all things." As if a dam had burst and all the water run out, he slumped into a heap. A verse floated through his weeping mind. *"If we confess our sins, he is faithful and just to forgive us our sins, and to cleanse us from all unrighteousness."*

"Thank you, heavenly Father." He forced his shivering body to stand long enough to crawl into bed, where peace wrapped him in a feather quilt and warmed him with his Father's love.

At five sharp the following morning, he came fully awake, as if someone had just called his name and shook his shoulder. His mind singing thank-yous and praises, he washed, shaved, and dressed in record time, and when he sat down at his desk, his pen flew over the pages. The story flowed as fast as he could write, his mind creating pictures and his pen recording the perfect words to describe them. By the time he needed to be on his way to the Rogerses' house, he had finished the chapter he'd promised and written another. He gathered up the pages and laid them on Phillip's desk.

On the way to the Rogerses' home, he toyed with Psalm 84, setting the words, "Blessed are they that dwell in thy house. . . . Blessed is the man whose strength is in thee. . . ." into a tune that played over and over in his mind before bursting forth into a whistle.

"My, you sure are a happy one this morning." Elizabeth met him at the door.

Thorliff stepped inside and leaned slightly toward her. "I finished my chapter and another one besides."

She stepped back and with a grin laid one hand on her heart. "Goodness, did you not sleep at all?"

"You wouldn't believe me if I told you."

"Come and eat so we can get going. And tell me your secret. I need to feel as cheery as you. Studying half the night gives me nothing but a headache." She rubbed her forehead. "I shall be delighted beyond measure when this test is over."

Cook took one look at Thorliff when he came into the kitchen and shook her head. "Something good surely happened to our boy." She took a plate out of the warming oven and set it on the table with a motion for him to sit.

"Is it that obvious?" Thorliff couldn't remember his face looking that different in the mirror.

"Well, I have not heard you whistling one time until now. My mor always said that when a boy whistles in the morning, he has sunshine in his heart."

"How come then my mother says, 'Whistling girls and crowing hens always come to two bad ends'?" Elizabeth set her book satchel on a chair.

"Whistling is for boys, not girls." Cook made her pronouncement with all the certitude of a philosopher.

"It's not fair." Elizabeth whistled three bars of "Yankee Doodle."

Thorliff sat facing the door where Annabelle appeared in the middle of the whistling concert. He waggled his eyebrows to catch Elizabeth's attention, but she went blithely on until she caught the shake of his head. She let the notes trail off and wrinkled her forehead, her shoulders rising in a flinch.

"Elizabeth Marie Rogers, what has come over you?"

"It's Thorliff's fault and Cook's. They dared me."

Thorliff and Cook exchanged wide-eyed, raised-eyebrows looks and turned as one to shake their heads at Elizabeth.

"Are you ready to go?" Phillip stuck his head in the back door.

"Saved by the bell," Elizabeth muttered as she grabbed her things and dashed out to join her father. "Have a good day, Mother," she called over her shoulder.

"That girl." But the slight smile on Annabelle's face belied her words.

Thorliff couldn't help but whistle as he followed her out to the sleigh.

"Mr. Bjorklund, could you please stop by my desk after class?" Mr. Ingermanson stopped by Thorliff's side.

"Ah, of course." He watched the slightly stooped gentleman make his way to the front of the room without pausing to talk with anyone else. *Now what?* But Thorliff kept his questions off his face and out of his mind and forced himself to pay attention to the lecture. At least he wasn't behind in this class, and his papers had been getting better grades. When the dismissal bell rang, he waited and let the others file out ahead of him.

"You got trouble now," Benjamin whispered as he passed by. "Meet me in the dining room when he lets you loose."

"Ja, I will." The "ja" gave his tension away. No matter how he tried to conceal it, a summons to the professor's desk made his stomach clench.

Mr. Ingermanson turned from talking with another student. "Just a moment."

Thorliff nodded and made himself stand still. His feet twitched to run, not walk, out the door. He studied the instructions written on the board as if he had not already copied them into his class book.

"Ah, good, thank you for waiting." Mr. Ingermanson shuffled through some papers on his desk and came up with what Thorliff recognized as one of the chapters of his story from the newspaper.

"This has been brought to my attention. I did not realize you wrote for the local paper."

"Ah, I started out cleaning the press and things like that. Mr. Phillips wanted someone to be in the building at night, so he offered me room and board in exchange for my staying there and helping."

"Very good." Mr. Ingermanson read a few sentences and looked at Thorliff over the rim of his gold-framed glasses. "This is a good story."

"Thank you, sir."

"Some places could be improved, but . . ."

Thorliff waited, sure that the next comment would elucidate all the shortcomings of his story.

"I was wondering if you would like to join our magazine staff. Usually we don't take on freshmen, but you have proven yourself more than worthy, or rather capable." He read a bit more.

Thorliff swallowed, even that small action sounding loud in his ears. *How can I do this? How can I not do this?*

"What other things have you written for publication?"

"Some other articles for the paper." He wanted to wipe his hands on his britches. "And *Harper's Magazine* bought a story last year."

"Indeed." Mr. Ingermanson laid the newspaper back down on

his desk. He half sat, half leaned on his desk and crossed his arms. "I had no idea we had a celebrity in our class."

Thorliff looked up from studying the back of his textbook to see if the man was being sarcastic. When he saw only approbation, he half shrugged. "One or two stories do not a celebrity make."

"Modesty is becoming in a man." Mr. Ingermanson leaned forward enough to look over his glasses. "The grades I have given you must have been hard."

"Ja, they were, but I have been learning, and that is what I came to school for."

"Good. Striving for excellence. Would that everyone would take that as his creed. Now, I come to my reason for asking you to stop. Am I clear in understanding that you plan on becoming a newspaperman?"

"That and write stories too. I like both."

"I see. Well, the normal rule here is that one must be a sophomore before being asked to join the *Manitou Messenger* staff, but we have decided to make an exception in your case due to your experience. Would you be interested in joining the staff?"

Thorliff swallowed, desire warring with practicality. "I . . . I'd be honored." *Tell him the truth.* "But I have a problem with the matter of time. Since I earn my room and board working at the newspaper, and I have that ongoing story, and I try to keep my grades up, well, I have so little time. . . ." *I s'pose I've really messed up now.* "I'll have to give it some thought. And prayer." *God, what am I to do?*

Chapter Twenty

February 1894

"Quarantined!"

At Thorliff's exclamation Dr. Gaskin turned from nailing the sign to the front door of the Rogerses' home. "Sorry, son, but that's what we have to do with the measles. Elizabeth came down with them last night."

"But what about Mr. Rogers?"

"He hasn't had them before, so he cannot leave either."

"And the newspaper?"

"I imagine he shall miss a couple of issues." Dr. Gaskin put his hammer back in the outside pocket of his black bag. "Mr. Rogers said to tell you that he will be talking with you on the telephone. Right now he is trying to find someone to take over or at least to help you."

Thorliff heard and felt his stomach rumble. Obviously Dr. Gaskin did too, for he smiled. "And you are to eat at my house."

"Ah." Thorliff could feel his neck get warm. It must be about as red as his nose. If there was some way to keep from blushing, he sure wished he knew it. "Mange—er, thank you." Stuttering too. "I'll go to your house, then on to school. If you talk with Mr.

Rogers, please tell him that." He strode off down the walk without a backward glance, his mind going ten times faster than his feet, which picked up to just short of a run.

How can I help him? How can I find help? Who will help me? I cannot put out the paper by myself and keep up with school. Lord, help me, please. I need a miracle—or maybe ten.

The faster his mind ran, the faster his heart pumped, and he knocked on the door to the doctor's house, puffing like he'd run five miles.

"Good morning. You must be young Mr. Bjorklund." The woman who answered handed him a brown-wrapped packet. "I figured you might want to head straight up the hill, but if you come earlier tomorrow, I'll fix you a hot breakfast."

"Thank you."

"There's plenty there for both breakfast and dinner. Come by here for supper on your way home."

He nodded. "Yes, thank you." And tipped his hat. "See you late this afternoon."

"Dr. Gaskin said about four?"

"Ja, that is good." He heard his accent deepen. *Careful, you have no time for fretting. That will only make things worse.*

"Worry, my dear Thorliff, is the work of the devil. Our Lord says to cast our cares on him, that He will redeem our hours and our efforts." Thorliff heard Pastor Solberg's voice as if he ran right beside him. He slipped once on the ice going up the hill to Manitou Heights and St. Olaf, so he kept to the snow-covered side of the path. He made it through the door to the classroom just as the bell rang, totally out of breath from running the two flights of stairs.

"Good of you to join us." Reverend Ytterböe's smile took any sting from his words. Often an assistant taught the class, since the good reverend spent most of his time on missions to the surrounding towns and congregations, working to raise the money to keep the doors of St. Olaf open.

Keeping his mind on the classwork took every stitch of Thorliff's concentration. Every time his mind skittered off to think about the newspaper, which needed to be put to bed that evening, he jerked it back until he felt like a yo-yo with a first timer tangling the string.

Down in the dining room after his first two classes, he inhaled his breakfast at the same time as his dinner and left his mates to go study. Ignoring their taunts, he huddled in a corner to prepare for the next day, since there would be no study time this evening.

In English class Mr. Ingermanson stopped by his desk. "Have you thought about writing for the *Manitou Messenger*?"

"I-I want to, but right now it is not possible." Thorliff felt his stomach do a flip. "Mr. Rogers and his family are all quarantined with the measles, and that means I need to get the *Northfield News* out by myself. It goes to press tonight, and I know all the typesetting is not finished. I'm still getting used to the new Linotype machine, so it takes me longer than it used to."

"Ah." Mr. Ingermanson stroked his pointed beard. "You do indeed have a problem. Is there anyone else you need besides typesetters?"

"We have a new press too, and I am just learning it. I did all right with the old one." No matter how Phillip raved about the new press, Thorliff hadn't gotten it all down perfectly yet. And tonight he would be running it alone.

"I'll see what I can do." Mr. Ingermanson turned to the rest of the class. "I'm sure you all have your papers ready. We will start with Mr. Hanson. Read from the front of the room, please."

Thorliff knew he was supposed to be making notes to improve the read manuscripts, but he found himself composing an editorial instead—on the vagaries of quarantines and how they could wreak destruction on businesses and lives. By the end of the class, he had a satire going on the doom of Northfield if all the residents were locked in their houses.

Would Mr. Rogers mind running something like that? Or had Thorliff just created for himself another hour's work that would be required to finish it? Let alone the hour he'd just wasted in class.

"This is utter nonsense." Phillip Rogers stomped around his study, his hair standing all awry from raking his fingers through it time and again as he vented his extreme frustration. Pulling his hair seemed preferable to pounding his fists on the desk, the walls, the doors.

"Now, dear." Annabelle stopped. She rubbed her eyes with fingers that had suddenly started to shake. One minute she was freezing cold, the next wishing to tear off her clothes and fling herself in a snowbank.

"Phillip, I-I think I will go upstairs now."

"How can I—" He stopped long enough to truly look at her. "Oh, my word. You have them too." He took her by the arm and led her to the stairs.

"I-I'm fine. I must check on Elizabeth." The stairs undulated before her, and looking clear to the top made her think of mountains she had seen on the stereopticon.

"Can you walk up alone?"

His voice came from a distance, as if he were standing in the basement perhaps, calling up the stairs. "I . . . of course." Annabelle set a hand on the banister, only to be attacked by another bout of chills that shook her head to foot.

"Here." Phillip put an arm around her waist and half carried her up to the landing. They both took a deep breath and made it the rest of the way up, then down the hall.

"I . . . have . . . so . . ."

"You are going to bed." He guided her to the four-poster in their room and held her up with one hand while he turned down the covers with the other. "Do you want me to help you undress, or. . . ?" She started to tip sideways when he sat her on the edge of the bed.

Tears pooled in her eyes and overflowed as she looked up at him. "I don't . . ."

"I know." Phillip unbuttoned her brown morning dress and slid the garment from her shoulders. Untying her chemise and the bow on her padded winter petticoat and removing the garments would have been easier had she been standing, but the stark white of her skin, dotted by red, warned him away from any untold motion. By the time he had her garbed in a flannel nightdress, he felt as though he'd been through a skirmish, only not with soldiers but with yards and yards of fabric. Perhaps dressing women in britches was not a bad idea after all. He laid her back on the pillow and swung her feet to the bed so he could pull the covers up to her chin. It would have been much easier to call Cook, but he had an idea she wasn't feeling too well either. Could everyone in the world have the measles at the same time? Annabelle definitely had the measles. He had seen the telltale red dots on her neck and shoulders.

Following the same orders the doctor had given for Elizabeth, he pulled the drapes closed, darkening the room, and headed for the kitchen to bring up a pitcher of water. Making sure she drank plenty of water was important, since he'd been warned the fever could be high.

By the time Phillip called Thorliff, darkness had fallen, and all three of his patients were asleep—for a change. He stood at the wall, waiting for the operator to connect him to the newspaper office. Thank God for the telephone at a time like this. His thoughts on the blessings of all the modern inventions included the gaslights he turned on when dusk dimmed the land, not of course in the rooms of the sick, but if he had to take care of kerosene lanterns like they'd had years earlier and haul in wood, it would be far too much for one man. "I've gotten soft with this life of ease, that's all."

"What did you say, Mr. Rogers?" Ina Odegaard, the switchboard operator, caught him by surprise.

"Nothing, just thinking out loud." He held the black receiver to his ear. "He must not be there, eh? Try Dr. Gaskin." He waited again.

"No answer, but I'm sure his housekeeper is there. I didn't see her leave." The switchboard was in a house right across the street from the doctor's, and Ina kept track of everyone in town from her seat in the bay window and the lights on her switchboard.

"Hang on just a minute, Mr. Rogers. I might have found him." A pause and she came back on the line. "Okay, your young man is just leaving the doctor's house, and from the speed of those long legs of his, he should be at the newspaper office in three or four minutes. You want to ring him again then?"

"Yes, that's what I'll do. Thank you." He eyed the oak box on the wall with distaste, as if it were at the heart of this matter.

The tinkle of the bell told him Annabelle was calling. Elizabeth had one with a more somber chime. After helping his wife to the necessary, he checked on his daughter, still sleeping, and made his way back downstairs to try Thorliff again.

The ringing phone summoned Thorliff from his seat in front of the keyboard. He lifted the earpiece from the cradle and glared at the monster he'd as soon consign to the nether regions as to keep working with. New wasn't necessarily perfect. "Yes."

"Ah, good, how are things going there?"

Thorliff shook his head. How to answer? If he admitted how stuck he felt, perhaps Mr. Rogers would feel even worse. The last time he called, Mr. Rogers spent five minutes apologizing.

"Slow." Now that was a good safe answer.

"You are typesetting." His tone said he knew Thorliff was having trouble.

"Ja, ja. But it is getting easier."

"I wish I could get someone to help you. This quarantine is . . . is . . ." Phillip sputtered to a stop. "But that is getting us nowhere. How can I help you?"

"I don't know. The paper will just have to be smaller if I am to get it out on time." The silence let him know what his employer thought of that. "I-I don't know what else to do."

"No, you are right. Smaller and a day late will just have to do. That is better than canceling altogether. Put a thirty-point header on the front page about the measles outbreak. And run about three inches telling the good citizens of Northfield about the importance of keeping those ill in a darkened room. You might get a quote from Dr. Gaskin. I will send my editorial over in the morning."

"All right." Thorliff hung up after they said good-bye and leaned his head against the wooden box. Good thing he'd brewed another pot of coffee. Even with the day's grace, it looked to be an exceedingly long night.

When his eyes smarted so he could hardly see the keys, he left off typesetting and tried to study his Greek textbook to prepare for the test he feared was coming. After another cup of coffee that now tasted like bitter sludge, he made himself run up and down the stairs to the basement to get his brain functioning again.

The clock bonged three when he crawled under the quilt; the hammer pounding in his head made his ears ring. And the paper was not done.

Lord, do I go to school or work on the paper? Both are important. I haven't missed any classes up to now, surely the . . . He dropped into the well of exhaustion with nary a ripple.

Thorliff woke to a pounding he thought to be his head with sun diamonding the windowpane. Leaping out of bed, he realized the pounding came from the front door, and a glance at the clock in the hall told him he was late for class.

Still pulling up his braces, he unlocked the front door to find Dr. Gaskin about to hammer the wood again.

"Are you sick, young man?"

"No, I just overslept." Thorliff stepped back to let the man enter.

"You are sure you do not have the measles? No headache, no aching, no dizziness?"

"I had a headache last night, but not now. I am fine." *At least I hope so, but if I felt sick then I would have an excuse for missing class.*

"Mr. Rogers is worried about you. Give him a call, and then get on over to my house for breakfast. You need to keep up your strength. I have no time for another patient." While he spoke, the doctor laid the back of his hand on Thorliff's forehead. "No fever." He started to leave, then turned back to pull a paper from his breast pocket. "I almost forgot. Here is Phillip's editorial. He'll be talking to you soon."

Thorliff nodded, then had the presence of mind to finally ask, "How is Elizabeth?"

"Pretty sick, but her mother is much worse, and Cook thinks she should be taking care of them when she can't even walk across the kitchen. Phillip has his hands full." Doctor looked over the top of his half glasses. "Something like you do." He raised one hand in a brief wave and strode off down the street to where his horse and buggy waited.

The phone ringing made Thorliff hurry back to the hall. "Hello."

"Why didn't you go to school?" Phillip's voice sounded more weary than the night before.

"I-I didn't wake up in time." Cold had attacked Thorliff's feet and was climbing up his legs.

"Are you going now?"

"No." Thorliff straightened. "I am going to get the paper out. I can miss one day."

"I hate for you to do that, but I most assuredly appreciate your dedication. I will make it up to you."

Ignoring the last comment, Thorliff cleared his throat. "I . . . ah . . . wrote an editorial too. Kind of a satire, but short."

"Are you pleased with it?"

"Mostly."

"Then do a final edit and run it."

Thorliff felt his stomach hit his socks. "Ah . . ."

"Yes?"

Thorliff swallowed, his throat clenching, strangling the words he wanted to say. *How can you trust me to not make mistakes? What if I misspell a word or . . . Stop it!* He jerked himself to attention. "Thank you, sir."

Phillip chuckled. "You'll do fine, son. Bring me a copy when you've run it."

"Yes, sir." A pounding at the front door made him realize he had yet to open the office for the day. *How could he manage the office and run the paper too?*

"Leave up the Closed sign. Anything too urgent, they can call here." He paused. "Anything else?"

Yes. I can't do this. His mother's voice echoed in his mind. *"You can do whatever you set your mind to. Remember, the Bible says 'I can do all things through Christ which strengtheneth me.'"* "No, I'll be fine."

"That's the way. I know what I'll do. I'll tell Ina to send all the calls this way. Then you don't have to worry about the phone ringing, and if it does ring, you'll know it's me."

Relief tasted sweet, like honey drizzled on a fresh biscuit. The thought made his stomach rumble again. Breakfast first, and then all the rest.

Thorliff's fingers trembled when he set the earpiece back in the hook. " 'I can do all things through Christ which strengtheneth me.' " He repeated the verse again as he finished dressing and thrust his arms into his coat sleeves. One of these days he needed to write a letter to his mother and tell her how often he heard her words in his mind. Perhaps that was the way it was supposed to be: the teacher or the parent taught, and the teaching stayed on in the mind of the one taught. Perhaps that was why the Bible said to eat the words as bread so they became part of one. If his stomach would quit demanding to be fed, perhaps his mind could cogitate on this learning thing some more.

CHAPTER TWENTY·ONE

Blessing, North Dakota

"Ingeborg, it is none of your business."

"I know, but . . ." She stared at her husband, wishing she could think of a good answer. If only Ivar Moen had not come to Blessing. Anji was such an innocent.

Haakan held the covers open so Ingeborg could slip into bed more easily. When she shivered in spite of her ankle-length flannel nightdress, he reached over and pulled her against him. With her head on his shoulder and her back fitting snugly to his chest, he nuzzled her neck. "Ah, wife, you always smell so good."

"Ja, soap and flour and—"

"And you." He kissed her right at the base of her braid that she had just finished tying with a string.

Ingeborg shivered again, this time not from the chill of the room. She snuggled closer, if that were possible, and sighed when he kissed her again. The breath from his question tickled the hairs on her neck. Tomorrow she'd have to talk to him about Anji. Tomorrow. Right now there were more important things to do.

Anji and thusly Thorliff was still on her mind when she woke in the predawn darkness. *Lord, how do I help them and yet not play the busybody Haakan warned me about?* A spark of anger struck out like flint on flint. Why in the world was Anji treating Mr. Moen so friendlylike when she was promised to Thorliff? Surely she didn't realize how it all looked. Ingeborg knew she wasn't the only one who noticed. Andrew had mentioned it after church the Sunday before.

Ingeborg felt Haakan shift beside her. She should get up and get the fire going. But lying in bed next to her sleeping husband was such a treat, one only allowed in winter before spring work began. The way the wind whistled around the eaves of the house, she knew that winter had not yet released its grip on the land, in spite of the warming sun of the day before.

"You worrying, my Inge?" Haakan always sounded wide awake with the first word, none of that sleep-shrouded voice like hers.

"How do you do that?"

"What?"

"Sound like you've been up for hours." She rolled onto her side, facing him. "And no, I'm not worrying." *Liar.* "I'm thinking this through."

"Ruminating?"

Ingeborg chuckled. Ruminate—to chew on, to ponder deeply. The word had been on Andrew's spelling list. She certainly had learned many English words that she'd not have known otherwise because of the children's lessons.

"Worry is like that, is it not? You burp it back up and chew some more, then you can't figure something to do, so you swallow it again, to be brought up later."

"Ja, but at least when the cow does it, she eventually gets her cud chewed enough that it goes on by. Not like worry. No end to that." He stretched, pulling one arm across his body with his other hand, then repeating the process. "Why don't you stay in bed a few more minutes. I'll get the fire going."

"Takk." Ingeborg pulled the covers up to her chin. *Lord, I am so blessed to have Haakan for my husband. Thank you from the bottom of my feet and every bit of me.* She sighed. *Ah, that my children will be as blessed. Father, take care of my son. Though he not be of my loins, he takes a big part of my heart. And I thought he and Anji . . .* She heard the rattle of the grate from the kitchen. Perhaps she was creating a tempest in a coffeepot. No, that wasn't the way she'd heard that. "Uff da." She threw back the covers and swung her feet to the floor. There would be no more sleep this morning. There hadn't been for some time, and here she'd been lazing around. *What would Mor say if she saw me?* Thinking of her own mother made her feel sixteen again and getting the usual lecture on scaring eligible young men off with her forthrightness. "Sorry, Mor, Haakan says that is something he likes—no, loves—about me."

"What did you say?" Haakan paused in the doorway, holding the lighted kerosene lamp in front of him.

"Nothing important. I think I shall go see Bridget today. Andrew said she didn't look well when he took the wood in yesterday."

"And that is all?" Haakan's right eyebrow arched in that way he had when asking a question behind a question.

"You doubt me?" She raised both eyebrows, hoping for the wide-eyed look of pure innocence.

"I'll go call Andrew, or we'll be behind on the milking." He patted her posterior as he went past, which after more than ten years of marriage, Ingeborg knew meant "You'll do what you'll do, but I love you anyway." She added another stick or two to the now blazing fire and filled the coffeepot with lukewarm water from the reservoir. Grinding the coffee took a few more minutes, and Haakan returned from calling Andrew.

"Is Hamre in the soddy or over at Kaaren's?"

"Kaaren's."

Hamre sometimes stayed over at the school to help Kaaren and Lars with the chores and the machinery, but he and Lars always helped with the milking.

"You think he might be there so much if Ilse weren't?" Ingeborg stopped in the middle of her coffee grinding. "Can't Hamre see she has eyes for George McBride? I have a hard time calling him 'mister.' "

"Leave off the matchmaking, if you please. These young'uns don't need to be in such an all-fired hurry to go courting." Haakan settled his wool chores coat around his shoulders and crossed a hand-knit scarf across his chest.

"How about I make an apple pie before the apples all shrivel up?" Ingeborg knew how an apple pie seemed to perk up her husband's spirits. "And ice cream."

"Sounds good. Keep the coffee hot." The wind took away whatever else he'd meant to say.

"Mor, did you see my history book?" Andrew meandered into the kitchen, still rubbing his eyes. Taller than his mother, but yet to fill out in the chest and shoulders, Andrew reached behind the stove for his boots, getting a quick lick on the hand from Paws, who rarely left the shelter of his bed anymore.

"How you doin', old dog?" Andrew paused to pat the dog's head. "Has he been out yet?"

"Ja, I think your father carried him out first thing."

"Pa said we should put him out of his misery. You think he's miserable?" His voice cracked on the words.

Ingeborg knew how much the dog meant to her son. Paws had come when Andrew was toddling around, and while Uncle Carl, Kaaren's first husband, said he was Thorliff's dog, Paws had loved both boys and watched after them both. Along with all the rest of them.

"I don't know, Andrew, but he's getting up there in years, you know."

"He'll feel better once spring comes." Andrew finished tying his boots and stood up. "My history book?"

"I'll have Astrid look."

Once the two children were off to school, Ingeborg peeled the apples, rolled out the pie crust, and within minutes had two pies baking in the oven. She washed the breakfast dishes and set a ham bone to boil. Later she would add the ham to the beans that had been soaking overnight. While thoughts of Anji and Thorliff kept trying to take over, she forced herself to think of spring and her garden instead. Was it too early to start the tomato plants? Glancing out the window at the blowing snow made her decide it was too early—far too early.

Paws got up and staggered to the door, looking over his shoulder to make sure she got the message. When she opened it, he stood in the doorway for a moment, as if trying to decide if all the effort was worth it.

"In or out, but be quick. The kitchen will be cold as the porch pretty soon."

He made his way out to the porch, and they repeated the process at the outside door. Ingeborg reached back to the rack and grabbed her shawl, putting the heavy wool knit over her head and shoulders. She was as bad as the boys. None of them wanted to say good-bye to Paws yet. She found him sitting at the bottom of the three steps, a telltale yellow spot in the snow saying he'd done his business, but the look on his face said the three steps looked mountain tall and insurmountable. She leaned over and, wrapping her arms around his haunches and chest, picked him up and carried him back into the house. As she set him down, he quicklicked her chin.

"I know you're embarrassed, but it's all right. Sometimes we all need a little extra help, especially in the winter."

The food Andrew had put down for him still sat in the bowl, but Paws drank from his water dish before curling up on his bed behind the stove. His sigh brought one of her own.

After taking the pies out of the oven and adding the beans and onion to the broth simmering in the kettle, she checked the weather again. Was it worth hitching up the sleigh, or should she ski into town? Or should she just stay home?

"Lord, is Bridget ill, or what was Andrew thinking of? Haakan doesn't want me to go, not unless it clears off. Unless, of course, I can talk him into going." She grabbed her black woolen shawl off the hook and headed out the door.

While it had stopped snowing, heavy clouds hovered over the land. The wind had dropped from a shriek to a murmur, so she could hear herself think. If she wanted to. Sometimes not thinking was far easier. Especially when it came to an aging dog, a son who was about to have his heart hurt, and a young woman she already thought of as part of the family. She swung open the door, grateful the snow no longer blocked the way.

"Haakan!"

No answer. The cows in their stanchions all looked her way, winter-fluffed ears looking like fuzzy paddles. One mooed, a cat mewed. "So where is he?" She crossed to the ladder. "Haakan!" With no answer and no hay being pitched down from the haymow, she turned back. He must be in the machine shed. Back out in the cold she checked the sheep shed on the way and found him tying off the tails of the frisky lambs. They'd had a good lambing this year, with many sets of twins and even some triplets. Andrew was good at getting ewes that had lost a lamb to adopt another by skinning the dead lamb and tying the hide over the orphan.

"What do you need?"

"I wondered if you want to go to Bridget's with me."

"What does it look like outside?" He put the cap back on the iodine bottle.

"Lowering."

"How about tomorrow?"

She shrugged. While that was not particularly what she wanted, he was most likely right. "You need some help?"

"I thought Hamre was coming, but he and Lars must have gotten started working on the steam engine." He wiped his hands on a rag. The ewe nuzzled her offspring, comforting him for the terrible acts done by the mean human. The lamb bopped her udder and began nursing, what was left of his tail twitching from side to side.

"Did you hear the wolves last night?" Ingeborg couldn't help smiling at the sight of two lambs jumping over each other.

"No, I slept like a log last night." The wink Haakan gave her made her cheeks warm.

"Sure made me glad we have such a snug barn for them." Thinking back to the early years made her shudder. The wolves nearly got her entire flock one winter. And the lambing—she and Thorliff nearly froze themselves after Roald had disappeared.

Life was so much easier now that sometimes she felt guilty. And this year Haakan and Andrew, along with Hamre, took care of the lambing.

"You're not dressed to work with the sheep. Go on back to the house and put the coffeepot on. I'll be along pretty soon, and if the pie is still hot, well . . ."

"Will warm do?"

"Perfect."

After dinner Haakan leaned back in his chair, this time without creaking the back legs, which drew a smile of approbation from his wife. "I need to talk with Olaf about some things, so you want me to check on Bridget? Or you want to come along?"

Ingeborg paused in her clearing the table. "I think I'd like to go along."

"You don't trust me to observe Bridget carefully enough?"

"Oh, you." She flapped her apron at him. "Of course I . . ." She paused again. "No, really I don't. She won't talk women-talk with you. When do you want to leave?"

He glanced at the clock. "Ten minutes, soon as I hitch up the sleigh."

"I'll be ready."

The jingling harness chimed with the sleigh bells as they flew across the heavily crusted snow. Their breath blew like miniature clouds of smoke, and the sun glittered on the drifts, making Ingeborg laugh in delight. "I'm so glad I came."

Haakan turned to smile at her, his special warm smile. "Me too." He dropped her off at the boardinghouse and returned her wave as she mounted the steps.

Ingeborg inhaled fresh bread perfume as she entered the door. "Bridget, are you here?"

"In the kitchen. Is that you, Ingeborg?"

"Last time I looked." Ingeborg removed her heavy coat and muffler and hung them on the carved coatrack by the door before taking her basket of cheese and eggs on her arm again. She pushed open the swinging doors to the kitchen, greeted by the warmth from the two big black ranges that dominated the room. Kettles hung from hooks on a rack suspended above the stoves, a red-and-white checked oilcloth covered one table, and matching gingham curtains framed the tall windows. Bridget, her white hair braided and coiled around the top of her head, left the dough she was rolling to give Ingeborg a hug.

"Excuse my flour, but it is so good to see you."

"Is there any time you are not up to your elbows in flour? What are you making now?"

"Pie, I can never get enough pies baked. Those railroad men would eat us out of house and home if we let them." She lifted the cloth and peeked in the basket. "Ah, soft cheese. I'm about out of cheddar too. I need to send that husband of mine out to buy more. And eggs. How did you know I ran out just this morning?"

While Bridget took out the gifts, Ingeborg studied her face and the way she moved. Andrew had been right. Something was different. "Are you all right?"

"Ja, nothing to be alarmed about."

"Then, what is it?"

"That hip of mine is giving me some trouble. That is all. That fall I took before Christmas—uff da. Some things just take time to heal."

"Ja, and if you would take a lie-down once in a while, that might help."

Bridget stopped in midstride. "Who has time for such silliness. Men want to be fed, no matter what."

"I tells her to take it easy, but she don't listen." Mrs. Sam, entering the kitchen in time to hear part of their conversation, shook her head, her dark eyes showing her concern. "We'uns could do for her for a few days."

"I'm not ready for the rocking chair yet, so you don't go getting any ideas. Come warm weather, I'll be fit as a fiddle again. In the meantime, let's have a cup of coffee and some of that good cake you baked this morning."

By the time they'd finished their coffee and chat, Haakan pushed his way through the door. "Time to head home."

"You want coffee?" Mrs. Sam hoisted the pot she was just returning to the stove.

"No thanks. Had some with Olaf." He looked toward his wife. "You about ready?"

"Ja, always in a rush." Ingeborg stood and patted Bridget on the shoulder. "How about I send you some of that liniment I made up. Burns going on but helps the aches and pains."

"You do that. I thought to buy some from that drummer that came through, but then forgot." Bridget shook her head. "Forgetting is just getting too easy."

"I'll send it with Andrew in the morning, and he can bring it over after school."

"Tusen takk." Bridget pushed herself up by bracing her arms

on the table. "You want some of this cake for supper?"

Ingeborg and Haakan exchanged a look that said he saw what she saw.

Bridget followed them to the door and waved them off. "Come again soon. I never see enough of you."

Ingeborg waved again as they drove down the street. "That place takes so much out of her."

"She wouldn't have it any other way. Perhaps we can talk her into bringing in more help, but you know how riled up she got the last time we suggested it."

"I know." *Another one I have to commit to God's keeping. Such a stubborn old woman.*

That afternoon she cut out a dress for Astrid and had all but the handwork done before the children came home from school.

"Oh, Mor, how pretty." Astrid held the blue-and-white-checked gingham up in front of her.

"Now you'll have something new for spring." Ingeborg eyed the hem length. She hadn't cut it any too long. "You are growing so tall."

"Mange takk." Astrid fingered the bow at the neck. "Blue is always my favorite color."

"Now, how did I happen to know that?" Ingeborg laid the dress across the sewing machine. "Perhaps you would like to hem it?"

"Mor." Andrew entered from the kitchen. "Paws didn't eat his breakfast."

"I know."

"Did he go outside?"

"Yes, but I had to help him back in."

"Oh." The small word hung on the air. Andrew clenched his hands at his side. "He's going to die soon, isn't he?"

Ingeborg nodded. "He's an old dog, son."

"Is he suffering?"

"I-I'm not sure." She thought back to the look Paws had given her when he needed help.

"Has . . . has Pa said . . ." Astrid's eyes swam with tears.

Ingeborg shook her head.

"B-but we can't even bury him." Astrid flung her arms around her mother and buried her face in her shoulder.

Ingeborg patted her daughter's back and watched the battle going on in her son.

"W-would it be kinder to . . . to . . ." Tenderhearted Andrew could not even say the words.

"I think so."

"Can we wait until tomorrow?"

"Would the waiting be worse?"

"I don't know." Andrew turned and started up the stairs to his room, his shoulders bowed, each step weighted. "Thorliff will be sad too."

"I know. We're all sad. Paws has been part of our family almost since we came from Norway."

"Mor, do dogs go to heaven?"

"Ah, Astrid, sometimes you ask such hard questions." Ingeborg tried to think of all she'd heard of heaven. "I don't know."

"But God loves dogs too, just like we do."

"Ja, I am sure He does."

"After all, He made them."

Ah, my Astrid, how to answer you. So many things I have no answers for. Please, God, you answer.

"So if God gave us dogs, why wouldn't He take them to heaven too?" The young girl rubbed her chin the same way her father did. "But we will still miss him here, huh?" The tears choked her voice. She turned toward the kitchen, and Ingeborg heard her murmuring to the dog.

Andrew clumped down the stairs and on outside without looking at her.

That night when she was getting ready for bed, she found Andrew sound asleep in his quilt behind the stove, one hand resting on Paws. Ingeborg bent down and stroked the dog's head. Paw's tail lifted only a little at the tip. He licked her hand, barely moving his head.

"I'm praying he'll be gone by morning," Haakan whispered when she joined him in bed.

"Me too."

She woke in the middle of the night to Andrew's shaking her shoulder.

"He's gone, Mor." Andrew sat down on the edge of his bed. She could hear the tears in his voice. "I woke up because he licked my cheek. I petted him, and all of a sudden, I knew. He'd quit breathing." Andrew knelt on the floor. "Do you think he was saying good-bye?"

"Ja, I do." Ingeborg dashed the tears from her own eyes. "That's the kind of dog he was. A faithful friend." She stroked her son's shoulder as he snuffled his tears.

"I have to write and tell Thorliff."

"If you want to." She felt Haakan's hand rest on her hip, so she knew he was awake.

"Can we leave him by the stove until morning?"

"Ja, that we will do." Haakan cleared his throat. "You go on up to bed now."

"God natt, my son. You were a good friend to him too."

Ingeborg snuggled into her husband's arms as she heard her son leave the room. "Thank you, God," she whispered.

"Ja, thank you, God, indeed. I didn't want to have to shoot him."

"I know." *Ah, Thorliff, I hope this is the saddest news we have to send you.*

CHAPTER TWENTY-TWO

Northfield, Minnesota

"How long have I been ill?"

"A week." Phillip spooned more chicken broth into his daughter's mouth.

"Can we please open the drapes? I'm not a good mole." Elizabeth tried to keep the petulant tone out of her voice, but she could hear a whine.

"Soon. Doc says as soon as your temperature is normal for twenty-four hours, you'll get well quickly. You are young and strong."

"I don't feel very strong right now, more like a newborn baby." She rubbed her chest where it itched. "I really need a bath."

"Tomorrow." The spoon clinked on the bottom of the bowl.

"How's Mother?" When he didn't answer immediately, she raised up on her elbows, only to collapse back on her pillows.

"She has a worse case than you."

"What are you saying?" She caught her bottom lip between her teeth. *Please, God, how sick is she?*

"Doc says that measles is harder the older you are."

"Mother isn't old."

"No, but . . ."

She could hear the shake in his voice. "Has it gone into pneumonia?"

"No, she's just very weak." He rubbed a hand across his forehead.

"Have you been sleeping at all?"

"Some." He caught a yawn behind his hand. "The good news is that Thorliff got the paper out only one day late, and a fine job he did. That young man has a real future in journalism. He wrote a satire on the measles that made even me laugh."

"Can I read—" She stopped and shook her head. "I know, not until . . ." Now it was her turn to yawn. "I wish I could be up helping you."

"Tomorrow maybe. Cook is able to be up a bit now. I warned her that if she collapsed on the kitchen floor, I was going to fire her."

"Father!"

"Well, I had to do something to keep her in bed. Doc Gaskin's cook is sending food over. Not that anyone but me is eating real food."

Elizabeth heard his voice from a distance as she slipped back into healing sleep.

Within three days she was up, and though moving slowly and resting often, she took over the care of her mother so her father could go back to work in time to put out the next paper. Thorliff and his helpers from St. Olaf had put out the second paper also, much to Phillip's relief.

Tenderly she bathed her mother's body, using cool water to help bring down the fever that spiked in the late afternoon.

"I am sorry to be such a bother." Annabelle's voice swelled no higher than a whisper, and Elizabeth had to lean close to hear.

"Oh, Mother, don't fret. Just rest and get well again." Elizabeth thought back to the night two days earlier. Barely out of bed herself, she had spent most of the hours at her mother's bedside, praying for each rise of the covers, grateful for each new breath. At times like this she wished she knew nothing of medicine, nothing of how close to leaving her mother hovered. And there was nothing she could do but pray and keep sponging away the fever. She only knew her father had carried her away from her vigil because she woke up again in her own bed.

"Father God, please leave my mother here for me, for us." That prayer turned into a litany as she sent her father to sleep in another room while she, feeling much stronger, took over sponging her mother's hot skin and dripping cool water between her mother's parched and cracked lips. "Please, God, we need her more than you do." Somewhere in the darkest hours of morning, she sensed a change, minuscule at first, the faintest cooling of skin, a deepening of breath. Fear clutched her heart. *Is this the end? Do I call Father? Lord, what do I do?* She smoothed tendrils of her mother's limp hair back from her brow, now definitely cooler. Was that color returning to her cheeks?

"Thank you, Lord God. Thank you. She has turned the corner, thank you." Tears dripped as Elizabeth sponged her mother's body once again and pulled the sheet back in place. She held a spoon of water to her mother's lips, and this time, Annabelle swallowed immediately. Several spoonfuls later, she moved her head slightly to the side, signaling Elizabeth to stop. But it was a beginning.

"How long have I been ill?" More hours had passed, and with each wakening, her mother's voice was stronger.

"I'm not sure. I got the measles first. Then when I started to get well, I . . ." She paused. There was no sense in telling her mother how close to death she had been.

Annabelle opened her eyes and glanced around the room. "So dark."

"I know, but not for long." Elizabeth folded the cloth and laid it over the edge of the basin. "Would you like me to read to you?"

"Yes, if you are sure your eyes are all right." With each word, her mother's voice grew more firm.

Elizabeth picked up the Bible that lay beside the lamp but found the light too dim to see the words. Were her eyes weaker, or was it the light? "I'm sorry, Mother, it is just too dark in here to read." But when she looked up, she realized Annabelle was sound asleep again.

Earlier, in her own room, she'd tried to read one of her textbooks but had fallen asleep before finishing a page. She had no idea what she had read. Now, hesitant to leave her mother, she kept one finger between the pages and thought back to all the Bible passages she had memorized while attending Sunday school. Needing to hear the words out loud, she whispered, " 'The Lord is my shepherd; I shall not want. He maketh me to lie down in green pastures: He leadeth me beside the still waters.' " She continued until "Yea, though I walk . . ." And her voice cracked. Tears burned the backs of her eyes and drained into her nose. So close, her mother had been so close. She tried to sniff them back without sounding like that was what she was doing, but when that failed, she dug a handkerchief from her apron pocket and blew her nose.

"I was in that valley."

Elizabeth stared at her mother, then took the trembling hand that reached out to her. "I know."

"And He was with me." A pause stretched from then to the present. "I will never doubt again." Annabelle kept her gaze on her daughter's face. "I could feel your prayers, and your father's. I heard him weeping one night, sitting right in that chair. I couldn't even open my eyes or say a word, but . . ." A soft sigh escaped just as she slipped back into sleep.

Elizabeth now let the tears run. She stroked the leather cover of the book still clutched in her hands. " 'Surely goodness and mercy shall follow me all the days of my life: and I will dwell in the house of the Lord forever.' " She repeated the words again, savoring them like sips of the finest nectar. "Lord, oh Lord, thank you for your mercy to us, your gracious kindness." She rose from the bedside to go telephone her father and, after giving him the good news, returned to her own bed for much needed restoration.

" 'Surely goodness and mercy'—Lord, a doctor needs those qualities in abundance." Good wasn't something Elizabeth was often described as being or even alluded to. Yes, she was good at her music and her studies, but this referred to something else, something that came from within. Good like Jesus was, not just a lack of bad or evil. She tried to keep grasp of the thoughts, positive they held a message of great importance. When they slipped away, she glanced at the pile of books on her nightstand. "I need to go back to school, and yet I am so tired."

Mercy, how did one become full of mercy? She slipped into

sleep, the last picture in her mind of standing drenched under a waterfall labeled Mercy.

⊛⊶⊛⊶⊛

The next morning Elizabeth served Dr. Gaskin coffee in the parlor. "Why is it taking me so long to get my strength back?" Elizabeth hated pleading almost worse than asking for forgiveness.

Dr. Gaskin shook his head as he placed his stethoscope back in his medical bag. "I told you to get plenty of rest."

"I am."

"You are taking care of your mother, who is still unable to get out of bed for any length of time. You are studying in spite of my recommendations, and—"

"If I don't study, I may have to repeat this term, and that does not fit into my calendar." She felt like stomping her foot and pounding her fists on the table but clamped them under her armpits instead.

"Elizabeth, I have no other advice for you. You should be eating more than usual, especially beef, to help rebuild your strength, not running up and down stairs—"

"I wasn't running."

"No? Perhaps not, but I could hear you struggling for breath from clear down the hall. Now, if you recall, I warned you that measles also puts a strain on the heart and lungs, even though for you, your lungs stayed relatively clear."

"Relatively?" Her attention zeroed in on the word.

"Meaning I heard only minor wheezing instead of a surfeit of fluid."

"So will my lungs be weakened permanently because of this?"

Dr. Gaskin shrugged. "I don't know." He spoke slowly, emphasizing each word, the look on his face warning her that further interrogation would be unwise.

Elizabeth sank into a chair, nibbling on her bottom lip. "And Mother is far worse off than I am." She studied her hands clasped in her lap, one thumb smoothing the skin of the other. Sometimes her eyes burned, and she wasn't sure if it was due to tears or overuse. But how to get anything done without using her eyes? And what made them hurt anyway? Granted they felt better in a dim room, but then she always fell asleep in a dim room, so of course they felt better when closed. Perhaps she could do an experiment on what soothed her eyes. The thought made her want to leap to her feet, but she knew Dr. Gaskin well enough that he would see through her and demand her strict obedience to his regimen. Not that he really had a regimen for her but to rest, eat well, and let time take its course.

"Do you mind if I play the piano?" At the lift of his right eyebrow, she knew she'd failed in keeping any trace of sarcasm out of her voice.

"Not at all, as long as you play from memory." Dr. Gaskin winked at her as he hefted his bag and headed for the front door. "I'll show myself out." He stopped under the arch and looked back over his shoulder. "And keep the sheers drawn, at least. It will be easier on the eyes."

"Yes, sir!" But she refrained from saluting, confining her ready-to-offend hand with the other. Wandering over to the piano, she sat down on the bench and let her fingers trail over the keys, searching out chords and melodies to match her mood. But melancholy didn't satisfy, so she segued to a march, then drifted into hymns, which she played for half an hour before her back complained to her that it was tired and she ought to lie down. On the way to her room, she peeked in to check on her mother.

"Thank you, dear. Those old hymns were just what I needed."

"You are most welcome. Can I get you anything?"

"No, I'm just floating on the music, wishing I had the strength to get up and do something, but it looks like I must be satisfied to think or sleep instead."

"I know what you mean. I'll be lying down if you need anything." Elizabeth blew her mother a kiss and left the door half open so she could hear a call if need be. Floating indeed. If that was what her mother needed, she would play again before supper. Strange how weary even playing the piano made her feel. Usually she gained strength at the keyboard, and that's what she'd been hoping for, not the need for another nap. At the very least she should go help Cook in the kitchen. Sighing, she lay down and fell asleep like a candle being puffed out.

Wrestling her way out of a nightmare left her dripping sweat.

Elizabeth leaped to her feet, swayed while she waited for the room to cease spinning, and made her way to her mother's room. Annabelle lay sleeping, her breath coming in short puffs but evenly and with little wheezing. In the dream, she'd closed her mother's eyes in death, and her father had not been far behind.

Sucking in a deep breath made her throat itch to cough, so she left the room and darted back to her own bedroom to cough until her chest ached and her throat burned with a scratching fire. She leaned against the wall, shivering in her damp clothing and from the aftermath of the coughing fit. Was she getting worse? Right now, that's what she felt beyond certainty. She made her way to the bathroom and turned on the faucets to fill the tub. Soaking, breathing deeply of the steam, would surely help.

Her father found her back in bed, alternately shivering and sweating.

"Ah, did too much, eh?" He laid the back of his hand on her forehead.

"No, I did not do too much. I have done nothing of any worth for almost two weeks now, and here this confounded illness is back again. I thought to go up to school tomorrow, and look at me."

"No need to bite the hand that will feed you tonight."

"I don't need feeding." She sounded like a cranky child and castigated herself for that too. "If I miss any more school, they are going to say I have to take this term over, and—" She exploded in another coughing spell and tried to catch her breath.

"I'm calling the doctor."

"There's nothing he can do. He'll just say bed rest, and drink lots of beef or chicken broth, and use the cough syrup he already left." She fought to catch her breath between phrases. *How had this come spinning back so quickly?* "I even played the piano for mother today and thought I was so much better." Tears wanted to leak from her eyes, so she rubbed them with her fists.

"Thorliff sent his greetings, and Thornton dropped by the office to see how you were. He was just released from quarantine at his uncle's house. The children all had the measles too."

"And he didn't get them?"

"No, he took care of everyone else. He offered to come read

some of your textbooks to you if Doctor will let him."

"Has he had the measles?"

"Must have, or he'd have them by now." Phillip leaned against the carved post at the end of her bed, his fingers absently stroking the pineapple carved at the top of the cherrywood post. "I'll send Cook up to bathe you."

"I just got out of the tub an hour or so ago."

"I meant to cool you off."

"Just open the window, and I'll throw back the covers and let the wind take care of me."

Phillip chuckled. "You must not be terribly sick. Your tongue is sharp as a needle."

She sighed. "Sorry. Please hand me that cough medicine. It will put me to sleep, and perhaps I will wake feeling better again."

Phillip did as she asked. "I'll fetch a spoon."

"No need." She raised the brown bottle to her lips and took two serious glugs, the medicine burning clear to her belly. When she could talk again, she rolled her eyes. "Must be enough whiskey or brandy in that to drop a horse." Handing back the bottle, she rolled over on her side. "Thank you."

Phillip stoppered the bottle with the cork and set it back on the stand. "Ring your bell if I can get you anything."

"I will."

"They say doctors make the worst patients." Dr. Gaskin replaced the now empty cough syrup bottle with another.

"How would I know? If I stay in bed all the time, I won't have to worry about becoming one." Two days had passed, and while Elizabeth knew she was better, she felt virtually unable to keep her mouth from spewing out her resentment.

"I think spring will show her face soon."

"Right, and I've spent most of February in bed."

"Better than the grave. I lost another patient last night, and you know how close your mother was."

Elizabeth bit the inside of her lower lip. "I'm sorry."

"I know you are. But please listen to me, and let's not do this again."

"Can I read now?"

"Unless it bothers your eyes. You're done with the measles, but the secondary infections are what death uses to carry folks off."

All right, quit being such a spoiled brat and behave yourself. "How bad has it been?"

"Four dead, two still borderline, and everyone else slowly recovering. Miss Browne has been a trouper. You found a jewel when you found her, and I thank you for it."

"Good." Elizabeth hacked and coughed up more phlegm. She checked her handkerchief. No longer green at least. "How is Mother?"

"Weak." His brow wrinkled. "You will be on your feet far faster, I'm sure." He shook his head.

"I'm far younger."

A one-shouldered shrug greeted what she had meant as humor.

"Is there something you aren't telling me?"

Gaskin checked his watch, then tucked the gold timepiece back into his vest pocket. "I must be going." And with that he was out the door before she could overcome another cough and ask him more questions.

Elizabeth threw back the covers to follow him but flopped back on the pillows, her heart pounding at the effort. "I hate being sick!" She felt tears burning her throat and coughed again. "And I will not cry!" She hugged her shoulders with both hands. "And please, oh, please, Lord, make my mother well again. All the way well."

CHAPTER TWENTY-THREE

March 1894

Dear Thorliff,

There is not much news here. I am sorry I haven't written more often, but I do appreciate your letters. It sounds like you are working very hard and getting the things you wanted, like writing and becoming published. Father is much the same, but Mr. Moen comes to sit with him, and they visit. That is why I am able to take time to write to you now. I am sure you will enjoy talking with him when you come home. He is so interested in the lives of Norwegians in America, and since you came as a little boy, he wants to hear your story.

Swen has asked Dorothy Iverson from south of Blessing to marry him. They will begin to build a house this spring and be married in the fall after harvest.

Again, thank you for writing.

As ever,
Anji

Thorliff read the short letter again. Was this the man his mother had also mentioned? It must be. But why was he talking so much with Anji's father? Joseph didn't come from Norway. His mother and father did. Joseph was American, not Norwegian. Wishing he could put his finger on what was bothering him, Thorliff folded the letter and put it in his pocket before heading up the stairs to the classroom. *Why can't I be more pleased?*

He laid his Greek text on the desk and reviewed the paper he'd written about Sophocles, not much different from the ones Pastor Solberg had required of him in high school. The good foundation he'd received in Greek made this class easier than some of the others. Since his school assignment was finished, he worked on the next chapter of *The Switchmen* for the newspaper during his study time.

"Hey, it snowed again," Benjamin announced as they left for the day. "You want to go tobogganing?"

"I wish I could. I told Elizabeth I would bring her assignments to her, and we print the paper tonight." Shrugging into his coat, Thorliff tucked his muffler inside and pulled on his mittens. "Unless you want to toboggan down the road to town."

"No, we're using the slope into Norway Valley. Sorry you can't come." Benjamin waved and headed off toward the valley where shouts and laughter could already be heard.

Thorliff looked longingly after him. The fresh powdery snow would be perfect for sliding. Instead, he turned his face toward town and hunched his shoulders against the wind.

"You have a letter." Phillip handed the envelope to Thorliff when he reached the newspaper office.

"Thanks." Thorliff looked at the return address and then at his boss. "New York. From Mr. Gould."

"Hope it is good news."

"I could use some." Thorliff took the letter opener from the pencil cup and slit the envelope. The heavy paper felt rich in his hands.

Dear Thorliff,

I am sorry it has taken me so long to respond, but I wanted to say congratulations on your article in *Harper's*. Imagine my delight when I saw your byline. There is nothing like starting at the top. *Harper's* has the pick of the crème de la crème, as you well know. I am very interested in hearing how your year at St. Olaf and your work on the newspaper are proceeding. I know the drought has been a hardship for those in North Dakota and the other prairie states, and I am sure it would have been very easy for you to remain at home on the farm. It is a tribute to your parents that they see the value of college for a young man of your talents. I look forward to hearing from you.

Sincerely,
David Jonathan Gould

"Good news?"

Thorliff nodded and handed the open letter to Phillip. Since he'd told him the story of Mr. Gould's beneficence, he knew the newspaperman would be keenly interested. Thorliff watched as a smile widened on Phillip's face.

"Never hurts to have a man like him in your corner." Phillip returned the letter and, tipping his chair back, locked his hands behind his head. "Amazing how things work out. Your mother gets lost in New York City, and years later you receive money for college from the man who helped her—you and the others you graduated with."

"And our school library received books. Don't forget that. Gould is a most generous man."

"He's also involved in railroads. . . ." A raised eyebrow accompanied the comment.

"I know, and not likely a union sympathizer." Thorliff thought a moment before adding, "Life holds many hard choices and few easy answers."

"And the easy answers don't usually follow the path of wisdom. Good thing you are learning this young, son. Lessons get harder the later you wait to learn them."

"That's encouraging." Thorliff shrugged out of his coat and hung it along with muffler and hat on the tree. "How are Elizabeth and Mrs. Rogers doing? Cook was so busy I didn't stop to chat. She still doesn't look well either."

"I know. Elizabeth is wearing herself out taking care of her mother, so she relapsed. Cook is fussing that she isn't doing a good job of caring for them, and I sometimes contemplate moving a bed to here in the office."

Thorliff smiled back at the self-deprecating grin from Rogers.

"I'll go make a pot of coffee if what remains is from this morning."

"Good. It's so thick now the spoon stands up." Phillip sat back straight and picked up his fountain pen. "I'll have this editorial finished soon."

That night Thorliff added another paragraph to his running letter to Anji.

> Thank you for the short letter I received from you today. I am grateful Mr. Moen is helping with your father. . . .

Thorliff paused, rethinking his next sentence. It would do no good to tell her of his displeasure—or was it concern?—at the place Mr. Moen was gaining at the Baard house. After all, no one had told him that Mr. Moen was young. His mind just created that picture. Perhaps Mr. Moen was old enough to be her grandfather, or father anyway.

> I received a letter today from Mr. Gould. He saw my story in *Harper's Magazine* and wrote of his pleasure in seeing that. I'm going to send him a couple of the articles I wrote for the *Northfield News*, and though I was thinking of sending him the beginning chapter of *The Switchmen*, perhaps since that is political satire against the railroads, it might not be a good idea. Back to my studies. I'm sending you copies of those articles too. I hope you enjoy them, and perhaps your father will too.
>
> I remain yours,
> Thorliff

After that he wrote a letter to Mr. Gould and included the articles he'd mentioned to Anji. While he was due to write another letter home, he put his things away and fell into bed. He'd almost fallen asleep studying at school, but when could he fit more sleep in?

And when could he find time to write in the journal he'd received for Christmas? Too few hours in a day and far more things he'd like to do, if he could find the time.

By March fourteenth, the day before winter exams, Thorliff, his head stuffed with a cold and his fingers aching from writing two research compositions and rewriting them a third time to make them perfect, was weary to the point of sleepwalking. He wanted nothing more than a week of sleep, off somewhere so no one could bother him. How can one person be so far behind, he asked himself. And then he thought of Elizabeth, recovered enough from the measles to go to school and so far behind in her schoolwork that she was asking for extensions. Not that asking for extensions was in any way unusual. Most of the students who'd fallen prey to the epidemic either gave up and went home to recuperate or asked for extra time. Exams for them would be in two weeks.

Since snow was falling again, Phillip took them up the hill in the sleigh. "Now that was the quietest trip we've ever had." His comment failed to elicit a response, other than Thorliff blowing his nose.

"Thank you, sir." Thorliff stepped from the sleigh and slid on the ice. He grabbed hold of the sleigh frame and leaned over to pick up his satchel that had gone flying.

"Careful there."

Elizabeth, cheeks looking even redder compared to the dark circles under her eyes, didn't even bother to smile, let alone laugh at Thorliff's near fall. "Thank you, Father."

"I'll be up to get you at noon. Don't want you skating down to Carleton."

"Good." She ducked her head against the snow and wind, letting Thorliff walk on the windward side without a comment.

"One more day." Thorliff held the door open.

"At least for you it will be over then." She brushed ahead of him and started up the stairs to the classrooms.

He stared after her, feeling pity for her load and pique at her brusqueness. But there was no way to help her. Right now he could hardly help himself.

The first two winter exams passed in a daze. While Thorliff

knew his papers were good, he wasn't sure he could even read the exam questions. He wrote all he could, staggered down the hill, and collapsed on his bed to sleep through the night and half the next day.

"Just checking on you, son." Phillip stood beside the bed. "Can't have you coming down with pneumonia or something."

"Oh. What time is it?" Thorliff felt as though he were trying to see through a frost-covered window. Everything blurred.

"One."

"In the afternoon?"

A chuckle greeted his question. "Yes. The sun rarely shines at one in the morning."

Thorliff let his face flop back into the pillow.

"I brought you some chicken soup. Cook says you have to take it now, like medicine, you know?"

Thorliff pushed his body upright and swung his feet to the braided rug on the floor. "Mange takk." He didn't hear Phillip go out the door as he devoured the soup.

The next morning, Friday, he showed up at the Rogerses' door, still sniffling but with a fairly clear head.

"Ah, the resilience of youth." Phillip greeted him, peering into his face to assure himself Thorliff should be up and about.

"Yes. I have another exam today and the last one tomorrow." He accepted the steaming coffee mug Cook handed him and took his place at the table, ready to devour the plateful she put before him. He didn't stop until he'd cleaned up a second helping. "I am so looking forward to the week off. When school starts again, we should all be in healthier condition."

The knowledge that he had earned two A's and the remainder B's made his vacation week even more enjoyable as he spent it writing, working on the paper, and writing some more—letters, chapters, articles, and more chapters.

The chinook winds blew like a blessing on all their activities after Elizabeth passed all her exams the following week.

"If only mother felt stronger, life would be perfect," Elizabeth said as she and Thorliff trudged up the hill.

If only I'd have a long letter from Anji—signed that she loves me still—that would make it perfect. But Thorliff kept his wish to himself, only murmuring agreement to Elizabeth as he slowed his pace to relieve her from puffing to keep up. The more disturbed he was, the longer his strides and faster he ate up the distance.

"A letter for you." Benjamin handed him the envelope as they strolled into class at the same moment as the bell rang.

"Good of you to join us, gentlemen." Professor Schwartzhause wore his habitually stern expression.

"Sorry." Thorliff and Benjamin scurried to their seats.

A glance at the handwriting said the letter was from Andrew, not Anji, so Thorliff stuck it in his pocket to read later. Later didn't come until his walk down the hill alone, since this was Elizabeth's afternoon at Carleton. He drew in a deep breath of air that promised spring on the way and, staying in the track melted down to the gravel, took the letter from his pocket, slit the envelope, and began to read.

> Dear Thorliff,
>
> I hate to be the one to write this to you, but Mor said you would want to know. Paws died in his sleep behind the kitchen stove last night. I took my quilt down there because Pa said we would have to put him out of his misery in the morning, and I wanted to be with him as long as possible. He could hardly walk anymore and had to be carried outside to relieve himself. He was so embarrassed at that. You know how he was. But in the middle of the night he licked my hand, and then I patted him, and he died just that quick with a little sigh. He was such a good dog, and we all miss him terribly. Mor said the house seems empty without him, and even Astrid's cat goes around looking for him.

Thorliff dashed a hand across his eyes, blurred to the point he could scarcely read the words.

> Far says we will get another dog, but one would have to go a long way to make up for Paws. I just know that I miss him, and I know you do too. When the ground thaws out, we will bury him in the corner of the yard under the lilac bush where he liked to sleep in the summer.

I hope you are liking school more all the time. Christmas went so fast, and just when I was used to having you home, you left again. We had twenty lambs this year, and Bess had her foal, a colt that thinks he is the king of the world. He is so funny. I named him Star because of the perfect star right between his eyes.

Mor made snow candy yesterday when we had new snow. Thank you for sending copies of your newspaper. You write really good articles and we all enjoy your story. Pastor Solberg is reading it during school.

Your brother,
Andrew

Thorliff folded the letter and put it back in the envelope. Sometimes letters carried bad news. Pictures of Paws through the years flashed through his mind. Paws as the half-grown dog with caramel ears and white feet; Paws herding the sheep and bringing in the cows; Paws dancing out his welcome when they came home from wherever they'd been. Paws climbing the ladder to the haymow and shocking them all; Paws, champion nose- and chin-licker. Thorliff could feel that lightning tongue on his damp cheeks. Paws never did like anyone to cry.

That night Thorliff sat down and wrote to Andrew and his family, and enclosed "A Tribute to a Good Friend," written like a eulogy.

Mr. Rogers says he'll run this in the paper, and then I'll send you a copy of that. Thank you for letting me know and for being the kind of brother who cares so deeply for all living things. I'll see you in June.

Thorliff

CHAPTER TWENTY-FOUR

Blessing, North Dakota
April 1894

"Mor, can—er, may I write to Thorliff?"

"Of course. You needn't ask." Ingeborg looked up from rolling out molasses cookie dough. "We will send him a package."

"He likes your cookies best. He said so." Astrid snitched a bite of cookie dough and left, giggling while licking her finger. She retrieved paper and pencil from the tray in the old trunk and closed the lid, a gentle finger stroking the flowers and other rosemaling designs painted on the trunk. She knew the stories well of her mother's ocean trip to the new world with Tante Kaaren and the Bjorklund brothers, who both died one winter. No matter how people tried to explain it to her, she still could not understand an ocean so large it took more than a week to cross. Others who came by ship earlier said the crossing under sail took much longer.

Taking a seat at the kitchen table, she set to her letter. Goldie the cat came and jumped up in her lap, kneading her legs with his front paws before settling into a purring that vibrated clear to her ankles.

"Should I tell him about Anji?"

"What about Anji?"

"Well, she came to church with that Mr. Moen from Norway."

Ingeborg rolled the dough a bit harder than necessary, causing a muttered "uff da" when some of the dough stuck to the rolling pin. She peeled the dough from the pin surface, patted it back in place, and dusted more flour on the rolling pin. How to tell Astrid no without making her think poorly of Anji? Not thinking poorly of the young woman whom she'd been so sure would be her daughter-in-law was taking an extra storm of prayers.

The rift between Thorliff and Anji is none of your business, she reminded herself for more than the first time. Easier said than done. But she'd caught her mother-in-law, Bridget, giving the young woman a glare that would melt the Red River in January.

Why should they be angry, or rather disappointed, with Anji? That man was the real problem. *That man* was the way she always referred to him, as if his name were of no account.

Actually, another reminder to herself, he was of too much account. He had everything that Thorliff didn't. According to the gossip she'd heard, that man had education, wealth, wit, and charm enough to turn any young woman's head. He'd certainly done it with women much older and more experienced than Anji, like nearly every woman in the region of Blessing. He also had two young daughters living with their bestemor in Norway.

"Mor?"

Ingeborg retrieved her mind from its wanderings and, before turning to her daughter, took a deep breath and let it all out. She made sure the consternation was wiped from her face, since Haakan always told her it was easier to read her face than a book with large print, and looked Astrid in the eye.

"What do you think?"

"I think Thorliff would be very angry to see them together, and maybe someone should tell him so he could come home or write to her or . . ." A frown creased her wide forehead. "I wish Mr. Moen would go back to Norway. That's what I wish." She tapped the end of the pencil against her teeth. "If Thorliff married Anji, she would be my sister. Right?"

"Well, your sister-in-law." Ingeborg removed a flat baking pan from the oven and slid the cookies off with a pancake turner. "Would you please sprinkle some sugar on the cookies in that pan so I can get it in the oven?"

Astrid nodded and rose from her chair to help. While sprinkling sugar with a spoon, she picked up bits of dough left from the edges of the cookies and ate them. Finished sugaring, she returned to her letter.

"Did you tell him how many lambs we had?"

Ingeborg shook her head. "You might tell him about the new foal born too. He always liked Bess." Bess was one of their older heavy mares, and Haakan feared she had not settled with the last breeding. All of them had been delighted when they learned of the imminent birth.

"We should let Thorliff name the baby."

"That would be nice, but I think Andrew already did." She slid more cookies into the oven and added wood to the firebox. "I'm going to need wood pretty soon."

Astrid sighed. "I'm never going to get this written at this rate."

"Is there a rush?"

"I don't know. I just had a dream about Thorliff last night, and he didn't seem very happy. You think he likes school as much as home?"

"You ask hard questions."

"I know, but I'm worried about him. Aren't you?" Astrid reached for a cookie and nibbled on the warm edge.

"Worried?" Ingeborg paused in cutting out more cookies. "No, not really. I know he is where he should be, and I know God can take better care of him than I can, so I leave him in God's hands." She stopped to study Astrid's face. "You see, the Bible tells us not to worry and—"

"Where does it say that?"

"Psalm 37. 'Fret not thyself.' God says not to fret. *Fret* is another word for *worry*, and over and over again we are told to trust God. Now, if we are worrying, we are not trusting. You understand?"

"So is thinking about Thorliff the same as worrying?"

"No, not at all. Worrying is . . ." Ingeborg shook her head. "Sometimes I think you and Andrew must get together and figure out ways to confuse your mor. Some things I can explain better in Norwegian."

"But we speak English. How come our language is called English instead of American?"

"Because it was spoken in England first." Stirring the pot of soup simmering on the back of the stove, Ingeborg enjoyed the relief stealing up from her middle. How to answer all this child's questions without quelling her curiosity. "I'm thinking you should look some of your words up in the dictionary at school."

"Like *worry*?"

"Ja, for sure."

"Thorliff would know."

"Perhaps. Now, no more cookies until after supper, or we won't have enough to mail to Thorliff. Why don't you get out the popcorn, and we'll pop plenty to fill his box."

"That way the cookies won't break. Right?" A grin flashed across her face. "Or at least, we won't worry about them breaking."

Ingeborg smiled back. "And with that you better put on your shawl and bring in enough wood to fill the woodbox."

"Are Andrew and Hamre still over helping Onkel Lars?"

"Ja. Getting the machinery ready for spring fieldwork."

"Do they want us to milk tonight?" Astrid paused before darting out the door.

"No, they didn't say that." Ingeborg scraped the leftover flour from rolling the cookies into her hand and dumped it into a bowl on the shelf above the warming oven to be used later for gravy. While Astrid brought in load after load of wood, Ingeborg picked up where she had left off on the spinning. With Bridget knitting hats, mittens, and sweaters to sell in Penny's store, spinning was always needed.

"There, I'm done." Astrid found her mother in the parlor at the spinning wheel. She glanced over to the basket of carded wool and shook her head. "And here I thought I could read for a while. Can I finish Thorliff's letter before I start carding?"

Ingeborg nodded. "If you don't take too long."

But Astrid's question about Anji stayed with Ingeborg until bedtime. She sat on the edge of the bed brushing her one hundred strokes, and the more she thought about the new man in town, the faster she pulled the brush through her hair. What was normally relaxing turned into a race.

"You planning on brushing it all out or something?" Haakan lay back on the pillows as he watched her, his hands clasped behind his head.

"No, why?"

"You look more like you are pulling that lovely hair out than brushing it."

Her brushing arm dropped to her side, then she clasped her hands in her lap, rubbing one thumb with the other. *How to say it. Quit stumbling over your thoughts and just ask.* She cleared her throat.

"Do you think . . ." She paused, sighed, and started again, not looking at him for fear he would see the heat creeping up her neck. "Astrid asked me . . ." *Just get on with it.* "She asked me if she should tell Thorliff that Anji attended church on Sunday with Mr. Moen. The man from Norway."

"I know who he is, and so do you, since he's visited here several times."

She looked over her shoulder to see Haakan's mouth quirk in a slight smile.

"Ja, I s'pose you do. And he's only been here twice."

"He is a fine man."

"Ja." *So, that is not the point. What is the point?* Her silent questions demanded answers that could be heard. And shared.

"So what do you think?"

"I think you should come to bed and let those young ones work out their own problems without our interference."

"I wasn't going to interfere." Her words snapped on the still air like a whip cracking above the oxen backs.

"Oh?"

She clenched her teeth and turned, sending a glare intended to burn flesh. "If you can't help me, then don't hinder."

"Oh." Haakan raised one hand as if to block the barb, then used that same hand to pull the covers back on her side of the bed.

Ingeborg laid the brush down and, with rapid motions, divided her long hair into three parts and braided it, snagging some on a fingernail. "Uff da!" She ripped the offending sliver of nail off with her teeth and finished braiding, tying off the end with a slim strip of cloth from the dress she'd been sewing. Flinging her braid over her shoulder, she climbed into bed, flopped on her back, and pulled the sheet and blanket up to her chin. She crossed her arms over her chest and stared at the ceiling. So was she worrying about Thorliff after all? After answering Astrid so glibly this afternoon, she could hear herself, *I know he is where he should be, and I know God can take better care of him than I can, so I leave him in God's hands.* It sounded good.

Haakan reached up and blew out the kerosene lamp, the smell of smoke pervading the room. He turned on his side and reached an arm over his wife to pull her close.

She pushed his hand away and humphed. She glanced to the side when a puffing noise indicated Haakan was already drifting asleep. Sure, and he couldn't stay awake three minutes to help her. Men! She flounced over on her side, taking half of the covers with her.

His snore deepened.

Ingeborg thought back to the Sunday afternoon Mr. Moen had stopped by after church to talk with her about what she remembered of the trip to America and the years after, when she and her family had first arrived in the new land. They'd been sitting in the parlor with Andrew and Astrid sitting cross-legged on the floor, always ready to hear the stories of the early days.

"Do you mind if we speak Norwegian?" Mr. Moen had asked as he took out a pad of paper and a pencil. "I can take notes faster that way."

"Not at all," Ingeborg answered in Norwegian. "When I came, I knew not one word of English."

"Did you come by sail or steamship?"

"Steam, but even big as that ship was, the waves threw it around like a rowboat. So many people were violently ill, and some died. Kaaren's baby daughter was born not long before we steamed into the New York harbor. Kaaren was so weak, we were terrified she would be turned back by the government officials. But thanks be to God, they let us all come into the new land. We took the train to Fargo, and Roald and Carl worked on the railroad to help earn money for a wagon and the oxen. I worked in a hotel, and Kaaren took care of the children in two rooms in a boardinghouse. When spring came Roald and Carl rode horses north to find a homestead and then came back for the rest of us."

"What advice would you give to those who want to emigrate?"

"Learn the new language before you come. Things will go much easier for them. Oh, and bring warm clothes. No matter how cold the weather in Norway, the wind blows here much worse."

"What do you remember of your first winter here?"

"Ah, we built those soddies you see outside—one for all of us, that was two men, two women, a small boy, and a baby, and the other for the barn. That was built first. We are still using them. One thing you'll most likely hear from others is that after my husband died in the blizzard and Carl and his two little girls died from the influenza, I discarded my skirts and went about in britches, since I was doing the work of a man and my skirts were a hindrance. I also hunted—was quite a good shot actually—and did anything I had to do to keep from losing the land we worked so hard to break and plant. Kaaren took care of the house and my two boys while the oxen and I busted sod. Ah, so many stories I could tell you. One of them you can read in *Harper's Magazine*, written by my son Thorliff. He is away at school in Minnesota, at St. Olaf College, and plans on being a writer."

"You will like Thorliff. He tells good stories." Andrew stretched his legs out in front of him. "Tell him about Metiz, Mor."

"Please do."

Ingeborg picked up her knitting needles. "When we came here, we found an old Indian woman who lived along the Red River. The only word we understood was Metiz, so that is what we called her. Metiz are actually a group of Sioux Indians with French Canadian blood. She taught us about living off the richness of this land, for example, the value of herbs for medicinal purposes, and she became a wonderful friend, along with her grandson Baptiste. She made our lives easier than they would have been without her."

"Metiz makes the best knives with deer-horn handles and vests and mittens out of rabbit skins. She sells them in Tante Penny's store." Astrid looked up from stroking the cat that lay curled in her lap.

"You have made a fine farm here." Mr. Moen glanced around the parlor.

"Ja, God has been so very good to us. The land is rich, and we are close to water, but that is why Roald chose this area. He knew what we needed, and this land was still available. Some gave up and went back East or returned to Norway."

"What made you start the cheese house?"

"My mor taught me to make cheese, so when we had extra milk, I made cheese, and it was good, so the business grew. People like good cheese. When the railroad came we had to keep making a bigger cheese house."

Mr. Moen closed his paper pad. "I think I could write forever just about your family. Could you perhaps give me Thorliff's address? I would like to send a copy of his story to my paper in Norway. I think they would like to publish it too. If they like it, maybe they would take more."

Ingeborg brought her memory back to the present, but by the time she finally fell asleep, she was no nearer to an answer about Thorliff and Anji. Other than this was none of her business, and she had to admit she had enjoyed visiting with Mr. Moen. Just like Haakan had said. Sometimes she wanted to take Thorliff by the ears and shake him, along with Anji.

"But do we know what God's will is in this matter, besides what you—we want?" Kaaren refilled Ingeborg's coffee cup the next morning.

"You think they are perfect for each other too, don't you?"

"You mean Thorliff and Anji?"

"Of course." Ingeborg tightened her jaw, then at the concern in Kaaren's eyes, she sighed and shook her head. "Forgive me. I know I must not let this bother me. How am I to know God's will in a matter like this? I just know what I think, and when even a child sees what is happening, I . . ." Her words trailed off as she raised the cup with both hands and sipped her coffee. The rocking chair creaked as she set it in motion. Kaaren settled into the other chair with a sigh, propping her elbows on the arms of the chair and inhaling the steaming aroma.

"Do you think Thorliff is aware of what is happening?"

"How could he be unless someone writes and tells him?"

"Are he and Anji writing to each other?"

"I don't know. She hasn't been over in weeks, months perhaps. And I wrote to him about this earlier and mentioned it when he was home at Christmas, so seems to me I've done all I should." Ingeborg looked over the rim of her cup. "Not all that I want, you can be sure, but what I should. According to Haakan this is none of my business. But Thorliff is my son, and I want the best for him."

"So—what if the best isn't Anji?" The question lay between them like a sunbaked clod of black dirt.

Ingeborg rocked and sipped, the song of the rocker comforting in the silence. *Ja, what if God has something or someone else in mind? How to know the mind of God? Thorliff struggled with those questions all last summer.*

"I know the answer is to trust that God knows best. I know the Bible verses, and one would think by now that I would not struggle with such a thing as this. 'Trust in the Lord with all thine heart; and lean not unto thine own understanding.' "

Now it was Kaaren's turn to nod. "Ja, that says it all."

"Saying is easier than doing."

The two shared the kind of smiles that only those who have gone through the muck and mire of life's hard times together can share.

"Our Lord has always provided."

"Ja, I know." Ingeborg rolled her lips together, the *tsk* buried in the motions. "But it still isn't easy."

"You think it was meant to be?"

"No, but by now it should be easier."

Kaaren set her cup on the floor and at the same time picked her knitting out of the basket beside the rocker. With the click of the needles joining the creak of the rockers, the two women went on to discuss the budding romance between Ilse and George, the seeds they'd started for the gardens, and how many hens were setting.

When Ingeborg strode back across the short pasture some time later, she kept to the grass to prevent gumbo from building up on her shoes. Geese honked in their vees overhead, calling out their song of freedom. A hawk soared against the blue, his wild *scree* tingling down her spine. A north wind pushed at her back, flapping her skirts against her legs and tugging at her black woolen shawl.

Oh, to take the shotgun out and bag a goose or two, or a deer like she used to. But game no longer lingered near their back doorstep, and the pull to hunt had fled and left her behind. No babies in their houses any longer, no need for her to hunt to keep them in food, and help enough to ease the drudgery of the early days. Things indeed had changed, and by the time she kicked her boots against the stoop and scraped the mud from the soles, she knew one thing for certain. Maybe she had given up some things, but what she'd gained far outdistanced the debt.

She stopped in her upward motion to study the old straw and manure that they used to bank the house. Now that much of the frost had left the ground, it was time to spread the banking material out on the garden, and when there was time, plow it under. The cycle continued.

She leaped up the stairs, skipping the one in the middle. Nothing cleared one's head like freeing the house from its winter insulation, and nothing would feel better than the pleasant ache in back and arms from working outside again. She'd been cooped up in the house for too long. That was it. And tomorrow, after she cleared away the banking, she'd start spring cleaning inside.

A spurt of wind tugged at her skirts, urging her to look toward the north. Heavy clouds mountained the horizon, gray tinged with near black, bereft of silver linings. She'd best hurry if she wanted to get at the banking, or perhaps she'd better hold off. Sighing, she pushed open the door and hung her shawl on the hook. She still missed having Paws greet her when she came home. Without him the house seemed quieter and emptier. She rattled the grate and lifted the stove lids to add more wood. Almost dinnertime and she hadn't started the meal. Whatever possessed her to think she could start the garden today? But soon, she promised herself. Soon.

CHAPTER TWENTY-FIVE

Northfield, Minnesota
May 1894

Dear Elizabeth,

I'm sorry to have taken so long to write to you but things have been exceedingly busy here at the hospital. Like everywhere else, the measles outbreak caused several deaths, and when one must quarantine a hospital such as ours, our patients suffer unduly, especially the elderly, of whom we serve so many.

To return to the purpose of my letter, I so enjoyed meeting you, and I sincerely believe that you have a future here with us at the Alfred Morganstein Hospital for Women. Therefore, I am extending you an invitation, which is in actuality a plea for help, to join us here in Chicago for as much time as you can manage this summer. I cannot offer you a salary but only room and board and a wealth of experiences for a doctor in training. I know you have been serving with your local physician and have gained much valuable experience there, but in a short time here, you will be amazed at all you can learn.

I know I am sounding like a salesman for my hospital, but

I believe God brought us together for a reason, and I'm hoping
that your coming here is part of that process.

No matter what you decide for now, I know that, God willing, we will be working together sometime in the future.

God bless and keep you,
Dr. Althea Morganstein

Elizabeth read the letter for the second time, her sigh growing
only deeper. Before having the measles, she would have answered
yes quicker than she could pick up the telephone. But now . . .
She sighed again. Now, unless she could pass the exams somehow,
she would need to go to school through the summer to make up
for the two classes she might have to take an incomplete in. All
thanks to the measles. And thanks to the measles, her mother still
had not regained her strength.

And Dr. Gaskin was planning on her helping him, as was her
father.

How to do it all? She made her way downstairs and over to
the piano. Listening to her play was one of the joys of her mother's
day, and since Annabelle didn't get out at all, Elizabeth could not
fathom being gone for the summer months. She lifted the lid and
sat on the bench, feeling like smashing something one moment
and breaking into tears the next. How could so many lives be so
messed up by such a stupid illness as measles?

But you are still alive and others aren't. The little voice in her
head added an arrow of guilt. *I should be rejoicing. I know I should,
and yet . . .*

"*In everything give thanks.*" The verse whispered, but it felt
more like shouting.

She let her fingers wander the keyboard without conscious
thought or plan. The notes floated around her like dust motes on
a sunbeam, but instead of soothing, they prickled. *I should be
studying. I should be helping mother. I should be catching up the
accounts for the newspaper, and I should—*

The telephone jangled. She listened for Cook's weary tread but
realized with the lack of response that Cook was outside or in the
basement. At the third ring she rose and crossed swiftly to the hall
where the oak box was mounted on the wall. Lifting the receiver,
she spoke into the black mouthpiece. "Hello." She heard the click

of the operator and then Thornton's voice.

"Hello, Elizabeth? I'm so glad you answered."

"It's good to hear from you too. How have you been?"

"I'm fine. Everyone else here is finally well, and I have something to show you. Do you have an hour or so?"

"I'm supposed to be studying."

"Me too, but even the draft horses get a day off once a week."

"So now you are comparing me to a draft horse?" The smile that twitched her lips felt good.

"No, I'm the draft horse. You'd be the darling daughter's Arab riding mount."

"I guess that is somewhat better."

"So I can come to see you?"

"Yes, of course. But Thornton, you know I hate surprises."

"Too bad. I think you'll enjoy this one." Only the hum of the line met her ear.

What is he up to now? The tinkle of her mother's bell brought her upright from leaning against the brocade-covered wall. "Coming." She raised her voice enough to be heard clear up the stairs and mounted the risers slowly. Whatever could Thornton be planning? His voice sounded pleased, so it wouldn't be a bad surprise. Not that Thornton would do anything the slightest bit mean anyway.

"Who was that who called?" Annabelle asked from her half-reclining position on the bed where she could look out the window to the backyard. Elizabeth had gathered a number of pillows to support her back.

"Thornton. He said he has a surprise."

"How nice." Annabelle let her head fall back on a pillow, as if, like a fully bloomed sunflower, it were too heavy for her neck. "I take it he didn't give any hints?"

"No, none." Elizabeth studied her mother's face in the soft light from the window. It was still so pale, her very soul seemed to shine through and, like an unshielded candle flame, to flicker instead of shining brightly. Her mother coughed, the hacking kind that had come with the measles and never left. The effort left Annabelle gasping and flattened against the feather bed beneath her. She'd lost so much weight that her bones seemed destined to poke through her skin in spite of the constant soothing of lotions and fragrant oils. The feather bed seemed the only thing soft enough to keep sores from developing.

Elizabeth handed her mother a glass of water and waited for her to sip before taking it back. "You need to drink more."

"I know. I need to do all kinds of things, but . . ." Her hand fell down to her side, the blue veins standing out like cords, and her eyes drifted closed.

Elizabeth laid the back of her hand against her mother's forehead. No fever but a slight sheen of perspiration from the coughing. How could she even begin to think of leaving her mother in a state like this? *I can't. That's all there is to it. I just can't, and if I tell her about Dr. Morganstein's offer, she'll insist I go. Lord, what a mess this is becoming. Are you trying to tell me that I am on the wrong track? That I am not to be a doctor?*

"Are you all right, dear?" Annabelle spoke in a voice so soft Elizabeth had to bend over to hear her.

"Yes, of course." But Elizabeth straightened so her mother could not read her face.

"Thank you for playing."

"You are welcome."

Annabelle patted the edge of the bed. "Please sit here with me until Thornton comes."

Again a tug of war. Sit and talk and let her mother see something was wrong, or make excuses as she had so often of late. "I need to freshen up."

"You look lovely." Annabelle fingered her daughter's dress and gave it a gentle tug at the same time. "We need to be arranging for our summer frocks. Since we were too sick to celebrate Easter, we have nothing new at all."

Elizabeth perched on the edge of the bed, wishing she had fled when she had the chance. "It's not like we have a scarcity of clothing, Mother." She looked into her mother's pale face. "But if ordering something new would make you feel better, I will do so tomorrow."

"One of these days"—Annabelle stared out the window—"I need to be out in my garden."

"Yes, you do." Elizabeth leaned forward, ideas buzzing like a swarm of honeybees following their queen. "Perhaps Thornton could carry you downstairs and out on the verandah. You can give Old Tom instructions from there. Thornton and I could help too." *Anything to get you out of this room.*

"Oh, I couldn't ask that of him. I'm too heavy for him to carry down those stairs. And besides, look at me, I'm not respectable for company."

"You are most properly dressed."

"I don't have my corset on."

"As I said, you are properly covered, and besides, Thornton isn't company, he's family."

As she said the words, she wished she could snatch them back. Thornton wasn't family yet, and he never would be, and here she was leading her mother on again. But all for a good cause, she reminded herself. And if this was what it took to help get her mother back on her feet, so be it.

"Can you brush my hair first?"

Elizabeth knew she had won. "Of course." She retrieved the brush from the walnut dressing table, unwound the bun at the base of her mother's neck, and began brushing, forcing her mind to allow the soothing motion to bless them both.

The doorbell rang just as she put the last hairpin in place. So much for fixing her own hair and donning a fresh gown. "I'll get it," Elizabeth called when she heard Cook closing the back door. She'd been trying to lighten Cook's burdens too, because she was not back up to her best either.

Passing the mirror in the hall, she paused to tuck a lock of hair back into the upsweep on the sides, then pinched her cheeks. Still too pale by far. She opened the door just as Thornton was about to ring the bell again.

"Caught you in the act, eh?"

"Ah, fair lady." He swept his straw boater off and bowed à la knights of old.

"Oh, silly, come in. I have something special for you to do."

"Not until I show you my surprise." He reached out a hand, and with a quizzical look, she placed hers in it. "Come," he said.

"I'm coming. I'm coming." She hung back against the tug on her hand. "What is it?" She followed him down the three brick steps and around the corner. He stopped in front of her.

"Now close your eyes." He took her hands and placed them over her eyes. "No peeking."

"Thornton Wickersham, what is going on?"

"Just wait until I tell you to open them." His voice was farther away.

The temptation to peek between her fingers made Elizabeth giggle. "What is it?"

"Okay, now! Open your eyes."

Elizabeth dropped her hands, and her mouth flew open at the same time. "Thornton, be careful."

Coming toward her, Thornton rode high on the seat of an old velocipede with a large front wheel followed by a small one.

"Where did you get such a thing?"

"Uncle bought it for the boys, but they are still too small to ride it. You want to learn how?" He rode past her on the brick-lined gravel drive and turned around to ride back when over he went, crashing into the privet bushes leafing out along the drive.

"Oh, Thornton, are you all right?" Elizabeth rushed to his side to help him pick leaves and stickers off his tweed jacket. She retrieved his boater from the bushes and, dusting it off, handed it back to him. "You're not broken anywhere, are you?"

"No, not at all." He checked his pants for rents and righted the contraption. "Takes some getting used to, but we shall see these or something similar all over the place very soon."

"I just saw it all over the place, thank you, and now Old Tom will have to do some judicious pruning to cover up your accident scene." She tried to sound stern but broke into chuckles instead, her merry laughter lifting like butterflies on the spring breeze.

"I'll teach you how to ride it."

"We'll talk again when you are more proficient." After he leaned the contraption against the house, she slipped her arm through his and led the way back up the front steps and into the house. "Now I do hope you have not injured yourself, for I am in need of a strong back, or rather my mother is." She took his boater and hung it on the carved walnut coat and hat rack that reigned in the corner of the staircase.

"How is your mother feeling?"

"I have decided, and she has agreed, for her to have a time on the back verandah. The only problem is that she is not strong enough to negotiate the stairs. So . . ." She let her gaze dwell on his strong arms and chest.

"Ah, I get it. I am to be the bearer."

"You are amazingly perceptive." She stopped three stairs above him and turned with a serious face. "This won't be too much for you, will it?"

"No, but it is a good thing your mother is not as tall as Cook." His whisper made her smile, but she eyed the curving staircase with concern. Perhaps they should set up a bed for her in the music room. Then it would be easy to take her outside and surely she would gain her strength back more quickly.

"First things first." She meant to keep her mutter to herself, but Thornton tugged on her hand.

"I heard that. What scheme is going through that lovely head of yours now?"

She started to answer, but the heat blazing up her neck at the compliment made her turn around again and scurry up the three remaining steps.

"Mother, look who's here." She led Thornton into her mother's room and over to the bed.

"How are you, Mrs. Rogers?" Thornton bent to take her hand. "You are indeed looking better."

"Better than what?" Annabelle shook her head. "Forgive me, I seem to be having a touch of the doldrums these days."

"So you will allow me to carry you downstairs and outside? It is a glorious day out there."

"Unless of course you are riding a velocipede."

When Elizabeth put a hand over her mouth to trap the giggles, Annabelle looked from her daughter to the young man and back again. "Whatever has been going on?"

"You wouldn't believe it if I told you, but when you are stronger, Thornton will give a demonstration on his velocipede."

"Or else your daughter will, for I am determined that she shall learn. Riding a velocipede is all the rage now."

"Surely a horse is much safer."

"But one needn't feed a velocipede. Nor groom it, nor clean up after it."

"Well, that is not quite so. There was some cleaning up to do after . . ." Elizabeth's eyes danced, and she broke into giggles again.

Annabelle reached out and plucked a leaf off the arm of Thornton's tweed jacket. "Were you rolling in the bushes?"

"Now, how did that get there?" If total innocence could be assumed, Thornton proved it when he took the leaf and dropped it into a wastebasket.

"I have no idea what is going on with you two, and I'm not sure I want to know, but if you would be willing to carry me, I would love to go outside."

"At your service, madam." Thornton bowed and, sliding hands under her knees and behind her back, lifted her with only a bit of a strain. "Now put your arms around my neck." He took a step backward and staggered slightly.

By the time he deposited Annabelle outside on the wrought-iron lounger, his charge was apologizing for putting him through such an ordeal.

"Now, Mother, you just rest while I bring out the tea. Thornton, I think Old Tom is working out behind the barn. Would you please ask him to join us?"

"Of course."

Elizabeth returned to the house in time to find Cook setting up the tea tray.

"You could have killed them both with a scheme like that." The teapot clanked down on the tray with more force than necessary.

"Now, not to worry. Thornton is very strong, and helping Mother like this will only make him stronger."

"And you think he can carry her up again?"

Elizabeth flinched the tiniest bit. "Now that you mention it, I wonder if we shouldn't set up a bed for her in the music room. We could bring down that Chinese screen from the attic and the single bed from the spare room. What do you think?"

"I think she will refuse, and then what?"

Elizabeth shrugged. "I guess we cross that bridge when we come to it, but while she is ordering Tom around, the three of us could set it all up, and she will feel too guilty about needing to be carried back up and will agree to our plan."

"Our plan?" Cook's eyebrows nearly met her graying hairline.

"You know how she hates to create a scene. I am sure this will work." Elizabeth picked up the silver tray and headed for the French doors. *Please, Lord, bring this about. I want my mother well again, and this is the best idea so far. Surely it is from you.*

"Well, my dear, you've certainly had a busy day." Phillip Rogers joined his daughter in the study later that evening.

"I know, and I'm grateful it worked out so well. If Thornton had tried to carry Mother back up those stairs again . . ." Elizabeth gave a delicate shudder, then a chuckle. "He surely was a big help. With him teasing her, how could Mother be anything but agreeable? And I know she will be happier down here where she can be part of life instead of stuck up in that gloomy bedroom."

"I tried to talk her into such a move a week ago, but she was adamantly against it. I think you are going to have to marry that young man sooner rather than later if he can charm her like that."

Elizabeth fought to keep the smile on her face. One of these days her mother and father were going to have to learn she and Thornton were only playacting. There was no imminent engagement, no future wedding. Guilt pricked like a hair shirt.

How could she ever tell them she thought of Thornton more like the older brother she'd never had than as a husband? She stared down at the sheet of paper that was supposed to be a letter to Dr. Morganstein. Would this be another secret too heavy to keep?

Chapter Twenty-Six

June 1894

"Thorliff, do you think you'll be able to finish the serial before you leave for home?" Phillip leaned back in his office chair, hands locked behind his head.

Thorliff stuck his head around the door from the pressroom where he was cleaning up after the print run. "I think so. I'm two installments ahead right now, and I see only two or three more before the end of the story."

"I sure wish you could manage to stay on through the summer. You've spoiled me, son. I haven't even looked for someone to replace you over the summer months." Phillip brought his hands down to the chair arms with a thump. "You will be returning, right?"

"Planning on it. God willing, as my mother says."

"I never would have made it through that measles mess without you."

"Thank you, sir." Thorliff lingered. "How is Mrs. Rogers doing?"

"Not well, but better. Elizabeth's getting her out of that bedroom and outside like she did was pure grace. I was beginning to think Annabelle would continue to fade away." Phillip cleared his throat. "I never realized measles could be so vicious." He swung his feet off his desk and pulled out a side drawer. "That reminds me, and for this I must beg your pardon. A letter came requesting permission to reprint your satire on the measles. You don't mind, do you? They would have to pay you for the privilege, of course." He dug through his files. "Here it is." He handed the letter across the desk. "Don't know how I can misplace things like that. Sorry."

Thorliff read through the letter, fighting back the grin that threatened to crack his face. "Legally you don't have to ask my permission. I work for you, so what I write for the paper is really yours."

"Maybe so, but that's not the way I work. If we go ahead and print your story in book form like we talked about, you will receive a portion of the sales, royalties if you will. This new press is opening up all kinds of possibilities for us."

Royalties. Thorliff swallowed to settle his pounding heart. Was the story really good enough to print in book form, or were the people of Northfield just more accepting of local talent? However, even Mr. Ingermanson at St. Olaf had commented on how good the story was. And as head of the *Manitou Messenger*, the school's monthly magazine, he was pretty critical. At times Thorliff regretted that he'd not had time to join the magazine staff, but just when he was about to do so, the measles epidemic broke out, and he'd been working around the clock to keep up at school and put the newspaper out.

"Should I give them the go-ahead?" Phillip waited for Thorliff's answer.

"Ja, of course. This just caught me by surprise, is all. I mean, that satire just came about so . . . so . . . "

"Easily?"

Thorliff could feel his ears heat up. If he said yes, he would sound like he was bragging, and if he said no, he'd be lying.

"It is not a crime to have a piece come to you like that. Consider it a gift, and remember that gift the next time you are ready to rip your hair out over another article that isn't so easy."

"Yes, sir."

The telephone jangled, and Phillip got up to answer it. "We'll talk more about the book another time." Nodding to the noisy instrument, he continued, "Most likely Elizabeth calling me home. Or rather us. You didn't stop by to pick up your supper, did you?"

"Ja, I did. I need to study for exams and finish another research composition."

The phone jangled again.

"All right, I'm coming." Phillip reached for the earpiece. "Rogers here."

Thorliff returned to cleaning the printing press and sweeping the floor, all the while swallowing the shout that wanted release. Mr. Rogers was serious about printing his story in book form. He'd mentioned it several weeks earlier, but when nothing more was said, Thorliff figured Phillip had changed his mind.

And he was to receive royalties. Just seeing his name on the cover would have been enough.

Anji, I've got to tell Anji—and Pastor Solberg. The thought died as quickly as it flowered. Why hadn't she answered his last letter? Three letters since Christmas was all she'd sent in spite of his apology for not being able to spend more time with her in December. Was it his fault there'd been such a terrible blizzard?

Like all the other times, he alternated between sorrow, despair, and rage. And like all the other times, he had a choice—sink into despair or put it aside and keep on working. He'd somehow found the strength to do the latter before, and he would do so again.

"Good night, Thorliff. Don't worry about the garbage. I'll take care of that in the morning."

"Good night and thank you."

"I'm not sure what to say you are welcome for, but you are." Phillip snagged his felt fedora off the hatstand and headed out the door, a cheerful whistle floating over his shoulder.

Promising himself that if he finished his paper he could write another chapter, Thorliff ate his supper without warming it and continued to cover pages with his research, thoughts, and conclusions on the Pullman strike. He'd chosen the topic because he was hoping that Mr. Rogers would allow him to write a series of articles on the subject, or perhaps it would turn into another serial story. Most likely it would have to be the second.

The thought made him write faster, otherwise his mind would

go off on another tangent, and he'd not finish the composition he was working on. . . . Maybe his characters from *The Switchmen* would be involved in the strike. What if one of them were wounded—or killed? What if. . . ?

***

The clanging of the milk wagon woke him in the morning after getting far less sleep than he needed. By the time he reached the Rogerses' back door, he finally felt awake enough to continue on up the hill.

"You're late!" Elizabeth met him in the kitchen.

"No, I'm not." Thorliff nodded to the clock. "It's only seven-thirty." He took the cup of coffee Cook handed him and sat down at the cloth-covered oak table.

"But I told you we needed to be early today."

Thorliff shook his head. "No, you said don't be late, and I'm not."

"You sit down and eat, miss. You still need to get your strength back." Cook pointed toward the place set at the other side of the table. Since Annabelle still slept later in the morning, the family had yet to return to breakfasts in the dining room.

Elizabeth growled but did as told, sending resentful looks across the table.

Thorliff glared back and shook his head. Whatever had gotten into her? He looked again and noticed the purple circles under her eyes and her pale face.

"You feel all right?" Ever since the measles, she'd not regained the vitality that made it hard for anyone to keep up with her. She'd most likely been studying too hard to try to make higher grades to make up for her winter quarter. But he knew if he mentioned anything more, she'd take his head off. Women. Inwardly he shook his head and ground his teeth. Outwardly he sipped his coffee and did away with the ham and eggs that Cook set before him. All without looking at Elizabeth again. On the way out he picked up her satchel at the same time as his own and held the door for her.

"I can carry my own, thank you." Icicles had returned in spite of the spring breeze.

Without answering, he nodded for her to precede him and struck off for the path up the hill. If she wanted to be obnoxious, let her. Two could play that game.

"I said I can carry my own satchel."

"Nice day, wouldn't you say?"

"Thorliff Bjorklund, you can be the most stubborn, exasperating man I know." She verbally stamped her foot.

"Thank you. I do hope your exams go well. It would be good if you could pull top marks to make up for earlier."

Her sputtering made him think of Astrid, for often he'd dealt with her bouts of temper the same way. When he heard Elizabeth panting to keep up with his long stride, he slowed imperceptibly so as not to be noticed.

Oak trees in full emerald dress whispered secrets in the breeze, their feet tickled by nodding grasses. Robins sang for their mates, and a woodpecker rata-tata-tated on a nearby tree trunk. After the hush of winter the songs and smells of summer played upon the senses like an oratorio in full crescendo.

At the door to Old Main he handed Elizabeth her satchel and sketched half a bow. At her glare when she passed him, he shrugged his eyebrows and followed her into the building. Her "humph" made him smile as he headed up the stairs. Sure enough, just like Astrid.

The thought made him whistle as he walked the hall to his first class.

"You certainly seem to be in a good mood," groused Benjamin, who caught up with him at the door. "You'd think exams were over instead of just beginning. Did you not spend all night studying?"

"More than half of it, and my paper is done. That alone makes the day worth a whistle or two."

"How you keep up is beyond me." Benjamin dropped his books on his desk and dug in his pocket for a pencil. "You can bet this will be all essay questions. I hate essay questions."

"You hate everything at this time of the morning." Thorliff took his seat and set out two pencils already sharpened and several sheets of paper. When Mr. Ingermanson entered the room, all conversation ceased, and the nearly late arrivals slid into their seats.

"Now, ladies and gentlemen, when I take down the sheet, you will begin to write immediately, and when you are finished, hand your tests to me, and you may leave the room. I expect you to do so quietly so as not to interrupt those around you. Are there any questions?" He glanced around the room. "If not, then good luck, and you may begin." He reached for the clothespins holding up the sheet, and the questions appeared before them.

Thorliff read through all five questions and stopped to both think and take a deep breath. He claimed to be a writer. Now all he had to do was write. Right?

By the time he'd finished the last question almost two hours later, his hand had permanently cramped around the pencil that he'd stopped to sharpen twice, along with its mate. While he wasn't the first to leave, he wasn't the last either, and when he turned in the pages, he felt certain he'd done well enough.

He made his way to the dining room, poured himself a cup of coffee, and headed toward a corner where he could continue working, hopefully without interruptions. Taking two cookies from the packet Cook had packed, he munched and sipped while reviewing his Greek and Latin notes.

At one point he looked up when he heard a familiar laugh. Sure enough, Elizabeth. Why was she so cantankerous with him and so jolly with the two young men accompanying her? He shook his head, sent a glare her way, and went back to his notes. Women!

"There's a letter for you," Phillip called from behind the press when Thorliff arrived at the newspaper office. "On the counter."

"Thanks." Thorliff picked it up and read the return address. "Moen at the Boarding House in Blessing."

Thorliff wandered down the hall to his room to drop his satchel on the bed. Letter in hand, he crossed to the window to have more light.

Dear Thorliff,

I am writing this to inform you that your story on the blizzard and the schoolchildren will be printed in the paper I work for in Norway. Your sister told me about the story, and since my paper is begging for news on Norwegians in America, I requested the rights from *Harper's* and sent it all on. You write a very good story, by the way. I am enclosing a small stipend for the privilege of using your story again. Perhaps when you come home for the summer, you and I can discuss other stories you might like to write for the Norwegian papers.

Sincerely,
Ivar Moen

Thorliff turned over the draft paper. Two dollars and fifty cents. Enough to make a good start on a quarter's tuition. Since he had deposited his hundred dollars with Reverend Ytterböe at the school and only used about half of it, he already had sufficient finances to start school again next fall, besides the money he'd received from Mr. Rogers, money that he kept in an envelope in his desk. *I am rich. Lord, thank you. I am rich beyond measure.*

Later that evening he felt like tearing at the roots of his hair. Two more days until he'd be leaving for home, and he still had not finished *The Switchmen.* Every time he tried to write the climax, he felt like he'd run into a barn wall. A stone barn wall.

He looked up at a knock on the door to his room. "Yes?"

"Thorliff, can I talk with you a moment?"

No, go away. Three days of grouching and now Elizabeth wanted to talk? Now when he was caught in the tangle of characters who refused to do his bidding. He gritted his teeth and inhaled, the smell of printer's ink pervading the air. He pushed himself to his feet and went to the door.

Taking a deep breath to keep from snapping, he opened it. "Yes?"

"I'm bothering you."

"I'm trying to finish the serial so I can catch the train the day after tomorrow." He knew he sounded rude, but then she'd been more than rude the last few days.

"I . . . I think I owe you an apology." Elizabeth stared at the floor, then glanced up to his face.

"Ja, you do." There, he'd said it. So much for good manners.

"Oh." She gathered herself and stood straighter. "Then, I'm sorry for the way I've been acting. I've been a . . ." She looked down again and shuffled one foot. "I have no excuse, at least not one worth anything. But I was pretty worried about my exams and perhaps having to go to summer school, but now I don't. I mean, my grades are all right and . . ." Now she looked him straight in the eyes. "I was rude to you and behaved like a child and . . . you can stop me any time you feel like it."

I would if I felt like it, but what you say is so true. "You're forgiven." *Now go away.*

"Thank you." She turned slightly and looked over her shoulder. "Still friends?"

He raised his hands and let them fall to his sides, shaking his head at the same time. "Next time you get in a huff like that, go yell at Thornton. Don't take it out on me."

"Why would I yell at Thornton?" She stared at him. "And for your information, I wasn't taking anything out on you." Her words bristled faster than a porcupine scenting danger.

"Okay, okay. Let's leave this alone. You've apologized, and I've forgiven you. Now I have to get back to work." He took a step back. *Have a good summer, and I'll see you in the fall, if, in fact, I choose to come back*

"I've done it again, haven't I?"

"Elizabeth Rogers . . ." Slamming the door in her face was definitely not the way to treat either his employer's daughter or a friend, or even an acquaintance.

"Perhaps I could help you."

He stopped, studied her for a long moment, and raising one finger to indicate that she should wait, he spun back into his room to pick up a sheaf of papers. "Here. Read this and tell me which ending you like best or give me some other suggestions or whatever."

She took them with a smile. "I'll be at my father's desk."

He watched her back as she marched out to the front office. What had he gotten himself into now?

An hour later, she marched back in, handed him the sheaf of paper, and announced, "The reason you can't write the climax is because you have too much story to tell yet, too many loose ends to tie up. What if you just relax, quit looking at the clock or calendar or whatever, and just write the story until you are finished?"

He stared at her and through her, his mind churning six ways from west.

She leaned against the doorjamb and crossed her arms over her chest.

After a long silence he nodded. "You are right. Perhaps I can finish it on the train going home, then mail it back." He thought some more, and when he looked up, she was still standing there. *Now what?* He thought back to their conversation. "Ah, thank you?"

"You are most welcome." She smiled sweetly and turned on her heel.

He heard her shoes tapping down the hall. He shook his head. Was it all women, or was he just blessed, or cursed as the case may be, to have two of the perplexing species in his life?

CHAPTER TWENTY-SEVEN

"I just don't know what to do." Elizabeth sat out on the verandah with Dr. Gaskin, who had just finished checking on her mother.

"What do you want to do?" Relaxed in his chair, the doctor crossed one leg over the other and, fingers steepled beneath his chin, studied his young protégé.

"I want to go to Chicago and work with Dr. Morganstein."

"So what is keeping you from doing just that?"

Elizabeth leaned back and stared at the branches of the ancient oak tree that sheltered them with limbs large enough to be oak trunks. Leaves still the fresh green of spring rustled in the wind, casting shadows that danced in the sunlight. Oh, to be free to do as she wanted and not be brought down by the guilt that threatened to cut off her breathing. "Good question, that. How can I leave my mother, frail as she is? If she were back on her feet, I would be on that train in an instant. Or at least as soon as I packed, and I can pack light."

"Your mother is getting stronger every day, just not so's you noticed, being with her all day every day as you are." Dr. Gaskin picked up his glass of tea from the table in front of them both and waved it for emphasis. "Besides, with you here to wait on her hand and foot, what need has she to push herself?" He drank from the glass and watched her over the rim.

"Are you saying Mother is faking her weakness?" Elizabeth's eyes widened.

"No, I never said any such thing. But I'm sure she doesn't want you to go."

"She doesn't know about the letters." *And I feel like a liar for keeping the secret.*

"Ah." Dr. Gaskin leaned forward, elbows on his knees, his hands clasped loosely, one finger pointing at her. "You listen to me, young lady. Your mother is on her way back to health, and she doesn't need you here to mollycoddle her. She does want you to stay home though, and that is her right. I want you to stay here too and work with me, but I know you could gain more by working with Dr. Morganstein, so I'm man enough to let you go." The twinkle in his eyes told her he was teasing himself as well as her. "So since you asked for my advice, I say go write that fancy doctor and ask if she still has a place for you. If so, you kiss your mother good-bye for a month or two and get on with your life's work. There, I had my say." He dusted his hands off and let a sigh escape. "Old fool that I am to cut my own throat like this." He shook his head as he lumbered to his feet. "Your father finds out I did this, and he'll slit my throat for me."

Elizabeth rose and, tucking her hand into the crook of his arm, leaned her head against his shoulder. "Thank you."

"Don't thank me. Thank Matilda. She said if I kept you from going, I was a horse's behind for sure."

Elizabeth fought the giggles that threatened to overcome her but finally cupped her hands over her mouth like a little girl and exploded.

Dr. Gaskin watched her for a few moments, then shook his head. "Personally, I didn't think it was that funny."

Elizabeth called up all her mother's admonitions on ladylike behavior, but none sufficed. One more look at the doctor's pained face set her off again.

"Well, I certainly hope and pray that by the time you earn your medical degree, you will have your emotions under control."

Was that a hint of devilment she caught in his eyes? She sucked in a deep breath and, letting it all out, pasted a prime smile in place and answered, "Of course, Doctor." Inwardly, she chuckled and chortled, and much to her surprise and his as well, she leaned over and kissed him on the cheek, right in front of his left sideburn.

"Thank you, my dear. That I shall treasure. Along with the sight of you giggling like a little girl." He cleared his throat. "Helen and I considered you as close a daughter as God gave us. I'm sure she's watching over you from heaven, the same as I will always be while I'm on earth. You will be a fine doctor, and I will be the first to shake your hand when you make it."

Now Elizabeth had to fight the tears that attacked her as swiftly as had the giggles. She reached over and laid a hand on his. "And for much of my knowledge and experience, I have you to thank."

He cleared his throat. "Best not be lounging here all day, no matter how pleasurable. You get on with that letter, and I'll be on my way." He stuck out his hand, which she ignored and gave him a hug instead. "Go with God's blessing as you learn to use the gifts He has given you."

Elizabeth put the letter in the mail the next morning and continued on to her father's office. Today she would get the accounts in order and remind him that he needed to find an assistant for the summer. There was no way he could do it all himself. Sure was a shame Thorliff could not have stayed on. She nodded and smiled to the folks she met on her way, and it wasn't until she reached the door to the newspaper office that the thought struck her. What if Dr. Morganstein had already filled that position? Perhaps she shouldn't mention her letter until she received an answer. But then, she had never told her parents about the first letter. She stopped stock still, her hand still on the door. Had Dr. Gaskin spoken with her mother? What a quandary, and all because she was trying to protect her mother. *Lord, no wonder you order against a deceitful heart, even when mine wasn't meant to be one.*

"I can't do this."

"Do what?" The deep voice from behind her made her turn with delight.

"Ah, Thornton, you are just the right one."

"I am? How wonderful, but why do I get the feeling I'm not going to like this?"

She tapped the third button on his coat. "You can play pastor and help me out of my dilemma."

"The last time I agreed to, and I quote, 'help you out of a dilemma,' I got more problems than I planned on."

She cocked her head to the right and gazed up at him. "Why do you think that? I kept you safe from all the young ladies who accosted you so recklessly."

"True. Never mind, I didn't mean anything by that." He took a step back, and by the time he looked into her eyes again, whatever she'd glimpsed there was gone, and his teasing laughter had returned. He took her hand, tucked it under his arm, and swept off his boater with the other. "At your service, milady."

"Thornton Wickersham, I'm not in the mood for your teasing. I need a wise answer and I need it now."

"Can we search for this wise answer over a soda at Mrs. Sitze's?" The ice-cream parlor nearby was well frequented by students from both colleges and the townspeople too.

"That will be fine, but I need to get to work too."

"On this fine day I thought perhaps we could go for a ride in the country." Matching his steps to hers, he smiled down at her.

With a sigh she shook her head. "I have to get Father's accounts in order. And that's why we need to talk."

"Because of your father's accounts?"

"No, no. This is a long story, so—"

"So perhaps we should order double sodas if we need fortifying for a l-o-n-g story."

"Be serious, if you can."

"Oh, I can. What flavor would you like? Black cherry?"

"That will be fine. Let's sit in the back under the awning." She pointed through the red and white decor to the sun-shaded porch in the back. "I'll go save us a table."

"And so," she said sometime later with the sodas nearly gone, "that's what my quandary is. What words of wisdom do you have for me?"

"I don't want you to go."

"Thornton, that has nothing to do with it. You're leaving for home and—"

"No, I'm not." He interrupted her. Something he rarely did.

She stopped sucking on her straw and stared at him. "I thought you were going home for the summer and then starting your first term at the seminary in the fall."

"I was, but now I've been offered a position in Minneapolis, and I was coming to tell you. It should give me enough money to cover my first year at the seminary." He dropped his voice and looked down at the table. "That is, if I don't get a call to the mission field first."

"What did you say?"

"Nothing. Nothing at all. Let us turn our attention back to your dilemma. I believe you should sit your mother and father down at the same time, so you don't have to go through it twice, tell them exactly what happened and why you did it that way, and then . . ." He gave a half shrug and raised one eyebrow.

"Yes, and then?"

"And then you have two choices: run like a scared rabbit and don't return until you are certain they have simmered down, or sit there and listen without answering back or justifying yourself."

Elizabeth leaned back against the heart-shaped, twisted wire back of the chair. "Is this the kind of advice you plan on dispensing as a pastor?"

Thornton took a slow draw on his straw. "Hmm."

"Hmm what?"

"Hmm, I'm thinking."

"God help us."

"That's what I forgot. I forgot to tell you to pray first." He leaned back, complacency written all over his handsome face.

"And that's it?"

"Yes, I think so."

"And of the two, which would you do?"

"Neither. I wouldn't have let myself get into such a pickle in the first place."

"Well, thank you, but everyone can't be as perfect as you."

"Now, Elizabeth, don't pout. It doesn't become you."

"I'm not pouting." She twirled her straw in the now empty soda glass. "I just want some other choices. No, to be honest, I just want it over, so I shall talk with them tonight." She looked over at him from under her lashes. He wouldn't be here when she returned from her month or two in Chicago. Funny, but the thought twinged on her heartstrings. *Sure, silly, it's all right for you to be gone, but everyone else should stay the same.* "I better get back to the newspaper. Father is going to be calling around looking for me."

"I'll walk you back."

"Not necessary."

"I know."

They exchanged news of the town as they ambled back to the office, and with a tip of his hat, he left her there and continued up the street. For a moment Elizabeth watched him go, then pushed her way into the office, blinking in the dimness, the bell over the door tinkling her entrance.

"That telephone is going to be the death of me yet." Her father brushed past her, reaching for his hat as he left.

"Where are you going?"

"Barn fire out south of town. If only Thorliff were here. He could cover it."

"Since when—"

But the door slammed behind him, setting the bell to jangling. Elizabeth wanted to rip it off the wall.

The note on his desk asked that she call the head of the women's missionary society from the Methodist church about their ice-cream social that had been held on Saturday. Someone was supposed to send in a write-up, and if they didn't do it today, they would miss this week's edition.

"Thorliff, where are you?"

While her father returned late, Elizabeth kept to her resolve. After supper she invited them both into the music room, where she sat down at the piano. Listening to her play always put them in a gentle mood. But while she tried to relax, her shoulders kept hitching up to her earlobes, and she could tell the difference in the way her fingers felt stiff on the keys. She knew her mother could too, but she persisted, playing their favorite pieces and ending with "Rock of Ages."

"Thank you, dear, that was lovely." Annabelle laid her needlepoint in her lap. "Shall I have Cook bring tea in here?"

This is the first time she's had her stitching out since before she got sick. The thought pleased Elizabeth, making what she planned even more possible. "Before she does that, I have something I need to talk with you about." Elizabeth left the piano bench and went to sit on the floor in front of the sofa where her parents sat close together.

"You want to sit here?" Phillip patted the seat beside him.

"No, thanks." *I need to see your faces.* Elizabeth wrapped her hands around her legs and rested her chin on her knees. "A few weeks ago I received a letter from Dr. Morganstein inviting me to come and work in her hospital for as long as I wanted to this summer. There would be no pay but room and board and the certainty of a variety of experiences I've not access to here." She raised a hand to stop her mother's interruption. "I sent her back an apology, turning the invitation down because of the situation we were in here due to the measles and the aftermath."

"Why didn't you tell us?" Annabelle clung to her husband's hand.

"I . . . you . . . ah . . ." Elizabeth wasted little energy on the minuscule shrug. "Be that as it may, I did what I felt was best at the moment. But now things are somewhat different. I thought to stay here, Mother, and make sure you kept improving like you have been. I know it is slow, but Dr. Gaskin assures me that you will regain all your strength and—"

"And you were willing to give up a summer at the hospital in Chicago to care for your mother?" Annabelle leaned forward to tip her daughter's chin up with one finger. "And I would have let you."

"Yes."

"Why didn't you talk this over with us?" Phillip crossed one leg over the other, ankle resting on the opposite knee.

"I . . ." Elizabeth sucked on her bottom lip. "I . . . it's time I begin to make my own decisions, and I didn't want to add any pressure to either of you or to myself, as a matter of fact." She raised her gaze to meet her father's. "I am growing up, you know."

"Only too well." Her father huffed and laid a hand on his wife's back. "We appreciate your trying to make things easier for us. Right, dear?"

Annabelle nodded but without looking at either of them.

Get it all out on the table. "I mailed a letter to Dr. Morganstein this morning asking if she still has a place for me, telling her I could leave as soon as she lets me know. I gave her our telephone number." Elizabeth laid her cheek on her knees and watched her mother. "I would really like your blessing, and it's not like a lifetime commitment. Only a month or a little more, and then I will be back home getting ready for my senior year."

"While I'm not thrilled that you didn't come to us from the beginning, I understand, and of course you have our blessing." Phillip paused and looked to his wife.

The silence stretched before Annabelle finally looked to Elizabeth. "I was hoping you would be content at home and we would have more time together, perhaps even go on another vacation as a family."

Elizabeth sighed. How could her mother make her feel so guilty with so few words?

"But, as your father has said, we give you our blessing."

Is there a but *hanging on the end of that sentence, or am I imagining things?* Elizabeth leaned against her mother's skirt and raised a hand to grasp her mother's. "Thank you. Perhaps if you feel up to it, you could come to Chicago when it is time for me to come home, and we could go shopping." *A fate near bad as death but if it will make her smile, it's worth it.*

"Perhaps. If I feel strong enough."

Looking at the purple shadows around her mother's eyes and the pale skin, Elizabeth tightened her grip. "You will." *Surely you will. God, please, please make this all right.*

CHAPTER TWENTY-EIGHT

Blessing, North Dakota

Driving the teams pulling the cultivator through the foot-tall corn left Thoriff with far too much time to think. Or rather, to remember.

Here he'd been home three days already, and still he had not had time alone with Anji. He'd gone over to the Baards' twice, but one time she'd been too busy with her father, and the other time Knute and Swen had talked him into going fishing with them. She'd seemed glad to see him, smiling and welcoming him home. But then her father called, and she ran to help him. Swen and Knute said she did that most of the time, in between caring for the two younger ones, cooking, washing, and all the other women's work.

The Mendohlsons had gone back to their own farm with the coming of spring and the need to get the crops in. So Mrs. Sam helped out at the Baards' as much as she could, besides working at the boardinghouse, and some of the other women lent a hand now and then, but Anji was the one whose shoulders bowed under the heaviest weight. Or so it seemed to him after listening to her brothers.

When he mentioned her name at home, it seemed his family changed the subject, or was it all his imagination? He tried to think it out, but between swatting at flies and keeping track of the team, nothing made much sense.

"Thorliff, you want buttermilk?" Astrid waved and called from the edge of the field.

"When I get around there." He clucked the team to a slightly faster pace and stopped them near her.

"I brought you cookies too and a chunk of cheese." She handed him the jug first, knowing how thirsty the men got riding on the machinery.

"Mange takk." He glugged another mouthful and took off his hat to wipe his forehead with the back of his hand. "Think I'd forgotten how dusty it can be out here." Leaning against the iron wheel bristling with lugs, he reached for the cheese. "Aren't you going to have some?"

"No, I'm not hungry." Her sunbonnet hung on the strings down her back, and the skirt of her cotton dress had a big three-corner tear on the side.

"What happened there?" He pointed to the hole.

"That barbed-wire fence snagged me. No matter how close I wrap the skirt to my legs, it just has to snag."

"You ever think of using the gate?"

Astrid gave him one of her you've-got-to-be-kidding looks, one she'd perfected even more in the last year. "And go all the way back there?"

Thorliff leaned over and gave a gentle tug on her braid. "You sure did grow up while I was gone."

"I grew three inches this year. We marked 'em on the spring-house wall, just like always. Andrew grew five inches. He's almost as tall as you. Did you grow this year?"

"I don't think so. My pants stayed pretty much in the same place."

"No, you grew, but this way." She spread her hands a couple of feet apart.

"You're saying I got fat?"

She rolled her eyes and gave him another dumbbell look. "No, you look more like Pa, you know, broader in the shoulders and chest. That kind of growing."

"Well, if I don't get back to work, this corn won't get a chance to grow. Thanks for the lunch." He took another cookie and climbed back up on the implement seat. "Mange takk."

"You're welcome." Her laugh floated back on the breeze as she ran back across the field.

Thorliff looked to the south to see where Andrew had his teams. Over to the Knutsons, Haakan and Lars were working on the steam tractor. Though the iron monster never tired like the horses and oxen did, it needed constant maintenance. Just like he did.

Even with heavy leather gloves on, his hands felt like ground meat. His legs cramped at night so bad he leaped out of bed and scared even Andrew awake. In spite of the brim on his hat, the sun burned his neck to a blaze, and if he could ever truly quench the thirst, he'd—what? He didn't know. Had he truly gotten so weak living in town that he never realized how much strength and endurance farming required? Strange, when he was in Northfield he had dreamed of home, and now that he was here, he dreamed of Northfield. He lifted his face to the breeze. Thank God for that at least. Now if only the wind would bring the rain. That's all the men talked about when any two or more got together—the needed rain and the low prices.

When he heard the dinner bell ring, he unhitched the double-trees, hooked the traces up to the rump pads, and turned the team homeward. Memories leaped from the soil itself: he and Andrew running out to ride one of the horses back to the barns, Paws coming to greet them, yipping and jumping in his excitement. Riding Jack the mule in to Tante Penny's store. He could barely remember his real pa, only shadows of a sober-faced man with a deep voice and gentle hands when he lifted a small boy onto his shoulders. So his memories of growing up always included Haakan.

"Hurry, Thorliff, or we'll start eating without you." Astrid cupped her hands around her mouth to help the holler carry clear to him.

"Go right ahead." Thorliff stopped the horses at the barn door and began removing the harnesses. Andrew grinned at him as he took a harness and hung it on the racks inside on the barn wall.

"Don't say a word," Thorliff cautioned him. "Not one word."

"Oh, I won't say that you look really bad, but if you want to go up and wash, I'll finish with the horses."

"Smart-mouthed kid." But even the grumbling felt good compared to staggering in behind the team. He should have ridden like he'd thought, but that would have meant admitting defeat.

"Another week and you'll be back to normal." Haakan handed him a towel and pointed to the washbasins that lined the bench on the south side of the house. "Astrid even poured you warm water."

Thorliff knew they were all trying to make it easier for him, and that made him feel even worse. He worked hard on the printing press. That was no slack job, but he had to be honest. It didn't continue day after day like this, and sitting at a desk writing did not build the kind of muscles the farm demanded.

They applauded when he made it to the table.

Instead of snapping like his insides demanded, he laughed along with them. When they bowed their heads for grace, he was most thankful for a chair that didn't move and a cushion to pad his rear.

"Tomorrow everyone will be here for dinner after church to welcome you home." Ingeborg passed the platter of fried chicken to him.

"Just like always." Thorliff took a thigh and a breast and passed it to Andrew. He took a bite and closed his eyes in bliss. "No one makes fried chicken like you, Mor."

"I fried the chicken." Astrid flipped her braids over her shoulders.

Andrew burst out laughing. "You should see your face."

Thorliff looked from his plate to his sister. "Really?"

"Ja, Astrid is a big help now. She can cook anything I can."

"Does she make cheese as good?" At their shrugs, he continued around his mouthful of chicken. "When I go back to school, I have to bring at least three wheels of cheese with me. I could set up shop and sell Bjorklund cheese to pay my way through school."

"That's at least one product we can keep selling at a decent price. I'm thinking we should keep some of the fields in pasture and buy more cows."

"Don't you still get milk from the other farmers around here?" Thorliff buttered a roll and ate half of it in one bite.

"Ja, Sam drives a wagon around and picks up the cans, then goes back to the blacksmith shop. We're going to have to add on to the cheese house again to have enough room to age it properly. We've been selling more of the soft cheese at Penny's store and in Grafton." Ingeborg refilled the basket of rolls and handed it to Thorliff. "I'm thinking of getting goats and making goat cheese as a sideline."

"Who would milk those smelly creatures?"

"There are two girls at the deaf school, and I'm sure George McBride would too. You won't believe the change in him."

"That's because he loves Ilse." Andrew chewed the meat off a drumstick and laid the bone down.

"How do you know that?" Astrid looked from her brother to her mother and back.

"I watch." Andrew reached for another chicken leg. "When they marry up, he will keep working for Onkel Olaf, and she will keep helping at the deaf school. You watch."

"Andrew, you amaze me," Ingeborg said.

You need to be more like Andrew, Thorliff told himself. *He sees more than anyone I know, other than Metiz.* "I haven't seen Metiz since I got home. Is she all right?"

"She moves more slowly sometimes but keeps plenty busy. I know she misses Baptiste, but she never admits it."

"We all miss him, especially all the game he provided. You never know how much someone does until they aren't there to do it anymore." Haakan leaned back and patted his stomach. "Not that we are starving or anything."

"Maybe I should run a line of snares for rabbits for Metiz. She runs out of skins sometimes." Andrew reached for another roll.

"That would be a good thing to do." Ingeborg held up the chicken platter. "Anyone want another piece?"

"When?" Haakan motioned for the chicken. "You work from dawn to dark as it is."

"Once the cultivating is done, the hay won't be ready yet. I'll do it then."

Thorliff listened with only one ear. Somehow he had to find time to write more chapters too. And that was the kind of thing one did in the winter on the farm. *Tell them, so they know you've made that promise.* He started to argue with himself, but after a drink of water, he leaned forward. "I promised to send Mr. Rogers a chapter a week for the newspaper serial until it is finished. He said if I had time to write any articles, he'd run them too. And funniest thing." He told them of his letter from Ivar Moen. "So if I can find time, I could send some things to his paper in Norway. He must be a pretty nice guy."

"Did you bring home the last two installments? That's sure been a good story." Andrew filled in the silence and turned to look at his older brother. "I guess I didn't know you could write such a long one."

"Guess I didn't know it either. One of these times I have to come up with an ending."

"Astrid has been reading it to us the evening it comes in the mail. Then we take it to school, and she reads it there too." Andrew nodded to his little sister. "She's a real good reader."

"I had no idea." Thorliff looked around the table. "You want to hear some good news about it?" At their eager nods he continued. "Mr. Rogers might print it in a book. He's gotten lots of requests."

"Oh, Thorliff, your first book." Ingeborg set a piece of custard pie in front of him, laying a hand on his shoulder at the same time. "And to think you are only one year in college."

"He didn't need college to write that book. He learned it all here on the farm." Haakan tamped the tobacco down in his pipe and waved the pipe for emphasis. "But his articles on the Pullman strike, now those are real reporting." He motioned Astrid to bring a lighted spill from the stove. "One day a man in Grafton asked if I was related to that reporter Thorliff Bjorklund. Can you beat that?"

"How did he get one of my articles?"

"I asked him. He said a relative from Northfield sent them on. The world's getting to be a smaller place every day." A cloud of smoke hovered above his head.

Thorliff inhaled the fragrances of home—pipe smoke, fresh bread, fried chicken, coffee. A rooster crowed from out in the chicken yard. The orange cat mewed and leaped up in Astrid's lap, chirp changing to purr as she stroked his head. Home. How he had missed it in the beginning. How would he be able to leave it again?

"How's your hands, son?" Haakan asked around the pipe stem in his mouth.

"Tolerable. Has anyone heard from Manda and Baptiste?"

"The Solbergs have gotten two letters, and Mary Martha went right over to Metiz' house to read them to her. They're hoping to bring another herd of horses home to sell this summer."

"Good for them. They like Montana?"

"I guess so, but you know Manda. She didn't waste too many words on paper either." Ingeborg took the plates from the table and slid them into the pan of soapy water steaming on the back of the stove. "Solbergs are coming over tonight to see you."

Thorliff glanced up from his coffee cup. That meant he couldn't go see Anji tonight either. When would they ever get a chance to talk? And yet he couldn't not be here. That would be insufferably rude. On the other hand, why did no one ask him first before planning out the time?

"We better get back out to work." Haakan stood and took his pipe to the stove to clean out the bowl with the tip of his knife, the residual tobacco falling into the coals in the firebox. He tapped the bowl against the rim of the opening and set his pipe back up in the pipe rack on the warming shelf.

Thorliff watched the ritual, filing it away for one of the characters in his story. Far was right. Most of what he wrote came from his life here on the farm, even though much of the current story was set in cities and towns along the railroad. He'd read that some famous writer said you write what you know, but while he knew the most about farming in North Dakota, he'd learned more than he wanted in reporting on the strikes and battling strikers. He could hear Astrid and Ingeborg talking, but the voices sounded farther and farther away until he heard them no more.

"Naptime is over."

"Huh?" He felt someone shake his shoulder at the same time

as he heard her speak right in his ear. He jolted straight up. "What?"

"I said, naptime is over. Pa said to let you sleep awhile, and then you are to take the oxen out to finish your field."

"Let me sleep?" Thorliff glanced around at the clean kitchen, table cleared, with salt and pepper, sugar bowl, and jelly jar all centered on the board with a lip he'd made for that purpose one year in school. The oilcloth tablecloth was wiped free of crumbs, the chairs pushed back in.

"How long did I sleep?" He rubbed the crick in the back of his neck that told him some time had passed.

"An hour or so." Astrid leaned against his shoulder. "I was afraid you would topple right off on the floor, but you didn't."

Thorliff rose and stretched, every bone and muscle in his body screaming in protest. He crossed to the water pail and raised the dipper for a drink. Wiping his mouth with the back of his hand, he hung the dipper back up on the hook.

"Guess I better get back on out there. I'll probably never live this one down."

"Maybe in a year or two."

"Yeah, sure, or ten or never." He patted her on the head. "Thanks for the good dinner."

"You're welcome."

Thorliff stood at the door to greet their guests that evening. "Good to see you, sir." He returned the handshake of the man who'd made so much of his education possible and become both mentor and friend.

"Ah, Thorliff, sorely have I missed you. School just is not the same without you there. I've had to work twice as hard since my assistant is in Northfield." His chuckle and a clap on Thorliff's shoulder said all the rest that his eyes added.

"Thorliff, you've grown up—er—out—er . . ." Mary Martha gave him a hug. "I'm so glad to hear you are doing well."

"Better by the end of the year, but . . ." Now it was Thorliff's turn to shake his head.

"Not easy, eh?"

"Ma." A towheaded boy tugged at her coat.

She pushed him forward. "Thorliff, this is Johnny; he is four now, Thomas here is three, and Deborah is holding Emily."

"They sure look alike." Thorliff grinned at Deborah, who smiled shyly back. "Except for you. And how come you went and grew up while I was gone?"

"She sure is a big help. I reckon I'd be right lost without her." Mary Martha reached for the baby. "You go on and play with Astrid, darlin'. I know that's what you all want to do." In spite of her years in Blessing, Mary Martha still had a trace of her Missouri accent and didn't try to hide it.

"So have you heard again from the Montana people?"

"Oh my, yes. In fact just the other day. I'll let you read the letter soon as I put this one down." She grinned up at him and thrust the baby into his arms. "You hold her for a minute while I take out the letter."

"I'll take her." Ingeborg reached for the baby, but Thorliff took a step back and shook his head. "I can manage." He looked down to see two dark eyes staring up at him, as if memorizing his face. Then a smile stretched her rosy cheeks, showing off two glistening white teeth above her lower lip. Emily reached for his face with a chubby hand and gurgled something. When he didn't respond, she put her finger on his lip and repeated the sounds. "Sorry, little one, I don't talk your language."

At the sound of his voice, she grinned wider and began kicking her feet, telling him something that he only wished he understood.

"She's beautiful." Thorliff looked to Mary Martha. "And so smart."

"Thank you." She handed him the letter and took back her daughter. "She's going to be a busy one, already rarely still for a moment and crawling after her brothers. I had to warn them to make sure the screen door was latched, or she'd have crawled right out the door."

Thorliff turned to see his mother watching him with a faint smile on her face. He raised an eyebrow at her. "Don't go dreaming about grandbabies yet, Mor. I have three more years of college, remember?"

"Oh, you." She shook her head. "Get on in there and talk with the men."

Thorliff found Johnny on Haakan's lap and Thomas on his father's, but they slid down and ran back to the kitchen when he sat down. "What am I, the scary man or something?"

John Solberg laughed. "Not to me, that's for sure. Tell me, what do you like best about school?"

"Well, I've learned not to ask Professor Schwartzhause about the contradiction of the God of the Old Testament and the God we see in the New."

"Oh, not open-minded about questioning students, eh?"

"No. My English teacher, Mr. Ingermanson, does not give top grades without suffering you through lower ones first. He did ask me to be on the staff for the *Manitou Messenger*, the monthly school magazine, but I had to turn it down for now. The city newspaper takes up a lot of time, but with the new Linotype machine and printing press, I might be able to do both this next year."

"You certainly are having a lot of experiences. Amazing how God has put you in that place in such times as we are living through. Your stories of the strikes and riots make one feel like they are right there. And your novel . . ." Solberg shook his head. "So much for such a young man. What a gift."

"Ja, we might set him to selling cheese in Northfield this year. We got another order in the mail." Haakan set his chair to rocking. "Sometimes I think we ought to grow only enough grain to feed our cattle and turn the rest into hay, so we can go into all dairy for the cheese making."

"Really?" Thorliff stared at his father.

"Something to think about." Haakan tamped down the tobacco in his pipe and sucked it without lighting.

When Haakan and Solberg started talking about something regarding the church, Thorliff fought to keep his eyes open. He covered a yawn with his hand and shook his head. He could hear the women fixing the dessert in the kitchen and the girls upstairs chattering. Andrew sat with his carving knives from Christmas and a block of wood that at this point looked only to be a source for the shavings dropping on the floor. And here he'd thought to spend some time on his chapter this evening.

"Excuse me." He rose and headed outside to the outhouse. Anything to get some air and wake up again. When he returned, he took his chocolate cake drenched in whipping cream to eat standing at the wall. Later, after all the good-byes were said, he stumbled his way up the stairs and fell on the bed, not even waking when Andrew crawled in a few minutes later.

As they drove up to the church in the wagon the next morning, he searched the crowd for Anji. When he saw Swen with a girl at his side, he wandered over to be introduced. After he met her, he asked, "Where's Anji?"

"Ah . . ." Swen looked over his shoulder and then kind of shrugged. "She was here a minute ago. Mrs. Sam is staying with Pa for today." He backed away. "Come on, Dorothy, let's go on in."

What's going on? Thorliff stared after his friend. He acted like . . . like . . .

"Come on, Thorliff." Astrid came to take his hand. He allowed her to pull him toward the front steps, nodding and greeting people he'd known all his life. When he sat down next to his mother he glanced forward to see Anji already seated. But from the back he had no idea who the man was sitting next to her. When she tipped her head slightly in his direction to hear something he said, Thorliff felt like a giant hammer clobbered him in the middle. They were together. Who was he? What was going on?

CHAPTER TWENTY-NINE

"Why did no one tell me?"

"Thorliff, there is nothing to tell. Mr. Moen has accompanied the Baards to church, whether Anji has been able to attend or not." Ingeborg kept her gaze steady on her son, a difficult task as he paced the parlor. His tortured face tore at her heart.

"Then why did it seem to me that they were together?"

"I . . . I'm not sure." As if outside her will, her fingers continued to knit and purl on the vest she was knitting.

"She was invited with the rest of the family to join us all for dinner."

"Of course, but someone always stays home with Joseph, and it most often is her. She is able to help him the most when his suffering is the worst. Besides, Mrs. Sam needed to get back to help at the boardinghouse. The guests there need to be fed no matter what day it is."

"And does Mr. Moen eat with them or at the boardinghouse?"

"Son, I cannot answer that. You were with Swen and Knute fishing. Why didn't you ask them?" She knew when she said that what kind of look she would get. As if young men, or any men, for that matter, would discuss something like this.

"I better get on out to the barn."

"You need to talk with her."

"I know, but not while I'm this angry. It was all I could do to be civil after the service. And besides, he's an old man."

"Well, I wouldn't call Mr. Moen old, and from all I've seen, he's a very fine man. We've enjoyed visiting with him very much." She glanced up to see that her caged son had stopped his pacing and was looking at her like she'd gone over to the enemy. "Thorliff, our house is open to everyone, just like it always has been. He has been interviewing immigrants, and we are surely that. He wants to talk with you too, as one of the younger generation and one who is going beyond the borders of the farm."

"Ja, when Norway sprouts palm trees." He turned, and she listened to his boots thud across the kitchen floor, the screen door slam, and the silence that seeped in from the corners and gradually filled the room like a shy fawn coming out to play in the meadow.

"Uff da. Lord, what is happening here? I know you see the future, and you know the path you have for our son, but does his heart have to be broken to make it so? Seeing him hurt like this makes my heart ache. You know how I love them both, and I did think Anji was to be part of our family." She drew in a deep, rather shaky breath. "Forgive my selfish prayer that they would marry and he would come home again and live here. We could build them a house so quickly." She sighed again. The cat rose from his place under the whatnot table, arching his back, stretching every muscle and sinew, then sitting in front of her, his chirp one of conversation.

"I know you want up in my lap, but I can't knit with you here."

He chirped again, staring at her from golden eyes, as if he could will her to pick him up.

Ingeborg pushed the two sides of the vest down on the needles and stuck the needles into the ball of yarn before setting the entire project back in the basket beside her chair. "All right, come here." She patted her lap, and the cat jumped up, gently bumping her chin with his head, already purring his satisfaction. "If only life were so simple—a good petting, purring, sleep, and stretch. What more could one ask for?" She stroked the cat's back and under his chin. "If only."

The morning after they finished cultivating, Haakan leaned back in his chair. "Thorliff, why don't you take the next couple of days off to work on your story? The rest of us are going over to the Baards' to help them out."

I want to go over there too. But he kept his face noncommittal and nodded. "Thanks, Far. I've not been getting very far in the evenings."

"I know, and sleeping with your head on the table doesn't give you much rest either." Haakan smiled around his pipe stem.

Thorliff raised his eyebrows and rubbed the back of his neck. "Doesn't do much for my brain either, no matter how much coffee I drink." He turned his head as far to the right, then to the left as he could and flinched at the crick.

Does Far know? Thorliff looked to his mother, who gave a barely perceptible nod. He felt his neck grow warm. They were trying to make things easier for him. He needed to go talk with her, that was for sure, but what to say? What happened to all those years of good and close friendship? Their long talks, the laughter, the . . . He jerked his thought back to the kitchen, where he reached for another cinnamon roll. "Where's Astrid?"

"Over helping Tante Kaaren. They are giving the schoolrooms a good cleaning." She refilled his coffee cup and held up the pot for Haakan. At his nod, she refilled his and sat back down at the table. "As soon as the cake is done, the box will be packed for dinner. Now don't let Anji talk you out of contributing. I'd go over there too if we hadn't started this cleaning thing."

"Of course." Haakan took another cinnamon roll from the plate. "When do you have to be back at school?"

"Fall term begins Wednesday, September twelfth. I told Mr. Rogers how soon I'd be back would depend on how fast harvest goes. He'd be glad if I could come back tomorrow. His letter said he hadn't found anyone to help, and with Elizabeth in Chicago, it must be pretty hectic there."

"Well, I'm glad you are here." Ingeborg rose and began clearing off the plates.

Andrew whistled as he came through the back door. "That sow is going to farrow any minute. I put her in the big stall."

"Then we'll go on without you. Did you see if Lars was about ready?" Haakan stood and began his ritual of putting the pipe away.

"He's got one team, and Hamre has the other. I harnessed the teams but didn't hitch them up." He scooped a dipperful of water from the bucket and drank it dry.

Thorliff felt like an observer or a guest watching the family go about their business. "How about if I watch the sow? I can write out in the barn."

"Good. Come on, Pa, let's get going."

"See what a slave driver he is?" Haakan slapped Andrew on the shoulder. "I'm coming soon as your mor has the cake ready. Let's go hitch 'em up."

"Thank you." Ingeborg nodded to Thorliff after the others left.

"I should go with them."

"No, you have a job to fulfill too. And besides, we all want to know what happens next."

"So do I." Her chuckle followed him upstairs to get his pad and pencil. *Tonight,* he promised himself. *Tonight I'll go talk with Anji.* But the picture of her sitting next to Moen in church made both stomach and fists clench, along with his teeth.

He waved the men off and took one of the milk stools into the farrowing stall. The old Chester White sow looked down her long snout at him, *oofed,* and went on piling the straw up in a corner. Andrew was surely right—she was making her nest and looked due to drop at any time. He read what he'd written the night before, crossed some out, and added a sentence here and a word there. He'd fallen asleep the night before right in the middle of a sentence. He glanced up when the sow lay down with a soft grunt. *Would that man be at the Baards' when the teams got there?* He forced his attention back to the pad in his lap.

Back in the story, his pencil stumbled and dragged across the page. He read aloud what he'd written and crossed it all out.

The sow got up and wandered around the stall, moving straw, pacing. When she lay back down, he set his pencil to the paper again and saw himself write "Moen." He scribbled that out and took a deep breath, read some of the earlier work, and the story began again. This time his pencil raced across the page.

He'd just gotten to the good part when he heard the sow

grunting and panting. He put his pad and pencil outside the stall and watched as the first baby slid into the world. Within minutes it was on its feet, staggering around the sow's hind legs to find a teat. Two came together, then three, one after the other. One of them Thorliff assisted, making sure it found a teat to nurse.

The sow lay flat out on her side, the piglets hooked on like leeches. When no more came for a while, Thorliff wiped his hands on a rag, got his paper and pencil back, and settled onto his stool back against the wall.

He just got going, and with another grunt two more babies slid out onto the straw.

She finished with ten, and after they had nursed, Thorliff guided them under the boards nailed across one corner of the stall. The sow rested long enough for him to write half a page, then surged to her feet to amble over to the water bucket.

"How about some mash and molasses too?" Thorliff put aside his writing again. He added water to the bucket of mash and molasses and whey Andrew had stirred up, poured it into the trough, and watched as she ate. "Good old girl, you sure know your business." Thorliff leaned over and scratched behind her floppy ears, then picked up a stick and scratched her back. When she lay down again, he herded the babies out and made sure they all nursed again, then sent them back to safety. Ten live pigs would be a good return, and he knew how easy it was to lose some to being stepped on or laid on. Some sows were more careful than others, and this one had a history of good mothering. Andrew often said she counted her babies before lying down.

When his stomach rumbled, Thorliff walked on back to the house and fixed himself a ham and cheese sandwich. He took that and a glass of buttermilk back out to the stall and sat back down in his corner to eat and write and observe his charges.

The sow went back to sleep, the babies slept in their corner, and Thorliff finished another chapter. He reread what he'd written, penciled in some changes, read it again, and finally realized it was getting too dark to read. He put his papers in a stack and, package under his arm, walked to the door. Heavy clouds darkened the sky, and the wind spun dust devils in the barnyard. Lightning forked the darkness, its brilliance painful to his eyes. In seconds the thunder crashed so close he stepped all the way outside to make sure the barn was still standing. His ears rang, and with heart pounding he stood in the doorway, waiting, praying for the rain to fall and not blow on over. The smell of ozone hung on the air. Rain veils raced across the land, pounding the earth into submission, washing the dust from leaf and branch, roaring as it devoured the dry.

Thorliff set his package down inside where it would stay dry and stepped outside into the life-bringing rain. He raised his face, eyes closed, and opened his mouth to drink. The lightning flashed off to the east now, and the thunder rolls came farther behind, but the rain continued. Soaked but jubilant, he returned to the barn and walked through the long aisle to the door to let the cows in. Rain or no rain, the cows needed to be milked. He fetched the milk buckets and the cans from the springhouse, dipped the grain bucket into the bin along one wall, and poured a measure in front of each cow, now straining against the wooden stanchions, long tongues reaching for the first grain.

"Okay, girls, take it easy. You'll all get yours." When he'd finished, he returned to the stall to check on the pigs. He counted, yep, all ten present and accounted for. He ushered the piglets out of their corner so they could nurse, and they plugged onto the sow's teats like they grew there.

He started at the far end of the line of cows, set his stool in place, and sitting down, lodged his head on the first cow's flank while he brushed bits of grass from the udder. Putting his pail between his knees, he started with the two rear teats, and with the pull and squeeze rhythm he'd learned as a little boy, he set the milk to ringing in the bottom of the pail. The milk frothed, barn cats mewed, and the sound of cattle chewing all combined with the aromas of milk and manure and grain to remind him that he was indeed home.

Having left the doors open, he heard the others return, and Haakan and Andrew joined him in the barn. Andrew ran to the pen to check on the sow.

"How many did she have?"

"Ten. Easy as could be. I brought them out from their corner to let them nurse."

"Ja, they are all piled on top of each other right along her belly." Andrew grabbed a bucket and took the cow next to Thorliff's. "Isn't the rain wonderful?"

Did Anji ask about me? Was that man there to help too, or is farm work beneath him? Tell me something. But he kept the thoughts inside, refusing to give them life by speaking them.

"I told Anji you stayed home to take care of the sow and write on your story." Andrew paused, then added, "Her pa is some bad. I don't know how he stays alive."

"Is he able to be up at all?" There, he'd asked a question that couldn't be construed as personal.

"No, hasn't been for months. They put a sheepskin under him. The bedsores are sure hard to keep from festering."

"Is Mor back?"

"Must be. There's lights on at the house. Did you get much writing done?"

"A good amount. Had to go stand in the rain though." Thorliff shivered in the cool breeze that tugged at his wet shirt.

"We stayed in the field until the lightning started. Got soaked on the way home, but no one cared."

"This might save us, at least give the fields a good start." Haakan took the next cow up. "Easy, Boss."

Thorliff finished stripping his cow out and, picking up bucket and stool, dumped the bucketful through the strainer, saved out a bit to pour in the flat pan reserved for the cats, and settled down for his second cow.

By the time they finished all the cows, dark blanketed the countryside, and the rain continued to soak into the thirsty earth.

"Fool sow smothered one last night," Andrew announced at the breakfast table the next day.

"She's usually careful." Astrid brought a platter of ham to the table.

"You'd think there would be some way to keep sows from lying on their babies."

"And ewes from lambing problems and chickens from . . ." Astrid shook her head. "Andrew, that's just part of life on the farm."

A knock on the door brought a "Come in" from Haakan.

281

Metiz opened the door and stepped inside, more hunched than ever but eyes bright as usual. "We go to Joseph now."

Ingeborg flipped the last pancake and turned to her friend. "Did they come for you?"

"No. I just know."

"Let me get my basket." Ingeborg kept a basket of medical supplies, bandages, unguents, herbs, and the things needed for birthing always ready to go.

"I'll hitch up the horse." Andrew left the room before Thorliff could volunteer.

"Rain is good."

"Ja, that is for sure. You want a cup of coffee?" Haakan motioned to the graniteware coffeepot.

"I'll go with you." Thorliff pushed his chair back and stood. He reached for the platter of pancakes, rolled two around a couple of sausages, and led the way out the door. This time he would be there when Anji needed him.

"He's gone." Swen met them at the door. "Went peaceful in his sleep. How did you know to come?"

Ingeborg nodded to Metiz.

"I had no idea the end was this close," she spoke around the lump in her throat, "or I would have come sooner."

"None of us knew." Swen wiped the back of his hand across his eyes. "I already got the box built. Pa asked me to do that weeks ago. I know he's with Ma now, but his leaving us is sure going to make a hole here."

Where's Anji? Thorliff wanted to ask but refrained. He could hear ten-year-old Becky crying and knew that was where Anji would be, taking care of the younger ones. "You want me to go for Pastor?"

"Ja, that would be good. We still got some chores to do. There's no rush though, if you want to talk to Anji first, that is."

Thorliff nodded to his mother and followed the sound of crying to the parlor. Anji held both Gus and Becky close beside her, their tears mingling as she crooned comfort.

What do I say? We all know Joseph is in a better place. "Your ma and pa are together again. That part is good."

Anji looked up and nodded. "But it is hard anyway." She held out her hand. "Leave it to your ma to come before even being called."

"Metiz came for us." Thorliff took her hand, wanting to take her in his arms and wipe away her tears. "I just wanted to tell you I'm sorry for—"

"I know. But he's not in all that terrible pain any longer. I have to remember to be thankful for that." She squeezed his hand and took hers back to stroke Becky's hair.

"I'm going for Pastor."

"Thank you." She turned her attention to her little sister. "Come now, we must wash up and get dressed. Gus, the chickens need feeding, and I know Swen needs your help in the barn."

Thorliff watched them for a moment, wishing there were something more he could do, but finally turned away and went back out to the buggy. Knowing his mother and Metiz would be washing and dressing Joseph's body, Thorliff clucked the horse into a trot, heading for the Solberg place.

After the funeral the next day, Thorliff found Anji alone for the first time since he'd come home. While the people of Blessing visited outside or inside or wherever, she was standing at the window in the bedroom where her father's chair had sat for the last year so he could look outside.

"Anji, can I get you something?"

She shook her head slowly, like the weight of care made it too heavy to move easily. "This is all he saw . . . out this window." She clutched the white cotton curtain with one trembling hand. "That's no life."

"No, but up until the accident, he had a good life. Good family, good farm, all he wanted."

"He never wanted to live after Ma died, then the accident. Took him a long time to die."

"But you took good care of him."

"I know. I did my best, but sometimes your best isn't good enough. I prayed, oh, how I prayed, asking God to make him better, to take away the pain."

"He has."

"But not the way I hoped or wanted."

Thorliff tried to think of something to say, but nothing would come. He laid a hand on her shoulder, but somehow she drifted away from him without hardly moving. *Anji, I want to hold you like we did last summer. I love you. You said you love me. But such a mess this has all been.*

"Anji, I . . ." Mr. Moen stopped in the doorway. "Oh, excuse me."

Thorliff bit back the words that surged behind his teeth. *Get out of here. You don't belong.*

"I'll be out in a minute, Ivar."

"Anji, we need to talk." Thorliff knew he was rushing in, but what else could he do?

"Soon, Thorliff. Let me get through the next couple of days, and then we will talk."

"But . . ." He saw the sorrow on her face and stopped. "Of course. If there is anything I can do, you will let me know?" Such stilted words and so useless. *God, give me the words. What do I do here?*

She nodded, closed her eyes for a moment, and straightening her shoulders, walked ahead of him back to the crowd.

A week passed. The wheat fields wore their mantle of green, gardens needed hoeing already since the weeds always outgrew the seeds, and several new calves in the pen bawled for their mothers.

"I'm going over to see Anji," Thorliff said after supper. "Do you have anything you want to send along?"

"Not that I can think of." Ingeborg glanced around the kitchen. "Astrid took over bread this morning."

"I'll be back later then." Thorliff set off, thinking back to this time last year. Should he have stayed home? He shook his head. Should he have come home? Again he knew the answer. She hadn't let him. So why had she not written?

Was there more to this whatever-his-name-was from Norway than anyone was saying?

"Come, let us walk out among the apple trees," she said after the first greetings were over.

He nodded and wished she would put her hand under his arm like she used to. But instead they walked side by side with a canyon between them.

She stopped at one of the trees and looked up into the leafy branches. "Looks like we'll have a good apple crop this year."

Why did you not write? "Yes, us too."

A silence, not the comfortable kind of two longtime friends finally having a good visit, but one fraught with twanging and crashings, felt but not heard.

"Thorliff, I'm sorry."

He left off studying the bark patterns of the tree and looked at her.

"For what?"

"For not writing, for not . . ." She stopped, cleared her throat, and tried again. "Things change, that's all."

What changed? He waited.

She blew out a breath. "I truly thought I loved you this time last year."

"Past tense." He swallowed, but nothing went down.

"I planned to write, and then time went by, and what with taking care of Pa and missing Ma and . . ." She lifted hands and shoulders, and when she let them fall, she looked close to collapse herself. "This is so hard."

Even in the gentle dusk he caught the glimmer of tears in her eyes and trickling down her cheeks.

But he could find nothing to say. His thoughts darted around like a hungry bat catching bugs in the evening, but he could make no order out of them.

"Thorliff, my dear friend . . ."

I am not your friend. That is far too common a word. I love you. Can you not hear me? I love you.

But how was she to hear words never spoken, especially when she struggled so hard to find words of her own?

She took in another deep breath and looked into his eyes. "I loved you with all my girlish heart, but now that I am a woman, I . . ." She didn't bother to wipe the tears away. "I . . . I have to say . . . I no longer love you more than as that friend of my childhood."

Thorliff closed his eyes, wishing he could close his ears. A picture of her standing beside Moen in church and then again at the funeral blasted through his mind.

"And you love another. Is your word so weak that you could not wait?"

"I take it all upon myself. I am sorry. That is all I can say."

"But why?"

"I don't know. I've asked myself the same question a hundred times. I think . . . I think it is that he needs me."

"And I don't?"

"No, Thorliff. You are building a new life, and I do not see you living it here."

"I would. I would give up school and—"

She drew herself straighter. "No! You will not. The price is too high."

"But what about the price I am paying now?" He felt a shudder start at his feet and race toward his head. "I cannot wish you God's blessing."

"I don't expect such right now, but someday. . ." She paused and gazed at him through her tears. "Someday you will know the dream to believe. I know you are on the right path for that dream. God gave you a big dream, and now you can grow into it."

"But we were to do this together!"

"I know. I'm so sorry, but . . ." She shook her head again and began walking back to the house.

He watched her go, knowing that to forgive was all that was needed, but the rage that soured his mouth and stomach burned the thought of forgiveness like paper in the fire pit. *How to get even? Make that intruder pay!* He locked on to that thought and strode off toward home, pounding the dirt beneath his feet, wishing it were Moen.

CHAPTER THIRTY

July 1894

Storm clouds do not rain make.

Thorliff stared at the black thunderheads on the western horizon. They looked just like he felt, but they could either send the life-giving rain or blow over. Neither of which seemed possible for him. About the time he got the hurt and rage under control, he'd see Moen with Anji at church or hear someone talk about what an interesting man they had living in their midst.

On top of all that, he owed the Norwegian a thank-you. He should have written a letter before he left Northfield.

He stopped the team to put some grease on the moving part of the sickle bar. All he needed was a breakdown to make the day complete. He climbed back up on the seat, now baked hot by the sun, released the lever to lower the bar, and nudged the horses forward. If the seat branded his own, what of it. One more pain that would be small in comparison to that of his heart.

Watching the tall grass fall behind the sharp chattering bar and keeping the horses going straight was not enough to occupy all of his mind. Too much of it had time to go off on schemes, schemes to get even, get rid of the man, or get back at Anji.

Black flies bit both him and the horses, and while the horses could swish their tails, he needed both hands on the reins. A fly landed on the back of his hand, the bite sharp and vicious. Sweat trickled down his back and blackened the flanks of the team. A meadowlark broke from the grass in front of the horses and sang in spite of the interruption. Rabbits hopped away, and gophers dodged back down in their holes.

The grass continued to fall, lying in sheets behind the mower. By the time he made a second pass around the field, the sun was already doing its work, leaching the green from the stalks, readying it for the rake. Right now during haying would not be the best time for rain, though the gardens and the pasture surely could use it.

"Why did he have to come here anyway?" The horses responded with ears that swiveled to hear him better. "Sure she wasn't writing a lot, and to be sure, she didn't want me to come help her, but that was Anji, thinking of what was best for me instead of herself." He gritted his teeth, nostrils flaring at the injustice of it all. "Lord, you know all things. You could have stopped this." He felt like shaking his fist in God's face, but what would be the sense of it?

The clanging of the dinner bell broke into his ruminations. He stopped the horses, unhitched them, and walked behind the team back to the barn. His hands and shoulders no longer ached from the labor, and calluses now hardened the skin. No longer winter hands, but the tan and toughened hands of summer.

Now if he could only harden his heart the same.

He and Andrew drew up their teams in the shade of the barn at the same time, the shade bringing instant relief from the unremitting sun.

Andrew nodded toward the west. "You think we'll get any rain?"

"I don't know. Doesn't smell like it." Thorliff unbuckled the harness and pulled it off, hanging it over the pegs on the wall for just that purpose.

"You all right?" Andrew paused in his return for the second harness and studied Thorliff's face.

"Yeah, why?"

"You mad at Anji?"

"Andrew, sometimes you ask things that are none of your business."

"And Mr. Moen?"

"Leave it alone!"

"I thought so. Mor said you would be all right eventually."

Thorliff clenched fists and jaw and swung around, the harness buckle slashing around and catching him on the side of the face. He uttered one of those words that he knew should never be used and almost threw the harness against the wall. It caught on the pegs but only because habit prevailed. A red glaze sheeted his eyes, and he charged at Andrew, head down and fists balled.

The snarl that came from his chest lent speed to his feet. He swung, and only through Andrew's quick footwork did the punch miss his brother's jaw and land on his shoulder instead.

"Thorliff!" Haakan's voice cut the charge before he had time to land the second one.

Thorliff plowed to a stop, shook his head, and stared at Andrew. What had he done? Struck his brother? In all their years growing up, he'd never . . . "I . . . I'm sorry, Andrew." Guilt and shame warred with each other, using him as the punching bag. "Please forgive me?"

"Ja, of course." Andrew rubbed his shoulder. "You pack a good punch for never fighting."

"What came over you?" Haakan, arms akimbo, stared from one son to the other.

"I nagged him with one too many questions." Andrew settled his hat back on his head and took two lines to lead the horses into the barn.

"Is that so?"

Thorliff shrugged and led off the other two. They'd water them after they cooled down. Andrew not only took the punch and didn't fight back but then took the brunt of his father's disapproval. Crawling under a sow's belly would be easy about now, and it would serve him right if she stepped all over him. He deserved every glare and recrimination sent his way.

He followed the other two up to the house to wash at the basins full of sun-warmed water.

"What was that all about?" Ingeborg asked when they entered the kitchen.

Did even my mother have to see me lose my temper like that?

"Nothing." Andrew responded before Thorliff could think of an answer. He looked up to catch that gleam in his mother's eye that said she'd not ask more now, but be sure this was not over yet.

That evening after the milking was finished and he was returning to the house, he heard Astrid ask their mother, "You think Thorliff is going to stay mad like this all summer?"

"I certainly hope not, but sometimes when your feelings are really hurt, you take it out on someone else."

"Like when Andrew got in trouble over Toby Valders, and he growled at me?"

"Just like that."

"I hate that Mr. Moen."

"Astrid."

"Well, if . . ."

Thorliff closed his eyes and scrubbed his face with soap on the rag, the burning of the soap in his eyes a just punishment. Out of the mouths of babes . . . What kind of a man was he that his whole family could read him like this? Shouldn't he be able to keep his feelings to himself? Were they being intrusive?

If only he had stayed in Northfield, none of this would be going on. He'd still be thinking Anji would be waiting. He wouldn't know about Moen. Ah, life was easier before the knowing.

The clouds blew on over without dumping their largess.

Sunday morning Ingeborg stared at her oldest son. "You aren't ready for church."

"I'm not going."

"But . . ." She crossed the room to lay a hand on his forehead.

"No, I am not sick. I'm just not going." He spaced his words carefully, not raising his voice but cutting each word precisely.

Ingeborg glanced at the clock on the shelf and back at her son. "But this is communion Sunday."

"I know." Thorliff tightened his jaw. "You go on now, or Far will be getting impatient."

"But what will I say when someone asks of you?"

He shrugged. "That I'll see them another time."

Ingeborg clamped her jaws together on a humph that said quite clearly what she thought of all this and slammed the screen door a fraction harder than necessary.

Returning home from church, Ingeborg greeted Thorliff.

"Pastor Solberg asked about you," she said, removing her hat and setting it on the shelf.

Thorliff looked up from the book he was reading. "Oh." He swallowed to get some moisture in his throat. "What did you tell him?"

"What would you want me to tell him?" She took her apron down from the peg and tied it around her waist.

"Nothing."

"He asked if you would come and see him this afternoon."

"Andrew and I are going fishing." Thorliff stared at the page in front of him, feeling his mother's concern wash over him. *I don't want to talk with anyone. Why can't they leave me alone?*

"Andrew went to Ellie's for the afternoon."

"Oh." He propped his head on his hands. "Guess I'll go alone then, unless maybe Hamre wants to go." He looked up. "Or Astrid."

"She went to Penny's to play with the baby." Ingeborg pulled the roast from the oven. She lifted the lid on the roasting pan, and the rich aroma filled the kitchen.

Thorliff heard and felt his stomach growl.

"Dinner will be ready in half an hour or so, if you want to go find Hamre."

"I'll ring the bell."

"Thorliff . . ."

He turned from opening the screen door. "Ja?"

"I want you to go over to Pastor's and talk with him."

Thorliff let the door slam behind him. *Why can't they just leave me alone? I'm not bothering anyone. So I'm not happy right now. If*

Moen would go back to Norway, I'd be a far more genial person.
If you'd forgive her, you'd be a far more genial person. And forgive
him too. The war broke out in his head again. *Forgive as you are*
forgiven. If he banged his head against the barn wall, perhaps he
could still the voices clamoring in his head.

Later that afternoon Thorliff finished his story. *I'll go tell Anji.*
He shook his head and poured himself another cup of coffee. *Wipe*
that thought from your mind, he ordered himself. *Never again. Don't*
think of her; don't dream of her. Never again. He edited the final
chapter and copied it over before sliding the sheets into an envelope and addressing it to the *Northfield News.* Tomorrow he'd run
it in to the store to mail after milking.

"George has asked Ilse if he may court her." Kaaren and Ingeborg were sitting in the shade of the house snapping beans and
catching up on their news.

"Well, about time. He's been working up to this since spring."

"He had to learn the proper signs first." Kaaren's smile said she
wasn't kidding. "He came to me and Lars in a quandary. Trying to
understand what he meant took some real figuring, let me tell
you, but when I understood, I showed him how to say 'May I
court you? Would you like to go walking out?' Then Lars gave
him permission to use the horse and buggy, and we figured out
how to sign *picnic.* So he was all set."

"We had better start a quilt for them."

"True. You should have seen the look on her face when she
came back from their ride. You'd have thought she'd been given
the sun and the moon too. I catch them in secret smiles and fluttering eyelashes. Ah, young love. Who even needs words?"

Ingeborg stopped snapping beans. "Ah, does Hamre know
about this?"

Kaaren paused and tilted her head to the side. "He's not said
anything."

Ingeborg cocked an eyebrow.

Kaaren chuckled. "I know, silly me. When does Hamre ever

say anything? But he must have noticed. You don't think he . . ." She shook her head and wrinkled her forehead. "No."

A slight shrug this time.

"Oh, my word. I never thought about that. Hamre has just always been around and . . ."

"And usually living in our soddy and eating here until this last year when he has pretty much moved to your place. Ever since the blizzard he hasn't moved back."

"Both Hamre and Thorliff, troubles of the heart over new men who came to Blessing. How to help them." Kaaren dumped the snapped beans in her apron into the basket. "Speaking of quilts, we need to get going on one for Swen and Dorothy. Think of all the time it used to take us to do a wedding ring quilt, and now it goes so fast."

"Thanks to our sewing machines. Now if someone would just invent as good a machine for washing clothes."

CHAPTER THIRTY-ONE

Chicago, Illinois

"Miss Rogers, they need you in the delivery room."

Elizabeth swung her aching feet off the narrow bed and sat up, reaching for the square cloth folded into a triangle that she wore tied over her head, hair bundled up off her neck. Bare skin cried for any breath of cool air to dry the perspiration that ran down her back. The heat and humidity in Northfield were like spring compared to this hospital in the slums of Chicago, where fresh air died before passing the windows. Slow rotating fans moved the air only enough to keep people breathing.

Wishing for a shower, Elizabeth shoved her feet back into her shoes and followed the messenger up the stairs to the delivery room, her home away from home. Sometimes she thought every woman in Chicago must be having a baby this July.

"I need your narrow hands." Dr. Morganstein looked up from the woman on the delivery table propped against a nurse who was braced against the wall. "If we can turn this little one, perhaps we can keep from doing a caesarean."

Elizabeth studied the situation, remembering a similar situation from a time back home. "Dr. Gaskin and I had one like this before. If we get her up on her hands and knees, that will take the pressure off the baby, and then I can turn it more easily."

"Well, I never. Of course." Dr. Morganstein motioned to the nurse and turned to Elizabeth. "Go see if there is anyone out there to help us."

Elizabeth darted back out the door, the woman's scream lending speed to her feet. "Patrick, come quick."

The old man who kept the floors spotless pointed a finger to his chest in the classic you-mean-me? pose.

She grabbed his arm. "Help us now."

"B-but . . ." He let her drag him into the room, all the while keeping his eyes averted from the panting woman on the table.

"All right, Mrs. O'Brien, we are all going to help you onto your hands and knees now. I know, I know. . . ."

The woman's wail echoed off the walls, and as they rolled her to her side, she screamed and clawed at their hands. "No, no, no, no . . ." They finally managed to get her to her hands and knees, her hiccups bouncing her hanging belly on the table, she was so huge.

"Thank you, Patrick. You can go now."

The man scuttled out the door, his face as red as a newborn's.

"Now listen to me, Mrs. O'Brien, you're a good strong woman, and we need to get this baby of yours turned so it can greet the world properly. Elizabeth is going to do the turning as soon as you've had another contraction, all right?"

The dripping woman moaned but nodded at the same time, then her shriek rose again with the next contraction. When she inhaled in relief, Elizabeth, her hands still wet from the basin of soapy water, went to work.

"Come on, baby, turn for me. Lord, please turn this child." She looked to the doctor. "Palpitate her abdomen and push to the left. Perhaps that will help." She felt something—the shoulder, a round dome—the head. "I've got it."

"Good, okay. Mrs. O'Brien, we're going to set you back up again so you can push. Quick, help her." The young nurse scrambled back up against the wall, and between the doctor and Elizabeth, they turned the woman just as another contraction rolled over her body.

"It's com-i-n-g." The woman panted and pushed, clenching her round face and grabbing the nurse's legs.

"One more push. Now that's a good girl." The baby slid into the doctor's hands and let out an offended wail that made them all laugh.

"I have a baby?"

"You most certainly do. A healthy big girl who's not going to take any sass from anyone. Listen to her—lungs like an opera singer." While she talked, the doctor massaged the woman's lower belly to get the uterus to contract and stop bleeding. With the afterbirth in a basin, the baby and mother studying each other chest to chest, and the bleeding already lessening, Dr. Morganstein turned to Elizabeth, who was mopping away tears. "Good girl. Can't see this miracle without tearing up myself, no matter how many babies I've brought into this world. You taught me something new, and for that I thank you. Not sure why it never occurred to me before, but that doesn't matter. I'll write it up in my journal so we can use it whenever needed."

"She was wide hipped enough and fully dilated, or it wouldn't work." Elizabeth moved up beside the bed and touched the baby's head. She looked to the mother, who smiled back. "She's perfect."

Young Mrs. O'Brien nodded. "I thank you now, but there for a bit . . ." Together they chuckled.

Elizabeth took the scissors the doctor offered and cut the cord just beyond the tie. Then Elizabeth gently washed the baby, who let them know what she thought of their moving her around, while the doctor cleaned up the mother. After diapering and swaddling the infant tightly in a clean sheet, they tucked her in the curve of her mother's arm.

"Doctor, emergency." The call came from the doorway.

"How bad?"

"Knife wound."

"Come with me, Elizabeth. The nurses can take over here."

They raced down the hallway—at least Elizabeth raced. Keeping up with the doctor's long strides kept her trotting. They hurried down the stairs and into the surgery, where they shucked their bloody aprons for new ones and started scrubbing at the sink.

"Tell me what we have."

The admitting nurse described the wound. "She says her boyfriend was fighting with someone, and she got in the way. It is her right arm. Slashed clear to the bone. Someone tied a tourniquet above her elbow to stop the bleeding."

"Can she move her fingers?"

"No. They are turning blue."

"Okay, loosen the tourniquet so we get some blood back to her extremities. We'll be there in a moment. We'll need sutures, clamps, the smallest sizes of everything. Make sure the lights are plenty bright. Have you given her any laudanum yet?"

"Yes, enough to dull the worst of it."

An hour later the woman was stitched, bandaged, and sleeping off the effects of the chloroform.

Elizabeth and the doctor drank two glasses of water each, then laid cold cloths on their foreheads and the backs of their necks. "Is it always like this in the summer?"

"Wait until August if you think this is bad."

When Elizabeth fell into bed for the second time that night, she threw back the sheet and laid a wet towel on her chest. Too tired to care, she fell into a chasm, dark and quiet.

Over the next two weeks, she ushered four babies into the world, only being forced to call the doctor to help stop the bleeding on one, set more broken bones than she could remember, and practiced her stitching on enough wounds to think there was a war going on. She diagnosed dyspepsia, a heart murmur, internal bleeding, and pregnancies. She ordered tonics for poor blood and oatmeal baths for suppurating sores. When she found a moment, she read the textbooks lining the walls in the doctor's study and looked up recipes for unguents and powders in the pharmaceutical books.

One night the doctor found her crying in the supply closet. "I know. Losing that woman and her baby was hard, but there was nothing more you could do. Nor I. Had she come to us sooner, we might have saved them, but when it's twins and one dies in utero early like that, it can poison the other and the mother too. Really, there was nothing more you could have done."

Elizabeth mopped her tears, but they continued to fall. "Sh-she fought so hard to live."

"I know." Dr. Morganstein leaned against the shelves of linens, absently taking down a towel to wipe her own face and extending one to her young assistant. "Nurse Korcheski will be back next week, and then perhaps you can take a day off. I didn't mean to work you to death here, but then I didn't know her mother was going to need her either. Illness never consults us for permission."

Elizabeth wiped her eyes again and then her neck. "It's just that we lost a woman like this at home last Christmas—the wife of our pastor. But she died as much from exhaustion as from blood loss. Poisoning, like this one . . . that smell. I shall never forget that horrific odor."

"The stench of decay and infection. That's one thing you learn. Different illnesses have different odors. Oftentimes your nose can help you make the correct diagnosis. Consumption has a slightly sweet odor, infection putrid, and throat infections not only show white on the tongue but smell like ripe and rotting fruit."

"Mostly what I smell around here is unwashed bodies. Urine on small children and feces if they haven't learned to wipe well."

"Many of them have no paper to wipe with. And barely enough water to drink, let alone bathe."

Elizabeth closed her eyes. There, she'd done it again, shown her ignorance in the face of all the poverty. Things she'd taken for granted, like clean water without restrictions, clean beds, and inside toilets. "I-I'm sorry. I . . ." She rubbed her forehead and blew her nose again. *Lord, give me strength.*

The next day Elizabeth entered one of the examining rooms.

"You have a letter. It is on my desk." Dr. Morganstein looked up from wrapping a splint around a boy's arm.

"You need help?"

"No, you go get something to drink. Put your feet up for a bit and read your letter. I'm about done here, and this young man can't wait to get outside again." She gave him a stern look. "But no more racing down stairs like that. Next time it might be your neck you break."

Elizabeth winked at the little boy, smiled at the mother who sat in the chair fanning her face with a paper, and headed for the quiet of the doctor's study. Guilt crept in and slid long fingers around her neck, trying to squeeze the enjoyment out of the stolen moment. No, not stolen, taken with permission. She brushed at her neck and, in the process of scaring off the guilt, realized she

had tendrils of hair curling damply on her collar line. She
smoothed them back into the bun and secured them with pins
that had been derelict in their duty. Picking up her letter, she
smiled at the return address. Thornton, bless his heart, had found
time to write to her. The only writing she'd done had been a quick
note to her parents to tell them she had arrived safely.

Barring emergencies, Doctor had promised her Sunday off, and
she planned to catch up on her letter writing then. She sat back
on the settee and swung her legs up as instructed. Just leaning her
head back felt wonderful. Eyes closed, she could feel the weariness
seep out the soles of her feet. If only she had a glass of iced tea
and some of Cook's lemon cookies. Feeling herself sinking deeper
into the upholstery, she forced her eyes open, slit the envelope,
and pulled out two pages of closely spaced writing.

> Dear Elizabeth,
>
> I know better than to ask how you are, for I've heard horror
> stories of some of the hospitals situated in places like the one
> you are in. Sometimes I wish you had not been so graphic in
> your descriptions of the hospital there after your first visit, but
> it keeps me on my knees praying for your safety and trusting
> that you are getting all the experiences you so desired.

She rolled her eyes. *If he only knew. No, better that he doesn't,
or he'd worry even more.* She'd been in Chicago for nearly three
weeks and had not stepped one foot outside the hospital since she
walked in. She returned to her letter.

> I have heard from my missionary friend, and he is encour-
> aging me to come as soon as I am able, but since I have not
> the sanction of the missionary board, I can put that on hold
> for now. I have agreed to apply, though, in case that is the route
> that God would have me take.
>
> Minneapolis has grown since I lived here a few years ago
> with my parents. I am convinced I would not make a good
> accountant but appreciate the summer's work and rejoice on
> the weekends when I can go bicycling, a sport that I have truly
> come to enjoy. Of course a bicycle is the chief form of trans-
> portation for missionaries in Africa, either that or walk, so I'd
> best enjoy it. When you return home I shall take an extra day
> and come down on the train.

He continued on, but Elizabeth could scarcely keep her eyes open to read. The third time she found herself nodding off, she folded the letter, put it in the envelope, and tipped her head back. Only for a moment would she close her eyes, but any minute helped. The doctor's office was the coolest place in the building, other than down in the basement.

She dreamed she was home in Northfield, lying on the chaise lounge under the widespread oak tree, her mother also sitting in the dappled shade working on her needlepoint. A butterfly landed on the rosebush by the veranda. Thorliff came whistling through the house. She jerked awake. *Thorliff, what are you doing in my dream?*

"Sorry to disturb you, miss, but Doctor is needing you." Patrick stepped back at her look of confusion. "I didn't want to wake you. You were sleeping so peaceful-like, but . . ." He shrugged, his skinny shoulders lifting the fabric of his sweat-stained shirt.

"No, no. That's fine. I was just dreaming of home, and I guess I didn't make the transition back here quickly enough." She swung her feet back to the floor and, with a hasty refastening of her head cover, followed the man down the hall, smoothing and retying her apron as she went.

"Sorry to disturb you," said Dr. Morganstein, "but I thought you might want to do the stitching on this wound."

"What happened?"

"Another fight. These Irish are a hotheaded lot, especially when the men have been without work. They stop by the pub and get liquored up enough to go home and take their frustrations out on their wives and children."

"He . . . he don't mean nothin' by it. Jist the way he is." The woman with deep auburn hair and fair skin that went with her red hair gazed out at them through green eyes swiftly turning black. Her lip needed stitches, as did the cut under one eye. When Elizabeth tipped the woman's head up to see better, she winced.

Dr. Morganstein left the room while Elizabeth continued the examination.

"Are there other injuries?" Elizabeth kept her voice gentle, but this wasn't the first time she'd seen this woman in for treatment.

The last stitches had been taken out two days earlier. She pushed the rioting hair back to check the hairline where she'd stitched before. The pink welt looked healthy.

The nurse handed her the basin to cleanse the wounds, which had pretty much stopped bleeding and, when that was done, handed her the curved needle with fine black silk thread.

"Do you want a bit of chloroform to deaden the pain?"

The woman shook her head, wincing again and blinking her eyes. Her indrawn gasp for breath made Elizabeth look to the nurse, who shrugged. She carefully stitched the wounds closed, applied bandages, and after washing her hands, probed the woman's neck.

"Did you hit your head or neck on anything?"

"The wall. It stopped me from fallin' down the stairs."

"I see." Keeping her face bland and her voice even took a discipline Elizabeth didn't realize she had.

"I . . . I lost me bairn from the last one. If he hadn't kicked me, I . . ." She sighed.

"Do you have somewhere else you can go? Get away from him until he cools down?"

A slow shake of the head was her only answer. "He's a good man, my Ian, until he drinks too much, you know?" As if that were all that mattered, as if that was just the way things were.

Elizabeth helped her off the examining table. "Would you like to lie down for a bit until you feel stronger?"

"No, I have to feed the young'uns. He'll be all right for a while now, you know? If only he had a job again. Nothing like this happened before all the trouble with the railroads."

Later, when they had finished supper, Elizabeth turned to the doctor. "There must be something we can do."

"Which something are you referring to?" Dr. Morganstein looked up from the paper she was studying. "Here, I think you should read this." She slid the paper toward her charge, pushed her glasses back up on her nose, and concentrated on Elizabeth, a trait Elizabeth found both intimidating and encouraging, depending on what had been the action or conversation just before.

"Thank you, I will. I'm referring to the number of women coming into the hospital suffering injuries at the hands of their husbands."

"Yes, it's the worst I've seen."

Elizabeth waited, certain her mentor would have, if not a solution, at least some suggestions. Finally the silence had stretched so long, Elizabeth had to say something or ask to be excused. "So?"

"So what do you suggest? Throw them in jail? Kidnap their wives and children? Implore the railroad or the mills to put these men back to work? Go to Eugene Debs and ask him to make the union men behave? Sic the government on them? The church?"

Elizabeth could feel her jaw drop and thud on her chest. "Ah." She sighed. "I'm being idealistic, aren't I?"

"Yes, and I wish I could help you stay that way, but short of bludgeoning these husbands and fathers who are most likely cursing themselves for not providing for their families, so they go drinking . . ." The good doctor clasped her hands on the table. "If only life were simple."

"I think it is more so in Northfield."

"Does this burden of suffering women and children make you want to run for home where, I'm sure, there are green trees, flowers and grass, clean cold water, and no black underbelly of despair?"

Elizabeth shook her head. "No. I want to make things better. I want to do more than patch people up. I want to keep mothers and babies from dying before they live. I want to understand what causes tuberculosis and typhoid and what can be done to stop them before they begin."

"Don't you believe all these are either the scourge of the devil himself or retribution for our many sins?" The words lay gently upon the table, but the doctor's eyes grew obsidian sharp.

Elizabeth thought only a moment. "I believe that God could take all this suffering away in the blink of an eye if He so chose. But when Adam and Eve sinned, sin invaded the world and brought with it all diseases of body, mind, and spirit. And we're stuck with them until Christ comes again. But in the meantime, God gave us brains to use and wills to fight for life. There have been changes in medicine, and there will be more. I want to be part of that, God willing."

"Well said, my dear. I pray that the battle doesn't change your mind." She reached across the lace-covered table and took Elizabeth's hand in hers. "I understand that God gave you the gift of music with these hands, but I have seen them bring comfort and healing, a far greater mission."

Elizabeth cleared her throat, tried to speak, and blinked hard. She tried again. "Thank you. I must go check on the little girl brought in late this afternoon. I wish I knew her name."

"I fear she is one of the street waifs. If we can give her enough nourishment to fight, we will have helped. I fear she is too weak to—"

"Annie is with her, spooning chicken broth and bathing her to bring down the fever. Might help with the vermin too. I washed maggots out of the ulcer on her leg."

"They at least eat the putrefaction. I read a paper that said that during the war, they learned that maggots could clean a wound better than anything man had yet to devise. Carbolic not withstanding."

Elizabeth shuddered. "I'm afraid I washed them away."

"Perhaps they had done their job. Alcohol is a viable alternative."

"Thank you." Elizabeth rose, and taking her kerchief out of her apron pocket, tied the triangle over her hair again. The two made their way down the hall to the children's ward.

Annie met them at the door. "I-I'm sorry, she's gone. There just wasn't time to help her none."

Elizabeth sagged against the wall. "What happened?"

"She just quit breathing."

"You should have called me."

" 'Twas too late."

Elizabeth nodded. "You did the best you could." *Why, Lord, did I stop for supper and a visit with the doctor? I should have stayed here. Perhaps I . . .* She slumped against the wall, lost in her recriminations.

"No, my child, you do not waste your energy on what has been. You save it to fight for the next one. Only God has control over life and death, in spite of how hard we try." Dr. Morganstein took her arm and led her back up to her room. "You go to bed early, and things will look better in the morning. Often I have to remind myself that weeping endures for the night, but joy comes in the morning. That's one of the verses I cling to when despair seems imminent."

Through the next three weeks Elizabeth had many opportunities to remember the doctor's words and take them for her own.

When the day arrived that she was to leave, she trailed through the hospital, imprinting each ward and room in her mind. She gave Patrick a hug, which turned his ears bright red.

"Th-thank 'ee, miss."

Back in the doctor's office, she felt like a little girl called before the principal.

"You'll have one more summer before you start med school. You are welcome to spend as much of it as you want or are able to here with us." Dr. Morganstein handed her an envelope. "Just a bit to show our gratitude."

"But it is I who must be grateful." Elizabeth stuttered to a stop. "You do want me to come back?" Joy burst like a firecracker.

"I don't want you to leave, but your mother will be here any moment, and I know she is looking forward to your time together. We will keep in touch, and I will send a letter of recommendation to whomever you need me to. Between my dear friend Issy Josephson and I, we will get you into a medical school somewhere. You can count on that."

"Thank you." *Please, Mother, come before I turn into a weeping puddle right here.*

That night at the hotel, her mother asked, "Was it all you hoped?"

"Far more than I could even dream, but I have a favor to ask. Could we have dinner brought here to our room so I could spend an hour or two in that lovely bathtub?"

"Of course, dear. But tomorrow we shop. You promised."

Elizabeth groaned but leaned over to give her mother a hug, cheek to cheek. "You look well again. Thank you for my summer." As if she would ever get it out of her mind.

CHAPTER THIRTY-TWO

Northfield, Minnesota
August 1894

"Elizabeth, I have to talk with you."

Thornton's voice sounded strange, even over the telephone.

"Fine, but I haven't even been home two hours." Elizabeth rubbed her forehead where a headache had started up during the last hours of the train ride. Or had it started during the long hours of shopping with her mother in Chicago? Why was it that shopping made her far more weary than the longest shift at the hospital?

"Would it be all right if I came over about three?"

"Why don't you make it four and plan on staying for supper?"

"We'll see."

Elizabeth hung up the earpiece and stared at the oak box. What was it she heard in Thornton's voice? She trailed one hand on the banister as she climbed the stairs to the upper hall.

"Who was that?" Annabelle asked, coming out of her room.

"Thornton. He'll most likely be joining us for supper."

"On our first night home?"

"I know. Something is wrong, I'm afraid, but he wouldn't say, just that he'd see me at four."

"Hmm." Annabelle peered more closely at her daughter's face. "Are you feeling all right?"

"A headache is all. I'm going to take a bit of laudanum and lie down."

"That sounds like a marvelous idea. Just what I planned too, the lie-down part, that is." Annabelle took her daughter's hand. "Thank you for the shopping and the concert. I feel better than I have for so long. And your Dr. Morganstein is an amazing woman. You are fortunate to have such a fine patroness."

"I know. Rest well." Elizabeth kissed her mother's cheek and crossed to her own room. In spite of the humidity of this August day, a breeze lifted the sheer white curtains at her window. After removing her travel clothes, she wrung out a cloth in the cool water of the pitcher and lay down with the cloth across her forehead and eyes. Within moments she was sound asleep, her last thought about Thornton.

"Dear."

Elizabeth felt her shoulder being shaken and her mother's voice but somehow failed to find the energy to respond.

"Elizabeth, Thornton is here. He's waiting out in the garden to talk with you."

Elizabeth opened her eyes and stretched her arms above her head. "I was having such a nice dream." She tossed the now dry cloth toward the basin and sat up. "Please tell him I'll be there in a few minutes. How I would have loved a bath first."

"I've told Cook to expect another for supper. I was thinking of a tray in my room, but . . ."

"Thank you. I know he wouldn't have called if it weren't something important."

Elizabeth slipped into a light robe and spent as little time in the bathroom as she could manage, resisting even looking at the tub, sure that her longing alone would turn on the taps. The fragrance of bubble bath would be such a treat after the weeks of running full speed ahead at the hospital.

Back in her room feeling some refreshed, she chose a dress of white lawn with bluebells sprinkled over it and a blue sash at the waist with matching trim above the skirt ruffle. After slipping it over her head, she sat down at the dressing table to brush her hair.

She'd worn it coiled in back for so long that brushing it out to flow over her shoulders felt almost sinful. She tied it back with a blue ribbon the same as her sash, slid her feet into doeskin slippers, and made her way downstairs. The piano called to her from the music room that no longer held the bed she'd set up for her mother, another visible sign that Annabelle was, if not back to normal, at least close. Half an hour at the piano would set her spirits to right; perhaps Thornton would rather listen to her play than talk.

"I have lemonade ready for you anytime you want and the lemon cookies Mr. Wickersham likes so well." Cook nodded to the tray.

"Thank you. I'll take that out with me." Elizabeth blew her old friend a kiss and took the tray outside, opening the screen door with her elbow.

"Elizabeth, I could have come for that." Thornton sprang to his feet and rushed to help her.

"I know, but I was on my way out." *If only he knew of all the truly heavy things I've been lugging around these last weeks.* She let him take the tray, the better to observe him for a moment. Surely something was bothering him. His eyes tattled.

"Won't you sit down?" He motioned to the wrought-iron chair padded with thick cushions in red-and-white check.

Elizabeth took one of the glasses and settled into the chair. "Cook made your favorite cookies."

He nodded without looking at her. "I . . . I know."

"Come, Thornton, whatever can be so bad? Tell me, and perhaps I can help." She kept her voice light and her smile ready.

Head hanging, elbows on his knees with hands dangling between, he looked like he'd been severely castigated.

"Thornton, what is it? You are frightening me."

"Ah, Elizabeth, forgive me." He looked across the glass-topped table. "I just don't know where to start."

"They say to always start at the beginning. That's easiest."

"Perhaps, but not necessarily in this case." He reached across the table and laid his hand palm up. She put hers into it, keeping her gaze on his face.

"I . . . I've received a call, a call to the mission field."

"Already? I thought you had decided to attend seminary first."

"Me too, but the pastor friend that I told you about has requested that I come now and work under him. He is that desperate for assistance."

"Is this what you want to do?"

"You know it is what I believe I am being called to, the mission field, I mean. Originally I had thought more to the Orient than Africa, but I will go wherever the Lord sends me."

"So . . ." Elizabeth turned her head slightly to the side, studying his face. *What then is wrong? He is just going early.* "I don't understand. Why is this bothering you so much, unless you no longer want to go."

"Sometimes things don't go the way we planned."

"So?"

He sat straighter in his chair. "Do you remember when you asked me to pretend to be falling in love with you?"

"Of course, and we've both been saved a lot of trouble because of our agreement." She leaned forward and tapped his hand. "Haven't we?"

"Yes, and we've had some good times too. But that is part of the problem."

"I don't understand."

"I didn't hold up to my part of the bargain."

"Of course you did. Why, we've become the best of friends and—"

"That's the problem."

"Thornton Wickersham, just speak out what you have to say. This pussyfooting around is not like you."

He went down on one knee in front of her. "All right. This is as plain as I can make it, but remember, this wasn't what I planned."

"I see."

"Elizabeth, I . . ." He took both of her hands in his. "I have fallen in love with you, and I'm asking you to marry me and come to the mission field by my side."

Elizabeth would have laughed but for the expression on his face. "In love with me? You think you love me?"

"I don't think so. I know so. Didn't you have even a hint?"

She shook her head, disbelief keeping the motion going. "No. I thought one time that if I were ever to think about marriage you would make a fine husband, but you know I don't believe that is what God is calling me to do. I am to be a doctor, and after my weeks at the hospital, I am more convinced of that than ever."

"But that doesn't have to mean you don't love me. I will go now and come back for you when you have finished medical school, or I shall stay here and finish school myself, and we can go together."

But, Thornton, I don't love you, not that way at least.

"Please, Elizabeth, darling, don't say no, don't even think no, just say you will think about this."

She opened her mouth, then snapped it closed.

"I do love you, and your agreeing to become my wife would make me the happiest man to walk this earth."

Elizabeth kept her groan to herself with the most diligent of discipline. "Thornton, I . . ."

He laid a finger along her lips. "Please, just prayerfully consider this." He picked up her hand and kissed the back of it. "I think I better be going."

"I thought you were staying for supper. Cook has prepared extra for you."

"Are you sure?"

"Sure of what? That you can eat with us just as you have in the past? Is this, ah, pronouncement of yours to change everything?" She knew she was only making the situation worse. A thought made her stop. "Thornton, did you ask my father for permission to ask me this?"

"A long time ago. When we first began the charade. I knew it would not be proper without it."

"O-h." The word became a groan. "I never knew that." No wonder her mother and father had been so unquestioning when she had gone places with him. They really thought a romance had been in the making.

A charade all right. Only now one of the players had changed the rules. And she was sure she didn't want to play anymore.

That night in bed, she replayed the scene in the garden. Had there been any thrill when he kissed her hand?

No, none.

Shouldn't there be if she were in love with him?

"Of course." She sat up and punched her pillows into a back-rest. "At least that's what all the books say. How would I know?" She crossed her arms over her chest. "The real question is, do I want to go to Africa with Thornton, as Mrs. Thornton Wicker-sham?" She waited for some answer to strike, then melted into the pillows. "No, the real question is, do I love Thornton Wicker-sham? Am I in love with him?" She waited again. The no that whispered through the breeze from the window echoed in her heart and head. "Oh yes, I love Thornton Wickersham all right, but only as the brother I never had. Not like a woman who dreams of marriage." She pulled the pillows out flat and curled onto her side. "I said I was never going to marry, and Lord, it sure seems that way. Now, how do I tell him this? I feel like a creature crawl-ing out of a slimy bog.

"Lord, forgive me for causing hurt to my friend. This isn't what I wanted to have happen. I didn't mean for anyone to get hurt." She got up and went to stand by the window, lifting her hair off the back of her neck, wishing for a cool breeze. Now, how to tell Thornton?

Over breakfast the next morning Elizabeth tried to explain the situation to her mother. "But I don't love him." She'd repeated her-self once already, but Annabelle didn't seem to be hearing.

"Love grows, dear. You will be a lovely bride."

"Mother, you are not listening to me. I am not marrying Thornton. I do not love him, and besides, I have said all along that I would not be marrying anyone. I am going to be a doctor."

"I see. Of course, but there is no need to say this right now. Give yourself time to get used to the idea."

If stamping her foot would get her the attention she needed, she would have, or slamming doors, but instead she just shook her head. She'd known better than to confide this to her mother, but she needed wise advice, not total lack of comprehension.

"I'm going to the office. I'm sure Father's accounts are in total disarray by now."

"No, they aren't. I've taken over that part of the business, and Phillip says I am doing almost as well as you did." At the shock on her daughter's face, Annabelle continued. "I think your father offered me the position as a way to get me feeling better, and it worked."

"Well, I'll be . . ." Elizabeth shook her head slowly from side to side as if in a state of shock. "After all these years."

"I know. I should have realized a long time ago that if I can manage the household accounts, I could manage the newspaper's also, but it wasn't until you were gone that I . . ." Annabelle shrugged and half smiled. "This will make the last year of college easier for you too."

"Yes." Elizabeth reached for the doorknob. "I think I'll go on over to Dr. Gaskin's then and pass on some things I learned at the hospital. I'll be home in time for dinner."

"Good, dear, and if you see Thornton, invite him to join us."

Stifling groans was becoming epidemic for her.

"Well, congratulations, missy." Dr. Gaskin looked up from his notes.

"For what?" Elizabeth stopped in the doorway.

"I hear you and Thornton Wickersham are engaged."

"Now, where did you hear that?" Biting off words was becoming easier also.

"Ah, oh-oh. And top of the morning to you too. I'm not sure who I heard it from, and I'd not tell you if I could remember. Also, I will make sure the news never passes my lips."

"Good, because while he has asked me to marry him, I have not given him a final answer."

"I take it the answer is not one that will make our young man overly delighted."

"First of all, he is not 'our young man,' and secondly, you are right. I've always said I would not marry, and just because I've been asked, that doesn't change my assertions. Now can we talk about some things I learned this summer that you might like to use for the good of your patients?"

"Sit yourself down and let's talk. I have fifteen minutes until they open the doors and the ill and injured flood in."

Later, when she left the doctor's office, she started downtown, but after the second congratulations, she turned around and went home instead. How had the word gotten out so quickly, and how was she going to stem the gossip before it got back to Thornton?

She stomped up the front steps to her own home and slammed the door behind her. Her heels made a satisfying click on the hall floor and across the parlor to the office where her mother sat writing a letter.

"Mother, we have to talk."

"In a minute."

"Now."

"Elizabeth Rogers, whatever is the matter? You are being rude, and your face is red as a sunburn."

"Mother, who have you told about this supposed engagement between Thornton and me?"

"Why, no one." Annabelle laid her pen down and put the cork in the ink bottle. "I haven't been out of the house."

"Then how does half of Northfield, including Dr. Gaskin, know to congratulate me and wish me all God's blessings?" Elizabeth sucked in a deep breath, running to a stop at the look of total confusion on her mother's face.

"Would Thornton say anything?" Annabelle shook her head as she spoke. "Of course he wouldn't."

"Then who? How?"

The phone jangled in the hallway. Both women turned to stare out the office door.

"The telephone. Your father and I talked about it on the telephone." Annabelle gave a small shrug and shook her head. "I'm so sorry, dear. I never thought . . ."

Elizabeth blew out her cheeks with a sighing breath. "I need to go talk with Thornton right now." She turned and left the office, barely acknowledging her mother's repeated apology. What a fine kettle of fish this had become. *One thing for sure, I am not using the telephone.*

"Elizabeth, your young man called, but I didn't realize you were to home yet. He said he'd be by in about an hour." Cook beamed at her. "Such a fine young man."

Elizabeth clenched her teeth but smiled in spite of it. "Thank you. I'll answer the door when he rings."

"Good. I've always known you would be a beautiful bride."

Elizabeth had rearranged the knickknacks in the parlor twice before the doorbell finally rang. She dusted off her hands and didn't bother to paste a smile on her face when she pulled the door open and stepped outside.

"Let's go around the house and into the garden."

"Hello to you too." He offered his arm, which she ignored and strode on ahead.

"Ah, I take it you are not overly joyous right now."

"No, I'm not, but most of my concern is for you." She turned and faced him as soon as they were far enough away from the house to not be overheard. "Thornton, in spite of what you may have heard this morning, I have not told anyone that I am marrying you." She stopped and looked up into his sparkling eyes. "For the simple reason that I am not marrying you. I thought and prayed much of the night, and while I love you dearly. . ."

His smile started at that, but she raised a hand to stop him. "And I do, but as a brother, not as a husband. I enjoy being with you, you make me laugh, and we have had marvelous times together, but I'm not cut out to be your wife."

"Many marriages start out with far less than this."

"I know, but I cannot be married to my brother."

"I asked that you give the thought some time."

She shook her head. "No, look what has already happened. I must beg your forgiveness for starting the charade in the beginning." She lowered her gaze to his third button. "I never meant for anyone to get hurt."

"There really is no hope?" He clasped both her hands between his.

"No, none."

"I see."

She looked up to catch the sheen of tears in his eyes. "I'm so terribly sorry." Swallowing tears of her own, she sniffed and blinked hard.

"I know. As am I." He took a deep breath and forced it out. "Then I think I shall write to my friend and tell him I will be coming as soon as things can be arranged. I would be grateful if when you think of me, that you write. I know letters from home are prized in the mission field. After all, you are my best friend."

"I shall write if you want."

"Then I shall be on my way. I have much to do." He tucked her hand in the crook of his arm. "Smile for me. I don't want to remember you sad."

And so she did the same one week later as he climbed the steps to the train. She smiled and waved until the train disappeared in the distance, then went home and cried for two hours.

CHAPTER THIRTY-THREE

Blessing, North Dakota

As summer progressed, the stunted wheat ripened early. Thorliff had four up side by side to pull the binder, and for the third time that day the twine broke. He whoa'd the horses and flung himself off the seat to again check what was wrong with the delivery system. He checked the tension on the bolt of twine, retied the ends, and closed the cover. Everything seemed to be in order, so why was the twine breaking?

"Got a minute, Thorliff?" Pastor Solberg called as he rode across the field.

"Why not?" He pushed the brim of his hat back with one finger and, grabbing the canteen, took several deep swallows.

Pastor Solberg leaned his crossed arms on the saddle horn. "Having a problem?"

"The twine keeps breaking."

"Did you grease the spindle?"

"Tried that, checked the tension, cleaned out the track, but it broke for the third time." Thorliff shot the offending machine a murderous glare.

"I'm no mechanic, that's for sure. Here, I brought you something." He handed Thorliff a packet of cookies. "My wife sent you these."

"She thought I needed some sweetening up?"

"Perhaps. I've missed seeing you in church. I was looking forward to some of our talks again."

"Ja, well . . ." Thorliff kicked a dirt clod with the toe of his boot. He stared at the ground, then raised his head to look toward the pastor, feeling the concentration of the man's gaze on the top of his head. "I've not been very good company this summer."

"Anji?"

He nodded. "And Moen." Bitterness bit his tongue and throat. Anger clawed the bites deeper.

"I was afraid of that."

"I'll be going back to Northfield soon. That should make things easier."

"Easier isn't always best. Our Lord says we must forgive those who trespass against us if we want God to forgive us our trespasses."

The words lay between them like a flame that coiled and flickered, seeking new straw to devour. One of the horses snorted and stamped a foot. Another followed suit.

"Ja, well, I been trespassed against all right. Well, I need to get this rig in motion again. Thanks for stopping by." He started to climb up on the binder seat, then stopped and looked at his friend and mentor. "But I don't have it in me to forgive him . . . nor her either." He settled his hat back on his head and, taking up the reins, hupped the horses forward without a backward look.

Forgive! But they did the wrong! Forgive, or how can God forgive you? The argument kept time with the horses' footfalls and the creak of the wagon wheels. The blade clattered, the wheat fell to the belt that carried it to the stretched canvas that delivered it to the bundler and the twine that tied the bundle. The bundle was dumped out on the stubble, the whole of it a plethora of squeaks and clatters and squeals, rattles and banging and dust. Dust that coated his face and neck, drying his tongue and lips. It sucked up the sweat from the horses and turned it to globs of mud. Sometimes he could go for an hour or more without thinking of Anji and Mr. Moen, or of anything at all. Just push the body to do the same work over and over. But his heart grew harder as each day passed.

———

Days were nightmares of heat and sweat and dust. Nights were battlefields of friends and rage and despair. He read the Psalms where David said his very bones were being sucked dry by the weeping, and he knew what David meant. Thorliff was too tired to write and too drained of ideas to express his feelings.

The war within continued. Friday night in the middle of the night, he threw back the sheet and leaped to his feet, his leg muscles clenching in knots. He paced the room he and Andrew shared, stretched his leg out, and finally made his way downstairs to get a drink of water. He took the cup outside and sat on the stoop, sipping and looking at the sickle moon sinking toward the western horizon.

"God, I cannot forgive him."

A dog barked somewhere far off. Coyotes yipped and sang from over on the river. Next week he knew they would take the steam engine and separator on the road. But he wanted to go to communion first. Only he couldn't. Confessing his lack of forgiveness would not suffice. He had to also do the forgiving.

He argued with himself all the next day, but evening found him on horseback on his way to Pastor Solberg. "I have a question," he said after the greetings and he and the pastor were seated side by side on the front porch.

"Shoot."

"How can I forgive when I don't have it in me? I mean, I can say the words, but Scripture says God sees into the heart, and all He'll see in mine is blackness."

"He knows you, remember, from the time He knit you together in your mother's womb."

"So?"

"So all you have to do is ask Him to forgive through you."

"But He already forgave."

"But you haven't. So you can ask Him to love someone through you. You can ask Him to forgive through you. A willing heart is all He asks for. Are you willing to forgive?"

317

"Yes, I think I am. I want to take communion again, but I don't want to see them together in church. I cannot do that. I mean, I've been thinking a lot. I don't like the way I am now. I get mad easy. I think bad thoughts. I want to argue with people, and I hurt others' feelings. This is not good, and I don't want to look on this summer as a time of hatred and anger."

"Remember, the Scripture says, 'If we confess our sins, he is faithful and just to forgive us our sins, and to cleanse us from all unrighteousness.' "

"Ja, you made sure I memorized that one and the one following. 'If we say that we have not sinned, we make him a liar, and his word is not in us.' "

"You learned the verses well. Do you confess you are sinning by not forgiving Anji and Mr. Moen?"

"Yes."

"Are you willing to forgive them?"

"Yes. Do I have to go to them and say that?"

"If you want. The Bible also says that if your brother sins against you, you are to go to him and—"

"Can I write them a letter?"

"If you'd rather."

Thorliff nodded. "I will do that tonight. Right now, though, I confess my anger and grudge. I seek God's forgiveness."

"Then by the grace of God and my holy calling, I declare unto you the forgiveness of all your sins and the cleansing of all unrighteousness." Pastor Solberg laid his hand on Thorliff's head. "You are forgiven, dear Thorliff, go and sin no more."

"Amen." Thorliff stood. "Think I'll get on home and get those letters written. Thank you, Pastor."

"You are most welcome. See you in church tomorrow?"

"Ja, at the altar."

Thorliff left for school again on the tenth of September, after weeks of harvest and the crew still on the road. He waved to his mother, brother and sister, and the others who gathered around to see him off. As the train chugged down the track, he saw the Baard farm off to the left. Someone was at the clothesline hanging out clothes, and he knew it must be Anji. "Go with God, dear friend. And may you find the right way for you."

Thorliff leaned back against the seat, letting the memories of the last weeks wash over him—his conversations with Pastor Solberg, his discussions with God, his fights with himself. Such tremendous changes, and none of them were even visible. If someone had told him what all would transpire over the summer, he would have laughed in protest. But what if . . . ? He tuned out the clacking of the train wheels and listened closely to that inner voice. What if a young man in a story went through what he had gone through? Would that make a story? Could he tell it this soon without it ripping out his heart? Would Anji mind? After all, it was part her story too.

He took the pencil out of his inside jacket pocket and paper from his valise. One good thing, he'd learned to always carry the tools he needed. Paper and pencil. His pencil flew over the pages, jotting notes, bits of dialogue, descriptions, titles.

Hours later, after changing trains and never losing track of his story, he put everything away as the train chugged into Northfield. Again there was that strange telescoping of time moving him from one life to the other. He swung his carpetbag down from the overhead rack and stepped into a blast of hot air, stirred by the steam boiling up from under the train.

Carrying both cases, he headed uptown for the newspaper office. While he'd told them which day he thought to arrive, no one had met him, and he'd not expected them to. Within two blocks, sweat rivuleted down his spine, behind his ears, and into his shirt collar. Oh, for a blast of that North Dakota wind right about now instead of a paucity of breeze that didn't even rustle the birch leaves, small as they were.

He pushed open the door to hear the bell welcome him back.

"Can I . . ." Elizabeth looked up from writing at the desk behind the counter. "Thorliff—er, Mr. Bjorklund." She surged to her feet, her smile flashing bright in the dimness.

"Mr. Bjorklund? Have I been gone that long?" He set his carpetbag down and tipped back his hat, wiping the sweat from his forehead with the back of his hand.

She stopped, tilted her head to the side, and studied him. "I can tell you've been out in the sun. Farming for sure."

"How can you tell, other than . . ." He held out his tanned and well-muscled arms.

"Your forehead is a dead giveaway."

"My forehead?" He touched it with one finger.

"The line—the hat line. All farmers have it."

He removed his fedora and set it on the valise. "Pardon me for my manners."

She shook her head. "Now don't go getting in a huff. I have made a resolution."

He eyed her as he would a critter he wasn't sure would bite or not. "Like what?"

"I shall not pick fights with you."

"You already are."

"No, I'm not."

"Yes, you are." Thorliff grinned at her. Things were certainly back to normal. "I have a story idea." He didn't mention the twenty pages he'd already written.

"So tell me."

"I don't think so."

"Thorliff Bjorklund, you are the most infuriating man I've ever known." She crossed her arms and waved one finger at him.

Ah yes, the new year was off to a fine start. "I'll give you a hint. It's about a young man and a young woman."

"A romance?" Her cocked eyebrow and tone clearly said she didn't think he could write such a thing.

"Guess you'll just have to wait and see." He picked up his bags and carried them back to his room. The window sparkled, and the floor shone with a new coat of paint. Even his desk had been polished, and a plaid cushion invited him to sit. New story, new room, new dreams. He hung his hat on one of the pegs by the door, sucked in a deep breath, and let it all out. New life.